PENGUIN BOOKS

BAD WISDOM

Bill Drummond was born in 1953 and grew up in Galloway and Corby. In 1987 he formed The KLF with Jimmy Cauty. By 1993 it had become the K Foundation.

Mark Manning was born in 1958 and grew up in Leeds. In 1985 he formed the rock band Zodiac Mindwarp and the Love Reaction.

Drummond and Manning's literary collaboration grew out of a long-standing friendship. In 1994 they founded the Curfew Press in order to publish their own work. Together with Sally Agarwal they have produced five volumes of correspondence, *The Letters*, and *A Bible of Dreams*. 'The Lighthouse at the Top of the World' is the first part of a *Bad Wisdom* trilogy.

Bad Wisdom

The Lighthouse at the Top of the World

BILL DRUMMOND AND
MARK MANNING

PENGUIN BOOKS

PENGUIN BOOKS

Published by the Penguin Group
Penguin Books Ltd, 27 Wrights Lane, London w8 5tz, England
Penguin Books USA Inc., 375 Hudson Street, New York, New York 10014, USA
Penguin Books Australia Ltd, Ringwood, Victoria, Australia
Penguin Books Canada Ltd, 10 Alcorn Avenue, Toronto, Ontario, Canada m4v 3b2
Penguin Books (NZ) Ltd, 182–190 Wairau Road, Auckland 10, New Zealand

Penguin Books Ltd, Registered Offices: Harmondsworth, Middlesex, England

First published 1996
1 3 5 7 9 10 8 6 4 2

Set in 10/12pt Monotype Baskerville
Typeset by Rowland Phototypesetting Ltd, Bury St Edmunds, Suffolk
Printed in England by Clays Ltd, St Ives plc

The otherworld is not a myth, but a reality,
and in all ages there have been souls who have been
willing to brave the great adventure, and to risk all
for the chance of bringing back with them some
assurance of the future life.

JESSIE L. WESTON

CHAPTER ONE

Atomic Blowjob

I am shit scared. Shit scared of almost everything.

It was the end of the twentieth century, a fin-de-siècle horror show unravelling like the stinking entrails of a long-dead dog. The Soviet Union had collapsed, transmogrified into a dangerously unstable collection of hard-line crypto-Fascist, weirdo ethnic states; Eastern Europe had mutated into a demented bitch Hydra, ripping off her ugly bread-queue, boiled-cabbage dead-heads and tossing them into the charnel houses of history. The pavonine and prismatic American dream had turned into a shit brown nightmare; cyber Nazis and techno-perves stalked the Internet; and Japan was producing good heavy metal bands. Something had to be done.

It's pissing down outside. The day is seven hours and fifteen minutes old and already it is crippled with the weight of my evasions, deceit and downright lies.

My name is Z. I am a Zen Master and, in one of my many mythical manifestations, I am part of a triumvirate of Magi known throughout legend as the Three Wise Men; the other two thirds are known as Gimpo and Bill. They, too, are Zen Masters; and are both shit hot at karate.

I go looking for a saw. Find it. Venture out into the rain without a coat – that's about as brave as I get. Cross the road, pick a small tree – no more than six feet high, slender and straight – a young elm. It keeps raining. Down the back of my neck it goes. I lop off the top of the young tree; cut three short staves.

We had a plan: we were going to save the world – the whales, the dolphins, the rainforests, Bambi, the whole damn Walt Disney bunch, babe; we were gonna free Willy, fuck chicks and slay dragons. We are Zen Masters and know what the fuck we are talking about.

Back in the cottage I drink another cup of tea; check one more time: passport, air tickets, money. All I need is packed into my small black haversack. Waiting for the taxi.

This was the plan: we would take a holy and sacred picture of the King of Rock 'n' Roll, Elvis Presley, to the very summit of the earth; once there, we would place it with sincere reverence amongst the chimerical shimmering palaces of ice and snow and then (accompanied by some weird Zen magic) we would light joss sticks, dance about making screechy kung-fu noises, get off our faces, and that would be it: Planet Earth saved. Simple.

The taxi arrives. This is it: the journey has begun – the North Pole or fuck all.

The divine Presleyesque vibes would slide down the myriad ley lines and dance across the scattered latitudes, transmitting instant love, peace and global understanding. All war would cease; McDonald's hamburger bars would materialize in famine-stricken Third World countries, dispensing free McDonald's Cola and Big Macs to the starving millions; the Dalai Lama would be made President of the Federation of Free Earth and harmony and excellent karma would reign over our beleaguered planet. In our hearts, we knew this to be true.

Lock the front door, then remember I have not switched on the answerphone; let myself back in and leave a cryptic message about 'Following a star' and 'I may be some time'.

Life as I have lived it has crumbled. Since last May, living alone in a rented railway cottage. There is no TV, radio or music-making machine; there is a telephone. Not quite the lifestyle of the romantic hermit – the outside world does exist – but removed enough from the stabilizing effects of a steady job, definable responsibilities, the *News at Ten* and football results at Saturday tea-time for the mind to slip and creak. Let's hope the hinges hold.

'It sounds more like an excuse.' A distant voice.

Jet Taxis, my favourite cab company. The drivers are mostly Pakistani. I have got to know a lot of them in the way that you can get to know cab drivers. The driver this morning is Faizal: late forties, his greying beard is shaved in a frightening but precise way – not quite how the Ayatollah Khomeini had it, but close.

Is there a secret, coded language stretching right across the Muslim world, developed since the Prophet first welcomed his revelations, all expressed by which bits of your beard you shave and which bits you leave? I don't ask Faizal if he has read *The Satanic Verses*.

It's still pissing down and we are off to Heathrow. Should take forty to forty-five minutes. Hit the traffic the other side of Amersham – we are going to be late. Conversation drifts from the all-pervasive American presidential elections (will success slip from Bill Clinton's grasp in the last few days before the poll?) to how the West doesn't give a fuck for the Bosnians 'cause they're all Muslims.

Conspiracy theory number 23 creeps in: the US is secretly in league with the 'ethnic cleansing' of the Serbs; and, of course, there's always the arms build-up between Pakistan and India that . . .

It is a miserable day. The Chilterns look crap. Although I am usually happy to discuss with Faizal the latest goings-on with the Kashmir Liberation Front (KLF), this morning I am riddled with insecurities masked by a thick skin of bluff confidence.

A wet windy morning in Uxbridge. People make their way to proper jobs, leading proper lives. Faizal asks why I am off to Helsinki. What do I say? I tell him that I am writing a book with a friend and we have to go to Finland to finish it off. I don't mention Elvis or saving the world or the Baby Jesus inside. He accepts the irrationality of my reply – I mean, it was Faizal who drove me to the airport the day I made my escape to Mexico. The conversation drifts off into safer topics – his father's farm in Kashmir, what his brothers are up to.

Heathrow Terminal 1. No need for me to tell you what that's like: you know the score.

Gimpo and I had arranged that we should meet up at the British Airways check-in desk at 8.45 a.m. I'm five minutes late. I pace about; keep my new Polar Explorer hat on, even though it's beginning to itch my forehead; make some more of these notes; buy the *Mirror* and the *Sun*; take my hat off, put it back on again; take off my specs. Maybe it looks best with the flaps turned up and my specs off; or maybe with the flaps down . . . ? Where the fuck are they?

Make a phone call. That's what I always do to calm my nerves – I make a phone call; it doesn't really matter to whom. It is less than four minutes since I made the call and sat down to write these notes, but already I have no idea who I called or even if I got through.

Lots of people going to lots of places. I watch the overhead TV monitors with the lists of destinations and departure times. I want a large fry-up breakfast. I want Z and Gimpo to be here.

9.32 a.m. Back at check-in desk 23. No Z or Gimpo. Make notes. Kate and James will be in school by now. Look up. At last, there is Gimpo bounding in through the automatic sliding doors and Z shuffling behind. 'Are we not men?' A line from Devo flits in and out. Embarrassed grins. We then perform a very sensitive ceremony right there with thousands of people milling to hundreds of destinations: I pull out three elm staves from my haversack and hand one each to Gimpo and Z, and with the other I whack myself (lightly) on the head.

'Zen sticks,' I say.

'Ya what?' replies Gimpo.

'*Zen sticks*. The three of us are Zen Masters. You know, you must have read about it – how Zen Masters used to have these sticks to whack their pupils on the head in order to help them on the path to enlightenment. We're the pupils as well as the Zen Masters.'

'Yeah,' says Z, not looking at me, clutching his stick in his right hand and whacking the open palm of his left hand. Gimpo looks at his, checks to see he has the best one (which he does), and immediately accepts that we are Zen Masters.

4

I hand over the air tickets and my chunk of the cash float to Gimpo. We check in and head round to the café for that fry-up.

Z is a singer in a Rock 'n' Roll band, Zodiac Mindwarp and the Love Reaction. They've had a bad weekend, as bands do. Z tells me he read Ecclesiastes again last night to try and get himself in a better frame of mind. How anybody could read the biggest downer of all the books in the Old Testament and find it uplifting is beyond me. He takes a sip from his mug of tea, pulls from his pocket a dog-eared pack of tarot cards and mutters something about a Golden Dawn and the need for us, the Magi returned, to have a reading.

The first card he lays is the Fool. He looks up at Gimpo and chortles. The second is the Hermit. He rubs his goatee, shifts the frame of his heavy black specs and gives me a sideways glance. The third is the Magician. I can see that self-satisfied grin of his spread across his face. I've always found this pagan symbolism stuff more than a little suspect – runs counter to my Presbyterian core. My contradictions run deep. I lose interest; return to these notes and my fry-up.

There was only one problem: how to finance this epic odyssey to the hyperborean wastes to secure the future of our species. Mega-bucks were in short supply. Bill had squandered the billions he had made from his KLF adventures on the usual shit: ex-wives, ex-girlfriends, prostitutes, cocaine, VAT and bad magic. I, too, was flat broke; the mothers of my two children and the vomity queers from the Inland Revenue were squabbling like septic alleycats in courts all over England for the paltry financial detritus of my Mindwarp escapades. Two niggers with blades had robbed Gimpo of his drug money.

It was like being in a dark tunnel surrounded by floating shite and squeaking vermin. But at the far end of this pus-dripping sewer stood a soiled angel holding a Zippo aloft in chipped nail-bitten hands: Tracey Beehive. Tracey had earned millions of dollars in her career as one of the world's highest-paid popular entertainers: one show in Vegas could net her more than Bill and myself had earned in our entire lives.

As a profitable sideline, she had also amassed a fortune equivalent to the GDP of several Third World countries by servicing corrupt American politicians and her father's friends with deviant sexual acts so abhorrent that even thinking about them threatens my typewriter with the half-digested contents of my last junk-food meal. Think of your worst sexual nightmare, multiply it by three thousand, and that's where the area of her sexual expertise begins. Her remarkable repertoire makes the most gruesome parts of Dante's *Inferno* and the collected works of De Sade pale into Beatrix Potter's *Squirrel Nutkin*. I shit you not, disbelievers, this bitch is hideous heavy.

Ten minutes later: 'Well, Bill, it looks like we did a deal with the Devil a long time ago, and you jacking in the music business ain't going to change that.'

'The thing is,' I tell Z as I put the last of the black pudding in my mouth, 'when we get back from putting Elvis at the Pole and finding the Baby Jesus, we should head off in search of the Devil. Perhaps we can trick him into giving our souls back.'

Z looks up from his spread of tarot cards, quotes a verse from Milton. I think he's trying to say the Devil isn't easily fooled.

Gimpo takes charge and we head for passport control.

At passport control I discover that I've left my jacket somewhere. The jacket has my passport, Zen stick and wallet in it. Panic. Rush back. Find it. Through security check – no guns or bombs about my person – up the stairs to Duty Free in search of Z and Gimpo. I hate Duty Free shops; want to smash them up; hate those golden glowing adverts for perfumes, bottles of . . . Hate, loathe, hate.

No Z, no Gimpo. Tear down to departure gate 23. Our names are being called. No Z, no Gimpo. Is this how far we are going to get? If they don't turn up now, I'm going without them. The fuckin' bastards. Anger wells up inside me. The nice ladies from the airline who tick your name off try to calm me down by telling me the plane will not leave without my companions. Fuck my companions, is what I think. If they can't get it together to get through Duty Free and on the plane without holding everything up, they don't deserve to save the world. They arrive. My anger evaporates.

They heave bulging carrier bags of Blue Label vodka. I hate vodka

– I hate all spirits – but that warm, loving grin of Gimpo's spreads across his face. He pulls from his bag a bottle of red wine that must have cut into a sizeable chunk of our limited float. Z tells me they bought it for me to drink at the Pole. Friends!

On the plane we get the stares from the regular business travellers – yes, it was us who held up the flight. We have been given seats right at the back. We settle down. Gimpo checks out the air hostesses to see which ones are worth shagging, Z flicks through my copy of the *Sun*, and I pull out my notebook to read through what I've already written. Write some more, fill in the gaps.

I lied just then: we *all* looked to see which of the air hostesses were shaggable – none of them were. The terrible truth is that whenever a male of the species boards an aeroplane, however short the journey, he indulges himself in the pathetically mistaken fantasy that all those welcoming smiles and drinks-trolley bonhomie are the come-on that he so justly deserves. Of course, when he observes that his air hostess is equally attentive to the fat German businessman in front of him and the Turkish guestworker across the aisle, he realizes she is nothing but a wanton hussy pretending to have a worthwhile career.

On re-reading these notes, I realize that a couple of things have to be explained: Gimpo and Tracey.

The reason why this unique American citizen bore the shining Zippo of hope for us three saviours of mankind is bizarre and bowel-churning. To fathom the psychological twists of this complex and depraved logic is nigh impossible, which leaves me with only the facts: Tracey found Gimpo irresistible; she had a grand and unrequited passion for our gremlin-like companion.

Whenever they found themselves in the same room, no matter what the social setting – a bourgeois soirée, a public house, a restaurant or even his mother's sitting-room – the voracious Yank would be on her hands and knees gagging on his gonads and punishing his blushing helmet. She would rip at his clothes, trying desperately to fellate the confused and distraught object of her desire, her scarlet talons reducing his shit-stained Jockeys to flapping curtains of tatters and blood.

It was obvious: Gimpo would have to inform Tracey of our noble

7

crusade and our consequent need for humanitarian cash; she would then place her entire fortune at our disposal. Simple.

Firstly, Gimpo. Gimpo, half-brother to Sandra. Sandra, mother to Z's first-born, although she is neither of Z's ex-wives (she came somewhere between them both). So Gimpo is a sort of erstwhile brother-in-law to Z. He is also Z's manager. That could be misleading – Gimpo is no Brian Epstein or even Malcolm McLaren.

Gimpo, in fact, was a squaddie, veteran of the Falklands War, Manchester born and raised, untouched and untroubled by any of the tempering effects of soft southern society. He's one of the warmest and most honourable men you are ever likely to meet, yet he likes nothing more than to carry out his stage security responsibilities with the utmost rigour.

Once upon a time I saw him grab a persistent stage-diver, drag him behind the PA stack and smash his face in before throwing him back into the seething slam pit. After the gig, information travelled backstage to us that a young lad, covered in blood, was screaming at the house management and local promoter, threatening litigation and all sorts as a result of his mistreatment by a deranged member of the stage security staff.

The promoter demanded to speak to the band's manager, front of house, in order to find out who had acted so unprofessionally. And yet Gimpo is nothing if not professional – by his own standards, of course. He got up, put down his can of Bud, head-butted the wall (twice), ensuring an instant and obvious battering to his forehead, and left the dressing room to sort out the messy problem. Five minutes later he was back sipping on his Bud. Explanation? He had admitted that he had smashed the young Rock fan's face in, pointing to the now swollen and ugly bruise on his brow and claiming that the poor lad had become uncontrollable and had hit him first, and that he had only been trying to calm him down.

I'm sure you think it rather crap of me glorifying such behaviour, but I just wanted to give you an example of the singular methods used by Gimpo to solve problems. I won't go into any of Gimpo's gut-churning Falklands stories here.

Gimpo left Her Majesty's Service some time in the mid eighties;

was working on building sites around London when he met up with Z; knew not much about Rock and had never been drawn to its crap glamour; but, because he liked lifting heavy things, started to work part-time for the pubescent Zodiac Mindwarp and the Love Reaction. He learnt to fill out carnets; he learnt to collect receipts; he learnt to get people out of bed, he learnt to . . . well, he learnt how to do all those unrewarding things that tour managers have to do. He then tour-managed, stage-managed, or merely humped gear all over the world for bands and artistes from the Dave Balfe/Food Records stable of would-bes. At the time, Z was managed by Balfe, who at some point over the previous eighteen months had felt unable to take Z's career any further. Gimpo leapt at his main chance, set up Pit Bull Management and took over the management reins.

How to describe Z and Gimpo's relationship? It's a life sentence. The bond between them goes deeper than any management contract – theirs is a dark respect, a loving commitment. They know each other's weaknesses and each other's strengths.

There is another thing you should know about Gimpo: drugs. Gimpo has a metabolism that can absorb vast quantities of drugs without any lasting effect on his physical or mental health. Let's talk about acid, LSD, or whatever you kids call it these days. Now, it's supposed to open the gates between the conscious and the subconscious mind, as well as fuck you up. Well, for Gimpo acid is just a laugh, no lifelong side-effects; unlike for Z and myself, with our acid scars ploughed deeply across our frail psychic frames, those gates between our conscious and subconscious irreversibly damaged, clinging desperately to the remnants of objective reality – something that existed for only a few short years between childhood and this – to steer our course between sunrise and sunset, hoping that shopkeepers and bus conductors don't look too far into our eyes.

'OK. OK. We get the picture, you think you're some sort of counter-culture superheroes 'cause you took acid once,' said a voice somewhere.

The room filled with steam and Gimpo started crying. Bill reached in his black leather doctor's bag, produced a large sack of supernatural cocaine and calmly unwrapped it. Gimpo threw his face into this evil crystal persuasion and inhaled, Scarface style. Staccato jungle bird noises shrieked from deep inside his bowels, his bloodshot eyes bulged and started to pulsate; he smelt of broken ozone and melting tin; a halo of fire appeared around his head and singed his eyebrows; a troop of homosexual chimpanzees appeared from nowhere, baring their horrible pink arses and farting hit tunes from Broadway musicals.

A Carlos Castaneda steamhammer had splintered Gimp's reality and was leaking into ours. 'Now!' barked Bill. 'Get him a cab, quick! We're visiting the American.' I didn't ask my tall Zen Master friend where he had obtained the strange occult crystals. Dark Bill has connections.

Gimpo's hyperactive mouth was raging out of sync with his head, a spiral dialogue about the Pope, Sgt Bilko and Philip Larkin churning in a kaleidoscope of intense verbal irrelevance. He was in no condition to refuse the ride.

Gimpo is also very strong; very, very brave – can look death in the face and piss in its mouth; does not smoke; has short wavyish hair, blue eyes, sensible clothes.

We bundled the scrabbling chemical tornado into the back of a black cab, his synapses fizzing audibly, his skull popping and eyes flipping spooky 360 *Exorcist*-style degrees. His logic had fallen down some hallucinogenic Mardi Gras shite-hole; he was masturbating openly and singing Eartha Kitt songs.

Our makeshift psychedelic ambulance skidded to a halt on the gravel drive of Tracey's Chelsea townhouse. The driver sped off without waiting for his fare, tyres on fire, trousers brown.

Bedtime reading for Kate and James over the past couple of weeks has been *Peter Pan*, so this analogy comes to mind: if Z is Captain Hook, racked by self-doubt and self-loathing and a lack of good form, then Gimpo is Smee, a pirate dog through and through, but still instinctively a man of good form.

I hammered on the oak door, the sacrificial Gimp gibbering between

Bill and myself. He had pissed himself, and his verbal pyrotechnics were surfing parallel dimensions to which only he had access. The butler ushered us into the drawing-room, where Tracey was spinning a crazed dipsomaniac waltz, a pint glass of raw vodka, ice rattling, clutched desperately to her clashing bosoms. Mascara ran down her tear-stained face; her hair was a mess. She was wearing a quilted pink satin housecoat, one fluffy slipper and sperm stains. She was singing out of tune to a crackly recorded rendition of Piaf's 'Je Ne Regrette Rien' and raving about penile dimensions and algebra (it was only later that I learned that her ex-boyfriend, the love of her life and possessor of a colossal chopper, was dating a professor of Euclidean mathematics). She didn't notice our presence for at least ten minutes.

The other thing that has to be explained is Tracey Beehive: Tracey Ray, Tracey Kennedy, Tracey Bryn. Tracey – a different name for a different day. Without Tracey, I think this expedition would never have become reality. Tracey is the singer, songwriter and front person for the pop group Voice of the Beehive, an all early-eighties Valley Girl with ten years' hard living, hard loving stuck on. Wise but foolish, spiteful but fun, she is a mature sixty-year-old, an immature sixteen. She is all faded Hollywood dreams. The brilliantly incisive woman's words in her songs are about the badness of boys and the fickleness of love. To be asked up to her 'platter' is the dream of many a young boy's heart – many are called, few are chosen. Yep Trace, if you're reading this, I'm sorry, but, like I've got to report the facts/lies how I see them, from where I'm standing.

To return to my Peter Pan analogies: if Z is Pan, then Tracey is Tinkerbell. Z and Trace may never have been lovers, but a lot of love has flowed between them. They have caused a lot of damage to each other's love lives; they have also provided a shoulder for the other to cry on. They both like to make new starts in life.

So why Tracey?

She spotted Gimpo. Bill and I ducked for cover. Imagine a sex-starved, rapist pitbull, Tasmanian she-devil hell bitch on meltdown; add the grossest, filthiest porno movie you've ever seen on fast forward; throw in nuclear sex-war, a gaggle of gobbling turkeys busting out of Bernard Matthews just before Christmas, and you get the picture. It was no Renoir. She was on him. Gimpo, blabbing about Elvis and one brave step for mankind, didn't stand a chance. We waited until she got a good rhythm going, steam heat rising, then made our move.

'Tracey,' Bill said calmly, 'we need two million dollars – we're going to save the world.' Without taking her mouth from Gimpo's shredded, bloody penis, the crazed fellatrix screamed deliriously: 'Take it! It's in the refrigerator.' Rasp, chew, bite, tear – it was horrific. 'And get the fuckouttahere!' We didn't argue.

Because although Tracey never loved Elvis, she believed in our crusade.

No, no, no – before all that. I've just remembered something else I should say first. When Voice of the Beehive were on tour in Australia (where, by the way, I'm told they are superstars), Tracey and her sister Melissa met up with this strange lady who sold them wings and magic wands. Tracey and Melissa became fairies. I have learned from reading *Peter Pan* that fairies swing between being all badness, deceit and conniving, to all goodness, honesty and love – all fairies have both these extreme sides in their personality, and it is thus with Tracey. Tracey is a perfect fairy.

I opened the door of the huge chrome refrigerator. It was stacked with hundreds of bottles of vodka, rotting hamburgers and piles of American dollars. At a glance, I calculated there were exactly two million: a sign. I stuffed all the money and as many bottles as I could into Bill's leather doctor's bag. 'We'll get the Gimp later,' I snapped, 007 with a money hard-on. 'Let's go – she ain't gonna be finished with sexboy till the poor bastard's liquid, drained and shrivelled. That stud's got work to do!'

We went to the nearest bar and waited.

Tracey had elected to make our icon of Elvis. Tracey is very good at making things. I had no idea what it was she intended to do. Z and I were summoned to her pad, where I refused to drink some lurid pink cocktail with a vodka base that matched Tracey's pink fluffy housecoat. I went out and bought myself a bottle of Jacob's Creek. Z drank the vodka neat. We were instructed to watch the video of *Hook*; told to eat chocolate cake that she had made for her father's birthday. (The strange thing about the birthday cake was that her father, who lives in Los Angeles, never got to taste it, nor even see it. Every year in honour of his birthday she bakes him his favourite chocolate cake and makes her friends eat it.) Z and I were hardly listening as she cackled on about unheard-of XTC LPs – we were both too engrossed in *Hook*, each hoping that the other would not notice our tears. A film for bad fathers.

Twenty or so beers later, a nice fug coming down, the torn shadow of Gimpo appeared in the room. His twisted visage registered a bizarre mix of disparate emotions: bliss and terror, longing and loathing, desire and disdain. 'I think I'm in love,' he blurted. 'It was horrible: shit, donkeys, blood, spunk, farts, everything. We're getting married.'

Bill took control. 'It's just the drugs, Gimp,' he said, reaching into his black leather doctor's bag. 'Trust me, I'm a doctor,' he added as he prepared an evil-looking syringe, then stabbed the malevolent implement straight through Gimpo's 501s and into his gnarled left buttock.

'God!' spurted Gimpo.

'No, just an antidote for chronic stupidity,' replied wise Bill, wiping and replacing the syringe in his black leather doctor's bag.

A word here about the seer Drummond: back in the seventies, Bill had been considered the world leader in the development of psychotropic drugs (it was Bill, in fact, who discovered the formula for MDMA which is proving so beneficial to the mental health of so many teenagers today). Unfortunately, Bill's promising pharmaceutical career ended suddenly in the early eighties when it was discovered that he planned to destabilize the world economy by manufacturing millions of tons of gold by means of alchemy and black magic. This magnificent global sedition was terminated only when he was caught stealing lead from the roof of his local Presbyterian church.

*

But back to Elvis and Tracey. What Tracey had done for us, done for mankind, was beyond all my hopes and fears. Hopefully a photograph of it will appear on the dust jacket of this book. If you can't make out the details, that printed stuff behind the image of Elvis in a black suit were miscellaneous pages ripped from the Bible, over the top of which she had stuck a couple of quotations from bits of Z's and my writings (I can't remember now what bits they were, but they were *relevant*); then all that stuff round the frame is top-grade paste pearls glued on and sprinkled with gold dust. Yes, yes, the thing dripped love; and right now as I sit on this plane, 35,000 feet above the North Sea, it is wrapped up safely in two Bon Scott T-shirts in Gimpo's holdall, not thirty inches from where I'm writing this.

Gimpo recovered from his fifth-dimensional sojourn in shaman country ten minutes later. The barman was giving us strange looks. Myself, Gimpo, Bill, the black bag and two million bucks headed for Heathrow. We were in business: next stop Helsinki.

Tracey, if you don't think I've been totally kind or fair to you in this portrayal, let me make it up to you by patronizing you further. Trace, I think you are the most talented woman songwriter in the world, and the most beautiful American woman I have ever met, and I am glad I know you. Thanks for Elvis. So that's it. That's Tracey. That's how we got to take an icon of Elvis to the North Pole as our gift to mankind.

CHAPTER TWO

The Legend of the Lost Chord

I've just thought I should tell you about the letters. Z and I have
been mates since some time in the mid 1980s. After I moved into
the cottage and all this life-spiralling-out-of-control thing started happening, I wrote to him. He wrote back; I wrote back; and a lurid,
lucid, drunken, mindless correspondence avalanched its way through
our respective letter boxes – up to five, six, seven letters a day. Men
of letters? A noble ambition, but many of these epistles were nothing
more than scribbled threats on peeled beer mats and ripped up fag
packets, dark truths and even darker lies.

Through these letters we entered a world where nothing was certain. I might write a letter full of chronic doubt, but Z would find a
chink in my fake self-effacing armour and sink his rapier. At times,
the two of us lived in fear of what other painful truths the postman
would deliver. These letters left no space to talk of the weather
or infanticide on the National Health. Yeah, and there was the
buddy-buddy stuff – the bitches, whores and angels stuff, and the
big stuff to do with God and His Arch-Adversary. I think we even
thought for a time that through our letters the ultimate forces of
good and evil were fighting it out for mastery of Creation.

All this time we never met up, never spoke on the phone. We
realized that to do so would bring us back to crummy objective
reality, to the façade of most face-to-face communications.

At some point, Elvis started to make his presence felt in our
missives. I dropped a copy of Albert Goldman's *Elvis* ('an abomina-
tion of a book') addressed to Z's Clerkenwell flat in the pillar box.
Scrawled across each of the 326 pages, in my large and clumsy hand,

was the word LIES. In my pretentious moments I read it as a mantra; at other times as just the excrement of a bitter soul. Thankfully, Z chose to focus on the mantra side and wrote back suggesting he would nail each individual page of the book, one at a time, to pine trees spaced out along the Arctic Circle, then fire a volley of shots from his Uzi 9mm through each and every one in turn.

What took us from that suggestion of his to the events that are now unfolding, I'm not sure. I know we asked Gimpo to come with us to deal with the reality side of things. Then, as there were three of us, we reckoned we must be the Magi returned. It followed that we might very easily meet up with the Baby Jesus, though perhaps not in his nappy-filling guise.

When the journey was first mooted, there was talk of our setting off for the North Pole on Christmas Day, thus fitting in neatly with the Three Wise Men/Baby Jesus stuff. I had visions of us reaching the Pole on Twelfth Night, with the Pole Star directly above us, at our feet a swaddling baby lying in a cradle made of snow, emanating the Way, the Truth and the Light. I argued with Z that we should leave on the Epiphany. Z retaliated by demanding that we set off immediately, before the Zeitgeist moved on or we got bored of the idea. That was four days ago – hence the lack of planning.

The drinks trolley has been round. Z and Gimpo are on their third can of Fosters and I am on my second quarter-sized bottle of a Cabernet Sauvignon. OK, but not great. I don't want to get pissed; I never do. I have an in-built something that prevents me from getting drunk. Three pints of bitter and I switch to halves; after the second half I start drinking water. Z hates me for it.

Z and Gimpo are playing with their Zen sticks. I get mine out. They are peeling the bark off theirs. I resist. A hostess asks us politely what our staves are for.

'Zen sticks,' Z replies. 'We're Zen Masters on the way to the North Pole.' He does the whole thing: how we are going to find the Baby Jesus inside ourselves and thereby save the world. I think she is impressed because she asks Gimpo to unwrap the picture from the Bon Scott T-shirts. And now, of course, with the help of a little tender alcohol, the wanton hussy falls into the shaggable category. (I see Z and Gimpo are thinking the same thing.)

I have the window seat. I hate people smoking. Well, sometimes I don't mind it. Occasionally I enjoy the aroma of a freshly lit roll-your-own, and I always love sticking my nose into a bag of Golden Virginia. But on planes I loathe smokers with a vengeance. Out of deference to Z we are sitting in the smoking section (actually, to be fair, we were late checking in because of my insistence on having a fry-up breakfast and these were the only three seats next to each other left anywhere on the plane). The fat German businessman in front of me is smoking. The air vent above my head fails to disperse the smoke.

The dinner trolley comes round. I refuse the shite. Yes, of course I hate in-flight food; always bring my own packed lunch and Thermos, but this time I forgot. Pick at Gimpo's tray; eat his biscuits, cheese and grapes. My knees are hurting from the cramped conditions.

I mean, what is Z dressed like? He has his baggy chequered lightweight trousers on, new only last month. Of course, these kegs are now stained with spilt beer, curries, skid marks (not shite, just good honest earth where he has fallen down when trying to make quick getaways from reality). He has one of those cheap Milletts checked shirts on, undone halfway to his belly button; no T-shirt or vest, revealing his grimy skin and his *pièce de résistance*, a tattoo you instinctively know that no one else in the world has: a plain, black Christian cross. The vertical is about twelve inches long and the horizontal about eight inches across, and both are a solid black, one and a half inches thick. The world is full of tigers and dragons, snakes and daggers, swallows and skulls, intricately displayed across ageing flesh (Z has plenty of these 'other' types of tattoos on his arms), but nowhere will you find something as simple and powerful as the cross on Z's chest. If you have ever had a tattoo, you will appreciate the pain that Z endured in having this solid cross carved into his proud, living skin. Earlier this year, after a rather harrowing foreign tour of duty, he returned to Blighty with the knowledge that he must have this final tattoo done. If you ask him why, you may get an answer, which might be that it works as a constant reminder that there is always something bigger than oneself – like that 'Deck of Cards' song, but without all the cloying American shite.

The 'Fasten seatbelt' announcement comes on over the intercom. We are now warned we will be flying into some pretty heavy air turbulence. I can boast that I am a man who enjoys a bit of heavy air turbulence. Gimpo and Z relate a horrifying tale about the Love Reaction flying back from Paris in a tiny, private, single-engine job, drunken drug-fiend owner at the controls. It seems they battered their way through the elements across the Channel like some returning but fatally injured Spitfire. This turbulence in the here and now is crap – I can even keep my pen steady as I write – no tumbling hundreds of feet down off the edge of one thermal then bang into another's upward thrust.

Lift my left buttock and let a silently sly fart slip free. Look out of the window; make sure the engine is still joined to the wing, as you do, and remember something that happened last night.

I had been driving through London in my pick-up truck with the radio tuned to Melody FM, 'the contemporary easy-listening music station'. The seductive music was pulling me into a nether world of dark chocolate and lonely nights, the lights of West London spinning by; Sergio Mendes and Brazil '66 performed their version of 'Fool on the Hill' and I was talking to myself. Well, not really to myself, but to an imagined audience. My voice had taken on the hushed, soothing tones of a Melody FM presenter with just a hint of Scottish lilt. Yes, for a few moments somewhere on the White City end of the Westway I knew what I wanted out of life: to be a night-time presenter on Melody FM. But the ambition lost focus and other thoughts seeped in: lies, deceit and self-loathing.

'Well fuck you,' is what I've got to say.

The odour has reached my nostrils. A good one.

Oh no, the air turbulence is getting real. Z strikes up a conversation with me: 'What are we going to do when we get there?' he asks. This is a loaded question, as there has already been a bit of friction about this. The original plan had been to spend the first night in an up-market Rock 'n' Roll hotel in Helsinki, go out on the town, hit the bars, pull some birds – you know, all that Brits abroad, male fantasy stuff. Never happens like that, but we can't stop the dreams, pre-programmed millions of years ago.

I don't care how many New Man affectations you take on board, the Cave Man isn't got rid of with just one generation of feminist propaganda. You know that slogan 'All men are rapists'? Of course it's true. Bloody obvious. But what are we supposed to do about it? Don't expect us to change in twelve months what evolution has taken millions of years to create – that's like suddenly deciding we should have six fingers on each hand to fit in with the survival necessities of the moment and expecting evolution to perform its tricks while we take a tea-break.

(That reminds me, why is the tea always so shit on aeroplanes?) They have just announced we will be landing in ten minutes' time and we have not resolved our differences. I think we should fuck off to the frozen wastes as fast as we can – none of this soddin' hanging round in hotel bars.

Disembark. International airports full of foreign people, global culture mixed with tell-tale signs of the stupidity of all those who are not us. It's weird, innit? No matter how many copies of the *Guardian* you read, it doesn't change the fact that as soon as you step on to foreign soil that little, blinkered jingoistic bigot starts to climb out of its hiding, releasing ugly thoughts about who won the war, 'Rule Britannia', the World Cup '66, The Beatles and how crap foreign pop music is. Quick, get my copy of yesterday's *Observer* out to remind myself how good a European I am, a citizen of the world ready to shape the twenty-first century as a safe and peaceful place for my grandchildren. We stand around waiting for Gimpo and Z's bag to come out of the baggage reclaim tunnel.

It is sometimes hard to understand what Gimpo is trying to tell you, not because of a speech impediment or regional accent, but because he will often start midway through a conversation, expecting you, the listener, to know what has gone on before. It's as if the linear flow of his speech has been broken up and then put back together in an inconsequential order before leaving his mouth. Maybe it's something to do with the shell-shock he suffered during the Falklands War, which made him permanently deaf in one ear. (His job was to load and fire cannons at Argie ships hiding out of sight on the far side of the horizon.) Mind you, it could be because he's from Manchester.

I'm a very Liverpool-orientated sort of person so, naturally, I hate

Manchester, loathe Manchester United. The only thing I ever liked about Manchester United was Denis Law. OK, I'll forget about football. But there is another thing I want to say about Manchester: it's fuckin' boring. I mean, it's so fuckin' worthy, solid; built out of honest, hard labour. The people are straightforward, they work hard or, if on the dole, they are properly poor. But Liverpool? That's another piece of duck-billed platypus.

Nothing is straightforward in Liverpool. It's a city where the conscious and subconscious mix freely, a city where the interstellar ley lines slither down back streets, a city built on ill-gotten gains. You can smell it in the air when you visit the place; you can catch glimpses of it on the hidden cornices of Victorian houses built for the sea captains home from the East Indies. Something of Jewish medieval culture was left behind by the pogrom-fleeing hordes as they made their escape from Eastern Europe via Liverpool to the New World. The Jews dumped a load of their 6,000 years of superstition, minor chords and mystery as they made their way down from Lime Street Station to Pierhead to catch those late nineteenth century Atlantic-crossing steamers. When Carl Gustav Jung dreams, he dreams of Liverpool. Only in Liverpool could you have a School of Language, Music, Dream and Pun whose school song is 'The Jung Ones'.

What the fuck has Liverpool got to do with our journey to the Pole with Elvis, finding the Baby Jesus inside ourselves and saving the world? Fuck all. What do you want me to do? Give you a detailed description of the floor tiles and light fittings used in Finnish baggage-reclaim halls? The thing is with real-life A-to-B external journeys, you can't stop those internal journeys spiralling off in strange directions at any given moment. It is down to you, dear reader, to sift through all of this and act as Editor-in-Chief. It may be that any one of these mindless observations contains the key that turns the lock and releases the Baby Jesus – and maybe I won't see it myself until days, weeks, years later; until, returning to ramblings, I will suddenly realize that yes, the secret of the universe, the road to Nirvana, is hidden in the floor tiles and light fittings. I am tempted to say unlikely, but I won't. Am I a Zen Master or what? But I am bored sitting here waiting for Gimpo and Z's bag.

Z shuffles his tarot cards.

The bag arrives. It's a beat-up affair, veteran of many a scuzzy tour, held together by at least three rolls of Gaffa tape.

Helsinki customs: no electronics, no screens – no problem. The World War Two issue Wehrmacht Luger and twenty rounds of ammunition secreted in Gimpo's rectum went undetected, as did the bad kaleidoscope contents of Bill's black leather doctor's bag.

Gimpo takes control. We stumble through customs and out into the grey light of early November 1992, Helsinki, Finland. We're not too sure what time of day it is. The time difference is two hours, but whether it is forwards or backwards we do not know. Mind you, none of us are watch-carriers. 'Time? Hey, that's for straights,' croaks a distant voice.

From the buses with unpronounceable destinations we somehow detect one that will take us to the railway station, where we hope to buy tickets straight to the Arctic. We clamber on board. It is great having Gimpo there, taking responsibility for our safety and paying for everything as we go. Z and I are like two little children, Gimpo is our dad and he is taking us on holiday to Skegness for the week.

Z has told me about how wonderful it is to go on tour with the Love Reaction. As the bus leaves John Henry's (rehearsal room and gear storage) with the band on board, they all wave out of the window, bye-bye to reality, and for two weeks it is tour-bus freedom: eighteen hours a day of porn films, two hours of *This is Spinal Tap* and four hours of sound-checking and gig. On the tour bus you sleep, shit, fart, drink, scream, wank, shag, eat, read, write, dream and watch the world slide by until Gimpo tells you it is time to get on stage. Then Gimpo sorts out which girls are allowed back-stage and of those which ones are to be allowed on the tour bus – I have even heard rumour that Z instructs Gimpo as to which girls are allowed to look at him and which are not.

Yep, all you feminists and post-feminists out there, if you want to stamp out all this male shite, don't bother with the Church of England, gentlemen's clubs and rugby changing rooms – stamp out Rock 'n' Roll tour buses. These small but perfectly formed cocoons of maledom are travelling the roads of your country, spreading a disease to willing young people everywhere.

We're on the bus now. We play with our Zen sticks and we wonder if anyone has noticed that we are Zen Masters, the Three Wise Men, the Magi returned. Z finds some scraps of paper, borrows a pencil from me and starts to scribble furiously – poetry, I assume. He writes poetry like other people kick dogs, breathe air and kack their kegs. There is no stopping Z when the muse hits.

During the flight Bill had proudly produced his Drummond tartan and decided to wear it. The Finns, of course, are totally unused to seeing tall Scotsmen in women's clothes, and consequently, within one hour of landing in Helsinki, we were involved in three incidents of unprecedented violence, the third of which culminated in the bloody death of an innocent taxi driver. I thought it was pretty dumb to shoot the guy through the back of his head while he was driving, but I didn't say anything. Bill is unpredictable at the best of times, but particularly when he's just committed murder and is still simmering in some neo-Celtic post-traumatic macho disorder.

Foreign buses full of foreign people. They never let you down – wherever you go in the world they are always there and always have that same foreign vibe. I suppose it would be a different vibe if we were in a Third World country – then it would be all people hanging off the sides and goats pissing in the aisle. Standing-room only for us lot on the bus. Gimpo has farted one of his specials. Outside, a Northern European city passes by.

It is time for me to come out, or at least for me to reveal to my two fellow Wise Men the magic costume I have stashed in my black haversack. I undo the buckles and yank it out. Z and Gimpo fulfil my hopes. They cheer my secret attire: my Drummond tartan kilt, given to me on my twenty-first birthday by my dad. (As there are three Drummond tartans and each can be dyed in either bright or subdued hues, there is not much call for any one combination, which means that when you want a kilt in a particular hue or a particular Drummond tartan, the material has to be woven specially for you.)

For a Scotsman, owning and wearing a kilt is very worrying

because it is an obvious statement of what you think you are. You fear the statement you are really making is that you are in fact a dickhead with some arrogant, blinkered Caledonian chip on your shoulder and can't help but be screaming: 'Look at me! Look, I've got a kilt on! Come on, ask me something stupid like, "What are you wearing underneath? What Clan are you? Oh, you do look good in it! Do you wear it all the time? You should wear it more often."' The worst paranoia is that there will be another Scots person whom you will make either doubly embarrassed or angry because in some way you are letting your common heritage down. So that's why I seldom wear my kilt, although I am very proud of it. I even make up lies about it – I tell people that it is an ancient custom for fathers to give their sons kilts on their twenty-first birthdays. Not so, not so.

In foreign parts, kilts are very useful things to have, up there with platinum American Express cards and small private armies. Kilts open doors and make friends, win admiration and scare off muggers. They get you seats in crowded restaurants without a reservation; they gain you instant admission to the crack dens in the Lower Bronx; they are loved and feared around the world, as long as you're outside the British Isles.

Last night, while driving my pick-up truck, I had an idea. I knew I was going to be taking my kilt to the Pole for all the above reasons; I also knew it was going to be freezing, so yes, I had this breakthrough vision: I would wear my kilt on top of my jeans. Nobody could then ask the question, 'What are you wearing underneath it?' I would still be warm, I reckoned I would still look hard, and there would be this added madman-out-on-the-edge vibe that would lend credence (false, maybe) to my artistic persona. So there you have it. Here I am standing on this bus and I strap my kilt on. I wait for the round of applause and yes, Z and Gimps give us the thumbs up. But what of the rest of the bus? Nothing . . .

Shit! Oh no! Here we go, the woman standing in front of me turns and confronts me. She opens her mouth. I want to climb into my haversack and hide in shame. She too is Scottish, from Banff, wants to know where I'm from and what we're doing over here. She's approaching her middle years. And I know, and I know that she knows, and she knows that I know that she knows, that by

23

standing here in the aisle of a foreign bus, with all these foreigners looking on, and strapping a kilt over my jeans, I am compromising an entire nation and its history. We didn't win Bannockburn so I could behave like this. Shame, shame and triple shame.

But Z and Gimpo don't notice. We play with our Zen sticks and we are soon at the station. Gimpo gets the tickets. We decide on getting the 9.15 p.m. It's about half four now. We are able to book a three-berth cabin and it doesn't seem as stupidly expensive as I feared. Next we put our bags in the lock-up; then to the phone booths.

I used to be in a band called The KLF. There were only two of us, me and Jimmy. Mega Records were the licensees for all the KLF product throughout Scandinavia. In our brief career Finland was the only country outside the UK where our 'It's Grim Up North' was a hit. Zodiac's records are also released through Mega in Scandinavia, and they too have met with a certain amount of success here. Last week I spoke to a couple of people at the Mega head office in Copenhagen, warning them of our pilgrimage and asking them to let the Finnish office know of our impending arrival.

If you're a recording artist you believe that it is your God-given right that, when visiting a foreign country, the people who release your records there should treat you like a conquering hero, or at least take you out to dinner, or at the very least let you drink the beer in their office fridge. They put up with your posturing bad behaviour because: 1) you could be The Next Big Thing; 2) you're there for no more than three days; 3) it is their job to be lackeys. All of this is disgusting, I know, and although I am tempted to qualify this admission of vileness, I won't. The thing is, you know that as soon as you leave town they are going to bad-mouth you rotten.

So Gimpo phones Mega. He gets on well with the promo girl there, but it turns out she got sacked on Friday. I'd heard rumour that Mega's operations in Finland were being totally restructured, relocated and refinanced. So when Gimpo gets through, they don't know who the fuck we are, and as he is talking in his shell-shocked, kill Argies, broken down and reconstructed language they don't understand what the fuck he is on about anyway. He tries to tell them something about Elvis, the world being saved, and a possible KLF *Greatest Hits* CD. But none of that matters, because I am sure they fall in love instantly with his warm and honest charm, and give him Mega's new address.

Five minutes later we are in the back of a foreign taxi, grudelburgers clocking up on the meter, failing light and miserable people outside. Z farts. We arrive at an unlit, empty backstreet; menacing dark warehouses loom over us. The address that Gimpo has been given is wrong.

We clambered from the taxi wreckage, soaked in black blood and speckled with tiny pieces of broken glass. We looked like exotic glittering birds from some violent, necromantic paradise. Bill was mumbling something under his breath about bastards, kilts, poofs and dresses; however, he quickly composed himself and apologized for his temporary loss of sanity. William Drummond: Scottish gentleman.

The taxi leaves us: rain, wind, and a sense that we have already got ourselves lost. I run a hundred or so yards down the cobbled street, cross over and bang on a warehouse door. I have a reason for this: the only lit window in the whole of the street is at the top of this warehouse. A voice from an intercom crackles and, yes, welcomes us to the new Mega office. I hail Z and Gimpo over.

We walked the rest of the way to our rendezvous with Mega Records. Neither Bill nor myself knew anything about them, but we assumed they would be like record companies all over the world – good for a free meal and an evening's entertainment of booze-fuelled bullshit. Fuck knows how we found the place, but we did.

We rang the bell of Mega Records Finland and were buzzed up. The elevator Axminster swirled around our ankles and crawled up the shiny mirror walls. Posh. We were greeted by the most beautiful girl I had ever seen: an angel from heaven with a word processor and sexy bad English. A profusion of Pre-Raphaelite russet curls cascaded on to her bare, alabaster shoulders; soft-focus lips like bruised cherries exhaled smoke from a French cigarette, and long, black lashes fluttered around eyes as blue as a child's crayon drawing. I was smitten.

I turned on the full volume of my lying-bastard, snake-oil super-charm. Five minutes later I had convinced her that I would marry her, that I wanted her to have my babies, loved her more than life itself, that she was the girl of my dreams and all the clockwork rest; ten minutes later I was giving her one up the shitter in the women's bogs. (I always use anal sex on girls I suspect of not using contraception: it's what I call safe sex − safe for me, anyway, with no chance of evil paternity suits or other female black magic.) I spat my sordid wad into her lower intestine, zipped up, told her she was a naïve little cunt, all men are bastards, she should stick to having sex with people her own age, and to think of this experience as a practical lesson in just how unfair and cruel life can be.

Between sobs and salty tears, she thanked me and told me that I was a true Zen Master and she felt honoured to have been buggered by a man so wise and noble. I was surprised at such wisdom and told her that when I returned from my heroic quest I might let her have sex with me again. She laughed and I dried her tiny tears.

Top floor, open-plan office. We meet, shake hands with the welcoming Ulla and Mulla. Ulla is the MD, Mulla is one of the other directors. No beer in the fridge. Drink foreign black coffee. I never drink coffee. Makes me shake. They apologize for not knowing of our visit. 'Hey that's OK,' is our vibe back. It is almost 6 p.m. Mulla cancels his squash appointment. They suggest they take us to dinner at a local restaurant. We accept. Ulla is in her mid thirties, she has a voluptuous figure and she's all open, warm, friendly smiles.

When I got back to the office, Bill was ejaculating over the handsome features of the female MD. Thick globs spattered on to her bold Nordic countenance. She smiled up at him submissively, sperm twinkling on her eyelashes. She reminded me of a Man Ray photograph. Gimpo was attacking his penis in an onanistic frenzy, his arm a juddering blur, eyes bulging, face blood-red. He screamed like a gelded pig and his lightning seed shot out like automatic-rifle fire and shattered a light bulb. Preliminaries over, Ulla, the MD, suggested a drink. An excellent idea, I thought.

Mulla may be younger, he is slim, cosmopolitan and, dare I say it, somewhat fey. On the surface they seem to accept us for what we are. 'What is that?' A voice.

We trooped around the corner to Oscar's, the local vodka bar where Ulla supplied us all with copious amounts of friendly alcohol.

Oscar's is a restaurant. Empty, but for us, on this miserable Monday evening. The menu: post-modern shite. You come to Helsinki, what do you want? You want traditional Finnish grub. What is this on the menu? Fake Louisiana swamp food: gumbo, black-eyed beans, crayfish pie and stuff. But hey, go with the flow. We order up, get stiff vodkas, bottles of wine and beer.

Why did they call it Oscar's? After Oscar Wilde? It is neither a very Finnish nor a very Cajun name. Music is pumping out from somewhere – The Doors, Big Jim mumbling something about taking it on through to the other side. The thing is with The Doors, you wanna hate them but they keep creeping back into your personal All-Time Top Ten Best Groups Ever.

What Z and I want is 'Immigrant Song' by Led Zeppelin, so we stand on our chairs and sing at the top of our voices: 'They came from the land of the ice and snow, With the midnight sun and hot springs flow,' and then the classic Robert 'Plant Pot' scream bit.

Of course we tell Ulla and Mulla the reason for and the meaning of our pilgrimage north, about the star we are following, about the Baby Jesus; and about Buddha sitting under his tree, about our Zen sticks and our icon of Elvis. But then I realize we have a problem, or we will have a problem: in my head we really are going to the North Pole, but Z keeps talking about nailing our icon of Elvis to a tree and having our picture taken in front of it, pointing manfully northwards. He has even been joking about spending five days in Helsinki and just pretending that we have gone to the North Pole, then something about the power of imagination.

None of this computes with me. What I understand we are going to do is get this train tonight; then tomorrow morning, in Rovaniemi, we will hire a vehicle and we will drive north, north and further north; and when we get to the Arctic Ocean it will be frozen and we will have a full tank of petrol and we will keep on driving north. Gimpo has a compass with him so we will know where we are going, and we will keep driving until we run out of petrol. Then we get out of the car and we keep going on foot until we die.

I think it is this last part that Z is dubious about. You see, I've never mentioned the dying bit to Z before, but I think he has detected that death-wish element in my psychical make-up and is a bit worried that I might drag him and Gimpo over the edge with me. Or maybe he hopes that by coming up with ideas like nailing the icon to a lonesome pine tree in some friendly Finnish forest I will go along with it and thus save all our lives.

The trouble is, I can entertain two opposing beliefs at the same time: I am certain we must push ourselves to the point of no return to achieve our goals – we have to die for our cause to prove to the world it was a cause worth dying for; I also believe that we will be using our return air tickets back to Blighty next Sunday. I mean, did Rupert Bear ever stop to question how he was going to get back to Nutwood when one of his adventures started to unfold? No, Rupert went on and on into the unknown; but he too, like us, knew that by the end of the story he would be back in Nutwood in time for tea. So, yes, I had promised Kate and James I would be back by tea-time next Sunday; and I promised the Divine Spirit that we would . . . Well anyway, enough of that.

Mulla has just recommended we should try some weird Finnish brandy. Finnish brandy? They don't grow grapes up here. I shut up and accept his offer.

A spectacular bout of drinking ensued, with magnificent and unpredictable results. Time and reality dissolved. Somewhere in the distance I could hear the theme tune to *The Twilight Zone*: doodo doodo, doodo doodo . . . I tuned into the weirdness, ditched the paddle and drifted downstream, laughing.

*

All through this meal I scratch away at these notes. Between quaffs of red wine, mouthfuls of Creole Swamp Duck and pleasant big talk somebody keeps catching my eye. I now have to recognize his presence. I look him straight in the eye and confront him.

Hanging on the wall opposite our table is a large black and white photo portrait, four foot by six foot, of Rock's greatest (bar one) living legend: Keith Richards.

Fuck loads of vodka later, I thought I recognized a skeletal figure drinking alone at the bar. He was slumped alky-style over a bottle of Rebel Yell bourbon, bleary-eyed and unshaven. A crow's nest of untidy black hair framed cadaverous, sunken cheeks and his mouth looked like a cemetery studded with askew and broken tombstones. He stank of bad breath and heroin and looked like Count Dracula with a hangover. The spectral ruin raised a glass of whisky to his mouth and missed. It spilled down his dirty white shirt, adding yet another territory to the stained map of his perpetual debauchery. He pulled on a bent Marlboro, and it was then that I saw it: a huge silver skull ring on the third finger of his left hand. Here was conclusive evidence: it had to be him.

'Keith?' I whispered cautiously, but he didn't hear me. 'Keith Richards? It is you, isn't it? What are you doing in Helsinki?' I was genuinely stunned to see him here. In Burroughs's Marrakech possibly; Conrad's evil Congo perhaps; New York City even; India, Bangkok, anywhere – but not fucking Scandinavia, home of genital hygiene and mixed saunas. His large, lizard head lifted slowly, malevolently. 'Fack off, cant,' he hissed through his Marlboro-destroyed larynx. His strong South London accent had miraculously survived the ragged wanderings of the past twenty-odd years. Stung at first by his uncalled-for rudeness, I calmed my macho pride and decided not to beat him to a bloody pulp – after all, he was one of a dying breed, a true living legend of Rock 'n' Roll; and, besides, he was obviously shit-faced and I was truly impressed. He did look bad, though. I mean really bad, like alky bad, like dead bad, like that bad.

The photo looks like it was taken some time in the late seventies/ early eighties. Keith Richards – I somehow feel the need to explain Keith Richards. It might take a few pages.

This isn't the reality of Keith as his mother or his wife or his son could tell you: this is the real reality. You see, Keith is our big brother; he is big brother to every boy who has bought an electric guitar in the British Isles since 1965. Stories, myths and legends, spread word-of-mouth through our little world of pre-CBS Fenders and Vox ac 30 valve amps. It is not that we wanted to be him or have a band like The Rolling Stones, but that Keith went out into the world and achieved everything we could ever dream of achieving in our adolescent Rock dreams, and he is still there and still doing it. As a guitarist he has never been flash, never played aerodynamic solos beyond our reach – just honest, straightforward stuff. He has fallen down, worn stupid clothes, made bad records; but he has never blown it, never lost our admiration. He has always been above and beyond current fads and fashions. He will never be part of any establishment. The basic haircut has stayed the same, now flecked with grey; the lines in the face have deepened, ripened and hardened, telling tales of a life well spent.

The thing is, although we know that Keith has never blown it, we also know he is not infallible, that he struggles on a daily basis with the things we struggle with – getting up, getting to rehearsals on time, getting your guitar in tune, making a record that doesn't sound shite, having to acknowledge that the record company pays your wages – but all of this just confirms his greatness in our eyes. He has never attempted to leave our world, never shattered our dreams by taking up with some stupid Eastern religion, gone all progressive on us, got into mime or made records for worthy charities. Even when he made an appearance at Live Aid's US show, backing up Bob Dylan along with his side-kick Ronnie Wood, you could tell that all three of them were so out of it and making such a terrible racket that they could never be accused of turning up and performing to help their own fading careers.

Then there is that other great weakness/strength of his. For thirty years Mick and Keith have pissed each other off, had rows, slagged each other in the world's media, both claiming to be the boss of the Stones, never resolving their differences long enough to make a truly great LP. And yet, and yet . . . We all know, even if they don't, they can't make any sort of a record without each other: they are the ultimate male partnership, chained together by a history of Rock that neither of them can unwrite. And we, we have all learnt from this; we, Rock music's foot soldiers, can see that however much Mick and Keith do not understand or are unwilling to acknowledge each other's strengths, that the adage is true: the sum is greater than the parts.

And that reproachful eye of his that gimlets out from magazine and record covers stretching across our lives. That look that keeps us in check, that keeps reminding us that it is only Rock 'n' Roll. But, but, but. Don't ever, never.

Keith, Keith! KEITH! What is it that we must never do? But he never tells us. So sometimes we don't keep ourselves in check and we go off and make a record with some South American rainforest people or decide that the electric guitar is too limiting in its ability to express the magnitude of our imagination. Of course, we make arseholes of ourselves and we come back and we are sorry; we pick up our guitar and some time soon we see a picture of Keith, and those eyes of his tell us, 'I told you so,' and yes, he did.

'Cant! Cant! Fackin' cant! Four-foot little barstard fackin' cants!' I realized that this wasn't directed at me and that he was talking about something or somebody else. 'Six million fackin' quid,' he continued, blind, stinking drunk. 'All my life, hic, lost, hic. Fackin' chord!' Keith lurched and heaved a hissing stream of black vomit on to his snake-skin boots. He wiped his mouth and continued. 'Lappish cants. The Lost Chord.'

He slumped on to the bar, unconscious. I was mesmerized. Anyone who has been at all connected with Rock 'n' Roll – from the lowest roadie lager rat to the highest-paid, hairspray-preening, stadium Yank wankbag millionaire – knows of the Legend of the Lost Chord. It is the Holy Grail amongst Rock 'n' Rollers of all generations. Bill and Gimpo slid across the room like anacondas spying a wounded rat.

'He knows of the Chord?' whispered Bill, serious as Moses.

'I think the old cunt knows where it is,' I replied, scared.

'Get him in the backroom, quick,' said Bill. 'We've got to sober him up.'

Gimpo hauled the stinking sack of bones and whisky over his shoulder and disappeared into the ominous shadows behind the bar. Bill picked up his leather bag and we followed him through the twinkling glass-bead curtains into the foreboding backroom of Oscar's bar. It was dark and smelt of consumption and satanic flatulence. The sickly perfume of dead flowers and tallow candles curled around the room, the Byzantine odours leaving me light-headed and slightly nauseous. Gimpo farted loudly, adding a vulgar note to the decadent, aromatic symphony. Weird Victorian furniture seemed to grow out of the walls and floors, all spiral turns and poison-ivy organic. Well-thumbed copies of the gay soft-porn magazines *Him* and *Zipper* were arranged in neat piles on an antique crystal coffee table. Flock wallpaper peeled from the walls, and between the damp and moss patches hung several faded photographs of a fey-looking blond boy, lovingly framed with faded green paper carnations. In the corner a huge bookshelf stuffed with ancient leather tomes on pederasty and all things Greek towered like a massive, shadow-dripping child molester. Malodorous green velvet curtains festooned with dusty cobwebs blocked out all natural light and sucked in the sound of our anxious breathing. An acrid plume of incontinence bent the hairs of my left nostril, and I noticed a sinister black cat with smouldering amber eyes spying on me from the top of the perverted bookshelf.

And here we are, Z, Gimpo and me, Zen Masters, all three, the Magi off looking for the Baby Jesus, sitting in Oscar's bar, and Keith Richards is up there on the wall giving us that reproachful eye. Have we gone too far; strayed too long from our Fender Twin Reverbs, Marshall stacks and Mesa Boogie amps?

Sometimes you have to tell a big brother to fuck off, and right now it is the right time to stand up and scream: 'Fuck right off, Keith!'

Bill broke the spell: 'Roll the cunt's sleeve up!' A thin arc of some esoteric pharmaceutical spurted from the needle of Bill's trusty syringe. He managed to find one uncollapsed vein and administered the drug. Keith sobered up immediately. Bill dug him again in the same vein with a large dose of sodium muscaria pethomanius, a notorious and highly illegal CIA truth drug. Keith's chemical monologue rambled and salivated like an inebriated sine wave for just over four hours. It would be impossible to repeat this speech exactly, but here is the gist of our new companion's strange tale:

Four years ago, Keith had paid a small fortune for a hand-drawn map showing the exact location and address of the Keeper of the Lost Chord, a shaman from Lapland. He had then travelled by private jet and platinum credit card to the shaman's home, a tepee in the middle of a snow-covered field.

Keith was welcomed into the old man's surprisingly snug Arctic home. Strange talismans, bones and magical tools hung from the reindeer-skin walls; cryptic diagrams and star charts were spread on the floor around the blazing fire, whose flickering yellow flames were straddled by a cast-iron tripod from which hung a black cauldron. A strange, viscous brew bubbled in the evil-looking pot. The wrinkled features of the ancient seer were covered in black soot and grease from the crackling blaze. His wise eyes peered at Keith across the turbulent liquid as he added odd roots and weird powders to his satanic stew. 'Drink!' said the shaman, dipping an earthenware ladle into the murky broth.

Beyond this, Keith could remember little. Piecing together the half-recalled events from his drugged, broken rant, it seemed obvious that the old shaman bastard had pulled one of the oldest tricks in the book: he had fed Keith the notorious hallucinogenic mushroom, amanita muscaria, commonly known in Lapland as the flesh of God, and had then palmed him off with a bunch of cheap Zen riddles. Our suspicions were confirmed when Keith started clapping with one hand and mumbling about the Secret Being in his heart and cherry blossom. As if this were not evidence enough, Keith cemented our fears by telling us of a bank statement showing the six-million-dollar cheque he had given the shaman had been cashed in Las Vegas just three days after their encounter.

'Do you still have the map?' Bill inquired with sympathy. Keith was sniffling, oily tears trickling down his leathery skin. The poor bastard.

*

33

My kilt falls down, revealing that my flies are undone and my knob is hanging limply out – this had something to do with me undoing the buckle of my kilt so I could sit and eat loads of grub with ease and to make things simpler when taking a slash. Keith made no reply.

But before Keith could reply to Bill's gentle probings, his hypnotic reverie was broken by the dramatic opening of a large oak door. Framed in the doorway, a phantasmagorical vision of decadent splendour: an eldritch, rotund figure in a pink crushed-velvet catsuit spattered with all manner of radiant jewellery, posing like a Shirley Bassey from some weird hallucinogenic nether dimension. It sparkled in the flickering yellow candlelight like a fat supernatural peacock. Waxy folds of flesh seemed to melt beneath an enormous blue-rinse bouffant wig. Its gums were bleeding behind garish pink lipstick and its pungent breath, reeking of sperm and onions, swam around the room like a dying catfish. It was as if the Baron Frankenstein had produced for us a new creation made up from the putrescent remains of Liberace and Quentin Crisp. This fabulous grotesquerie spoke, cracking its layer of thick orange foundation into a terrible map of debauchery and anal pursuits.

'Gentlemen,' a creepy, high-pitched vibrato. 'Please, be seated.' It gestured grandly, spilling copious amounts of laudanum from a dirty brandy glass. 'To what do I owe this pleasure? It's been so long since I had visitors,' it continued in a girlish soprano, totally uninterested in the answer to this question and obviously loving the sound of its own voice.

It fished a banana from a nearby crystal fruit bowl and proceeded to peel the fruit with lascivious relish. 'My name is Oscar Wilde,' it squawked loudly. It tossed back its head and threw both arms and the banana in the air. 'And I am alive!'

'Fuck!' muttered Bill.

'*The Picture of Dorian Gray* – it was all true!' continued the yapping poof. 'I,' he declared, 'am immortal!'

'You're pissed,' chuckled Keith derisively, swigging from a fresh bottle of bourbon.

A gentle gust of wind blew in through the beaded curtain making a sound like Chinese wind chimes and adding new perfumes to the already heady atmosphere of Ouija boards, cemeteries and farts. I don't know why, but for some unfathomable reason I believed the weird homo-monster was telling the truth.

'Faggot twat,' muttered Keith resignedly from behind his black teeth.

'Ignore him!' snapped Oscar, 'he's still bitter about Michael and me.'

'How come you look so old?' I asked, confused. 'I thought it was the picture that was supposed to age.'

'Darling,' sang Oscar camply; 'you think I look bad. You should see the painting! It makes old leather-face there,' pointing at Keith, 'look like a baby's pink little bottom, hee hee.' He balled his pudgy fist to conceal an acrid belch. 'Excuse me,' he continued, pardoning himself. 'It's the same old story, I'm afraid: deals with the Devil, Mephistophelean maleficence, purloined souls, etcetera. But, yes, I, Oscar, am immortal!' Oscar rattled off a perfumed fart.

'Alas, my corporeal residence, this ageing carcass I am forced to inhabit, it, I am sorry to say, is not.' He refilled his brandy glass and lit a Turkish cigarette. Blue smoke billowed into the inky void of the impossibly high ceiling. 'It's my own fault, of course. Small print and all that. I really should have checked it more thoroughly. But I was only a slip of a girl at the time, and His Satanic Majesty is rather gorgeous. I mean, I thought I was getting a bargain: it wasn't even my soul the horny bastard was after – just a piddling little sexual favour, a little bit of . . .' Oscar pushed his tongue into his cheek, miming fellatio. 'Small potatoes for what I imagined to be a graceful dance through the sherbet fountains of eternity with the pink bloom of youth forever upon my delicate cheek.' The Freddie Mercury swan-song, 'Who Wants to Live Forever', swelled in the background and Oscar started to cry.

'You sucked the Devil off?' asked Gimpo, mildly shocked. It was obvious from Oscar's raised left eyebrow that this was the first he had noticed of our Zen companion sitting quietly on the chaise longue in the corner. Oscar's predatory eyeballs swivelled and locked on to Gimpo like bumhole-seeking missiles. He tossed back his head with an operatic flourish, finished his potent brew and smashed the glass into the fireplace. He poured himself another glass and slithered across the room, an eel in Swarfega, and plopped himself on to the seat next to Gimpo like a jiggling plastic bag of congealed blood. Gimpo recoiled like a .44 Magnum, homicidal homophobia blanching his face like sheet lightning.

'Boy,' dribbled Oscar sloppily into Gimpo's ear, 'you remind me of someone I used to know.' He placed a pudgy hand on Gimpo's knee. 'Alas, he's dead now: *mort*, gone, gone like all the other beautiful things I have known.' The tears were rolling, Oscar was performing. He rose to his full height, the back of his left hand held at a dramatic angle to his forehead, right hand on his hip and, without any warning whatsoever, struggled from his pink catsuit, wrestled with the tumultuous curtains of blue flesh that were his stomach and fished out his cadaverous cock, a thick flaccid worm covered in warts and slime. The zombified dandy then attempted to mount Gimpo's face. I was nearly sick.

'Bosie!' Oscar's high-pitched scream screeched down the plate-glass window of my and Bill's unmitigated horror. 'My love who dare not speak his name!' Oscar's whining screams bored through our heads like a power drill. 'Pleasure me!'

Gimpo violently disentangled himself from the writhing octopus of his admirer's corpulent embrace. Gimpo's eyes had started to spin and I could smell ozone and portents of disaster: an apocalyptic force of nature visiting brutal carnage, tidal waves of blood, earthquakes and torn ligaments and shredded sphincters. Homophobic lightning bolts flew from his hair, black ectoplasm rocketed from his mouth and span around the room like electric locusts; feral screams and video footage of wild animals disembowelling each other; close-ups of tissue-clogged shark's teeth and evil, black eyes swimming through oceans of pink blood; vivid colour-enhanced photographs of open heart surgery; Charlie Manson; Son of Sam; chainsaw massacre; Jack the Ripper; Ted Bundy slicing up torsos; child murder; gore, blood, shit and sperm.

Gimpo swung Oscar's severed head around by its trailing spinal cord, the twitching, mutilated torso wobbling at his feet. 'Homo! Shit! Stabbing! Arse! Bandit! Bumhole! Sucking! Toilet! Creeping! Fucking! Sexual! Fucking! Pervert!' Gimpo punctuated his acts of violence with every swearword known to man. He was pulverizing the little that remained of Oscar's flesh into a grotesque miasma of blood, shit and arse stains, violent strokes on a Jackson Pollock canvas of carnage and splattered bumholes.

Suddenly Keith's whisky croak cut through the bloody mist hanging in the air. 'It's no good, man. You can't fackin' kill him. I should fackin' know, I'm always tryin' to top the dirty old bastard. I've fackin' shot him and everythin'. Look, the dirty cant fackin' loves it. He's got a fackin' hard on!' We looked across to the bloody mess and, sure enough, the twitching, slimy heap of gore was masturbating. Horrific rasping giggles emanated from his bloody, toothless mouth. Gimpo vomited. 'Oh thenk you, Bothie,' lisped the decapitated, toothless head perched upon the prostrate eviscerated heap. Gimpo screamed and kicked the heap once more. A scarlet orb popped from the gruesome shape and landed on my knee. I looked down into Oscar's staring eye, bemused. I thought of George Bataille's *Story of the Eye* and Kerouac's *Satori in Paris* and allowed myself a little literary chuckle. Keith lurched through the carnage back to the bar. Bill and I followed, allowing Gimpo time to cool his bloody heels.

Back at the bar, Keith had started on his third bottle of bourbon and was dribbling and laughing quietly to himself. We joined him. 'That was really funny,' Keith snorted happily. 'Here, man.' He passed us a small piece of parchment. 'That's the shaman's phone number.'

Bill unfolded the piece of yellowing paper with sincere reverence. His eyes widened then narrowed. He looked Keith seriously in his out-of-focus eye and placed a firm hand on his shoulder. 'Thanks Keith,' he said, gravely.

'Ah, forget it man, hic, Rock 'n' Roll,' Keith replied, and promptly fell flat on his face from the bar stool.

'Yes, Keith, rrrrrock and rrrrrroll,' said Bill rolling his 'r's in an exaggerated Scots fashion, looking down at the prostrate rock legend. 'To the Pole!' he proclaimed dramatically and strode manfully to the door, trailing a particularly foul SBD in his wake.

'Fack! Who's dropped one?' called Keith from the floor, the broken Marlboro still hanging from his bottom lip. We smiled and stepped out into the Arctic night.

'Good luck, lads,' he added.

As it turned out, we would need it.

It is time for us to catch the train. Ulla and Mulla hail a taxi. We all five climb in. Ulla sort of sitting on my lap. I admire her chunky thighs and some evil thoughts dance unrestrained through my mind.

CHAPTER THREE

Teenage Virgin Supermodels Eat Shit

We left the squalid carnage of Oscar's bar with a new determination and fire in our bowels. Clenching our teeth and gritting our sphincters against the freezing cold, we marched through the desolate Helsinki streets looking for a star to guide us. Heroic music swelled from the sewers and the snows swirled. Potent vodka heat swam through my veins like benign electric violence, a toxic anaconda warming my guts and making me feel at peace, in a superior-fire-power kind of a way, with mankind and the world. Helsinki railway station loomed in the distance: a pink granite, brass and wood palace styled in the national Romantic Gothic.

At the station we empty our locker, lovingly unwrap our icon of Elvis from the Bon Scott T-shirts and show it to our hosts. They are awed/confused. We each, in turn, hug Ulla and manfully shake hands with Mulla. We promise to visit them again on our return from the Pole. We have known them only three hours but we instinctively know they are good people. 'Don't you think that's a bit of a shallow assumption to make?' The voice. Maybe.

Inside the glorious marble mezzanine, stray Laplanders in piss-stained national costume – four-pronged hats, colourful jackets and curly-toed boots – clung to dark corners, eyeing us suspiciously from the perimeters of their cursed alcoholic world. Bad portents of personal apocalypse and grim futures pushed, kicking and incontinent, into the more paranoid quadrants of my imagination. Bums in unshaven clothing bearing down on me with the evil eye always spook me out. I shivered and set one of them on fire, which made me feel better instantly – there but for the grace of God go you pal, heh heh. I laughed as the old man screamed and flapped like a blazing Santa Claus trying to extinguish his roaring beard. My pyrotechnic malice embarrassed Bill and Gimpo, who scuttled off into the ticket office. The scorched vagrant started crying and shit his pants.

In the ticket office I could hear Gimpo shouting and swearing. It seemed that there were no trains to the North Pole; the most northerly destination was a Lappish town called Rovaniemi; the train was due to leave in five minutes and the journey would take eighteen hours.

We decided to purchase a few items with which to combat the inevitable ennui of such a long ride – alcohol and pornography. I bought a deliciously dripping edition of *Junior Gash* 23, Gimpo bought *Fat Scat Dumpers* No. 13, *Anal Rampage* 11 and a particularly ugly copy of *Excreta Sexy* 98; Bill bought ornithology magazines and a copy of *Sadistic Rape*. My penis felt thick in my trousers, an evil Cyclops weeping in secretive anticipation of sordid solitary pleasures. Gimpo had a similar wanker's glint in his bloodshot eye.

We downed a few quick beers and made our way to the train, where a stunted Lapp dwarf with bad teeth and evil breath showed us to our small cabin. He grinned like Gorgonzola as he pointed to our three-tiered bunk beds. I think he thought we were queer. I thought he was.

We wave goodbye to Ulla and Mulla and climb on board the train that is waiting to take us to the edge of the Arctic. What's great about many stations on the Continent is that the platforms are much lower than our British ones, so just the act of clambering up the steps into the railway carriage, a mere three feet six inches at the most, fills you with a sense of adventure, of derring-do, of danger up around the bend.

The cabin: neat, compact; wash-basin in the corner for pissing in; three bunks one above the other; crisp white bed linen – always a turn-on. Gimpo has the top bunk, Z the bottom, and me the middle.

The bunks were small but allowed ample space for masturbation.

*

We dump our bags and retire to the buffet carriage with our Zen sticks at the ready. Gimpo orders a round of ridiculously over-priced lager. Z scribbles poetry and lies and I scratch out this God-given truth for you to read. Mock if you must. The train trundles out into the Nordic darkness. The night is awakening.

The long Finnish steam train pulled slowly out of the station, swaying with a sensual rhythm. I lay down on the bottom bunk. The train's erotic vibrations pushed a serious blood rush into my long-johns; my plasma-gorged tumescence chafed uncomfortably within its thermal incarceration. I unzipped the jail doors and the purple criminal sprang free, throbbing happily. Gingerly and with reverence I peeled open *Junior Gash* 23. It was time to parade my panoply of paper whores before the hypercritical judge of my feverish imagination.

An initial cursory skim escalated into a myopic examination of little Heidi and her friendly Alsatian, Max. Heidi's impudent rosebud lips wetly enclosed a huge German Shepherd's blood-raw bellender, delicate dew-drops of dog spunk glittering magically on her mascara-matted lashes. Deeper into the magazine, hiding stickily between the fetid leaves, bad adventures unfurled in the wicked porno-forest: gentle little Suzy gazed out from her Kodachrome bondage with a confused and submissive expression as big Raoul slid his enormous salami up her backside, her exquisite four-colour pain captured in pristine Pentax black magic.

A nauseous heat emanated from the immaculate reproduction and melted my guts. I tried to seek refuge in the squalid banality of the prose, but even this clanking mundaneness could not cool my perverse fever; rather it poured gasoline on the sick fires of my primeval wanker's desire. '*Bodl says to Karl, let me suck you and wank your prick till it's hard, then you can fuck my cow. Karl knew Bodl, his half-sister, was as perverted as himself, they had been having sex with farm animals since they were kids . . .*'

So it spluttered on, jerking my engorged Cyclops into a strained trembling frenzy of anticipation. I yanked at the skin stretched across its shiny purple dome till a spurt of viscous white paste spat angrily from its solitary Asiatic eye, filling my belly button. I wiped the guilty emission on to the stiff disinfected sheets and placed my paper porno playmates back in their plastic bag. I heaved myself up from the bunk and slunk to the bar, a sperm stain spreading across the front of my trousers like the damp fingerprint of a wet dream.

There's a sense between the three of us that doors are beginning to open, that we will never be the same again.

Bill and Gimpo were swimming through their third beer and gently stroking the fragile surface of reality's creaky hull, doodling dipso-maniac hieroglyphics on her rickety mast and toying with her torn sails. I joined them and struck a match on the anchor. The bottle broke and SS *Madness* was launched on to the swelling waves of another ocean of tumultuous bad alky craziness. I noticed Bill's black leather doctor's bag nestling between his legs like a truculent pitbull waiting patiently for trouble. It wouldn't have to wait long.

I hate lager – as I mentioned before. Both Jimmy and I drank bitter; it bonded us together against the great lager-drinking masses. When it comes to beer, Z and Gimpo drink nothing but lager. I drink this round with them only out of a sense of camaraderie. I have one more round then I hit the tea, much to their disparagement. 'Call yourself a man? Fuckin' Jessie! Ye can't drink tea in a train buffet!' So the first hour of the train ride north is taken up with Z one moment questioning my manhood for not drinking lager and the next complaining about the shite quality lager they sell on the train. Z is, in fact, a world expert on lager – he knows the proof of every lager sold commercially on this earth.

I was sitting by the window, the train steadily rocking and rolling at about seventy miles an hour. I sipped my seventh beer and gazed out into the blue Arctic night. The sodium yellow lights from the Helsinki suburbs were twinkling amongst the black houses and swirl-ing snow. I could hear the swooping gasps and sighs of wife-swapping kissing our carriage window.

The buffet carriage is a rather Spartan affair: functional tables, fixed benches, stark lighting – makes travelling second-class British Rail seem decadent. Mind you, it is all Scandinavian clean, pine-top spic and stainless-steel span. We try to cheer things up with our rendition of 'Immigrant Song'.

Gimpo was sitting opposite me, perusing his pornography and casually stroking his crotch. I glanced at his magazine, *Anal Rampage*, spread-eagled across the table. It was truly horrible, a veritable pantheon of scatological Third Reich, shit-eating horror: pictures of naked nubiles strapped to torture contraptions, old men with semi-erections and Nazi armbands defecating on their hairless, pubescent pudenda. Gimpo unceremoniously removed his penis from his trousers to flick a gob of todge fluid on to his T-shirt. Without a word, he closed the magazine and finished his beer. The horror of other men's wank fantasies.

Bill and I worked on our Zen sticks. We were Palaeolithic tribesmen recording the hunt on ivory. The train's bar began to fill with fellow travellers who brought their farts, belches and fish odour with them. I heard a loud, muffled thump from behind me, followed by a spiralling, wailing noise. I turned round to see what had caused the disturbance: a raggy, Finnish drunk had fallen to the floor, his flies were undone and there was fag ash on his breath.

There are three or four others in the buffet, quietly tending to their thirsts. After some time one stumbles forward to join us. He must be in his mid thirties, a shock of frizzy black hair, blue-tinted aviator specs and a voice that sounds like a bad imitation of Bluebottle from The Goons (if you don't know who Bluebottle is, you will never know what this bloke sounds like). We assume he is on his way to being blind drunk.

I ignored him and carried on whittling magic symbols on my stick. I tied small pieces of leather around one end to fashion a handle, then admired its satisfying weight. I slipped my right hand through the handle and brought the stick down heavy, like a weapon, on to the table. It made a nice violent noise, like someone's head splitting open.

The loud bang roused the drunk, who clambered shakily to his unsteady feet and, in a vapour cloud of 100° proof halitosis, sat uninvited at our table. He demanded our attention by spilling all our drinks and addressing us in a voice like a klaxon. Despite this intense decibel ferocity, the cloud of fart-dust surrounding him, his vile acne-ravaged visage, and his fright-wig Afro, he appeared harmless.

I offered him a shot of vodka and a cigarette, which he lit at the wrong end. Bill engaged him in some drug talk while I flipped through Gimpo's clammy pornographic grimoires. I was trying to figure out the covert eroticism hidden within the strange scatological imagery and was just starting to feel a slight reptilian movement in my under-wear when my depraved concentration was disturbed by a quiet voice riding on the back of soft perfume. I slammed the sticky sperm-hell pages together and looked up into the face of a teen angel.

'Excuse me,' said the blonde, 'my name is Claudia. This is Naomi, and Linda.' She indicated her equally seraphic companions. 'We are naïve Finnish girls on our way to supermodel school. We couldn't help noticing your Zen sticks – are you Zen Masters?' An aromatic nimbus of flowers and milk floated around the three divine girls. I could smell summer and perfumed cunt. Bill had tented his kilt and Gimpo was in a trance, hypnotized by their supernatural beauty.

'Why, yes,' I replied after several seconds that felt like hours. 'Why do you ask?' I eased out the snake oil, my Cyclopean second sense telling me that something good was about to happen.

'We are virgins,' breathed Claudia quietly. The turkey neck twitched; the bald-headed champ was entering the ring. 'We wish to know of love, Zen Masters,' she continued, eyelashes fluttering like Bambi. Full bone and raging, the champ limbers up. 'Please . . .' she licked her raw rose lips, 'could you show us how?'

Things are surely getting out of hand – distant alarm bells are ringing. I may not be able to keep up these notes. Events are beginning to unfold, and I must direct my energy towards self-preservation.

Whack! Gimpo has just cracked me over the head with his Zen stick.

*

My zip cracked like thunder as I pulled out its teeth. I flobbed my swollen salami on the table, its angry veins blue and pulsing, a single glycerine tear leaking from its evil eye. The three girls gasped and covered their mouths with their hands. Frightened excitement dilated their twinkling pupils. 'It's so big!' whispered Naomi behind her long fingers, excitement dampening her innocent lacy underwear. Evil Bill and Gimpo had also released their puds and thwacked them on the table.

Bad sexual electricity skittered across the ozone-heavy air. Slow blue flames like Christmas-pudding brandy fire fluttered around my bell-end. Rising animal heat disturbed the air around the girls like rippling water, black ectoplasm leaked from Gimpo's Jap's eye. My sandpaper tongue scraped away from the roof of my mouth and my voice was lower than a submarine: 'OK ladies . . .' I could feel my heart beneath my T-shirt, a distant African drum slowly beating the rhythms of the swamps. I gently pulled Claudia's head on to my prick. Liquid velvet.

'Zen sex education: lesson one,' I announced loudly.

Hastily Naomi and Linda fastened their virgin lips on to Bill and Gimpo's gruesome stonk-ons. 'Work those tongues, girls!' I continued in my best porno gym-master voice.

It was hard to believe that Claudia had never sucked dick before – her bobbing head made my knob feel as though it was plugged into a can of electric worms; her wet tongue flickered like a professional, and pretty soon my platoon of spermatozoa warriors were lacing their boots in preparation for the taking of the breach. I placed my hand gently on Claudia's nape to restrain her enthusiastic rhythm.

'Whoah,' I said kindly, crisis point skilfully delayed. 'The art of good sex is to suck your man's dick till he *nearly* comes.'

All three looked up confused. Claudia wiped her perfect mouth. 'But how will we know, Zen Master?' she asked, wide-eyed.

'Pure instinct,' I informed my earnest student. 'Trust me.'

I flipped the Finnish kitten on to her back on the floor and ripped off her pants. 'Then your man will do – this!' I fucked Claudia and came inside her almost immediately, a monster glob of jizz flying up inside her to the eternal target. For demonstration purposes, Bill and Gimpo did the same: synchronized shagging, an ancient Zen discipline. I pulled out my shining wet prick. The delicate bouquet of ruptured hymen fluttered like the last butterfly of summer above her downy minge.

I leap to my feet, knocking my tea over. The liquid runs off the table on to my kilt. Over goes somebody's lager. Here I am, notebook in one hand, the other brandishing my Zen stick.

I observed that our impromptu sex education lesson had drawn an appreciative audience of leering, masturbating fools. I ignored them and continued with my lecture: 'That, dear supermodels, is sex.' The girls sighed, the audience applauded appreciatively. A couple of them spurted weak spunk on to the floor. I placed my deflated member back in my trousers and noticed that Gimpo was still erect and toying with his gnarled weapon which was pulsating like a horrible John Carpenter movie. 'Oh,' I added, 'one more thing. If you ever hear or read anything about something referred to as the female orgasm, ignore it. It's a vicious and evil lie propagated by a band of terrible and evil women known to mankind as feminists. Their sole intention in spreading this terrible, malicious untruth is to make you unhappy and to convert you to the dread crime of lesbianism.'

The little darlings gasped with shock: they couldn't believe they had sisters of such a malevolent bent. I fixed them with a fatherly frown. I noticed Claudia sneaking secret glances at my parcel and continued sternly: 'Remember, ladies: sex, when practised correctly and with due and proper respect and obedience to the male, can be a very beautiful and rewarding thing. Its primary function, however, is to keep men happy; and to produce children. A real woman knows this and performs her natural duty with gratitude and joy.' The young girls gazed at me with admiration. 'Now girls, if you will excuse us, we are tired and need to tend to our drinking.'

Claudia gathered together her silk underwear, a tear of love and gratitude swelling in her eye. 'Oh thank you, Zen Master. I thank you with all my heart – now the heart of a woman!' The deflowered beauty gazed up at me like an entranced novice before Christ. I shrugged and feigned modesty.

'It's nothing, my love,' I laughed. 'Now, the three of you, run along. Supermodels need their beauty sleep, don't they?'

Gimpo stands there, his eyes gleaming, grin splitting his face, giving me the total-violence come-on. He wants me to whack him back. My instant anger fades as I realize that if I fulfil his wish he will go totally mental with me. Gimpo is teetering on the edge of something and I refuse to fall with him. I sit back down and resume these notes.

'Just one moment.' It was Gimpo. A halo of blowflies had gathered around his head and he was smiling beneath flaming eyebrows, the smell of his bad intentions hung acrid on the fragrant, cunt-scented air.

'With all due respect, fellow Zen Master,' his voice dripped like evil treacle, 'sexuality is a far more exotic dish than the trifle you have served these fine maidens.'

Somewhere in hell the Devil farted; Myra Hindley sits in Holloway eating cold mackerel. The ghosts of aborted babies cry in limbo.

Gimpo elaborated: 'You do these girls a disservice, Zodiac my friend. I think we can show them a few more . . .' He balled his fist and covered his mouth politely. 'Ahem,' he continued, 'more . . . how can I say, advanced lessons.' He stretched the last syllables like a ham actor in a melodrama, his left eyebrow arched. I had a bad feeling. Gimpo unbuckled his belt; a red mist hung in the air. Bill was smiling through pointed teeth.

Oh no, Bluebottle is now on his feet, squawking in some language that surely isn't Finnish, his blue aviators sliding down his nose. But before he has time to do any more, Gimpo whacks him on his thatch of black frizz. He keels over into the aisle.

In Broadmoor, Ian Brady is masturbating over his memoirs in dirty underwear, his hands smelling of piss. In New York City the chicken ranches are thriving as the tabloids' interest in child sex abuse has sparked a revival of that quintessentially Victorian pastime.

*

Now, it had always been a laugh hearing about Gimpo's exploits – dead Argies and beaten-up Rock fans seemed no more real than an Alan Moore graphic novel – but right here and now when I am having to deal with the reality of the man . . .

Without the slightest warning, Gimpo slammed a shocked Claudia to the carriage floor, slid a black turd from his arse and laid it steaming across her breasts. Naomi and Linda started crying. Bill was laughing. The foul stench of public lavatories and old men's beer farts seared the compartment and took the skin off my eyeballs. The black odyssey into someone else's wank hell had started. The pitbull doctor's bag scented blood.

A hot horse's flow of steaming piss pulsed from Gimpo's ugly distended member; he was urinating over the incredulous super-model, his venomous flood mixing with the black excrement to create a vile brown paste. A demon from the greasiest slime pit of hell, Gimpo was stripped naked, a demented shite eagle, Priapus, Lord of the Blowflies, smearing slippery ordure all over the poor girl's body. He wrestled with her and, in the process, covered them both in loose stools. Sloppy lumps congealed in their eyebrows and pubic hair, the diarrhoeic paste streaking their bodies like a cheap fake sun-tan cream. The buzzing of the blowflies was deafening.

Gimpo was completely out of control, body surfing in a sliding universe of Stygian depravity. The torrents of liquid shite, pulsing come and rolling bloodshot eyes confounded any rational thought process that attempted to confront such feral behaviour.

To be fuckin' honest, I don't know what the fuck to say. Has Gimpo got to get his own back on the world for some terrible mishap that befell his life at a tender age? Is there a snake-pit of seething resentment writhing behind his warm, honest, evil grin? Or is he a natural man, untouched by all the softening that our silly, safe and simpering culture has wrapped us up in? Here, standing before me, is the missing link: a pure and true man, unfettered and unfallen.

Not to be outdone by this scatological Grand Guignol, his Celtic machismo pride rising like a sewer after heavy rain, Bill lifted up his kilt and threw his head between his knees. A Vesuvian cascade of faecal matter exploded with an atomic wet blast of Krakatoan volume. The gargantuan barrage of black shit volleyed across the room, knocking Naomi and Linda from their feet and covering the walls with dripping excrement. Bill laughed so hard that he vomited. The orange spill mixed with the black manure and painted ghastly brown psychedelic swirls across the carpet.

'Shut up, Bill. It's just Gimpo.' A voice.

Yeah OK, it's just Gimpo, but what are we to do with him? The voice does not answer.

So what is Z up to when all this is happening? Not taking a blind bit of notice. He has peeled all the bark off his Zen stick and is admiring and stroking its gentle curve. It is the shape and colour of one of those Japanese swords or knives where the handle and scabbard are made from one single piece of ivory and fit together so smoothly that there is no break in the line when the blade is snugly home in the darkness of its sheath. He has nicked a black Pentel off me and is becoming engrossed in decorating his stick with intricate patterns – sort of like how Maoris tattoo their faces, or Eskimos carve on walrus tusks. He shows me what he is doing.

He is proud of his work. He thinks he has now the best Zen stick. He is wrong, because I have – mine contains the Way, the Truth and the Light and doesn't need any heathen glorification. I don't tell him any of this, I just nod approvingly and hide my jealousy of his obvious artistic talents. 'Fuck you Z!' says my pen. 'You wait, my Zen stick will be revered down through history. Our children's children's children will build an ark to carry it in, as they escape from earth to explore deepest space to find a new home for a dying, crippled and deeply stupid race.'

Enough of this. We're above all these small, bitter smallnesses. Are we not Three Wise Men come to save the world from all this petty shite?

The train trundles on further north and further into this night.

Bluebottle is now scribbling poetry, squawking his inanities and laughing at the badly drawn cartoons he is scratching on our one and only map. We did try to explain to him who and why we are, but he just accepted it as the norm, as if he catches this train every night and every night there are three blokes on the train who claim to be the Three Wise Men on their way to the Pole with an icon of Elvis.

'Look Bluebottle, you don't understand. We're Zen Masters. You should be falling at our feet, overawed by our magnificence.'

He just giggles and demands a beer.

Z and I are now beginning to indulge ourselves in a rather strange fantasy. We realize there are three female members of the Cliff Richard Fan Club from Luton on the train. They too have a picture of their saviour with them, and they too are on their way to the Pole. Our fear is that they will get there first, nick the Baby Jesus for themselves and get all the credit for saving the world. It would be like Scott reaching the South Pole to find that Amundsen had got there first.

Oh no, who's this? A large bear-like Finn with a US Marine-style haircut has just clambered between Z and Gimpo. He has a grin almost as big as Gimpo's. He puts one arm round Z's shoulders and one arm round Gimpo's, gives them a big hug and then lets out a huge roar of a belly laugh. A half-second later the halitosis hits me.

This man speaks English and tells us Bluebottle is a famous madman. He begins to bait him. We think this is bad form and get quite protective of our buffet-table companion. We attempt to engage Bear Man in conversation. He turns out to be a union leader from some northern city who has been attending a conference in Helsinki. Bear Man likes to laugh and shout, to stand up to make his point, to jut out his lower jaw, to scratch his almost shaven head and to stare you out with his wild eyes. The train will be stopping at his station at four in the morning and he plans to drink until then before returning to his wife and two slumbering daughters, age twelve and ten. Z and I have a father-to-father talk with him and then Z demands that Gimpo fetch a bottle of the Blue Label vodka from the cabin.

The vodka bottle is now almost empty and we are all lifelong best buddies. But halitosis Bear Man is demanding that we provide him with another bottle of Blue Label (and these are the big litre-size bottles). Now, the fact is we do have another three bottles back in the cabin and Z is up for getting one, but Gimpo, yet again, takes control. 'Rations, rations,' is Gimpo's answer. Z begrudgingly accepts his wisdom.

I was tempted to write just then, 'The night wears on,' but it doesn't. It just erupts and explodes and simmers and then collides.

The guard passes by, smiles, stamps our tickets; a friendly sort of chap. Bear Man, frustrated at the lack of Blue Label vodka, picks up Z's Zen stick and starts to admire it. Yes, he is blind drunk by now and, luckily for us, the vodka has somehow negated the power of his halitosis. He doesn't want to hand the Zen stick back. Is this going to turn nasty? Bear Man turns to Gimpo, cracks a corker on Gimpo's skull. Gimpo thwacks back. Gimpo has found his man. Whack!

Crack!

'You fuckin' bastard!'

Whack!

'Oh no, no!'

But they're not stopping.

In a funfair nightmare a fat man brings down a hammer and rings the bell.

Bill and Gimpo were now naked and rampant on the table. Rummaging through his leather doctor's bag, Bill selected a satanic tangle of rubber pipes and glass balls, held them aloft and started masturbating violently with a broken bottle.

'Enema, anyone?' he cackled dementedly, as frightening and intense as classical music. Spiralling down and out of control, he bounded from the table like some vermin-encrusted bat from porno hell and landed acrobatically on Naomi's butt.

Bill and Gimpo's Dionysian frenzy inspired the rest of the shit-besmirched passengers to acts of escalating depravity. A helter-skelter ride backwards into hell. Men and women ripped themselves fiercely out of their ski suits and farted huge arcs of beer shit across the carriage. Someone had murdered the barman. Vodka and beer flowed in rivers.

The floor was awash with lakes of vomit, blood, shite and booze. My foot skidded on a raped corpse and I decided things were getting out of hand. Visions of flashing blue lights, horror tabloid headlines and gallows creaking in hell flashed a brief bolt of reality through my seared brain. I plucked poor ravaged Naomi from the sea of ordure. She was bleeding from the desecrated trinity of her ass, mouth and cunt; her face had swollen into an over-inflated football.

The train trundles into a station and pulls up. The smiling guard returns, this time accompanied by two armed policemen who, I have to admit, are dressed in a very police-state sort of way, and they pick on our poor friend Bluebottle. He tries to defend himself, we try to defend him; but his madness confirms his guilt. He goes sadly but willingly and is led off the train.

Bear Man just laughs, so we turn to the three arty-looking girls who are sitting at one of the other tables for an explanation. It seems that Bluebottle, being mad, was taken for the ringleader, so to make an example to us all they threw him off the train.

'But what will happen to him?'

'There is another train in four hours' time. He can catch that one,' replies one of the girls.

And that seems to be that. Z, Gimpo and myself feel rather ashamed of ourselves – it is because of us that this poor bloke has been turfed off. This all seems a bit real for us, a bit of a reminder that death camps and secret police knocking on your door in the dead of night are a reality for millions of people.

Our reality crisis fades as the train begins to trundle back out into the darkness (yes, I know I keep using the word 'trundle' but that is exactly what the train is doing – it never feels like it gets above fifty miles an hour and each individual clatter is audible, none of that distant muffled speed rumble that you get on an InterCity 125).

There is something I have failed to mention – maybe out of embarrassment, maybe because it didn't seem worth mentioning before – but now I will. Through the day we have developed a rather 'impressive' male-bonding war cry. It is a sort of cross between a Morris Men's stick dance and the Three Musketeers' 'All For One and One For All!'. It involves the three of us standing in a circle facing inward, Zen sticks in our right hands. Z whacks my stick, I whack Gimpo's, Gimpo whacks Z's. Then we all throw our right arms into the air 'like we just don't care', Zen sticks pointing to the heavens, and cry: 'To the Pole!', followed by our stamping the ground thrice with our right feet or banging the table thrice with our fists (depending on whether we are standing or sitting) and then finally bellowing at the top of our lungs: 'Elvis to the Pole!'

Would Elvis have been proud of us? Would our womenfolk be proud of us? Do we give a shit? Not tonight.

Bear Man and Gimpo are back at it, but something is changing. Gimpo seems to be trying to redirect Bear Man's violence towards me and Z. The bastard seems to be in favour of this. In fact, Z is trying to steal my stick off me so he can join in the unwarranted attack. Things are getting out of control again. Obviously, all sobering memory of what happened to our friend Bluebottle has vanished. Drastic measures need to be taken, and fast. Gimpo thinks it is all my fault that his head has been pummelled by Bear Man just because it was my idea to bring these Zen sticks in the first place; and he assumes I am wearing this thick, felt Arctic hat to cushion any Zen-stick blows. It is now time to put down my pen and defend myself.

I carried Naomi to our carriage and placed her on my bunk, then returned for Claudia and Linda. I found Claudia crouching under a table. She was in shock. I reached out to grab her but she recoiled in rape trauma. Gently, I managed to talk her into coming with me. Linda was dead. I saw a huge Russian sailor pull her slack mouth on to his penis. Bill was doing a Highland fling while Gimpo had regressed into cannibalism, munching away at someone's head, laughing between meaty morsels of eyeball, nose and lips. I grabbed the leather doctor's bag with one hand, gathered the traumatized Claudia with my other arm and made my way back to the carriage, where I cleansed the excrement from her broken and bruised body using the hundred-dollar bills from Bill's bag. I gave Claudia and Naomi a mild sedative, read them a bedtime story, calmed their fears and put them to bed.

I have just climbed back down from standing on the table, banging my head on the ceiling, and I now have all three of the Zen sticks triumphantly in my possession. The road to enlightenment beckons. I sit down and celebrate by writing a haiku:

The Nord train.
Zen sticks in hand.
Outside the snow falls in the Arctic night.

'Beat that, Basho!' is what I say. The others do not accept my victory, but we make up and indulge ourselves in another round of 'Elvis to the Pole!' I order some tea.

Something else has been going on for an unquantifiable time. There is this geezer who has been sitting with the three arty-looking girls. He is the classic-looking hippy type – long, straight hair parted in the middle, vaguely eastern-looking clothes, sandals (hasn't he heard of Arctic winters?). But anyway, this geezer has got a portable video camera and is filming everything that is going on, getting close-ups, even asking questions: 'What are you doing? Where are you going? Who is your name? Are you mad? Don't you think you will die?'

For Z and myself this is totally normal, which is why we hadn't noticed him earlier. Being involved in the pop process for so long, you get used to people filming you, taking pictures and asking you inane questions; you take it as a given. Some days you may be walking down the street, feeling rather chipper with yourself, sporting your brand new fake rhino horn on your forehead, and then you notice that nobody's filming you or asking you 'Why?', and you feel rather foolish and naked and ashamed.

If it is like that for Z and me, what must it be like for Madonna? She must sit there having a shit and wonder where the camera crew is.

Z leaves his scribbling of poetry and lies, leaps on one of the other tables, Zen stick back in hand; like a chimp he climbs over the tables and chairs to where the three arty girls are sitting. They look rather frightened but, I have to admit, rather excited as well. He asks them: 'Are you from Luton?'

'Pardon?'

'Are you from Luton? Come on, we'll show you our picture of Elvis if you show us your picture of Cliff.'

'Cliff?' They look rather confused.

'I know you're hiding it somewhere. We know what you're up to.'

These three arty-looking girls are in fact not girls at all, but mature-looking independent women in their mid-to-late twenties. One sports a rather staid pair of spectacles, another a bad case of post-adolescent acne and the third I will not describe. Of course, they are rather confused as to whether Z is behaving in this manner in an attempt to pull one of them or as good footage for the film-making hippy's camera; or, is he, in fact, spreading Zen wisdom to his fellow passengers? I will never know. For the sake of posterity and legend, I guess it is the Zen wisdom-spreading.

Z has given up asking about the Cliff Richard Fan Club and poses a more obvious question: 'Are you on your way to the supermodel finishing school in Rovaniemi?' I didn't hear their reply but somehow I don't think they are. I am now catching him out of the corner of my eye showing them his tattoo. Yes, I have to admit it, I think they are impressed. 'What about my kilt, you little tarts?' I don't ask.

The time is right to bring the night to an end. We round each other up, head for the cabin, take it in turns to piss in the sink, climb into our bunks. But in that moment just before sleep falls on us, I hear Z whisper his prayers.

When Naomi was asleep, I crawled into the bunk next to her; she purred drowsily.

'Z, one day your prayers will be answered.' Sleep. Sleep.

My dreams were weird, the cold and dizzy vertigo of fashion: brittle beauty imploding like collapsing stars at the end of plastic seasons; incandescent freezing fires of pornographic desire; Dante's damned lovers spiralling like mad starlings on the tempests of hell. Angular icons of female envy glide along catwalks sporting millinery made from human shit; haughty and aloof, their blank, cruel eyes blink before the crazed strobes of the fashion paparazzi, pack-like behind the phallic grotesquerie of their tele-photo hunger. The stage lights flicker blood-red George Grosz sickness; cannibal teeth chatter in time to loud disco music. The skeletal wives of wealthy multinational industrialists hold their breath and discharge yellow pus from their surgically tightened vaginas; they fart secretly on chairs made from human skin and fan themselves with their husbands' credit cards. Outside, the Third World stinks.

Piss in the sink.

I wake up sweating. Somewhere in Algeria, an American tourist photographs a young Arab weeping beneath a palm tree, lamenting his damaged soul.

Sleep, all night long, like three little cherubs. All bound for morning town.

CHAPTER FOUR

Saunas, Fags and Blowjobs (The Love Feast)

The dream fades back into the subconscious as my conscious self struggles to take control of these waking moments. The conscious mind wins and I am fully awake, hardly a trace of the dream saved. Daylight creeps in through a crack in the blind. Pine trees heavy with snow, a milky sky, and the train still trundling on at a steady pace.

I read my ramblings from yesterday, add in some forgotten facts and smile at our recorded exploits. There are some lies in there: there were only two arty-looking girls, but saying there were three seemed to balance better. I try to pick the bogey lying deep in my left nostril. It remains out of reach.

Sadness descends. My children and loved ones have not played any part in the last twenty-four hours; not one thought has been spared for them. It's as if I've shut out reality and its problems; or as if this journey, which we so flippantly describe as a path to Enlightenment, is nothing but us running in the opposite direction, grown men unwilling to accept the fact that life is hard.

Gimpo is gently snoring above me, Z breathes his smoker's rasp below and I've been pondering life's changes. No, not pondering – pontificating, maybe even attempting to lecture you, dear reader. So I've just ripped up five pages of my pontifications into a hundred guilty pieces.

Do you ever get that thing where you believe you correctly hold a certain opinion, which you may have had for years, but, once you've written it down and read it back, you realize that it is a load of arrogant self-righteous bollocks and that the only reason you believed it in the first place was to make yourself feel morally superior to your girlfriend, or brother, or something? Well, that's what's just happened to me. The fact that I'm lying in my bunk writing whilst Z and Gimpo indulge in the decadent art of sleeping in after 6 a.m. has, I suppose, given me a platform for my falsely superior pontifications.

The train rolled into the buffers at Rovaniemi, knocking a grizzly fart from one of my sleeping companions. Gimpo hawked up a chewy one and spat it on the floor. I covered the corpse of last night's weirdness and got up to perform my ablutions.

Bad drain smells wafted. Bill was still asleep as Gimpo struggled from the tangled carnage of his Jackson Pollock bed linen, a grim expressionist fart smear of bodily excretions and black blood. He groaned. He had a black eye and two split lips. I heard shuffling and a shriek. Bill leapt from his malodorous litter, a look of horror daubed across his blanched features, chopped liver dripping from his forearm. He covered up something on his bed and sped from the cabin fast-forward nervous. I cracked a violent, stinking, thunderstorm morning fart and followed.

There was something in the stuff I wrote that I wish I hadn't ripped up; something about how I like to believe that even though our bodies grow old and fall to bits, there is a flower inside that carries on growing and blooming right up until the moment we die. I take a break; look out of the window: pines laden with snow, milky sky. The sadness lifts. The world is there and I feel all right. I'll try and pick up my threads.

The last bit I tore up was about life being like climbing a hill, and about how in the past year I have got over a large, looming crest so that I can now see the summit. Yes, the road gets steep, there are icy patches and loose rocks, but I can see what I hope is the pinnacle and I know that this is the path I must take to reach it. I realize that taking a picture of Elvis to the North Pole isn't going to change anything; that, in a sense, Z, Gimpo and myself are just running away from the mundaneness of day-to-day squalor, having a laugh at the expense of loved ones. I bet even the original Three Kings were running away from some bits of nastiness in their lives, had some tensions and undercurrents going on between the three of them as they made their way to Bethlehem. And yeah, even they would have been comforted by the smell of their own farts. But perhaps we are bit by bit getting closer to that summit. Yes, I may never get there, but I am on my way.

There is a knock at the door. It is the guard. We will be pulling in to Rovaniemi in fifteen minutes. Time to get up. Self-doubt and introspection evaporate. The train hits the bumpers: it's as far as the line goes. We stumble about and spill over into the corridor, admiring each other's long-johns. Z and I talked long-johns before we left. We'd hoped to be able to get those all-in-one undergarments that you see cowboys wearing when they sit around drinking coffee in the cabin, or just before they get shot-up in the bordello boudoir.

We fell from the train into the gorgeous snowdrifts. The sensation was religious: I was cleansed and reborn in cold snow; the air was dry and smelled of metal and settled like frost on the inside of my lungs; the light swooped in at seventy degrees, casting long golden shadows; the sky encircled us in pink and peach robes; there was no wind.

Of course, we are the last to step down from the train. Shit! Those last five words have just kicked in an emotional surge and in my head I can hear Tom Jones singing 'The Green, Green Grass of Home'. It's one of those songs that often comes to me, and I identify totally with the main character. Like him, I too am sitting on death row preparing myself for the great unknown as I fantasize about a golden childhood that may or may not have happened many years ago. There is no green, green grass in Rovaniemi, but there is certainly a sense that we are leaving behind the familiar and walking into the unknowable.

As our boots crunched through the crisp powder snow I thought of torture and long black leather Gestapo overcoats. I walked to the ticket office aroused.

*

Back to the here and now, an end-of-the-line station yard. A meagre daylight and tiny snowflakes falling on our eyelashes welcome us to the Arctic. The air is still and very cold, but in a friendly sort of way.

We crunch over the night's fresh fall to the low concrete station building, where we stand around for a few minutes wondering what to do with ourselves. Gimpo is complaining that his head is covered in lumps and cracks from his Zen-stick exploits of the night before. He has booked us a car via his travel agent back in London and has the address of the local Budget depot. We get directions from the street map on the ticket-office wall and head up the road towards the sprawling town of Rovaniemi. On the way we cross an empty highway and then pass a derelict steam train, reinventing itself as a piece of heritage culture. Half a mile on we spy a truckers' café where we sit now, clutching mugs of tea and bemoaning the fact that they don't do massive fry-up breakfasts.

A group of Lapp college-girls were waiting to greet us, dressed in full national costume: weird four-pronged hats, curly reindeer shoes, everything. They carried cigarettes and bottles of vodka with a distinctive pentangle design on its label. A large banner screamed WELCOME ZEN MASTERS.

A very attractive undergraduate rushed excitedly towards us. I noticed the copper and tin smell of her fresh period see-sawing on the icy air like Turkish delight. She caught her breath and, in a voice like melted marshmallow, told us that the students were our official magic greeting party. Somehow, word of our clandestine and noble philanthropy had preceded us. Spooky music like Peruvian pan pipes and icicle wind chimes jangled on a sudden gust of the north wind. Bill farted nervously.

Back out. A weak sun streaks the southern sky with pleasant and pale shades. Beautiful schoolchildren dressed in brightly coloured snow suits laugh openly at us as we trudge by; their blonde lashes blink off the soft snowflakes and their china-blue eyes tell lies about their innocence as they take the last drag of illicit fags before turning the corner into the school playground.

*

We were driven to the halls of residence where beautiful college-girls greeted us with warm handshakes and large shots of the weird Pentangle vodka. It seemed that the only person who spoke English was the menstruating marshmallow girl.

We find our address, but it seems to be a shop specializing in curtain rails. It is closed. Next door is a ladies hairdressers. It is open. I pluck up courage and manfully enter this establishment with Gimpo's travel agent's docket. The coiffeurs don't speak English and, of course, if you haven't guessed by now, Z, Gimpo and myself, being true Brits, don't speak any other foreign language whatsoever. Pointing to the address on the docket, they point next door and nod.

Just then somebody seems to be opening up the curtain-rail shop – a young lad in his mid teens, exhaling lungfuls of tobacco smoke. We bundle in after him. He does not speak the international language of Rock 'n' Roll. What's the point of living in a post-modern world if everyone on earth does not speak English, I think selfishly. Yes, this is the Budget Rent-a-Car agent for Rovaniemi. He makes a phone call; indicates, using sign language and the clock on the wall, that our vehicle will be here in thirty minutes.

It's just gone 10 a.m. and we sit down in an empty restaurant two doors up from the curtain-rail shop. They stopped serving breakfast three minutes ago and, to our dismay, they won't bend the rules and prepare for us fried bacon, egg, mushroom, black pudding, sausage, beans and toast; instead we have to choose from the all-day 'theme' menu. What the theme is, is a bit confusing. Seen from the street, the four-storey building is post-war northern European: concrete, functional; inside, the restaurant walls are covered with pine logs and hung with elk heads, stuffed racoons, storm lanterns, red and white checked curtains and, in a place of honour above the fake open fire, a badly painted portrait of the Duke himself, John Wayne. What all this means, we don't know. Perhaps we feel cheated – here we are, come all the way from the decadent, crumbling cosmopolitan media capital of our own arsehole of a country to the very rim of the Arctic Circle and we foolishly, naïvely, want a bit of reality. And what have we got? A restaurant that has tried to cash in with a poorly understood Hollywood image of what restaurant interiors must be like in the snowy wastes of the North West Frontier.

We're tempted to nick the portrait of the Duke, to take him with us. His firm jaw seems to tell of a worldwide US stranglehold conspiracy – Hollywood, Arms for Hostages, Bay of Pigs, Nuke Hanoi, D-Day Landing, The Cavalry will Save the Day, Let them drink Coke, Mickey Mouse for President and I want to fuck my blow-up doll of Jackie Kennedy now – better than any televised fireside chat from Ronald Reagan. But we don't, 'cause the lady has come to take our order and we are all smiles and nods and pointing to the bits on the menu we have chosen.

She took my hand and led us to the huge communal sauna, which was full of naked flesh. The marshmallow girl told us to remove our clothes. Cyclops rose again as the three of us wordlessly dropped our kegs. I noticed that Bill and Gimpo were also stiffening. 'More weird sex – great!' laughed Gimpo, stroking his scarred organ, his knacker-sack tightening around his evil eggs.

Gimpo has reindeer steak, I have reindeer stew, and Z has the closest thing on the menu to a Big Mac.

'In Lapland, this is the traditional way of greeting Zen Masters,' said the girl.

'What is?' I asked, distracted for a second.

A girl of seventeen had dropped her cigarette and was bending over to pick it up. Her brown eye winked at me.

'I do not know the correct English, but it is called in Finnish *Il perverto Eucharisto*. The maidens of the village offer the visiting Masters a cigarette,' the marshmallow girl replied, 'then they perform oral sex. When you have tired of one maiden, you must extinguish your cigarette and the girl next in the circle will continue the ritual fellatio. It is considered polite to allow at least three maidens to perform the ceremony before you ejaculate your jizzom. It is said that once the Lord Jesus came to Finland and that his followers instigated this ceremony.'

I inhaled the smoke from my first Marlboro. A nymph gnawed at my phallus. Her teeth scraped the underside of my glans and I put out the cigarette. Another girl who was considerably more adept took her place, but there was something spasmodic about her rhythm. By the tenth amateurish pugwash I was becoming distinctly bored and my cock was deflating. I stubbed my cigarette out on somebody's behind in an attempt to perk my drooping member into a spurting position. Bill was having more luck. The ghost of pleasure honey spasmed across his concentrated features, his left eyebrow twitched and a post-graduette appeared from beneath his kilt, coughing on his spunk.

Gimpo had started his horrible shitting sex again. A glistening turd stuck its nose out of his arse like a vile rat from porno hell.

It is all shit.

It stank.

So is the fish and raw onion salad we nick by the handful and eat on the street outside.

'Please, your friend – it's not nice!' said the marshmallow girl. 'This is a very ancient custom and we take it very seriously. This is sacrilegious. Please make for him to stop!'

'Pathetic. Juvenile,' the voice.

The poor thing was almost in tears. Gimpo reluctantly nipped off his ugly stool and shot a gob of watery sperm into his fellatrice's mouth. She gagged and sneezed snot and spunk out of her nostrils. I punched her in the face out of pure meanness and she started crying. Bill was looking at his watch and straightening his kilt. We thanked the women for their hospitality, took their offerings of hard drugs and liquor and bade them farewell. They waved us off from the college gates.

'What a noble custom!' remarked Bill, heading north.

'Do you think followers of Jesus really invented such a ceremony?' asked a puzzled Gimpo.

'Sure,' I replied. 'They drank blood and stuff, didn't they? They could be weird fuckers when they wanted to be.'

'Hmmm,' mused the Gimp.

CHAPTER FIVE

Creeping Misogyny, and the True Faith
(Epiphany No. 1)

The streets of Rovaniemi were full of frosty angels smoking French cigarettes. Snowflakes fell out of a blue sky. Huskies pulling sleighs barked as they went past, curly tails and dirty bung-holes in clouds of powder snow. Old Lapps in crumpled four-pronged hats and piss stains, drunk on moonshine, farted on street corners.

We hired a car: an Escort with big spiked tyres.

Our car has arrived and to my shock it is an Escort, just a bog-standard one at that. We are about to drive to the North Pole in an Escort! Gimpo becomes quite defensive, explaining to us that even this model will cost us ninety-seven quid a day. 'And anyway it has got these metal studs on the tyres which will ensure we hold the most treacherous of roads,' says Gimpo. I am not convinced; mentally re-plan the last leg of the journey using huskies and sledges.

We are now heading north out of Rovaniemi following the signs to Ivalo, 228 kilometres. The road, a two-laner, is frozen over. Trucks heavy with timber roll by, fashionable 4×4s full of fresh-faced Nordic types, and us, in an Escort. It's past 11 a.m. and Z thinks that's enough of a reason to crack open our second bottle of Blue Label.

The car sailed north. We gunned a petrol-black swathe across the virgin snow.

Is there any point trying to describe the landscape? You will have seen it plenty of times as a back-drop in *Dr Zhivago* and films like that. So, yes, it is dense pine forest, heavy with snow, with the occasional clearing for a clapboard house, painted rust or white or pale blue. Ten kilometres out of Rovaniemi the road is practically deserted but for the odd lumber truck and us.

We have been driving for less than thirty minutes and a sense of boredom has descended on the car. It's as if we're driving up the M6 to Manchester from London for a night out: we've got past Hilton Park service station, have run out of things to say to one another and nobody's that keen on going to Manchester anyway.

I could hear Bill's teeth grind and his ball-point pen scrape. He was noting Arctic realities on an ice tablet: Moses of Antarctica, his imagination sliding with eternity's pyramids, each one indelibly etched with the legend 'Bill was here'.

The stunning landscape outside is boring because you don't expect to see any view for more than ten seconds before it cuts to something even more spectacular and you have a voice-over by David Attenborough telling some amazing fact about the Arctic fox and how it has a life-span of 423 years, two months, five days, seventeen hours, six minutes and fifteen seconds, a bark that in the mating season can be heard over a 300-kilometre radius (but only by the ear of a vixen on heat); then it cuts to the Amazon Basin. I am just about to say, 'David, we need you now,' when I become aware of a strange vibe. Gimpo is hunched over the wheel, his concentration on the road in front.

Gimpo gripped the steering wheel, his penis erect and pointing north. His hatred of the meaningless ephemera of modern life manifested itself through noxious fumes blowing blue flames from his rabid sphincter: this was his car and it was headed for death or glory. I got the impression that he didn't care which.

Me, I'm writing up these notes and staring blankly out of the window at my billionth snow-laden fir tree. Z is a bundle on the back seat in his black-quilted anorak, heavy black-framed glasses, mat of black hair sprouting from underneath his black woollen hat, Blue Label bottle in one hand and stub of pencil in the other.

I had the weird Pentangle vodka on the back seat; I poured some dreams . . .

His scribbling of poetry and lies is becoming so intense that it seems to be spilling out of his imagination and into the reality of three grown men sitting in a Ford Escort heading north to the Pole.

Creeping misogyny and the true faith tumbled from the cold skies and leaked through the car window, spilling evil semen on to my naïve perceptions of romantic love.

I've just skimmed through these notes. I'm shamefully aware of the self-centred nature of most of the stuff and how little regard I have paid to my fellow Magi, especially Z, so here's some background:
I believed that Zodiac Mindwarp and the Love Reaction would herald and ride the crest of the wave of a stadium-filling Rock renaissance. I felt the world was not only ready for, but needed, the Love Reaction; needed the unforgiving sexual godhead that Z had created in his Zodiac Mindwarp persona; needed the poetry of his visions that encompassed Cadillacs drawn by swans across star-filled skies through to the sadly real Lager Woman from Hell; needed the Love Reaction's grinding power chords that resonated with the hosannas of a thousand dark angels.
But stadiums didn't fill, and if a renaissance happened it must have been while I was having a tea-break. So, when I describe the shambling heap on the back seat slugging on the bottle of Blue Label and shuffling his pack of tarot cards, just remember the above is what I also know. (Enough of the patronizing bit.)
I catch a sneaky grin crack across Z's face and then scribble, scribble, scribble, as he documents another of his evil fantasies.

Guinevere coughs up Lancelot's spunk; her shitlocker is still sore from the violent buggering he gave her the night before. 'Of course,' said the Creep, 'the male orgasm is the only one that counts.'

I was slimily seduced, a smelly schoolboy dipping pigtails into dirty inkwells.

'The female orgasm,' continued El Creepo, 'is merely God's method of making sure that the bitch doesn't run away.'

The schoolboy agreed. It made sense: woman and her vile sucking cunt fires off meaningless machine-gun multiple orgasms into the pleasure-dome sky, whereas serious sniper turkey-neck squints his Cyclops eye and takes careful aim, a single shot bearing down on the miracle of creation, a howitzer bell-end blasting the egg. Thus spake the Fat Thruster. 2001: A Space Orgasm, Sperm Almighty. The giant foetus revolves in space; the old man eats his chicken dinner in bright silence, his wad shot, the job done; he waits for death in the canteen of futility. Philip Larkin joins him and spreads margarine on cold toast. The wolf zips up his fly and lurches into the forest of no fixed abode. The she-wolf lactates and claims Income Support.

I chugged another shot of the sacred Pentangle vodka. My hands shook. The vodka warmed my guts and stroked my fear. I cracked a wet fart and was pleased that I didn't follow through. Gimpo fiddled with the radio: some woman reading 'The Burial of the Dead', the first part of *The Waste Land*. Misogyny skulked off into the fir forests.

He starts to burble. He seems to be affecting a South London hippy drawl. To begin with, it is directed towards the scruffy notepad on his knees in which his right hand continues to scribble; after a minute or so of me pretending not to listen and just concentrating on the landscape, I become aware that Z is talking to me.

'Fack you Mick, fack you! I'm goin',' he says. 'I've 'ad enough of your fackin' wanka friends. You can fackin' keep the band. I'm goin' to Lapland to find the fackin' Lost Chord. If anybody deserves to find it, I fackin' do man. Are you lis'nin' to me Mick, you fackin' twat? You and your fackin' cricket and national fackin' music day. Who the fack do you think you fackin' are anyway? Cant!'

I turn my head discreetly, hoping Z will have returned to his scribbles, but no, I'm met by his evil stare, which convolutes into his 'bad boy' sly grin.

*

The King slid in on an FM frequency. 'And his momma cries . . .' Elvis sang of life in a Chicago ghetto and the heroic struggle of the poor. An oily tear rolled down my cheek and I remembered why I was there, risking my life amidst this coldness and madness, surfing into tragedy at full speed. Adonis, Attis, Elvis, the Fisherking of Rock 'n' Roll; *Le Roi est mort, Vive le Roi!*

Z seems to be directing all of the conversation at me. I turn sharply away, pretending there is something in the Arctic wasteland that I have just noticed and must record here on paper. I take a sneak glance at Gimpo to see if he is registering any of Z's protestations.

Gimpo gunned the engine; the wheels spun; the road was glass. I glanced at the speedometer: ninety mph. Blue flames and black smoke blasted from Gimpo's deranged butt. Bill conducted a military parade through the Valley of the Kings.

Gimpo is just total concentration on the road in front, his hard blue eyes not flinching from the task in hand. Z mumbles on for a while, occasionally chortling to himself. If he blurts any more of irrelevance, you can count on me to record it.

The vodka was strong and brought a shimmering vision in fairy dust, slow motion with Vaseline on the lens, out-of-focus and gold, of the King himself sitting next to me on the back seat. He is 21 years old, strumming an acoustic guitar and murmuring, 'Love me tender'. Our disparate dimensions mesh. The King sees me and smiles. His teeth dazzle like God. Religion rushes through me like a warm locomotive stoked on morphine. I feel like a schoolgirl before a manifestation of the Nazarene. A tender lightning bolt of understanding and wisdom cracks from the King's flashing eyes and groks into my soul.
  I finished the bottle.

How to resolve the format of the Book continues to nag at me. Do we use the letters that led up to this journey? There's so much stuff in them that may be totally libellous. Do we publish and be damned, or do we change the names to protect the guilty? And this whole journey section – Z and I never discussed how this was going to work out. Are we still sending each other letters? Is this a letter to him? Or is this a letter to my children? Or, as Z suggested, should we be both writing back to Tracey?

Then there was Z's idea that both our logs should run in parallel columns down either side of each page. Or should there be a chunk from Z and a chunk from me? Or would we just end up repeating whatever the other was saying? Or should we take it in turns to document the unfolding events? Of course, as I say, nothing is decided; both scribbling away, putting off the moment when we have to resolve our differences.

Wisdom and hallucinogenic realities pour like the Bible, an avalanche of poetry, crazier than Revelations and wiser than Solomon, neon words flashing from the fifth dimension. Elvis the wish myth: pink Cadillacs and old ladies and spontaneous acts of hillbilly kindness; the mundaneness of his corporeal existence transcended by modern mass-media apotheosis. Every cheap souvenir bought from the Graceland Lourdes speeds the King's ascent on Olympus. In a billion imaginations, in dripping rhinestones and massive religious flares, Elvis radiates like a Technicolor TV saint. On the Golgotha of prescription drugs, betrayed by those closest to him, the King is spread-eagled and crucified on his fame. The King is dead: long live the King on reissues and videos and a trillion memories. From Moscow via London to Memphis, Elvis Presley will still be the King of Rock 'n' Roll to me.

'Cant! Fuckin' cant!' Z has started again. Now he's beginning to take on another voice, a sort of authoritative, TV-documentary voice: 'Keith was a broken man, a pale, drug-addled shadow of his former self, living out his sad days in the bars of Helsinki, talking to anybody who cared to listen and even those who didn't.'

Voice returns to laid-back South London drawl: 'I offered him six million quid. Cash. I had it there in the flight case. He wouldn't fuckin' take it.'

He scribbles and cackles some more, takes a large swig from the bottle of Blue Label then, all of a sudden, bursts into a camp, affected actory-type voice: 'Oh Bosie! Bosie, where have you been, dear boy? This dreadful Keith character keeps telling me you were never going to come back to me!'

And then the thunder speaks: 'Datta! Dayadhvarn! Damyata!' Like a diamond bolt of lightning straight into my soul, Elvis talks to me and disappears back into the fifth dimension.

I rummaged through my bag and grabbed a fresh bottle of Blue Label Pentangle crystal dreaming fluid and chugged greedily. Our sacred image of the King stared at me from inside the bag. I removed it from its wrapping and stared hard at His Holiness. Any doubts I had were swatted like the bugs they were. 'Shantih,' I said, 'Shantih, Shantih, Shantih!' And I meant it.

Luckily for me, this all seems to be directed at Gimpo. Gimpo still makes no acknowledgement of his friend/client/sometime-brother-in-law's outpourings.

I opened the window and vomited religiously. I was purged and cleansed. This was the true faith.

CHAPTER SIX

The Blind Chainsaw Fishermen of Finland

The car ploughed on. The sun was a pale disc, alive and taunting us with evil games. Unlike the warmer latitudes with their sunrises and sunsets, this hellish hyperborean vista possessed a malignant orb that perpetually circled the horizon like some patient airborne predator waiting for the kill. It was never really day and never really night; a half world in varying shades of gold, silver and red, shifting gory hues in permanent twilight. The snow reflected the sky's ominous beauty as if in a soft mirror. Gentle winds blew the coloured flakes into whispering eddies like psychedelic smoke. The road vanished into a million possibilities.

Fuck! Gimpo has just regained control of the car. The car had swerved, hit something in the road, spun round, driven over something else. Z had screamed: 'Arctic crocodiles!' My heart is pounding. Adrenalin rushes round my body, searching escape. My brain tells me we will die a horrible death. My guilt tells me I deserve to. My pen documents that I swing my head round to look out of the rear window to see what it was we ran over. There is nothing there.

Gimpo still unflinching, and Z is off again in his documentary voice-over voice: 'They were first made aware of the reality of the mythological beast, the Arctic crocodile, when they ran over one and killed it while travelling at over 110 mph on the ice-packed road heading north.' Then Gimpo says something like: 'Got him! One less Argie!' I have a terrible feeling that other people's realities/unrealities are getting too close to mine.

Somebody has farted but nobody admits to it.

I'm trying to push out whatever else that is going on around me and concentrate on my concerns: this book. We still have not got a title. *The Literary Arseholes: The Collected Letters, 1992* or something similar had been the sort of working title, but now we are doing all this Polar stuff, it doesn't quite fit. Titles like *Last of the Summer Acid* and *Poetry, Lies and Gimpo* jump into my head and amuse me before limping off as the pale pastiches they are. If we were to call it *Last of the Summer Acid* people would think it was about three crazed, ageing hippies – like the Furry Freak Brothers, but British – and, although I like *Poetry, Lies and Gimpo*, every half-arsed sub-editor has been using the *Sex, Lies and Videotape* movie title as the basis of their smart-arsed headlines over the last few years. So *Zen Sticks to the Pole*, *Elvis to the Pole*, *The Men Who Saved the World* and the other titles that should in no way be recorded, now have been.

Whilst staring out at the passing Arctic forests, I have just said something aloud for no apparent reason: 'Siberian sabre-toothed tiger! That's what it was!' I don't think Gimpo heard me, but Z certainly did. He is off again, describing some weird scene that includes being attacked by howling polar bears and packs of Arctic crocodiles while mammoths quietly forage for pale green shoots on the fir-tree branches. Then he gets on to the fields of Arctic chickens. After each line or so he breaks down into grunting chortles.

I'm becoming more afraid. The further we go, the more Z seems to drift deeper into his own imaginary world. It's as if he is standing on quicksand being sucked down into it. Where am I drifting? Z told me a couple of weeks ago that Gimpo would save us from the death jaws of reality; but who will save us from our own unrealities? How will we find the Baby Jesus if we shipwreck before we reach him? Or is he waiting patiently on the far side of the smoking, hissing wreckage of our sanity?

I take a peek at the other two to make sure they are not looking before I make another attempt to dislodge that encrusted bogey in my left nostril. Fail.

I stop writing to enjoy the passing mantra-like scenery: no mountains or surprising landmarks. The road sweeps on: broad curves and gentle cambers, frozen lake to the left, then frozen lake to the right. Then . . .

*

In the trance-like state that is the transition from sleep to wakefulness I noticed that the car was turning smooth elegant circles on the deserted icy road. Gimpo had hit the brakes and we were sliding a graceful automobile waltz. I didn't panic. The car eventually slowed to a standstill and Gimpo wound down the window. The cold air curled into the car as Bill stared, entranced, towards the horizon. We had stopped on a vast frozen river.

A tiny blue spark cracked about an inch away from Gimpo's ear. He kicked the car into first and started driving towards two black figures barely discernible in the half light, a mile away in the centre of the frozen waterway. As the car crawled towards them I instinctively reached for my mysterious Pentangle vodka. Bill had removed his antique telescope from the doctor's bag and pointed it towards the figures.

'Gimpo! Look! Stop the car, Gimpo! Can you see those two men over there in the middle of the lake?' That's me talking.

'My God,' he whispered, 'it's true! The northern pygmies!' I grabbed the telescope and focused it on the object of his reverential awe. Two naked men in sunglasses stared back at me.

Gimpo pulls the car up. Z crunches back into his huddled reality and grumbles. I declare that the two men must be fishing through the holes in the ice and it is our duty to introduce ourselves to them and find what wisdom they have to impart to us.

We drove to within ten yards of them and saw that they were completely naked apart from sunglasses and penis gourds made from some kind of fish. They stood about four feet tall, their stunted torsos covered in Maori-like tattoos depicting five-pointed stars and fish. Both carried enormous, intricately carved gold chainsaws. They were totally bald, their scalps smeared with some kind of animal grease. They sported long, shiny black beards dressed in plaits. I opened the door to speak to these unique human beings but, before I could get out of the car, they had dived into a hole in the ice and disappeared.

*

We bundle up as warm as we can. Z is still clutching the Blue Label; Gimpo, the icon of Elvis; me, my notebook and pencil. Outside it is bitterly cold (it could be a lot worse – there is no wind), sub-zero silence and snow. We stride out across the frozen lake towards the two figures. The lake must be half a mile wide and the men are in the centre.

I ran up to the two-foot-thick hole and stared down into the black silent water. It lapped against the ice and looked as cold as hell. A large ugly fish flared its gills and floundered at the edge of the hole. It had black scales and stank of shit. I jumped back a yard when it started barking like a dog.

We extend our hands in welcome. They remove their gloves to shake hands. Z offers, and they decline, a swig of the Blue Label. I take a swig. The two hardy fishermen seem nonplussed by our appearance.

Fish and fishing have been a lifelong passion for me, but I've never heard, seen or read of a more strange or sado-masochistic form of fishing than this. I had always imagined sitting at a hole in the ice with a fishing line, a Thermos of hot soup and an Eskimo grin as rather a romantic thing to do; but that isn't what these geezers are up to. The first thing we notice is the chainsaws, primed for action; then the four-foot pike lying on the snow, struggling against death, gasping for oxygen but getting only air.

'Electric ice pike!' exclaimed Bill, examining the revolting specimen. 'Its flesh is hallucinogenic. Our shy friends believe that the meat, eaten raw, enables them to communicate directly with the spirit world. This is a pregnant female, by the way.' He flipped the fish over on to its side with his Zen stick. It writhed disgustingly, its eight gills opening and closing like a syphilitic whore's ruined cunt.

'The roe, when eaten out of the belly of a live fish,' said Bill, adjusting his sporran, 'supposedly enables the fishermen to communicate telepathically with God himself.' I was intrigued. Bill took a shot of my mystic vodka and continued in an erudite fashion, stopping only to pose heroically from time to time, photographing himself for posterity in his imagination. The ugly fish bucked and twitched like a spaz prozzy connected to the mains.

There are two holes in the ice, about eighteen inches across and eighteen feet apart. A rope disappears into the black water of one hole and resurfaces through the black of the other; fitted to the rope is a light nylon netting. The question that requires an answer is, how did they get that rope under the ice from one porthole of doom and back up through the other? The men cannot speak English; the question has to be left unanswered.

'The blind chainsaw fishermen of Finland,' began the treatise, 'for, if I am correct, that is who these strange fellows are, were thought to have become extinct some time during the last century. Little is known of them since, like their distant cousins, the Hottentot Kalahari bushmen, they are a nomadic people who, it is believed, migrated north long before the Jurassic shift which separated Europe from Africa. They are an ancient and deeply spiritual people. When a male child is born, he is blinded. This practice, so it is held, sharpens the child's inner vision and enables him to communicate better with the spirits.'

The pike gasps and flips itself over. I think of the sweet, white flesh of Pike and his hair bones. I think of the death he has meted out daily to Roach, Rudd, Bream and Dace. The law of the jungle dictates that some creatures kill for fun, pike and humans included. That doesn't stop my heart going out to this freshwater shark as it gasps and flips one more time.

'The diet of these fishermen is limited to fish of the kind you see before you.'

The geezers have a couple of kipper crates; in them are two more smaller pike and three other types of fish. These have all passed on to the great lake in the sky.

'You mean,' interrupted Gimpo, 'they're out of their fuckin' heads all the time?'

'An interesting way of putting it,' said Bill, arching an eyebrow and puffing on a pipe he had found somewhere. 'And, in a way, I suppose you're right. But if I may put forward a slice of personal philosophy . . .'

Are these fish to be sold? Do these men make a meagre living from this hard-won catch, or is this regular Tuesday fun on a winter's day? Gimpo unwraps Elvis and tries to explain.

He didn't get the chance – Gimpo had bitten the fish's head clean off. He fell to the ground juddering weird fish spasms and, with a fart blast of green ectoplasm, left his body completely. He was either at one with the universe floating on the cosmic space winds with the Silver Surfer, grooving to Hawkwind, or suffering severe toxic poisoning. There was only one way to find out. Bill filleted the female dreamfish and ate a handful of the slimy red eggs. They looked like the haemorrhoids of Satan and smelt like a Grimsby shagbag after a hard day's night. Bill gagged and fell to the ice, twitching like an epileptic struck by lightning. Within seconds he too had left his corporeal body and was up into the icy Arctic skies.

I looked down at the two twitching bodies.

Blank expressions.

Both of them had shat and pissed themselves and were flailing around like incontinent elephant seals, gibbering in a language I'd never heard before. I scooped up a handful of the still-living fish and swilled down the eggs with vodka.

CRAAAAA A AAAACCCCCCCCCKKKKKKKK ! ! ! ! !

The universe exploded. I was sent screaming straight into Revelations, Saint John the Divine's screaming bummer porno nightmare: purple-headed women drinking the blood of saints; seven-headed blue penis dragons; God, Magog and the Devil himself ripping the shit out of everything; weird bug-eyed animals and Motorhead music; swarms of locusts with human heads; politicians defecating glistening bloody eyeballs; Mickey Mouse and Donald Duck castrated with blunt tailor's shears and crucified on huge dollar bills; supermodels fellating monster poison jellyfish; child molesters eating offal from tabloid newspapers. Princess Diana's severed head bubbles and splutters in a microwave oven. It was like flipping channels on some satanic TV set.

I couldn't see Bill or Gimps anywhere and I was spiralling off into even stranger weirdness. Max Ernst's *Temptation of Saint Anthony* merged with all kinds of gruesome Hieronymus Bosch horror gremlins; monkeys with batwings dive-bombed into my head, screeching and baring their huge vampire teeth; demented Hindu deities were throwing severed heads at me; horrible masturbating Priapuses were spurting burning acid semen into my eyes. I approached the perilous chapel. If this was telepathic communication with God, I guess I must have caught him on a bad day.

This shit went on for hours. On and on piled the horror. Fortunately, I'd done plenty of bad acid in my time, so it didn't faze me too much, although seeing Adolf Hitler being sucked off by Jim Morrison did make me wonder exactly whose spirit world this was. Mad chainsaw-wielding LA gang members raped white women; Hollywood film crews masturbated in mortuaries; the Yorkshire Ripper with a weird smile strummed the strings of a woman's eyeballs; sado-masochistic homosexuals stuffed baby bull terriers up each other's bumholes; and again the chimpanzees, farting an *Evita* medley.

The three of us rejoined our bodies two days later. The Chainsaw people had kindly washed most of the shit, piss, vomit and God-knows-what other bodily fluids off us, so we didn't smell too bad – just that lingering, cuntish, dreamfish odour which gets you at the back of the throat like a dead ferret and nail-varnish remover.

Pick up the dying pike, little life left in its struggle.

Bill wrapped the remains of the disgusting aquatic nightmare in newspaper and placed it in his doctor's bag, mumbling something about a proper chemical analysis when we got back to England.

Gimpo has a disposable camera. I am embarrassed to report we have our photograph taken.

We nod, smile, convey our farewells and good lucks across the cultural barriers; trudge back across the frozen lake to the Ford Escort and the road north. The riddle of the rope and the two black holes is the wisdom we sought and will take with us on the road north.

Back in the car, Gimpo gunned the engine and we peeled northward. In the rear-view mirror I caught sight of the shy fishermen peeping out of their hole in the ice. They waved timidly as we drove away.

CHAPTER SEVEN

Nazi Kung Fu Sex Bitches with Rottweilers

Back in the car, and I am now sitting in the rear seat; Z is in the front. Bring these notes up to the minute. Gimpo pulls out into the empty road. The day is looking weary. And then, and now and as always I notice Elvis staring up at me. The unwrapped picture of the King is lying face up on the rummage of coats beside me.

I flipped on the car radio. A Finnish punk rock band were playing a song called 'Sexy Roy Orbison'. I was amused by the oxymoron, but the incessant punk rock beat bored me shitless. I switched channels and Wagner crashed on to the radio like a Teutonic avalanche of pure sex. Bill reached across and pushed up the volume. Big fat Valkyries were screeching Germanically about war and sex and blood and death. This was more like it: fine Nazi music to blast away the ennui of the beautiful but tedious Finnish landscape. The warm stink negotiating its way around the interior of the car indicated that my friend Bill had been adding his own woodwind solo to the Germanic symphony. I opened the window. Lighting a Finnish cigarette, I cracked open a bottle of Blue Label Pentangle vodka and drifted into another daydream.

Elvis. 'Why Elvis?' they will ask. And of course there is no need to answer: it is plain for all to see why Elvis. But something far deeper in myself asks, 'Why Elvis?', and I know I have to confront the eight-year-old boy sitting alone in a picture-house in a small market town in rural Scotland as the fifties drag themselves into the early sixties. Up on the screen was the opening sequence of the main feature: a truck gliding along the gentle twists and turns of a wooded mountain road. In time we see the truck from the back. We see a man sitting on the tailgate, guitar on lap. There my memory of what this small boy is watching fades. Of course, the small boy was me. The film was *Roustabout* and the man on the tailgate was Elvis.

I'd heard of Elvis before, knew he was a singer, but nothing else. I hadn't gone to see this film because it starred Elvis – I went because I went to the pictures every week. For one shilling you could get a ticket on the hard wooden seats near the front. My pocket money at the time would stretch to allow me to spend a further threepence on a poke of chips and to give another threepence to the collection at church on Sunday. No, I learnt nothing of where Elvis came from, or what these songs he sang were about or where or what he was for – he was just this man in these films that appeared every few months over the next three years until we moved to a different part of the country where there was no picture-house and The Beatles exploded into my life.

Back then, at the age of eight, there were no pictures of pop stars on posters, mugs, T-shirts and calendars; no video cassettes or box-sets, not even pictures on the single 45 sleeves. Where I lived, the only way a boy of my age could get to know anything about Elvis was through these films. I have never since seen any of the films and have no desire to. Yes, of course, I know that by the standards of the all-seeing, all-knowing, post-modern man these films were crap – I can't articulate any sort of argument to prove otherwise – but that's beside the point.

Through Elvis, something was communicated to me; not through any one thing in particular, but through his whole being. I know nothing of man's psychological need for gods, but the presence of Elvis in any form – a picture, the sound of his voice or just his name, those five letters ELVIS – was enough to set something in me free. I left the picture-house that night, crossed the main street, bought my threepenny poke of chips drenched in vinegar and found my way home in the darkness, never, ever, to be the same again.

As I struggled through the sixties, withdrawn and behind at school, Elvis struggled with me. Somebody said he was no good any more, then I saw a trailer for a film with Elvis singing 'His Latest Flame'.

How wrong that somebody was. But The Beatles came and haircuts changed and Elvis records didn't make it so high so often in the Hit Parade. 'US Male', 'Guitar Man': solid, worthy and real, but not No. Ones.

8 January 1965: standing in my mother and father's bedroom, staring out of the window, the radio news somewhere in the background. The announcer tells us that it is Elvis's birthday – he is thirty – and I thought, somewhere else in the world is Elvis and he is having his thirtieth birthday. It felt strange.

And then, some time else in another room, I stood staring out of another window and in the background the radio newsman's voice told us that Elvis had just got married to a lady called Priscilla. It is only now as I sit in the back of this Ford Escort heading for the North Pole that I wonder why I felt weird, strange and disturbed about hearing those two brief news bulletins at least twenty-five years ago. Was it because they confirmed that Elvis was real and ageing and not immortal; that yes, Elvis lived somewhere; had a mundane, day-to-day life?

One August morning in 1977 I awoke in my sleeping bag on some scrubland on the coast of Brittany. The morning was mild but murky. I climbed out to go and look for a baker's shop. A fat bald man was sitting on the ground outside a tent reading a newspaper, a French newspaper. The headline: ELVIS MORT. Now, I can't speak or read French, but I knew what that meant. That strange feeling came back, full force, and I thought, how can Elvis be dead when the feeling is still alive in me? I saw those five letters on the newspaper headline and it shot something through to the deepest recesses of my soul, just like it had always done. And as I stood there something fell to my feet from out of the sky: it was a baguette. I picked it up. It was freshly baked – no need to go to the baker's. Saved myself a franc or so. It was on that Brittany morning that I remembered how, at seventeen, I had wanted to be the actual record 'Hound Dog'.

Look, this is all a bit confusing for me. I can feel those tears welling up again so I'll write down some facts and hope they help me through this and sort it out:

1. I have never bought an Elvis Presley record.
2. I do not want to go to Graceland.

3. I have never owned any Elvis merchandise.
4. I have never sat and listened to an Elvis LP.

Over the years since picking up that baguette, the pull of Elvis has never left me, but I only ever want to experience him by accident. Hearing an Elvis record blaring out of an open window as I walk down the street, driving up the motorway and glimpsing a truck heading in the opposite direction with ELVIS written in chunky white letters across the windscreen visor, passing a shop to see him looking down from an exploitative merchandise calendar, is all it takes to throw the switch. I never went to Elvis expecting something. He always came to me, when I least expected it. I never wanted to possess Elvis, or to define Elvis. Yes, I knew that Elvis was a real person, a person that aged and made bad records and bad career moves and was a dickhead and didn't write his own songs and wasn't a guitar hero and wore stupid clothes and got fat and died. But, but . . . But all that is a reality that gets in the way of that other thing beyond all the crap.

That other thing beyond all the crap is mythology. Classical and pagan mythology was displaced by Christianity and poor old Jesus could never have embodied the whole pantheon of gods answering all our human needs and desires. When I say 'we', I mainly mean us of white European descent or, more precisely, northern European males. It is we who, over the last two thousand years, have bit by bit lost our contact with mythology. We allowed it to be taken away, but the hunger for it remains. No, not a childish hunger for heroes with which to identify – something far bigger and deeper than that. Because the symbol of Jesus Christ was unable to satisfy our need for myth we came up with the saints and their lives, we came up with Mary the Virgin Mother, but this is still not enough. So we battened down our needs, ignored our hunger, banished great chunks of our soul and made ourselves guilty about the bits that seeped through.

In our inner heaven, the old gods are all still there: Odin, Thor, Zeus, Athena, Artemis, Dionysus, Buddha, Allah and yes, of course, Jesus Christ and the Virgin Mary too. But these are just names and, if we burden them with too many facts and figures, whats and wheres, whens and whys, we will get no further than Albert Goldman did in his book *Elvis*: we will just be left looking at the bloated corpse of a Southern lad allowed to live a life of selfish excess, instead of recognizing the man who shared all our own closed doors and inner hungers. The difference between us and him is that this man's doors were flung open by the influence of the untamed dark continent, and inside him was Dionysus in perfect working order, bursting to get out. And he did: Dionysus was made flesh.

The sleeping Dionysus in all us young tender white males understood the clarion call. This clarion call grew and grew, went out around the world. Echoes. Echoes of echoes answering back from continent to continent, from year to year, from generation to generation. Gangs of young men went out into the world armed only with the buzzing, howling and chiming of single-coil and Humbucker pick-ups and the clatter of drums, screaming their war cries and moaning their laments.

Of course nothing is born pure, let alone stays pure; corruption of every kind seeped in and dribbled out of this noise, this clarion call, this Rock 'n' Roll. The archivists and historians can argue the facts and dates, they can talk about delta bluesmen, Little Richard, Bill Haley or white boys fuelled by guilt-ridden liberalism and loads of other shite; but all that misses the point.

Now, I know Elvis did not sit down and invent Rock 'n' Roll (Elvis didn't invent anything, nor did Sam Phillips with his slap-back echo – these are all incidentals). Elvis was Elvis because within him so much was right: the time, the place, the looks, the heartache, the rage, the depth, the shallowness, the hips, the fire, the ice, the voice, the name, the wantonness and the tragedy; and all of these separate elements were in each other, each contained the seed of all the other components.

Fads and fashions fanned flames then flickered away. Intellectual snobberies muddied the water. Technical prowess tried to hold us – the hordes – at bay. But through all that, Dionysus swaggered on, leering and lurching. He was on the loose for the first time in almost one thousand years. He had been banished since the last Viking raids, since the old gods, the Norse gods, the Olympian gods and the Celtic gods, banished but not killed, just locked deep in our souls.

So don't look for him in Elvis's quiff, or his tough-but-tender looks, or John Lennon's ache or Dylan's rhymes, or Bolan's boogie or Bowie's masks or Johnny Rotten's disdain, or in any other of the thousands who have heard the clarion call and made arseholes of themselves across the world's stages. Generation after generation has grabbed this mantle as a birthright – and yes, it is a birthright – but some forget that before Elvis there was nothing, well, nearly nothing, for a thousand years. Rock 'n' Roll in all its ugly, debased and exploited forms, torn out of and built up from the black man's basic twelve-bar blues, is the soundtrack to every Viking voyage. Once again the white boy can rape and pillage, lie and lick, lust and kick, swagger and swear across the known and unknown universe, the chains of Christian doctrine smashed on a pagan altar.

In today's eyes Elvis may be a figure of kitsch fun, a remnant of a bygone era, worth no more in that sense than the dry classical mythology taught in schools and colleges, so this argument of mine, this diatribe, this outpouring, lacks a logical thread. An intellectual case may be held more safely in a leaky colander. But what I am trying to ram home is that the power that has come through the man Elvis Presley is very, very, very . . .

'Facts, Bill, facts. Give me some facts, Bill.' A voice.

All I know is . . . Do I know that? All I know is . . . Do I know that? I hope I'm not losing it 'cause I've been on one here. The wantonness and selfishness of Dionysus will always end in tragedy?

The reason we Three Kings are hurtling towards the North Pole with this icon of the King is in recognition of the fact that we have thrown away our young men's years on his very altar. We now want to smash on through to the other side before the tragedy drags us down with him. Baby Jesus, here we come!

Elvis is dead. But it was through Elvis that we were able to experience one of our inner gods we had denied for a thousand years; it was on to Elvis and all those who followed him that we were able to project our undeveloped secret gods. We need those kings and gods and superheroes.

I look up from these words I am scribbling, peer through the half steamed-up windows to the now familiar landscape and wonder how far we are going to travel. Our maps have little detail.

Z mumbles something and we start up some sort of a banter about how great we are – regular male-bonding shit: shagging, drinking, poetry and the possibility of enrolling at the Ivalo School of Shamen. The conversation becomes quite lucid. We exchange ideas about structure and style. The threads get lost and again we return to hide in our/these 'words of wonder, words of joy'.

I re-read the pages on Elvis and think 'What the fuck was all that about?' I mean, Elvis means fuck all to me. It's as if what I'm really saying is: 'I'm me. Look, I'm me. Look, I've got all these deranged theories. I'm different from you – I'm me.'

'Don't try and wriggle out of it. We know you meant it.'

Some people try to prove that they're different by being faster, fitter, fatter, smaller, taller, cooler, hotter, smarter, richer, poorer; but me, do I try and prove it by having more half-baked theories? The thing is, while having them I'm totally there; then five minutes later it's all gone, like a dream slithering back down into the subconscious at the moment you wake. People who write proper books with a real structure and a thought-out concept with a message they want to impart to the rest of the world, are they able to hold the threads together? When they get to the end do they think, 'Well, I got that one sorted'? Do they re-read their book and feel proud? Or do they feel sick and sad and lost, not knowing what it was they were hoping to say?

Just before the cum shot, I was jerked harshly awake by the slamming of the car door and found myself face down in some of Gimpo's shit-stained underwear.

Gimpo pulls the wheel round.

I shook my groggy head to see Gimpo hurtling across the ice towards a huge sinister building.

Skid off the main road on to a bumpy track, bounce down and twist through the forest for a half kilometre or so and pull up at some timber cabins. GOLD PANNING – a notice.

It rose out of the swirling snow like dread Pandemonium, the evil parliament of hell. Gimpo was snapping away with his disposable camera. I noticed black and yellow signs screaming at the side of the road – they were festooned with death's heads, angry Germanic typefaces and violent exclamation marks.

A tourist trap of sorts through the summer months, I guess. The café is open. We are the only ones.

It's a sick place – more post-modern shite. It's pretending to be a gold-rush trading post up the Yukon half a world away, selling post-cards of Father Christmas, old-time '49ers and reindeer. We order our tea, coffee and weak beer. We pontificate about crapness, buy a chocolate bar, a second and third cup of tea. Bearskins on the wall, hurricane lamps, Red Indian tom-toms. A sleeping dog on the floor is there for me to trip over when I search out the bogs.

As silent as one of death's farts and with even less warning, a huge black shape leapt from the darkness and pinned Gimpo to the floor. I could see razor-sharp teeth bared in a carnivorous snarl and yellow eyes blazing with canine death lust: Rottweiler. A fucking big one. Three shadowy bipeds emerged from the darkness clutching machine guns; they barked in German to the frozen Gimp. The car was surrounded by thirty or more menacing shadows. Now they were close enough for me to identify the silver insignia and red armbands. I feared as much: Nazis.

Spooky orchestral music spiralled out of nowhere; a high-pitched voice screamed at us to get out of the car. Bill turned to me and said: 'I'll handle this, Z. I was born in Germany. I understand these people.' He got out of the car and spoke in fluent and authoritative German. The tallest Nazi snarled at him and, without warning, crunched him to the ground with the butt of a rifle. I was yanked violently by my hair from the car and swiftly felled by a jackboot karate kick to the face. My nose broke before I hit the deck. I noticed that our captors were all women.

When I regained consciousness I was at a distinct disadvantage: I was butt naked and chained to a dungeon wall with jump leads attached to my nuts. Blue flashes skittered underneath the adjoining steel doors. I could hear baboon screams and angry electricity crackling from the next cell; the screams sounded chillingly Scottish. The noise of electric torture split across the air and was followed by more Gaelic howling. The acrid smell of burning flesh insulted my nostrils. Those fucking Nazi bitches were doing something terrible to my Celtic friend. I heard more torture zaps, but this time followed by silence. The longest hour of my life slid past in a deafening silence. I could hear the white noise of my blood rushing around my adrenalin-flushed body; my heartbeat hit fours on the floor.

The place is sad and dusty, but I am sure in the summer months it is full of happy families. Yes, I could see that Kate and James would love it and I would feel good, in a fatherly sort of way, explaining to them how they used to pan for gold.

The iron door crashed open. Two six-foot Nazi bitches strode in wearing full Gestapo regalia, complete with monocles and duelling scars. They stood rigidly to attention on either side of the door, clicking and stamping their stiletto-heeled jackboots. A stunning six-footer catwalked into the room, pulling on a pair of surgical rubber gloves and snapping the fingers one at a time. Her thigh-high boots clattered menacingly on the stone floor; the SS officer's cap was tipped at a jaunty angle; her black tunic was unbuttoned to the waist, revealing a stern black bra emblazoned with two red swastikas; she was smoking an expensive cigarette from a silver cigarette holder. You get the picture. Oh yeah, black shiny tights and studded leather panties . . . stiffy, stiffy, stiffy.

She moved in closer to me and lifted my chin with her riding crop. I could smell Chanel and ozone. Her eyes were chemical blue. She blew smoke in my face through wet pornographic lips. 'So . . .' she breathed, caressing my balls with her gloved hand. My cock scoped Medusa and turned to granite. She started to toss me off gently and tongued my left nipple, then suddenly pulled back her head and laughed out loud. I screamed 96 decibels of sheer agony as my dick exploded. Sparks were flashing off my bell-end like a firework. She yanked up the voltage. My prick was flailing around like a possessed jackhammer; my knackersack was two blazing suns about to go nova; huge blue lightning bolts flew out of my Jap's eye.

She turned off the machine as abruptly as she had turned it on and I stared down at my smoking charcoal frankfurter in total disbelief.

'You like my little sex toy, handsome spy?' she purred.

'I'm no fucking spy, you stupid Nazi bitch!' I spat a huge wad of green phlegm into her face. I wanted to kill her. She brought her riding crop down on my frazzled knob and laughed at my screams. When she turned the machine back on, lightning bolts, two feet long, zapped from my seared member. 'I'm a polar fuckin' explorer! I'm going to save the fucking . . . AIEEE! . . . world!'

'You really expect me to believe that, you spying French bastard?' She spat in my face and cranked the voltage up even higher. The pain was beyond description.

By now the Nazi dominatrix was starting to enjoy herself. She was laughing feverishly and rubbing her hand against her studded crotch, masturbating vigorously. I reached down into the very essence of my being to find something primordial with which to combat the screeching agony surging through my genitals. I quickly regained my calm and said, 'Listen baby, turn this thing off and I'll show you some real fun.'

The Nazi torture bitch stopped mid-frig, snapped off the machine and, narrowing her blue eyes, gazed at me, a look of begrudging appreciation softening the Teutonic hardness of her features. 'Remarkable!' she smiled admiringly. 'You have just had over 2,000 volts pumped through your wedding tackle and now you proposition me as though we were in a night club.'

'Baby,' I continued confidently, a fiendish plot hatching in my brilliant mind, 'check the tattoos. I can take pain, I'm from Yorkshire, the hardest county in England.'

'Release him!' she ordered the kung fu Nazi goons.

I had her! Z knows what women want, even if they don't.

'Commandante Marlene . . .' said one of the Nazi bitches, hesitatingly.

'Now, you fucking whore!' snapped the Commandante, more ferocious than the Rottweilers.

The goons unshackled me. I knew exactly what I planned to do: turn on the snake-oil super charm, fuck her, kill her, rescue Bill and Gimp, blow up the castle, kill all the women – just like James Bond.

Marlene's boudoir: expensive French perfume and oak furniture; oil paintings of an idealized Führer dressed in armour on a white steed, a log fire fluttering in a fireplace the size of a council house. The only disturbing element in this elegant room was the presence of the tattooed lampshades. Marlene poured me a massive scotch as I languished on the black silk sheets of her towering four-poster bed. 'Hey baby,' I called, 'bring the bottle. I'm feelin' kinda dry.' She laughed and said, 'I love a man who can take his drink.'

In fact, we had seen this place before only two weeks ago on the telly! Michael Palin's *Pole to Pole*. He visited this place in his first episode. The cunt! When Z and I first heard about his up-and-coming series we nearly cancelled this whole trip. Then we thought back to the year zero and the place Mesopotamia and thought, would those original Three Kings have ditched their plans, ignored the Star, just 'cause some contemporary story-teller was doing the rounds with a tale about a geeezer that headed east for no reason other than . . . Fuck. Cunt. Shit!

She had changed into a black lounging suit with a red swastika emblazoned on the back of the jacket. Her large breasts swung freely beneath the silk, generating enough static to power a small town. As she crossed the room she patted a sleeping Rottweiler which was curled up by the log fire, luxuriating in the intense dry heat. She reached across the bed, undid my trousers and began to massage a scented tropical balm on to my fried penis, cooing and making cat-like noises as she admired its considerable length and girth. 'How did you learn to take such pain? Your friends were unconscious at only a tenth of the voltage you withstood.'

'Baby,' I laughed, my penis stiffening like basalt, 'I'm from Yorkshire. I'm rock!'

She laughed, lowered her glistening mouth around my wounded bell-end and gently cupped her soft hands around my nuts. Her head started bobbing gently. It was like having my chopper plugged into a can of electric worms. Her tongue flickered like a wet butterfly. She removed my penis from her mouth and started to nibble at my ball-bag. I could feel my spermatozoa battalion straining to erupt, so I relaxed the muscles in my stomach to extend this unique experience of Nazi sex. Marlene stopped her fellatio and sank to her hands and knees; she was in the full throes of feline Deutsche lust.

I took advantage of her abandonment and threw one up her shitlocker. As I banged my frazzled turkey neck up to the nuts in her stretched sphincter, she squealed with a mixture of pleasure and pain. She threw her head back and bit the edge of her hand. It was starting to hurt her. I eased it out slightly and started riding her delightful little fudge tunnel more gently. She sighed with relief as my vigorous thrusting became a light throb. I could smell her skin perspiring like sugary milk and honeysuckle. She was murmuring love words in her native tongue when I pulled back and plunged my blood-gorged tool as hard as possible, ripping up her colon and into her lower intestine. She screamed in agony as I whipped out my shit-covered dick. Her butthole was torn and spots of blood trickled down her legs. I apologized for my over-enthusiasm and, after a few tears, she seemed to forget. 'Make love to me like a woman,' she purred. I mounted her in the conventional manner and gave her the best fuck of her life. She came seventy-three times – I counted – before I spurted my virile seed. 'You are the greatest lover of all time!' she sighed as she languished in post-coital ecstasy. I laughed: she wasn't the first woman to have made that observation.

I got up and wiped the cunt juice, shit, blood and other stuff off my cock and poured another scotch. 'Drink, baby?' I asked. 'Yes lover, a large one,' she replied. I fixed her a monster scotch from the drinks cabinet and returned to the bed, patting the sleeping Rott on the head as I passed the smouldering fire. She had wrapped the swastika-emblazoned dressing gown around her shoulders and was lighting one of her fancy cigarettes. Blue smoke surrounded her. She looked beautiful. The flickering light from the fire danced across the beads of perspiration clinging to her tits, giving them the appearance of glittering, erotic jewels.

'So baby,' I said, draining my scotch, 'how does a beautiful woman like you get to be the head of a bunch of female kung-fu Nazi sex-torturing bastards?'

'Oh, Mark,' she murmured, using my real name, 'everything is not what it seems.' She wiped a tiny tear from her soft cheek. 'There is something I must tell you.'

'There there, baby, take it easy. What is it?' I comforted her, placing a protective arm across her shoulders.

She related a long and complicated story about the Fourth Reich holed up in South America where they had initiated the first stages of their bid for world domination. They were holding her frail grandmother hostage after discovering that the best way to bring their enemies to psychological breaking point was to use stunningly beautiful women to apply the torture. Her real name was Heidi, and she had worked with handicapped children before the Nazis captured her and forced her to do these vile things. She broke down in tears as she recounted her terrible tale of woe. I held her sobbing frame close to me and comforted her as she bit her knuckles. 'I'm sorry, Mark, I really am,' she sniffled.

'It's all right sweetheart, sshhh, I believe you. Don't worry, I'll get you out of this mess.'

I slid the knife into her belly and pulled it up to her chin. Her guts fell out. 'Lying Nazi bitch!' I screamed. 'Nobody sets fire to my knob and gets away with it!' I shoved my hand into the red and purple mass of her stomach, reached behind her ribcage and pulled out a flobbing lung. 'Here boy,' I called to the sleeping Rottweiler and tossed him the human offal. The hound scarfed it up in three greedy gulps, wagged his little stump of a tail and was up on the bed devouring the spread-eagled carnage. Playfully, he leapt from the bed with the end of Heidi's intestinal tract in his teeth. I laughed: it looked like some revolting toilet-paper commercial as he ran around the room unravelling her intestines.

I decided to join in the fun and started to work on Heidi's eyes with the knife. Amazingly the bitch was still alive, so I stuck the long SS dagger into her mouth to stop her gurgling. The knife passed through the back of her neck and she was nailed to the pillow, still wailing and groaning. 'Fucking amazing,' I remember thinking. 'Women, they never know when to shut up.' I took the knife, which was now slippery and greasy from all the gristle and gore, and hacked her head off completely. I severed the last tendon thinking about Anne Boleyn and tossed it into the fire. Fido was chewing on something disgusting and wagging his stump.

I took a large hit of the scotch and admired my handiwork. There wasn't much left of her – I had destroyed all the usual sexual orifices with my knife and her head was in the fire. A small step backwards for mankind.

CHAPTER EIGHT

Love Comes Down

And he took a cup and when he had given thanks,
he gave it to them and they drank of it. And he said unto them, this
is my blood of the Covenant, which is shed for many.
MARK 14.23

It gets dark. The map on my knees. We must have passed through
a place called Sodankyla but I can't recall. We make vague plans
to go to Russia. We see signposts for Murmansk and it sounds romantic in a dark, frozen-shipyard sort of way. Ivalo sixty kilometres.
Silence.

My dick was a metaphor for agony. It felt as though it had been
hanging on its own cock-sized crucifix for three days and three nights,
a penis Christ on sandpaper Golgotha. Bill and Gimpo whimpered
every time the car hit a bump, confirming that they too had received
similar treatment. We hadn't slept for two days.

Headlights. Ivalo thirty-four kilometres. Gimpo tells us: 'We will find
a cabin to stay in in Ivalo.' Z and I agree. Ivalo: eight kilometres.
The snowflakes scurry. The thoughts drift. Snowploughs bear down
on us then tear past into the day-night behind.
   Ivalo now: filling stations, supermarkets, a large hotel, a cathedral,
but no town, no place for the people to live. Where are all the
people? In seconds we are through. Handbrake turn. Gimpo laughs,
his love of others' fear in his eyes. Back to the crossroads. Decision
time and Gimpo makes one: Tourist Information.
   The shopping mall: snow babes and sullen youths, brightly
coloured snow suits, babies dragged along on plastic sledge-buggies.

Inside the mall: fag machines and last summer's posters for local discos. It's sorted. Back in the Ford Escort.

Two kilometres back out of town the way we came in. Handbrake turn across the frozen road. Crunch down a track. Dark. Fresh fallen snow, a line of chalets, made chocolate-box style out of pine logs, dotted around the edge of a lake.

Gimpo spotted a motel in the middle of blizzard nowhere and pulled in. The hotel's neon sign blinked a bleary red through the madness of snowflakes spinning through the centrifugal forces of the wind howling through the car park. The dim gleam from the reception windows looked as if it were a thousand miles away. The bald-headed champ hurt like hell and I was too tired to be scared. I just wanted to drink the rest of my Pentangle vodka and swim into a dead coma for at least three weeks.

Pull up and stride into the chalet park H Q, all manly and 'don't mess with me', Zen sticks in hand. Open, but personless. Flick through the postcards. Quite a place in the summer: blue skies, children playing, water-skiing and the midnight sun.

Bill and Gimpo hit the sack immediately, fully clothed, boots and all. Within thirty seconds they had started work on their usual nocturnal symphony, a rousing fanfare of farting and snoring, moaning and wanking. I caned the vodka and joined them. The dreams started.

A pretty teenage cripple enters stage left, speaks perfect English. Sordid fantasies.

'Four-way airtight, bagsy the jacksie!'

The battered pine door creaks open. Heat and the smell of hot fat hits me on my cold face. Standing behind the reception desk, two weird-looking twins: supernatural Arctic fairies – Down's Syndrome chicks. Their thick-lensed spectacles magnify their oriental eyes. They radiate a subnormal grace. I like mongols, they seem to inhabit a child-like half-world, free from the responsibilities of adulthood and that over-rated mental condition known as sanity.

Bill approaches the desk, fumbling in his doctor's bag for his credit cards. He asks them if they speak English. They nod and give us a charming smile. Speaking in unison, they tell us that there are a number of pine cabins available and that their father could book us in as soon as he arrived.

'Hmmm,' I reply. Cyclops twitched. I noticed Gimpo staring at their overdeveloped breasts. Apparently, Down's Syndrome sufferers are incredibly sexual beings. Staff in their special hospitals are reputed to receive extra wages because of the chronic trauma they suffer from having to separate rutting mongs.

Her father will be through in a minute and we will sort the cabin business out with him. In the meantime she helps us choose the perfect reindeer antler tip on a leather thong. We take three. Giggle giggle. Tourist trinket charms. We hang them around our necks.

The father, Papa Spaz, enters the reception area patting away snow from his ski suit. His eyes are too close together and he, too, looks inbred. The girls glide from behind the reception desk.

There is something odd about their carriage – a graceful roll, like ice-skaters. They are joined at the hip – Siamese twins. Siamese mongol twins. Siamese mongol twins with big tits and humungous libidos. The erotic possibilities snap my testosterone computer into overdrive; pin-ball bells and flashing lights illuminate my underwear. Gimpo looks frightened; a bad smell indicates that he has dropped his guts. Papa Spaz checks us in and the freak shows us to our room. My purple-headed reptile leaks glycerine. Bill looks flustered; red-faced, he locks himself in the bathroom. The faint, strangled moans echoing from the tiled room remind me of small dying mammals.

The sordid fantasies subside when her father appears. Strange beard, amiable. Gimpo deals with it. Sorted.

The cabin: one room, a pair of bunks, a bed, a cooker, basin, shower, radiator, hot water – all very snug and cosy, all very family holiday on a tight budget, so we will have to lie about it when we embroider our tales. It is one of a row of identical cabins: Scandinavian pine, clean and clear. No, none of the corners cut or last year's grime of British seaside holiday lets; no mean little badly typed messages sellotaped to the wall with the dos and don'ts and 'empty the bin before you leave'.

Outside, the blackness is hushed and still. A lamppost stands scooping the darkness away, leaving a pool of light into which a few silent snowflakes tipple down. A pair of children's swings hang motionless, the seats piled six inches high with virgin snow. A climbing frame stands waiting out the winter months for the return of tumbling toddlers, laughing girls and rocket-ship boys.

Inside we decide to have cabin fever. The fever hits hard. We have been cut off from all civilization for the past six months, hungry polar bears are howling outside and we are living on a diet of frozen skunk meat and bitter leaves. Our chances of surviving the winter are slim. So we make plans, get in the Escort and head back to Ivalo to supermarket and supplies.

Of course the supermarket sells everything, but what we want is eggs, beans, bacon, bread, butter and black pudding. We look at what appears to be burnt fish in the freezer and thank God that we are not foreign. Brits abroad, and we get the suspicious looks that we deserve as we pick things up and laugh at them. Heavy-metal magazines in Finnish, all blow-dried hair jobs and Japanese guitars. How do these American blokes manage to grow their hair like that, learn to play the guitar in such a mind-numbingly brilliant but totally boring way, whilst still appearing to believe in it all?

Any check-out girls worth shagging? No.

Z and I stop by the hunting-knife counter. We take our time pretending we know what we are looking for, inspecting the merchandise for quality and workmanship. Of course, what is going through our heads is Commando comics: slitting Japs' throats in the Burmese jungles, taking on a dozen Jerries and killing the lot with just the one bone-handled blade. The fantasies slide off into darker territories which I will leave unrecorded. Do boys/men ever get over their love and lust for sharp knives that could do serious and instant damage? Z and I both go for the cheap and nasty-looking ones with purple plastic handles and ruthlessly sharp blades.

'Stroke it. Stroke it.' The voice.

The temptation to draw my own blood is overcome. Oh yes, the knife has a grey plastic sheath. All very functional. Will do a clean job, be rusty in days. Throw it away, get a new one. Reality, reality, fucking reality. Back with Gimpo and the trolley at the check-out counter.

Out of the stark, unforgiving supermarket light into the dark and now bitterly cold night. A fine snow and hard wind sting our faces. We dump the groceries in the boot of the Escort, head across the street to what looks like a bar. More shite, but it's warm. More log-cabin vibe in a concrete box; more crap lager at twenty quid a glass.

'He exaggerates.'

Later that evening we visited the local strip joint. Weird hobbit-like women in full national costume performed a high-speed striptease to Finnish punk rock records and dildoed themselves with reindeer antlers. Novel, but I've seen better. The gnarled old local Lapps sat around drinking beer, masturbating openly and shooting up heroin. A bit like Kilburn, I remember thinking to myself. Despite the inventive porno show, interesting knife act, etcetera, I couldn't stop thinking of the strange, magical creatures back at the hotel, the Claudia Schiffer look-alike mongol Siamese twin things with those huge paps, Nordic porno ghosts from some parallel erotic universe. Gimpo was laughing at our erotic hosts, drinking strong Lappish lager and farting loudly. Bill looked distant, preoccupied; he was stroking his sporran, smoking his pipe and talking to himself. I noticed he was lovingly caressing the blade of a small purple-handled knife.

We sit up at the bar all sullen outsiders, just hit town looking for trouble, good times and satori. We've seen the Westerns, we know how it is supposed to be, but all we get is mood music, a pair of comfortable-looking middle-aged couples wondering what the fuck we are. Where's the threat? Where's the danger? Where are the whores with hearts of gold who we can save from their sordid lives and dump a week later? In my head I'm sitting up at the bar with Clint Eastwood and Lee Marvin in *Paint Your Wagon*.

*

'You're thinking what I'm thinking, aren't you, Bill?' I asked, malevolence curled around my syllables. He grinned through pointed teeth.

In fact, the mood music is now straining the melody of 'Wandering Star' and I'm mumbling along with it.

We reluctantly agree with each other to drink another glass of lager. Behind the bar is one of those loathsome collections of foreign banknotes stuck on the wall. I struggle to breathe some new life into my Paint Your Wagon/Wandering Star fantasy, but it won't take shape. I'm just left with the sad reality that we have now spent 120 quid on quenching a thirst that wasn't there in the first place.

'You're still exaggerating.'

Bored. Write notes.

We headed back to the hotel, weighed down with heavy vodka take-aways. The blowflies had started buzzing again. Papa Spaz got drunk real quick, but the freak could really guzzle. Papa Spaz downed two bottles of neat vodka and snapped. 'Four-way airtight, Papa gets the jacksie!' laughed the parent from hell. Bill pulled out his purple blade and cut the thing down the middle. He was pretty drunk and I think he thought he was doing it a favour. The father started wailing and pathetically trying to push the two halves of his gurgling daughter back together. Freaks like this, man, they were a perversion of nature and have no right to exist. I hate sentimentality, so I killed him with a supersonic karate rabbit punch to his temple. His eyeballs jerked out and splattered on the wall like soggy marbles. He shat his pants – I could smell it. We cleaned out the till and left.

Back in the cabin and the fever is coming along a treat. Massive fry-up, bucket of tea, great hunks of rye bread, warmth and blessings to the Chief up above. The cabin's a tip – all farts and fag ends. This is the life! We tell crap jokes and massive lies. Outside, the polar bears are still howling and the Siberian sabre-toothed tiger roars. Gimpo is now at the table sorting out the day's receipts. Z and I tend to our logs, filling in the gaps. We play with our knives, blades five inches long, knifey on the wooden floor; whittle our Zen sticks; pontificate about whatever takes our fancy. Gimpo is now asleep on his bunk, gently snoring. A day of driving and responsibilities.

Cabin fever, man. Weird shit.

Later. The cabin park bar: modern school-hall vibe, everything is pine, pine and pine. Two crap lagers but not so expensive. Families are sitting at tables playing cards, not poker or anything wayward or seedy – a gentle whist drive. Silence, whispers and the odd chortle. Feelings, I have a few, but then again too strange to mention.

Z and I struggle to converse. Make notes; wonder why, after the high drama of the night before on the train, this is all . . . well, not much. I could make up lies, indulge in fantasies, but Z does it so much better. Bored shitless with each other's company we stare blankly at the TV screen. Some sort of strange male beauty contest, all very hard-core gay. My homophobia is aroused but the liberal in me gets it under control. Is this family entertainment? Strange. The sound is turned down, but depressing Finnish folk music drones and crackles from a speaker high above our heads. We are at that point where you could be in any bar in the world and you have nothing left to say and you realize for the final time that life is dull. Then Gimpo walks in with his grin.

We head into town. It may be a nowhere Tuesday night, but Gimpo with his squaddie training and eternal optimism could eke out the secret good-time lurking in the cracks and crevices of the most solemn suburb, dying resort or ingrate's garrison town. Stuck at the end of a parade of closed shops, Gimpo spies a small neon sign flashing its arrow to a subterranean rear entrance: 'Music Disco Night Club'. Looks promising in a foreign sort of way. It turns out to be shit. Eleven quid to get in. It's empty and a bad Rock band struggle with a cover version of a Bachman-Turner Overdrive song. We fuck off before they make us pay.

Twenty minutes later. This is better! The floor is filled with middle-aged couples doing the foxtrot, a three-piece cabaret band provides the sounds and we are perched on bar stools getting them in. We are pleased with ourselves: we have found The Vibe, right here in this big empty tourist hotel on the north road out of town. There is laughter and smiles, warmth and good cheer, happy couples are gliding gracefully across the floor. Ballroom dancing is, of course, huge in Finland, along with Siberian sabre-toothed tigers, burnt frozen fish and low-alcohol lager.

Soft lighting, a friendly barman shaking strange cocktails. The room is large, well-planned, nothing seedy or cramped. We look around and our gaze is met by the welcoming smiles of well-dressed members of a respectable hard-working community. We don't feel like outsiders or frauds or threats or scum. The far wall is plate glass. Outside we can see the bitter night, the dark forest that stretches thousands of miles around the top of the world from here to the Bering Straits. It's weird how moods can shift and lift only a moment away.

The dream shifts gear: Epiphany No. 2. Angel-white light and electric sunflowers cascade like slow-motion cherry blossom; the warm lightning of absolute comprehension of everything runs through my veins like a morphine steam train; a humming generator of enlightenment lights up every single nerve ending in my body. I am a scintillating galaxy of tiny fibre-optic stars dusted by dreamstuff, the voice of the universe singing through my blissed-out body, hallowed be my name.

I could see the blind fishermen swimming through space. They had grown wings and were smiling beatifically; their tattoos were radiating brilliant, swirling colours and they had haloes. They started singing 'Love Me Tender' in beautiful, angelic soprano in telepathic communication.

Songs for Swinging Zen Masters, track 1: 'Strangers in the Night'. I struggle with my pen not to tell you lies about . . . or about the fact that Frank Sinatra is not of Italian descent but of pure Finnish blood. Where do you think his blue eyes and blond hair came from? The whole Italian thing was a deal he had to cut with the Mafia. You did see *The Godfather*? Frank, as it happens, is back in his home town Ivalo for a short stay, catching up with friends and family and, as a favour to his cousin Ulrich, is singing 'Dooby dooby do, Do Do Do Do Doooo' at his golden wedding anniversary.

*

A dreamy epiphany floated through my very essence and I knew that God truly was love, he loved me as a son and the fishermen were our guardian angels on this most perilous of journeys. I was surrounded by thousands of the blind angel fishermen, smiling and radiating warmth and heavenly affection. I brushed away a dream tear and fell to my knees, powerless in the face of such monumental good vibes.

In fact nothing much happens. The warm glow spreads and settles within. Gimpo keeps his grin, Z happily scribbles his Poetry and Lies and I have my arse pinched by a lady of uncertain age who then gives me the eye for the rest of the evening, much to the amusement of Z and Gimpo. The power of the kilt, is what I say. A fat but friendly businessman joins us for a chat. He's in mining, up here to exploit his mineral rights. He gets his round in: a weird fresh-snow-and-vodka-based cocktail. It is disgusting, but we don't let on. The floor jitterbugs then slows to a waltz. Tunes we recognize, others we don't. 'Fly me to the moon, let me float among the stars . . .'

I woke with rivulets of happiness streaming down my grateful face. Bill was frying eggs; his normally serious visage had lost its look of grimly heroic determination and was radiating love and happiness. Gimpo was dancing and singing hymns.

It was as if I had woken into a new world, a world free of the paranoia that had always clung to my shadow like an evil vampire. Gone were the feelings of bitter self-loathing that fed the salivating misanthropy I had carried like a disease throughout most of my adult life. Gone, gone like cobwebs blown away by a sea breeze. I no longer feared and secretly hated women; I no longer felt the need for heroin and pederasty. I was reborn a better man. I looked outside the window on to a scene of pristine sparkling beauty. I wept for the first time in my life.

Somewhere else a world is at war. Somewhere else a bunch of lads decide to form a band. Somewhere else a thirteen-year-old girl changes channel to see if *Home and Away* has started yet. But right here we decide to go: we want to be up and off early in the morning. We plead with Gimpo for no more handbrake turns.

Back in the cabin and the fever rages.

I turned to Bill, who was smiling so broadly I thought his face would split in two; his eyes were damp and shining and about to overflow with tears of holy joy. I grabbed him by the shoulders like a Christian.

'Bill!' I ejaculated. 'The dream!'

I was ecstatic. He smiled into my face and said, 'Yes, Zodiac, my noble friend, the dream.'

I spun round to Gimpo – he too was beaming like an amphetamine believer. He hugged me to his manly bosom. 'Yes Zed,' he laughed. 'The dream!'

Behind the mysteries of our REM slumber, we had all by some fantastic miracle experienced the same revelation. We embraced each other closely and started crying like women. 'God bless the fishermen,' blubbered Bill. 'They truly love us, they love us, they love us! And we them, everyone! We love everyone!' He dried his eyes on a pink silk handkerchief and handed it to me. 'Yes,' I added, 'we love everyone – even queers.' I wiped my nose and started to tidy the room. Gimpo was arranging flowers and Bill was applying lipstick. We ate our vegetarian sausages, paid for the drinks and happily set off for the Pole singing Boy George tunes. The world was beautiful and we loved everyone. I was wearing a bra.

We take photographs of ourselves, posing in our long-johns, standing on the table like conquering heroes: the Arseholes return. The possibility of the Lost Chord is discussed. Zodiac with his Keef 'Broken Man' Richards voice, me with my theories. Gimpo ignores us. Gimpo and I are for kip. Z sits at the table nursing the bottle of Blue Label, a candle lit, pencil stub in hand. He promises late-night lucidity poems. Gimpo snores and I tumble to sleep.

'Wake up you bastards, we're going to a party!' The bed is kicked and I am woken. Z is raging. The vodka bottle is almost empty.

'Fuck off Z!'

'You boring cunts!'

CHAPTER NINE

The Road of Fear and the Tunnel of Doom

Back to sleep. Well, something like that, but now it's the next morning and I'm filling in these notes. Have I mentioned how we are beginning to refer to ourselves as the Literary Arseholes? You know, like Wordsworth and Coleridge were the Romantics, Kerouac and Ginsberg were the Beats. Well, us and whoever else ends up in our gang are the Literary Arseholes. Z and Gimpo still asleep on their bunks, farting and snoring.

Daylight and fag ends. Have a shit, the first in three days, strap on my kilt, cook a breakfast fit for kings, wake 'em: 'Grub up!' Scoff the scram and we are off. Another day in paradise and no irony intended. A milky pale sun struggles then gives up; but we don't care.

When the E wore off, we all felt truly ashamed. The interior of the car hung heavy with a macho silence like the gentle sway of a bull's bollocks in a country meadow. We drove on, the Clint Eastwood atmosphere broken only by the occasional raising of a single buttock to rattle the small space with a manly fart.

Z has some tales about the magic international language of vodka. Where Esperanto failed, Blue Label came through. It seems that we had in the next cabin to us a neighbour who had spied Z in his puddle of candlelight and bottle of clear spirit and invited him round. This was the party. Z is taking the piss out of himself in that glorious way that only he can. He describes the scene in the geezer's cabin: a travelling salesperson with a leather waistcoat and a half-drunk bottle, Z with his bottle, each laughing and ranting at their own left-over legends, each understanding the other perfectly. It is only now that he recalls that the geezer with the leather waistcoat was speaking in Finnish, himself in Yorkshire and, in fact, that neither had understood a word the other was saying. Is this important? Of course it is – vital to the very subtle sub-plot that will become clear to you only after you've waded through at least seven volumes of the Literary Arseholes' collected works. So take note: leather waistcoat, Esperanto and the international language of Blue Label.

The landscape is more magical, unreal. Boulders the size of houses litter the side of the road, frozen lakes with strangely shaped islands lurching skyward, crooked pine trees grow out of cracks in the rocks. You know those Japanese and Chinese watercolours with the radical mountains all verticals and mist? Well, that's what the passing landscape looks like. I wonder if it's anything to do with us being Zen Masters on our road to satori. Must be.

The day is heavy and grey. We discover the car has a radio. The dial is turned. Static, then:

> You know the day destroys the night,
> Night divides the day.
> Try to run,
> Try to hide,
> Break on through to the other side.

Yep, it's Big Jim and the Finnish Doors telling it like it always has been. If I bad-mouthed Big Jim elsewhere then, please, let it lie, because right now . . . Right now! Well right now is right now.

'This is Radio Mafia!!' And we let it take over, providing the soundtrack for our inner journeys. Perhaps the landscape is only there to enhance the aural experience of this radio station, from The Doors to badly produced sixties psychedelic pop Dracula's Daughter, a track I have never heard before in my life, spindly guitar riff and a . . . The road is a toboggan run of uncertain death. Outside is an unreality that we are protected from by Radio Mafia.

*

The meteorological conditions mirrored our own concrete hardness: a screaming tempest scoured our windscreen like manic static on a detuned TV, headlight visibility was down to zero.

What's this? They've got some actor reading some weird shit in English.

> When shall we three meet again?
> In thunder, lightning, or in rain?
> When the hurly-burly's done,
> When the battle's lost and won.
> That will be ere the set of sun.
> Where the place?
> Upon the heath.
> There to meet with Macbeth.
> I come, Graymalkin.
> Paddock calls.
> Anon!
> Fair is foul, and foul is fair:
> Hover through the fog and filthy air.

This is followed by a heated in-depth debate, in Finnish of course, which lasts for twenty minutes or so. The sound of the language is wonderful – nothing like the other Scandinavian languages, or Slavic, or Teutonic or Latin or any of those other European sounds we are used to hearing – almost Middle Eastern. Finnish punk rock, all badly produced, angry, spiky and they mean it. Loads of this stuff and more unknown sixties garage bands. The name of one, Sexy Roy Orbison, grabs my attention. Then weird Finnish poetry with eerie sound effects. No adverts. They seem to be playing what they want. Who else is listening to this station? Is it only us?

Another reading, a long Finnish poem. It has a refrain that crops up every sixteen lines or so: 'What price to pay for wisdom?' The E Street Band hits in – all those big Springsteen chord changes. But then the singing starts: it's Finnish.

What the fuck is going on? If this is some Finnish sound-alike band, how can they afford to do it? They've got a million-dollar production there. How can the cost of making such a record be justified for such a small market? This is the record-business realist coming through in me; but you've got to understand that a record selling 25,000 copies up here is the same as one selling a million in the States, and a record like the one we are listening to would have to be on an album that would have to sell a million copies just to pay for the recording.

Shit. Fuck. Shit. Shit. Fuck! I don't want any of this music-business crap in my head at the moment.

OK. I'm just getting my head around this lot and picking holes in the Clarence Clemons sound-alike sax solo, saying if Clarence was really playing it he would do this, not that, when in comes the last verse, and it's Bruce for real this time singing in English or New Jerseyese or whatever it is he sings in when he is not singing in Finnish.

I'm confused. Is there a conspiracy theory going on in reverse? On principle, I don't go along with conspiracy theories – people seem to hide behind them so they don't have to take responsibility for what's happening to the world. One theory I have is that if conspiracy theorists stopped smoking dope, the conspiracies would disappear. Right now a strange jigsaw is falling into place: not only did Finland win the War, a fact we learnt at some point over the last two days, but it also invented punk rock. Johnny Rotten is Finnish: fact. Frank Sinatra is Finnish: maybe fact. Bruce Springsteen has a Finnish mother: got to be fact. Jim Morrison is not dead but living in Helsinki. What does all this mean?

There is a signpost. Z checks his tarot cards. We have to take a left-hand turn for Karigasniemi and the Norwegian border. Gimps pulls on the handbrake, spins the steering wheel. The rear wheels skim the ice and we are off down a different road. Gimpo's getting good at this.

Immediate landscape change: it is all rolling high-plain tundra, no trees, the road is narrow and rough, no trucks, no signs of habitation, no life. The road hurtles on from here to the horizon in one straight line, diving and climbing the dips. Seen from above, we disappear from view then reappear a hundred yards further away. You've seen that stuff in the films, Levi's ads, Coke commercials.

*

Gimpo lit a small cigar and stuck it between his grinding teeth, clenched his buttocks and accelerated aggressively. 'Can't this crate go any faster?' demanded Bill, cheroot between his teeth. He was whittling away at his erect penis with a huge bowie knife and chugging greedily on a bottle of cowboy whisky. Gimpo snorted a derisive laugh and, in a shower of sparks, slammed the pedal to the metal, reached between his legs and pulled out a blindfold, tied it across his eyes, removed both hands from the steering wheel and began masturbating. We careered headlong like electric suicide into the dangerous night, conducting a screamed conversation above the relentless power grind of the engine about what a great guy Adolf Hitler was.

Gimpo is now touching speeds I would not advise in the best of driving conditions. Fear creeps in but I kick it out. The endless pine forests had become a security blanket of sorts. Up here on the tundra we feel naked and vulnerable. Great huge chundering acoustic guitars, rolling drums and a deep resonating Russian voice fill the Escort, which right now is the whole known world. This is brilliance: this is what U2 should sound like. These geezers mean it in a way that Bono and the boys can only dream of. The Edge can buy up every living blues legend but will never have this. Z and I acknowledge this greatness; we expound on how sad it must be for these lads, knowing that they will never get the breaks and fill the stadiums in The Land of the Free. But our thoughts are cut short as the track segues into a droning bass riff. A voice warbles in: affectations to the left, affectations to the right, and an artist hits every nail going. 'Every day is like Sunday/Every day is silent and grey.' I close my eyes. A beautiful mushroom cloud lifts into a distant sky. They open again. It was only a dream I once had. We are pulverized with emotion. All the arrogance and knowing has been swept from us. This is Morrissey at the pinnacle of his precious best. And it is not only we who are moved: the heavy sky cracks open, a shaft of sunlight hits a far snow-covered mountain. Our hearts lift above the fear. 'Armageddon – Come Armageddon/Come Armageddon! Come.' And before the song closes the clouds have all but disappeared from the sky. The tundra sparkles a thousand shades of pink, two thousand hues of blue, thirty thousand glints of gold.

The midday news: Bill Clinton has won the US presidential elections.

From far above I can look down on our little car, tearing along this ribbon pulled tight across the world from horizon to horizon. I whisper a short poem to us, the Three Kings, far below. Of the three wishes I was granted at birth I have yet to use any. Sleep comes over me.

As our fear of having any vaguely feminine emotions gradually subsided, so did the speed of our car. Eventually the Viking ferocity of the weather also eased up, the relentless blizzard turning into huge flakes drifting gently to earth. The delicate, pastel hues of a virgin dawn beckoned on the horizon. Relaxed, we drove into the dreams of a new day.

I wake half-way through one of Gimpo's handbrake turns. We are pulling in for petrol. Is this a town? Buildings, trees, other vehicles, clapboard houses with powder-blue and white trimmings, a white wooden church steeple against powder-blue sky. Ponder on the denomination.

My feet are cold. Sun's still shining. Somebody has farted and not let on. Check the map: Karigasniemi. We have now come to the edge of this, our very undetailed tourist map of Finland. What the road does across the border we know not. Forward planning? No, not us.

A café. Z is hoping for lager with more than 2 per cent ABV. He does not get it. I'm hoping for a solid grub-up and I don't get it. Gimpo wants a break. Truck drivers but no mountains of mash, sausages and cabbage, which is what I need right now. Foreign tea. Of course I'm a tea-leaf man, made in the pot, the full traditional thing, so a glass jug of tepid water standing on a counter coffee-warmer and a box of mixed-flavoured tea bags on string are not what I want.

We rise above our petty disappointments. A high-powered snow bike roars past outside. We are filled with wonder that nobody has told us to stop yet. The bell hasn't rung for the end of playtime; nobody has shouted 'Come in number 57! Your time is up!' Are you really allowed to behave like this? Have we drawn the long straw or the short? The snow bike tears back the other way. All thought of making the final leg of the journey with husky and sledge is out of the window as visions of our three liberated snow bikes hurtling to the Pole almost give me a hard on.

The encrusted bogey is still there. Making sure first that nobody in the café is looking, I once again try to pick it. Fail. Comfort myself by picking an easier catch in my right nostril. Check again that nobody is looking before sucking it off my finger. Salty, a bit chewy, but not totally satisfying.

A cheese roll, a cup cake and four cups of tea later we leave the snug confines of the café; hit the cold crisp air, cross the road and dream into the snow-bike showroom: Hondas, Mitsubishis, Yamahas – of course the Japanese dominate the market. The showroom is closed. Next door is an all-purpose mini supermarket. We want maps of northern Norway; they have none. We buy supplies: fags, gum, boiled sweets. Try to get money changed; can't. Z and I follow Gimpo back out to the Escort.

The border crossing is on the edge of town. They don't even want to look at our passports, let alone stamp them. What the fuck is the point of having a British passport and travelling to foreign lands if they don't stamp exotic national emblems in it, then strip-search you looking for secreted silk-worm cocoons? We are waved on and across a high bridge over a rocky ravine (the Anarjohka) into the northern chunk of Norway that caps off the European mainland. Instant landscape change: pockets of snow-blanketed arable land in sheltered valleys, scattered farmhouses of primrose yellow and pale pink. Either I imagine cultural differences between the Finnish and Norwegian choice of farmhouse paint, or my . . .

Radio Mafia is beginning to fade and break up but we are still able to hold on to an interview with Cindy Stereo, in English. Z and I share a cynical fantasy about the half-bottle of vodka secreted in Cindy's handbag, her failing career, the special man in her life who has to carry all the blame, her having to do promotional tours in meaningless territories long after the album has been released and disappeared, bombed, gone, never even made it to the bargain bins.

Cindy is doing what 'we' all do: we do our interviews, displaying our well-rehearsed veneer; we trot out our anecdotes, we tell the lie that we are now in control of our careers, that our art is a precious, fought-for, special thing; although our personal lives may have hit some rocky patches in the past, we're now sailing a truer course; we are rational, concerned, even 'normal' people.

Lies, all lies. Every human being on earth has the raw material to become an artist – the living of life is all one needs, whether or not we have concert pitch, a way with words or an impressive sketch pad. But those of us who find a need to mine those seams of blood and gold also undermine those regions of the soul that keep us humans sane, allowing the ego to surge from towering superman (Nietzsche not Clark Kent) to cowering, gibbering wreck, open to any addiction that can offer a glimmer of stability in a storm-tossed life, seeking comfort in kitsch or cosmetics, alcohol or asceticism, chocolate or religion, sex or sadism . . . Or is all of this just a fantasy of the artist's life; a hand-me-down legend; an excuse to use when we lack the wherewithal to manage the day-to-dayisms of life?

And here is Cindy, on the radio, talking nicely about where she grew up, about who played on the album and what her next project is going to be. Cindy, the DJ doesn't fucking care, the listeners don't care; me and Z almost care 'cause we know it could be us. You're just doing your bit in helping to fill all this media space that has to be filled every week: all these local radio stations, all these magazines, all these TV arts programmes, all these record release schedules. More and more and more mindless information being pumped out. No, I've not got some conspiracy feelings about the powers that be, trying to deaden our minds with it . . .

'Ah, shit, forget it Bill. Just look at the landscape, drink the Nordic splendour.' A voice.

What was the name of the hit Cindy had anyway? Z and I drift into a conversation, one we could be having anywhere. The conversation develops and seems to be about who is the greater of the Romantic poets – out of the two Williams. I'm fighting Wordsworth's corner; Z, Blake's. We are not getting very far. It seems to be more about wanting to elevate shared love of poetry above its rather effete, willowy image, as if we were debating who was the greatest heavy-weight boxer of the pre-war era.

Now Z is able to quote whole chunks of Blake's *Marriage of Heaven and Hell* and *The Book of Urizen* at me and then without breaking for breath recite, in an affected girly voice:

> I wandered lonely as a cloud
> Blah blah blah blah
> Blah blah blah blah
> A host, of golden daffodils.

'Bill, there is no contest. One is man's poetry and the other is for little girls.' I'm not rising to the bait and return to these notes hoping I can pin down here why Wordsworth is, for me, the man.

Don't get me wrong – I love Blake; he sends shivers down my spine. I stand in awe, shuddering with fear at his abstract depiction of the abyss. The trouble is, most of it goes straight over my head – I get the drift but then lose the plot. The thing is, I can't really argue the case with Z, 'cause Z is Los, and Z's approach to his work is the same as Blake's. He is inspired by what he finds in his ever-expanding imagination, whereas I find that when April comes and I stumble on a bank of primroses glinting at the sun, all my senses reach out to the mystery at the heart of Creation. Blake criticized Wordsworth for paying too much attention to the details of nature at the expense of the inner realities. But what can you do if it is through the real, natural 'out there' world that God finds his way to you?

I want to be able to quote a section of Wordsworth's *The Prelude* but I can only remember those few lines about dipping oars and the silent lake. The image of the 'craggy steep' between me and the stars is the unseen power revealed in the natural world, just like those wild primroses in April. Now that I've got this written down, I feel more confident at trying to argue my case for Wordsworth being the heavyweight champ of the Romantics.

I open up the conversation with Z by asking if he has ever read *The Prelude*. He can't remember. I try to describe the stolen boat and revealed mountain scene, but I don't sound convincing. Z tells me that he knows what I'm trying to get at but Blake could do that stuff better when he wanted. 'He understood the mystery of the natural world. Wordsworth never came close.'

In the end, I suppose it comes down to the fact that I can identify with Wordsworth, the nature boy, as I aspire to a quiet, rural life, feigning a veneer of respectability and making do with the common language and the sights and sounds around me for inspiration; whereas Z, as I have already stated, identifies with the metropolitan Blake with a tangled and tortured inner Sodom and Gomorrah and glimpses of the shining ideal if he could only grasp that bow of burning gold and grab those arrows of desire.

I don't think I will ever reach the palace of wisdom via the road to excess. If I ever stumble across a bank of primroses again it will be to Wordsworth that I turn to make form of those yearnings aroused. But enough! I propose a toast: 'Up with the Romantics, down with the Age of Reason!' And we kiss the joy as it flies.

We descend into Karasjok. It claims to be the capital of Lapland: a crossroads, a modern shopping mall, two service stations, an impressive fifties church, stainless-steel steeple reaching for something in an already fading sky. Gimpo finds somewhere to change currencies. Me and Z trudge ('Always trudging, aye?') down supermarket aisles, the light from the freezers turning our faces pale green. Little hobbit women gobbling about, pushing trolleys almost as high as themselves. These women are shaped and dressed in clothes from some corner of our fevered imaginations.

'Try to be objective Bill.' The voice.

Well, they look like something between a Tolkien grandmother and a photo feature in *National Geographic* on living national costumes of hidden Europe, which is, in fact, what they are: Lapp women dressed in traditional costume for no reason other than it is what they wear when they are heading down to the supermarket for a mid-week shop. Z should draw a picture of them. We get accosted. A woman not in hobbit garb, somewhere down behind the burnt frozen fish aisle, opens her cheap coat to expose a dozen or so packets of Marlboro sewn into its lining. She babbles in a pleading way, pushes a loose strand of her lank hair from a pale brow. We scuttle away to a far aisle.

Why are we in this supermarket? What are we looking for? We don't find it. Gimpo has found some sort of map, but with nothing like the detail that we need – no Ordnance Survey here. Obviously we are heading into uncharted territories.

Lapland! What the fuck is Lapland? And what are Lapps? I dredge up some information about Lapland from a half-remembered *Blue Peter* feature from the late sixties; expound knowingly to Z and Gimpo about the history of the country and its people, about them being an Arctic–Asiatic people without a nation state, marooned in northern Scandinavia; dark-haired, high-cheekboned, narrow-eyed, short, stocky, hardy folk; a semi-nomadic lifestyle following their herds of reindeer as they have done for thousands of years, living the summer months in tepees, not acknowledging the national borders between Finland, Norway or Sweden. Z shuffles his cards.

We fill up the tank and take the north road. This could be the last we see of civilization, I imagine heroically. Mind you, we seem to be rather worn down already. I don't think we have done an 'Elvis to the Pole' chant all day. Elvis who?

Drive, drive, drive into the dreary afternoon hours. Landscape boring with no sunlight to cast drama. I bet the other Three Wise Men got bored out of their skulls sitting on their camels plodding across a featureless desert. Their resolve sapped by the monotony of the movement, their numbed minds would have been more focused on their saddle sores and the need for a good night's kip than the star still burning brightly in the sky. Headlights on at 2.15 p.m. We pass a large military signpost with much written information, some translated into English. We try to excite ourselves by this, even stop the car, reverse back to read it fully. We seem to be entering a military practice zone. Z, I can tell, is trying to weave some fantasy around this, that we may be swept up in secret military manoeuvres. There are times when I don't know whether Z's story-telling is meant to entertain us or to try and make light of his dark premonitions.

We drive on. Nothing happens. The three of us drift off into our own worlds, Z in the back seat spluttering and crackling as he attacks his paper with the stub of his pencil. I try to find a radio station as good as Radio Mafia.

Three hours later and we were back to the horror. The roadsides were festooned with lacerated corpses frozen in jagged disarray. Spears and swords protruded from flayed ribcages at mad angles; petrified intestines unfurled like frosted blue serpents; severed extremities and abandoned weapons lay all around. Shafts of dawn sunlight splintered off a vast lake of frozen blood. Hell had been here. The burnt-out husks of ruined automobiles lay like the exoskeletons of giant iron beetles half buried in the gore-spattered snowdrifts. Wrecked snowmobiles, burnt tyres, twisted bits of exploded metal. Strange banners and clattering bunches of human skulls fastened to poles blew in the wind. The whole scene resembled some bizarre combination of medieval aftermath and hyperborean auto dump. The grim carnage sprawled down both sides of the road as far as the eye could see. We drove slowly, mute with horror. I felt like Marlow gliding along a frozen river into some dread heart of Arctic darkness.

Time wears on. I offer to drive. Gimpo declines my offer. Elvis as the meaning of our mission to the North Pole is losing focus. Even two days ago, nothing on earth could have diverted my tunnel vision away from the imperative for this journey. The clearly defined reason we gave ourselves a week ago is peeling away. Now that we are on our way, the idea of a pilgrimage is beginning to unravel. It's served its purpose, like a spaceship travelling to the moon and dumping its booster rockets after breaking free of the home planet's gravity.

I stare down at the tourist map on my knees and try to work out the mileage to the next town. Are there any more interesting routes we should be taking? It's as if we are on an English motoring holiday in the English lakes. I try to pick my nose again.

' "The quality of boredom is not strained," somebody once said,' said Elvis, almost.

We pass out of the military zone. And on and down.

The lights of Lakselv. Low-lying, straggly blocks of concrete buildings. Pull into run-down service station. No beer for Z, no tea for me. Buy chocolates in desperate bid for comfort. Can't even be bothered to bring my comrades' characters to life in this prose. Lakselv, according to the map on my knees, is a town at the base of the most northerly fjord in Norway. The plan now is to drive up the road that follows the western shore of the fjord which becomes the most northerly road in mainland Europe. Thoughts like, 'Shall we drive out on to the frozen Arctic Ocean tonight?' or 'Should we get a night's kip before we head out and die in the morning?' don't bother entering my mind.

I try to stimulate myself by thinking about all the shite I have left behind. Nothing: no guilt, no self-loathing, no joy of escape. We drive. Civilization straggles on for a bit. My eyes scan the slow-failing light of the frozen fjord. There it is: a white sheet in the grey light, first sight of the frozen Arctic Ocean. My heart flutters, but just a bit.

We were on a narrow coastal road, winding our way around the edge of a huge black mountain. Thick clouds shrouded forbidding peaks and I could smell Satan's black fart-dust curling around the car. The weather grew mean again.

Seconds later. Fear is confirmed: the frozen Arctic Ocean stretches out into the fjord for only a few hundred yards.

I peered nervously out of the side window: three hundred feet of sheer death descended jaggedly into a sickly, slow-motion ocean of boiling molasses. The snow sliced in at 180 samurai degrees, sixty miles per hour and rising. The north wind was pissed off, howling like a wolf with its balls caught in a bear trap.

There I can see the black, unfrozen sea. Are we to be cheated out of reaching our destination because of a freak of nature? It is November. The Arctic Ocean should be frozen right down to the mainland. Reaching the North Pole across the Arctic wastes is now impossible. Those visions I had of us driving our Escort out over the Polar ice cap until we ran out of fuel, then trudging on with our snow-shoes until we either die or make the Pole, will never be realized. Could it be that our research on weather and geographical conditions was not thorough enough? I decide to blame the greenhouse effect and not any arseholing in our planning. This seeming nail in the coffin of our success has the reverse effect; something stirs deep inside. Fuck failure, fuck success! We're carrying on, frozen Arctic Ocean or not. I say nothing to Gimpo or Z. Z now seems to be sitting in the front and me in the back.

I feel reality begin to fade. No, no, reality is getting stronger, the senses sharper. Darkness has finally fallen all around us. The landscape is more magical, more unreal. The road is now down to a single lane, treacherously snaking its way along the Porsangen Fjord coastline. To our left and above us, bare rock and ice mountain; to our right and below, bare rock and a black swollen heaving sea. The road is, of course, frozen, crash barriers non-existent, the odd rock marking the sides of the track. Gimpo teases death with each touch of the brakes and turn of the steering wheel. I don't say anything. It's weird, I'm not even feeling fear. It's as if we're hurtling through virtual reality when we are in fact approaching eternity and leaving behind a couple of inches about the last known whereabouts of a pair of faded pop stars in next week's *New Musical Express*.

My bowels turned into wet shite and I tried not to fart. Bill had finished his cowboy whisky and was now singing the theme song to the Rupert Bear TV series, 'Everyone Sing His Name!' Mad laughter. He was rolling around on the back seat, hitting himself across the head with his Zen stick. If Gimpo was scared, he didn't show it. He drove steadily, cigar clenched confidently between his teeth. A small, warm emission leaked from my gritted arsehole.

What back in Lakselv was a gentle snowfall has now grown in stature and ferocity to a blizzard. The wipers pump and scrape some vision out in front of the glass. Each snowflake smashes itself on to the reinforced windscreen, screaming: 'Go back, go back, go back!' Headlight-beams focus our attention on the six or seven yards in front of all we can see of the world.

Suddenly, the sky went nova: a psychedelic death fart; a satanic bad acid, Pink Floyd pyromaniac cloudburst shit-browned across the neon clouds, a cosmodemonic, pulsating vomit thing erupted in the ether. I seriously kegged it.

Things are closing in; dark forces are trying to push down on us and the snowflakes keep screaming their warnings. Still we don't speak; we heed nothing. Back wheels start sliding to the left. Reality switches to slow motion. Gimpo spins steering wheel. We don't die. Or not yet.

'Fuck me!' murmured Gimpo, awe-struck. He stuck his head out of the window: 'Northern lights!'

His face flickered demonically beneath the spectacular effects of the aurora borealis. He forgot that he was driving and let go of the wheel and we swerved out of control at eighty mph towards the cliff edge. I grabbed the wheel and crashed the car into the rocks on the other side of the road. Bill was laughing hysterically, leaning out of the other window and howling like a dipsomaniac werewolf. The car sheared down the cliff, throwing off a grinding cascade of yellow sparks. The sky had gone badly apeshit; Satan walked the earth. I had shat my pants, we were all going to die and those two cunts thought it was bonfire night in Disneyland. The last thing I remember seeing was Gimpo catapulting like a crash-test dummy through the windscreen in a sparkling shower of torn trousers and broken glass. The Shangri-Las were screaming: 'Look out! Look out! Look out!'

The car was an orange and black fireball. By some infernal miracle I was thrown clear of the blazing wreckage. I could see a bewildered Gimpo some ten yards away, but there was no sign of Bill. Then I heard his screams escaping from the inferno. I leapt to my feet, ignoring the white-heat intensity of the pain like tiny piranha fish swimming through my veins and dashed heroically towards the blaze. I covered my face against the scorching heat as, from inside the carnage, I heard Bill screaming, 'Rupert, Rupert the Bear, everyone sing his name!' He was in shock. Ignoring my own safety I dived into the autogeddon and rescued the picture of Elvis. Bill followed me out. He was black and smoking, his leather doctor's bag in one hand and the empty cowboy whisky bottle in the other. He was laughing and his kilt was on fire. The blazing remains of the car exploded and flew into the air, arcing over the cliff edge like a meteorite before crashing into the black sea three hundred feet below. 'Wow!' said Gimpo who, apart from having no eyebrows and no trousers, seemed completely unharmed.

*

The car comes to a halt. In front of us is a huge iron door in the mountainside, a tunnel entrance closed off for the winter. So this is it; this is as far as we get and no further: the Green Door that's not so green or the hidden entrance to the Secret Garden. You want symbolism, there's plenty to choose from. Ask Ali Baba.

I looked around for the cause of the collision and what I saw made me fill my pants once more: a huge iron door, forty feet high, set in the mountain. It was covered with massive bolts, cast-iron skulls, devils, bats and all kind of weird Dracula shit; an enormous ring knocker shaped like a Viking's head hung dead centre. On either side of the door, two mammoth tusks framed the entrance. The ground started to shake, an ominous rumble, a deafening metallic whine of giant bones, Victorian machinery, distressed metal, grinding chains and levers. The door was slowly inching its way from the ground into the rock above. A vile blast of fetid air rushed out of the black hole. It was warm and stank of copulating skunks, blood and death. Margaret Thatcher in a porno movie pulls her piss flaps apart, green liquor trickles from her dead womb and her withered arsehole issues forth a blue flame. I retched. It was Bill's turn to shit his pants; and he did, big time.

But we are not dead. We don't smash into this door at the end of the road or go spinning off the edge down into the black abyss below. The iron door starts to open, portcullis-style. We spot a small, tell-tale infra-red light beaming down at us. We still don't speak. The door opens fully, revealing a tunnel hewn out of the bare rock, no comforting concrete smoothing the jagged edges. Yellow tungsten lights like a line of tracers illuminate the tunnel to where they disappear over the interior horizon, about half a kilometre from where we are.

The weather was turning dangerous: we could either freeze to death or take our chances in Thatcher's cunt.

Gimpo was the first to enter the foul labia of hell. The iron door slammed behind us; a heavy metal clang echoed down into the Stygian bowels of the mountain. Bill produced a torch from his bag and shone it across the walls. They were covered in strange carvings. 'Over here!' blurted Gimpo.

Gimpo slowly edges the Escort into the tunnel, twenty-five yards or so. Switch off the engine and get out.

I heard a loud bang and the hum of an old black and white Frankenstein generator.

We watch the iron doors close behind us; pull out our cocks and have a slash against the rock walls. The steam rises. Z lights a fag.

Lights flickered – Gimpo had thrown a lever. A sickly, sodium yellow flooded the place. I took a closer look at the wall carvings: alien alphabets, weird hieroglyphics, bizarre erotic carvings of spooky monsters having it off with humans. They put the willies up me. Bill was also studying them. He had sobered up and was looking knowledgeable, stroking his chin and muttering to himself. We set off into the eldritch labyrinth, twisting and turning on a steady downward incline. Slime dripped from the bare rock walls and vermin skittered around our feet. The stench got worse and worse, an acrid shiteish smell that shredded the skin on the back of my throat.

Eventually we reached the source of the ruptured drain perfume: sexually mangled corpses, about seven or eight, apparently female (I say apparently, as decomposition and rats had clearly been working on them for some time). They had all been spectacularly eviscerated. The mystery Ripper's artistry was quite impressive, showing considerable skill and imagination. I felt myself stiffen at the sight of one or two of the better preserved specimens. I noticed that Gimpo's interest was also not entirely scientific – he had his hand in his underwear and was shuffling rapidly, a dreamy look of abandoned creepiness sweated across his brow.

So we are the children of Hamelin for a cynical age; Elvis, the Pied Piper; but who was the poor cripple boy who never made it into the mountain before the door closed?

Journey to the Centre of the Earth, Orpheus in the Underworld,

Alice in Wonderland. Dante, come show us your Inferno; we are in an accepting mood.

'Let's see what's next,' says Gimpo.

We climb back in. Gimpo fires the engine and we slowly move on. The above-mentioned horizon is foreshortened as the road dips down in a convex way. Have I described that properly? I count the kilometres on the meter – we've done about five since entering the tunnel. The objective compartment of my mind tells me the iron door is there to prevent snowdrifts blocking up the tunnel, but the higher part of the mind is now in overload. Another couple of kilometres of tunnel and we approach another iron door.

After seven or eight hours wandering through this stinking tunnel of bad love we came to another huge iron door – the same weird Dracula shit, skulls, bats' eyeballs, the Devil's arse, etcetera. Gimpo threw a lever.

Will this one stay shut? Will we be left in this bleak tunnel to starve slowly to death? Iron door II begins to open in a similar portcullis fashion. Gimpo edges the car forward out into a waiting world.

The enormous portcullis ground into the roof. Stinko Bill ripped off another one.

Something is different. No! Everything is different.

CHAPTER TEN

Sons of the Horned One

The omnipresent snow blasted through the tunnel like ice buckshot and knocked us flat on our freezing arses. I could hear the sound of distant aircraft and see faint lights on the black horizon. The dread hum of powerful engines, like Messerschmitts, gradually became louder and the lights grew brighter. When they were about a mile away I realized they were headlights, about eighty of them, approaching rapidly.

The bass throb of the engines hit me in the guts, fat diesels clogging up the space between my ears. Eighty big men covered in snow and riding ski-bikes thundered up the tunnel, overwhelming and surrounding us: Ice Bikers. The iron door slammed shut. Shit. The bikers were wearing battered black-leather ski suits festooned with metal studs, swastikas, death's heads and iron crosses. Icicles hung from the massive reindeer-skin cloaks draped over their shoulders. Huge, blond beards dressed in plaits and smeared with grease, mirrored ski goggles, Viking helmets. Enormous chainsaws decorated with runes and Germanic script swung from their heavy leather belts. Studded gauntlets enclosed massive forearms. Calf-high, skull-crushing jackboots covered in buckles and zips. All I could see of their faces, just a couple of inches between the snow-encrusted beards and their impenetrable goggles, appeared to be covered in fearsome Maori-style tattoos.

The huge machines they sat astride were equally awesome: extended front forks that ended in skis, huge tank tracks instead of back wheels. They had reindeer-skin saddles slung low; a collection of human and animal skulls dangling from the front forks; chrome exhaust pipes exquisitely carved with strange runes. Flags flew from the backs of their machines, samurai warrior-style. I recognized the design depicting a black swastika with four lightning bolts flying from the centre as similar to that we had seen earlier flying amongst the carnage on the Road of Fear. Beneath the symbol emblazoned in Germanic script, the legend: 'Sons of the Horned One'.

The biggest guy, who I assumed to be the chief or president, raised a gauntleted hand. Instantly the deafening drone of the engines ceased and echoed off down the black tunnel. Bill, Gimpo and I shuffled, smiled and farted nervously. A silence as ominous as a hangman's breakfast froze time for a full five minutes. The big polar man slowly removed his gauntlets and pushed his mirrored ski goggles up on to his forehead. He fixed us with a rigor-mortis stare. His eyes were as blue as death. Steam drifted from his nostrils. A huge brass ring pierced his septum.

'My name is Ragnar. We are the Sons of the Horned One. We know of you.' His resonant voice was as deep as a submarine cruising the bottom of black oceans. 'The weather is not good, your car destroyed. You will stay with us.' This was not a request.

Three bikes broke formation and pulled alongside us, indicating that we should ride pillion. The big man barked a command in his native tongue; eighty ski-bikes started as one; the iron door rose. In strict formation, swathed in a cloud of black fart-dust and noise, we cruised into the storm. The Sons travelled at a steady thirty mph through the ever-present blizzard. The acrid stench of reindeer fat hung around my humungous chauffeur.

Under a full moon we drove slowly through a spectral cathedral of bending fir trees until we reached a clearing in the forest.

Stillness, no blinding blizzard, no threatening ice mountain, no swollen black sea. Undulating snow pastures gently stretch out in front of us, bathed in a soft light. Gimpo drives on with reverence.

I put down my notebook and lay my head on the back shelf under the rear window and stare up into the sky, and there above all the heavens dance Aurora's race in full flow. Soft colours swirl through the sky. Tears well up and trickle down the cheeks of my upturned face. 'Paid in full' is my thanksgiving to the Chief. I imagine sitting on my camel 2,000 years ago drenched through from the thunderstorms, frozen, frightened, hungry and lost; then suddenly the clouds in the night's sky begin to break up, pull apart, revealing that the half-forgotten star's still shining. Well that's the effect the aurora borealis is having on me. Gimpo drives. Ten, twenty, thirty minutes pass before I can bring myself to say anything to the other two.

'Have you seen the sky?' Me.

'You what?' Gimpo.

'. . . . .' Z.

'The aurora borealis, have you seen it? Stop the car. You've got to get a good view of it. Z? Gimpo?'

'What?' Gimpo.

'No! Keep driving!' Z.

I shut up. Gimpo keeps driving. There is a strange tension in the car. Nobody says anything else. Z sits in the front passenger seat motionless, staring straight ahead. The aurora borealis is the sort of thing that usually gets him into full flow; for fuck's sake, he even named his daughter after Aurora, goddess of the dawn. I tend to these notes, try to capture the events and emotions of the past hour. Fail.

We drive on through this winter moonscape. The Northern Lights flit and fade, the road twists and turns, danger seems to have ebbed. I try to rationalize recent events, search my mind for parallels in ancient stories; try to dramatize them into legend, elevate it all into some magical . . . What the fuck am I saying? This *is* magic. This is all magic. Just 'cause it's just me, Z and Gimpo and our damp, scuzzy lives with 'no direction known' and no neat plot line keeping us in tow don't mean . . . Move over Homer, the Literary Arseholes are here, and when we get home, Penelope better have stayed honest, true and faithful.

'Drive on. Drive on,' I hear Van Morrison emote. Time slips by. The tourist map on my knees meaningless in these obviously uncharted territories. We round a gentle hill and there below us we can see some lights. The road twists down. A small pier, lit by a row of hanging lamps; a cabin, light shafting out into the night from its uncurtained windows. As a film set it would be unconvincing; as reality, it isn't.

Inside, radiators blast heat; hot water on tap and a wall chart with ferry timetables in three languages, none of them English. But, seeing as we have no idea of where we are or where these ferries may be going, it makes no odds to us. We laugh, throw hot water on our faces. Z smokes a fag, I swig from a bottle of water, Gimpo stretches out on a fixed functional Formica tabletop. We don't let our minds formulate thoughts like 'What the fuck do we do now?'

An almighty sonorous blast from out of the night. A second follows. We rush from the cabin. Out in the sea, a huge ocean-going ferry pulls around and up to the small quay, its rear drive-on entrance lowers. Back down to the Escort. Light from the ship's interior pours out. We drive up the ramp and into its hold like Richard Dreyfuss at the end of *Close Encounters of the Third Kind*. From nowhere an articulated truck thunders up the ramp and joins us in the hold of the ferry. A seaman approaches us. Gimpo, in control, buys tickets. No English spoken, still no idea where we are going. The chunder of ship's motors in reverse.

We climb empty staircases. Stale air, diesel fumes, rather run down; worn and chipped cream paint. It feels like it must be in the wee small hours but no way of telling. Large empty canteen, friendly tea-lady type behind the counter; speaks no English. No beer for Z, no pile of hot steaming mash and stew for me. Plastic cups, tepid water, tea bags, open-top cheese sandwiches with gherkins and dusty puff-pastry apple turnovers.

Gimpo gets in a rake of the inedible stuff; Z clasps a bottle of Blue Label that has appeared from somewhere. Gimpo and I sort of talk but try to stay off subjects like 'Where the fuck are we going?' My mind is cranking up, flashing back and forth over the events of the last couple of hours, from the despair of the unfrozen ocean to the fear of the blizzard and the unmarked road to the unreality of the tunnel riddled with its symbolism and the faith-restoring wonder of the aurora borealis . . .

If I labour my incredulity, you won't believe me. Gimpo disappears for a wander. Z is shaking; tries to explain something. I don't understand. He bursts out laughing. I laugh too. What are we laughing at? Z confides. He was convinced that we were going to die, that neither Gimpo nor I had the intelligence to take in the reality of our situation; that all he had wanted to do was phone his loved ones and tell them he was sorry for all the shit he has caused and that he loves them from the pit of his being. Z means it. I am embarrassed by Z's emotional state. I turn to my notebook and make notes.

'Bill! Hey Bill, come out here! Lights!'

I look up. Gimpo is back and he's beckoning me to follow. I do. The deck is frozen over, tons of ice cling to the rigging. The ship heaves through the black. A gale blows, but no snow or even rain. The sky is still clear but no aurora borealis. Gimpo skips and skids about, fearless. Visions of losing my balance and sliding under the deck rail to the Bible-black below. Two thoughts cross my mind: 1) that perennial boyhood question: How many seconds does it take to freeze to death in the Arctic Ocean?; and 2) Robert Maxwell's bloated body sliding under the rail, falling shapelessly into Davey Jones's locker. I cling to the rail, salt spray at the back of my throat. Gimpo, with arm outstretched, screams through the gale: 'Over there!' My eyes follow the direction of his pointing arm.

The first thought to hit my mind is 'One Night in Torremolinos', a rare song by a rare seventies band, Deaf School. When I hear that song I always have this vision of the broad sweep of a Mediterranean bay daisy-chained with twinkling lights as viewed from the deck of a luxury yacht: kitsch romance. This is as far from that sort of camp pastiche seventies shite as you could get: this is *True Grit*. Brain flicks into rational mode and deduces that lights must be those of some large Arctic oil refinery. They do look pretty impressive and I appreciate Gimpo getting us out to have a look.

Back in the canteen I try to get Z to come out. 'No fuckin' way, I'm not going out there. How many lives do you think I've got?' He has a spread of his cards on the table; they make the shape of a six-pointed star. Gimpo and I head back out. We seem to be getting closer – we can see the outline of buildings, docks, movement.

Mood swing: disappointment once again starts to fill my . . . No, it's not Torremolinos or an Arctic oil refinery – it's Bridlington out of season. Now Bridlington-out-of-Season is all very commendable in a poem by John Betjeman or a song by Morrissey, but for the sort of journey we are on it is of no use whatsoever. We can now even see normal people walking about as if they were living in the real world, with jobs to go to and lives to lead. Fuck it! Fuck it! Fuck it! Minutes later we are disembarked and the truck driver whom Gimpo has befriended, despite lack of a common language, lets us know that we should follow him and he will lead us to a place where we can get a bed for the night.

The road into Bridlington-out-of-Season is well lit. Can't make out the terrain beyond. Z is becoming more animated, even laughing. I sink, sink into the accepting arms of failure. My anger circles around. How the fuck can Z be happy when we have come all this way with our portrait of Elvis to save the world? To find the Baby Jesus inside ourselves? Fuckin', fuckin', fuckin', fuck it! Why do I have to resort to the F-word all the time? Fuck that as well. I don't give a shit if I use it every second line. I fall silent, stare out of the back-seat window: houses painted happy colours, middle-aged woman walking a poodle, children playing. OK, it isn't actually Bridlington-out-of-Season, but it may as well be. Try to shut my mind down.

We arrive at a hostel, closed for the winter. We are welcomed by a tall, bearded chap. Speaks English. He has a three-berth room for us: blankets, sheets, hot shower, electric kettle. He chats. It turns out we are in a place called Honningsvag on an island called Mageroya somewhere off the north coast of Norway. If you look at your atlas, find a place called Nordkapp – that's where we are. It's only about 8 p.m. Gimpo gets instructions about a gaff where we can go and eat. 'Up on the main road across from the gas station,' our friendly host instructs. He hands us a key to let ourselves back in.

I could smell wood smoke and roasting meat. A huge log cabin, 200 feet long by 50 wide, made from whole pine trees, its roof covered in thick slabs of turf. A horizontal plume of smoke spirited away from the chimney on the back of the storm. Yellow glowed through the cracks in the door and window blinds. An array of pikes festooned with bloody human heads stood guard at its huge double doors, which were dressed with bones and strange carvings. A few scrawny dogs scattered at our arrival. The Sons performed elaborate manoeuvres on their ski-bikes before lining them up against the side of the grand hall. As one, the cyclone drone of the powerful engines ceased and the baleful moan of the northern gales rushed to fill the vacuum.

We crunch up well-lit, freshly snowed-on streets, pass the gas station, cross the main road, up some steps into a starkly lit functional bar.

'Sven! Olaf!' Ragnar barked. Two huge men opened the doors; orange light and sparks from open fires leapt out of the hall. I could feel the heat on my freezing eyeballs. Laughing and slapping each other good-naturedly about the head and shoulders, the men strolled into an enormous, medieval banqueting hall.

A pretty and attractively rounded lass appears out of the kitchen and takes our order: lager or lager, ham salad and chips or microwaved chicken and chips?

The hot smell of sizzling fat attacked my olfactory system with a machete. An immense wooden banqueting table dominated the centre of the hall. It dripped with acres of food and ale, a veritable cornucopia of gluttony: pies, fruit, the carcasses of whole animals with apples in their mouths, bread, eggs, massive round cheeses, whole salmon, trout, ice pike, gargantuan skinned polar bears roasting and dripping sizzling fat on dozens of spinning spits.

My emotions are so low there is no way I can describe my feelings about what is on offer. I don't know what to choose. I turn to survey the scene.

Mangy dogs chased chickens across the straw-strewn floor. The daub and wattle walls were covered with savage-looking weapons, swords, shields, machine guns, axes, the heads of various animals, bears, deer (I even noticed several human specimens).

Feral children dressed in leather and fur tortured a wolf cub over one of the fires, giggling delightedly at its howls of agony. A buxom blonde serving-wench poured us steaming horns of ale from an earthenware jug. Ragnar's submarine tenor cracked into a booming laugh. He poured the brew roughly in the direction of his mouth, guzzling down the ale and spilling half of it over his beard and chest. 'Har, har, har. Drink!' he commanded, good-naturedly.

The only other customers in this shit-hole are two youngish blokes in the far corner. Above them hangs a large TV set, held in place by matt black wall-brackets which are screwed to the wall with posidrive screws. I notice the minuscule irrelevant details: the Busy Lizzie that needs watering, the chintz curtains, open and gathering dust.

We imitated Ragnar and poured the foul-tasting brew over our faces. The men threw their leather ski suits on to the straw and several young women with tattooed faces raced in from what I assumed to be the kitchen to tidy up after them. Ragnar draped a beefy, tattooed forearm around my shoulders, which unnerved me slightly as he was now wearing only a small kid-leather jockstrap emblazoned with SS runes. He pushed me towards the table.

'Come, har, har! We feast!' His breath reeked of beer and dog farts. We sat at the large wooden table. The big women brought more food and ale. We fell into the acres of bloody meat and frothing ale with bare hands and voracious appetites.

Without warning and out of nowhere the whole fucking freak show exploded. A Viking heavy-metal band ground out a monster-decibel version of Led Zep's 'Immigrant Song' through quaking Marshall amps. Cart-wheeling dwarf strippers, jugglers, knife-throwers and sword-swallowers appeared. For the next six hours gluttony was the order of the day. I started in on the beer.

After the fifteenth horn it started tasting fine. The party was flying. I noticed Gimpo sodomizing a fat serving-wench. He was sticking her head into a huge vat of ale; she appeared to be drowning. Bill, naked and covered in beer and blood, was impressing our hosts with a particularly vicious Scottish war dance. His feet were cut to ribbons as he stamped up and down on a pair of crossed cutlasses. He was screaming about Frazer, *The Golden Bough* and vegetable gods.

Then the chair in front of me gets kicked over; the table upturns; a scream breaks free from my throat and I collapse on the floor.

*

Naked women smeared in beef dripping wrestled in front of a huge fire, the grease shiny on their skin. One seemed to get the upper hand and pushed her opponent's head into the flames. Her hair exploded. The Sons thought this was hilarious; Ragnar fell off his chair laughing. Small children performed mock executions for the amusement of their parents.

Gore, grease and beer drooled down my chin. I noticed that I laughed loudly at Ragnar's jokes before he reached the punchline. I was completely fucked. So was Ragnar. He was experiencing rapid mood swings. He slammed a huge tattooed fist hard down on the table. A whole roast pig leapt a full foot in the air. Some of the women looked nervous. He was past the first two stages of drunkenness – elation and depression – and at the third and potentially most dangerous.

'So!' His submarine tenor was thick and slurred. 'Skinny warriors!' Ragnar was fighting drunk, 'You want to save the world?' This was not a question, it was a challenge. I remembered my misspent youth drinking in the violent working-class pubs of Leeds and the advice of an old scrapper on how to deal with men afflicted by the fighting-drunk condition. 'Take the initiative,' he said, 'and be extremely aggressive, subtlety and reason being the first qualities that the sieve of alcohol filters from the affected drunkee.' I took a deep breath: 'Fuck you Ragnar, you stinking fat cunt!'

Oscar Wilde it wasn't. Ragnar's death-blue eyes, glassy with drink, flickered rolling rigor mortis. A look of confusion sailed across his countenance like the passing black shadows of thunderclouds; his thick lips pursed then parted. He bared his teeth, feigned a pass towards his chainsaw and let out a huge, bellowing laugh. My sphincter relaxed.

'Har, har, har. You are funny man!' bellowed Ragnar in his terrifying Viking accent.

I said a prayer for the old scrapper.

The party was farting along just fine. The Sons were laughing and in high spirits, beer flowing like an intoxicating river. The serving-wenches were being raped and taking it all in good spirit; animals were being playfully tortured; vomit splashed gaily.

Suddenly a blast from a conch shell cut through the bacchanalia.

I assumed the blast was ceremonial, as the hall fell into an uneasy silence, only the odd fart or belch breaking the expectant stinky atmosphere. Ragnar gripped the arms of his wooden throne and rose unsteadily to his feet.

'Sons!' he roared, balling his fist and shielding a Krakatoan belch. 'Visiting warriors!' He cast a blurred gaze in our direction and jabbed a stumpy finger. 'It is time for, hic . . .' Ragnar wobbled and continued, 'the evening's entertainment!' His voice was thick like creosote and severed ox tongues. He laughed, evil with a wet mouth, shreds of white meat caught between his teeth. 'The prisoners!'

Pandemonium visited earth. The Sons went apeshit big time: impromptu ritual dancing with much stomping of heavy jackboots and beer-throwing. The whole hall was on its feet. They all seemed possessed by some collective psychosis, particularly the women, who were pulling out their hair, baring their breasts and wailing. The main doors were flung open. A freezing blast of snow and ice chased the damp heat into the corners, fire and ash flying everywhere. Ten pathetic men stood thin and bedraggled, dressed only in rags and chains. The doors slammed shut behind them and all eyes turned to the new arrivals.

The carnival atmosphere subsided into silence. A mist of hatred hung tangible in the air. Ragnar fixed the raggedy men with his rolling, death-blue stare. He chewed his bottom lip violently, black waves of hatred emanating from his cold eyes. His bottom lip started bleeding. He stumbled toward the chained men, drew back, balled a hairy fist and smashed the tallest full in the face. Something broke. Huge gouts of blood described black arcs through the tense atmosphere. The man wiped his splattered chops and spat out pieces of broken teeth, gristle and blood. He fixed Ragnar with a contemptuous stare, his eyes clear and insolent.

'Skallagrim!' bellowed Ragnar. I could smell his breath from twelve feet away. 'You betrayed me! How do you plead?'

It appeared to be some kind of trial. Skallagrim pulled himself to his full height, attempting to retain some semblance of dignity despite the ignominy of his situation.

'Guilty!' he snapped. 'Ragnar,' he spat, 'we know the sentence, but brother, let us die like men, like Ice Bikers, with a chainsaw in our hand and fire in our balls. Do not deny us Valhalla!'

Ragnar moved closer and stared directly into the prisoner's eyes. 'Open the pit!' he barked and smiled like poison.

A small troop of dwarves scurried from the shadows and started to clear the banqueting table. The Sons stirred from their absorption in the proceedings and moved the oak table to one side of the hall. The dwarves swung on a chain connected to some hidden machinery which moved the floor in the centre of the hall. The floorboards scraped ominously and parted to reveal a large pit at the centre of the room. A bad smell like sour milk and lice, sperm, onions, blood and shit felt its way around the room. Yellow-eyed wolves prowled inside the pit, snarling and salivating. Skallagrim smiled. Ragnar, with a macho Viking gesture, bellowed into the tense air: 'You and your men who talked to my wife, you brigands of insolence, you will die like dogs! The lowest latrine of Valhalla shall be your destiny. You will be the vilest shit-shovellers of eternity. This fate awaits all those who are dispatched by beasts.'

Ragnar paused for a moment, allowing the full weight of this terrible fate to sink in. 'Or,' he paused again to crack a fart, 'you may die like heroes . . .' With the slightest flicker of his beer-and-carnage eyeballs Ragnar indicated Bill, Gimpo and myself, 'at the hands of these men . . .' A murmur of excitement rippled around the room. 'The Sons of the great King Presley!'

Once again Pandemonium visited earth – beer horns were held aloft and laughter and cheers of encouragement filled the fuggy room with intimations of violence. 'Shit,' I murmured to myself. Bill leapt to his feet and started throwing noble poses, staring at imaginary horizons, hand heroically placed on his hip. He broke into his weird Highland-fling war dances, stomping up and down and waving his wedding tackle at the serving-wenches – the bastard was into it, his macho Celtic pride inflamed.

Egocentric dramatic pose or a soul crushed beyond breaking point? Maybe both.

He removed all his clothes, poured beer over his head and directed grotesque hip-thrusting copulatory gestures at the captives.

'Ragnar!' he bellowed, deepening his voice as much as possible. 'Your judgement is sound. It would be an honour to slay these dogs for the terrible crime of chatting up your missus. However, please allow me to eviscerate these scum alone for I am afraid that, though noble in every other respect, my companions, Gimpo and Z, are crap at fighting.'

The screen beams across the room at me, sniggering, cackling, gibbering its jibes at me. There, in all its putrid Technicolor shite-glory is M-fucking-here-I-am-TV. Right now MTV is everything in the world I loathe, reject, want to be as far away from in the universe as possible; everything I want to rise above, put behind me, pretend never existed; and there Pip Dann stands with her nasal voice and haircut-of-the-day, introducing another video clip. I hate, I hate, I hate, I hate The Beatles. I hate dance labels formed yesterday. I hate eager A&R men. I hate the *NME*. I hate 'knowing' journalists. I hate foreign licensees who talk about the Rock 'n' Roll they have known and loved. I hate Virgin Megastore. I hate promoters with their tours nearly sold out. I hate smart logos. I hate other people who make great records and are not dead yet. I hate women who work in the music business who sound pleased when you phone up their office. I hate CD players, I hate the smell of vinyl. I hate NWA, Public Enemy, Ice T T-shirts, Crowded House, The Kinks, Techno Techno Techno, Bob Dylan, people talking about James Brown, The MC5, David Bowie, David Byrne, U2, Muddy Waters, BB King, everything I've ever been involved with. I hate all the records that I have ever loved. I hate everybody who associates the word 'scam' with what me and Jimmy have done – you lie, bleed, decry, give it everything you have got and these fuckers think it's a prank, think that you must be having fun. I don't have fun. I hate fun. The idea of fun makes me want to hit somebody.

Look, last year me and Jimmy made videos for 'Justified and Ancient' and 'America: What Time is Love?' back to back on the 007 stage at Pinewood, the biggest indoor studio in Europe. We had it all: cast of thousands, Viking ships, Tammy Wynette, sets bigger than the fall of Rome, catering vans feeding the five thousand, Winnebagos, technicians pandering to our every whim. Why did we do all this? We didn't do it for ourselves, we did it for MTV.

I can't write about it any more; I'm getting violent. Hated every fuckin' moment of it. It broke me, crushed me. I was left helpless, freezing, my life out of control, crashing down. You try and hold on, make it look like you know what's going on, get a grip. It maybe took a few months before I finally lost it and found myself alone at the top of a pyramid in Mexico, 12,000 feet above sea level, watching the sun rise.

Two days later after a 2,000-mile drive up through Mexico with no sleep and no food, I was walking through the outskirts of Brownsville. The night air was thick and hot; the trees were full of loud exotic bird-calls; there were pancake houses, pizza parlours, burger bars, steak restaurants, screaming 'It's all here for you! All the shit you wanted and more!' Those poor wet-back Mexicans, crawling across the border – for this! I heard a rustle in the grass at my feet. I looked down. A movement. Four or five foot of snake moved off, swishing, gliding across the grass. He looked back at me, we caught each other's eye and he was gone. Gone for good. I found a phone booth. I made a collect-call to Jimmy and told him I was OK.

'Wonder what the fuck he thought?'

I was relieved. Gimpo, however, took severe umbrage. He leapt to his feet, removed his erect penis from his trousers, grabbed the nearest chainsaw and proclaimed: 'Drummond! Do not demean me!' He swallowed a huge draught of foaming ale. 'I am,' he paused very dramatically, 'a worthy,' more ale, 'executionaaaar!'

But right now it ain't OK. Right now MTV is in the corner laughing at me, squealing, 'You thought you could get away, escape, get beyond. You, with your pure dreams of Elvis and the Pole, of the Baby Jesus inside, your infantile Zen Master illusions and blasphemous claims of the Magi. You have come as far as you are ever going to get, and we got here before you. We are everything! There is nothing left for you!' Although the snake was no illusion, maybe I misread the sign, because here in this TV screen is the same serpent writhing and wriggling at the fun he is having at my expense.

*

The bikers went crazy, they loved drama.

I took one look at the two crazy fuckers and told them straight: 'Count me out, noble ones. You are brave warriors and don't need a useless cunt like me. I'd just get in the way.'

Skallagrim sneered at me. He threw his head to the noble angle and spat defiantly: 'Like heroes!' Much cheering and throwing of ale, farting and wanking.

'The arena!' bawled Ragnar.

The arena was a dark room off the banqueting hall that contained another sunken pit. Blood-stained sawdust was spread over the floor and it was lit by flaming torches. The Sons were at fever pitch. Ragnar handed Bill and Gimpo a huge sparking chainsaw and told them to strip naked. The ten guilty men were, to their shock and disbelief, each handed a small plastic canteen cutlery knife. The Sons thought this was a great joke and ribald laughter rippled around the room in a cruel wave. The men were kicked unceremoniously into the pit, where they stood huddled in the centre, each clutching his pathetic little kitchen utensil. Several of them had defecated their rags.

Gimpo, naked, with an erection, patrolled the perimeter of the pit like some gremlin Priapus from a mad homosexual dream. He was swinging the spitting, sparking chainsaw in huge arcs above his head and laughing sadistically. He paused now and then to throw strange poses and lasciviously stroke his revolting erection. He mimed thrusting movements with his hips as if to tell the poor unfortunates that he intended to sodomize them after he had killed them.

Bill started doing his bizarre Scottish war dance, chainsaw held high over his head, stamping the sand like some terrible Hindu deity, flicking his tongue in and out in a horrible Haka sex-jig. He threw poses like a sexually insane Chris Eubank and occasionally stopped to oil his erection with grease from his chainsaw.

Ragnar rose to his feet, and once more reverential silence fell over the hall in deference to the chieftain. He lifted his beer, drained it and shouted: 'Odin!'

The Sons joined him. 'Odin!' they bellowed.

'The kill!' screamed Ragnar.

'The kill!' screamed the Sons.

'The kill,' I joined in.

The room erupted with primordial bloodlust. Bill and Gimpo were sucked into the lustmort frenzy and performed excellently. Gimpo jumped into the pit and charged at the pathetic huddle, his chainsaw held low. He took the legs off six prisoners just below the knee. Their screams popped my eardrums. A huge spray of blood gushed from their stumps, covering Gimpo's naked body in ruby rivulets of shining gore. The other four bolted in panic and tried to climb out of the pit, only to be kicked back in by the laughing Sons.

Bill vaulted into the pit and casually sauntered towards the pathetic creatures who were on their knees, crying and begging for mercy. He laughed and urinated on their faces before decapitating all four of them with one graceful sweep of his chainsaw. The Sons applauded his style. Bill bowed like a matador to the cheering throng, picked up the dripping trophies, threw them to the ecstatic audience and then sauntered over to where Gimpo was making a grisly meal of his slaughter.

Whereas Bill's kill was elegant and almost humane, Gimpo's gruesome butchery was positively bestial. He severed all the limbs from his charges and threw the spurting trunks into the air, drop-kicking them as they landed. The six men were still conscious, and it seemed that Gimpo took great pleasure in their screams of agony. He was wet with blood from head to foot and sodomized each torso in turn, dragging the poor creatures by the hair in a semicircle around him to witness the hellish torture of their fellow sufferers. After buggering each torso he set about castrating them, finding it particularly amusing to place their severed members directly before their horrified gaze. Finally, swinging his chainsaw in huge arcs, he set about reducing his victims to bloody hamburger, driving the blade through their ribcages and digging inside chests searching for kidneys and beating hearts. When nothing remained but sludge he beamed idiotically at the crowd, seeking approval, a shiny purple necklace of intestines draped around his neck. The Sons were ecstatic and leapt into the pit to lift him on to their shoulders. 'Gimpo! Gimpo! Gimpo!' they chanted. Bill smiled, proud of his friend.

*

I pick up the chair and straighten the table, apologize to the room, sit down with Z and Gimpo; sip my lager and eat my microwaved chicken and chips with salad on the side that is placed in front of me and stare calmly at MTV, beaten, crushed and broken. Can't even make notes.

Ragnar turned to me, laughing. 'Zodiac, my friend, now it is your turn, ja?' My heart sank. What diabolical party trick was I supposed to perform?

'We have had the violence,' Ragnar winked and elbowed me conspiratorially in the ribs, 'now we have the sex! Ha ha harrr! Clear the arena!'

Gimpo, an honorary Prince of Violence, beaming, naked and covered in gore, was placed next to Ragnar on a throne. Meanwhile the arena was cleared of the appalling carnage.

Four hirsute dwarves cartwheeled in, followed by a fifth leading a statuesque Negress and another girl on a double dog leash. The black woman was over six feet tall; her oiled body shone in the torchlight. She looked like Grace Jones, while the other girl resembled the supermodel Kate Moss. One of the dwarves pulled a cut-throat razor from his leather trousers and slashed the black woman's Achilles tendons. She fell to her hands and knees, screaming. Blood spurted from the back of her heels in two perfect fountains. A second dwarf sat astride her as if riding a horse and started to pull her teeth out with pliers. The dwarves banged nails into the holes where her teeth once were. Ragnar and the rest of the Sons laughed loudly. 'Kate' made a run for it but was caught by a lasso. She was pulled to the ground. One of the dwarves tore off her panties and started to bugger her. Another cut off all her fingers and gouged out her eyes. It resembled some kind of clownish performance in an evil circus. The dwarves cartwheeled and somersaulted, lopping off first her ears, then her nose and finally her lips. The Sons leapt one by one into the arena and hacked holes in the women's bodies, copulating with the wounds.

Can't even make notes. Bizarre colourful images flicker before me; nubile bodies cavort; genres are pastiched and Ray Cooke tells a joke, or is it Pip Dann smiling? I think Z is aware that something is up with me but ignores it.

There was much jollity in the air. Ragnar slapped me on the back and told me to get in quick while their hearts were still beating. Not wishing to offend our host, I removed my trousers and jumped down into the pit. Gimpo cheered. The black woman had been opened up and the Sons were laughing and throwing her innards good-naturedly at each other. I awaited my turn on the still-breathing 'Kate'. I grabbed her by the hair and started to fuck her in her ruined mouth. While I was thrusting away, just about to unload my seed, one of the Sons cut off one of her buttocks and jokingly rubbed the soggy side against my face. A dwarf unravelled her intestine and ran across the arena, stretching it like a huge elastic band. He let it go and it cracked towards me, covering me in black excrement.

I try to get rational. 'Look Z, we have come to the wrong place. We can't leave Elvis here. Elvis in this place ain't gonna bring about peace in the Middle East.'

Z is in an agreeable mood. We are not dead; we are in a bar that sells lager above 2 per cent ABV. 'Yeah, fine Bill, where do you think we should take him?'

Is Z humouring me? I wouldn't even shag Pip Dann. Gimpo gets another round in. I try to make some notes.

'Maybe Africa,' says Z. 'King Solomon's Mines or something, or that place in Ethiopia where the Arc of the Covenant is supposedly holed up.' These remarks drift over me. I think about Kate and James, how they will be tucked up in bed, asleep. What do they make of their father heading off to the North Pole? What will they think of it all in years to come?

The Sons fell about laughing, tears rolling down their cheeks.

I noticed Bill had joined the fun and was dancing around with the black woman's severed head impaled on his penis. Gimpo too had left his throne to join the party and had fashioned himself an artificial cunt in one of the other women's breasts. His pounding backside made me laugh. I shot my load into her dead mouth and pulled off her head with my bare hands. I started jigging a barn dance with Bill. The heads attached to our penises had Ragnar on his feet, clapping and cheering and wiping away tears of laughter with the back of his hand. The dogs and children leapt in the pit and joined in. The arena was full of laughing, happy people having fun with dismembered women.

The throng of debauched revellers gradually made their way back to the banqueting hall, joking and singing traditional Ice-Biker songs. Whilst our good-natured primeval passion play was unfurling in the back room, the serving-wenches had replenished the table with yet more roast meats and flagons of ale – all that slaughter had stoked everyone's thirst and appetite. We fell upon the fresh offerings with renewed manly gusto.

'So!' Ragnar boomed, thwacking me on the back and knocking a chunk of half-chewed meat from my mouth, 'Zodiac, my friend, how do you like our hospitality, huh?'

'A most cultured and informative evening, Ragnar my friend,' I answered honestly.

'Good. Good,' he replied, gnawing on a polar bear's hind leg. 'Now,' he continued, 'it is time for the more serious part of our evening.'

One of the two local lads calls over to us. 'Do you mind if we switch off the television?' Pretty good English.

'Uh?' Me.

I noticed a general quietening amongst the more raucous elements of the biker fraternity. The Sons' eyes were drawn towards Ragnar, a look of anticipation on their gnawing, smiling faces.

'Tell me, my friends,' Ragnar smiled, 'do you like poetry?'

Bill coughed and spluttered out a jet of splashing ale. 'Poetry?'

'Yes, poetry,' answered Ragnar, slightly annoyed at Bill's incredulous tone. 'Warrior poetry! Viking Ice-Biker poetry!'

'We want to switch on the radio. Radio bingo is about to begin.'

*

I groaned inwardly as I realized what he meant: Nordic sagas, ream upon ream of hard-man boasting; drunken tales of what a complete mental, vicious, conquering hero bastard was the subject of the poem. Fortunately, Ragnar's poems were relatively short. He rose unsteadily to his feet and called for the poetry bucket. Two men brought in the huge earthenware bowl containing at least fifteen pints of frothing ale. Ragnar held it in his huge tattooed hands, drained it dry in one draught and began his poem.

'I, Ragnar,' he began, pointing grandly at himself, 'am the hardest man alive!' He spat a lump of something horrible on the floor and continued.

> Any Son who wishes to challenge me,
> Shall feel the sting of my chainsaw, Brainbiter!

Ragnar raised a cheek, ripped off a carrot-cruncher and continued:

> As an infant, feeding at my mother's breast,
> I bit both of them clean off.
> At two years old, I slew my father.

The Sons of the Horned One applauded respectfully.

> At three years old, my penis was that of a fully grown man,
> I fucked my natural born sister,
> And shat on the devil's face.
> My farts drop cows dead in the fields.
> I can outdrink the gods. Thor is a poof compared to me.
> I can outshag, outfight, outwank, outfart,
> Any member of the Nordic pantheon you care to mention.
> Once, I had a fight with Odin, the fat bastard.
> I stuffed his three horns up his arse.

Ragnar burped and lost the plot.

'Yeah, fine,' Gimpo.

'Yeah,' he carried on. 'Once, right, when we raided Yorkshire, I fucked 8,000 women and buggered 2,000 men, some sheep and . . .'

The lad who does the speaking gets up and switches off the TV;

switches on a small Bakelite radio that is on the shelf high on the wall
between our two tables. He is short, good-looking, high-cheekboned,
moustachioed, a cheeky face, a bit of a swagger, a glint in his eyes.
You just know that girls are going to love him, mother him and find
him sexy all at the same time – just what they want. He moves over
to the bar and makes the barmaid laugh. She pulls out a stack of
eight-by-six-inch buff-coloured cards from beneath the bar; hands
them over.

I'm still wondering what radio bingo is when Gimpo calls over to
him: 'Can we play?'

'Yeah, sure. We will sit at your table, I will show you what to do.'
Him and his mate move over and the girl behind the bar joins us.
She brings over a phone and places it at the end of the table. The
three of them are sitting down one side, us lot down the other.

I take it most people are familiar with the rules of bingo, so I
won't explain it. Radio bingo turns out to be pretty much the same.
The radio announcer calls out the numbers in Norwegian, our new-
found friend translates them into English and we put the crosses on
our cards. If any of the listeners gets a line, they phone in and there
is much cheering from the studio audience, and the game carries
on.

On and on it went. And these were the better lines.

Bingo is boring, has a passing place in our culture, but here I am,
at 8.55 p.m. on 4 November 1992, playing it; even getting caught up
in the game. Z, Gimpo and I soon begin to recognize the Norwegian
numbers and can fill our cards in before the numbers are translated
for us.

The presenter is a sparky character. People who have won lines
are phoning in. He makes them laugh. We laugh. The game is rolling
on. Z asks if they have ever won. 'No, nobody on Mageroya has
ever won. Everybody plays radio bingo every Wednesday night and
nobody on the island has ever won.'

Several hours later the poems slurred to an end. Ragnar turned to
me, his eyes blazing like a forest fire, like a burning tenement. 'This

is the top of the world,' he said gravely, ultimate machismo, trembling violently like a Venus flytrap. Time stood still.

'Bingo!' screams Gimpo.

The girl gets on the phone. You can hear her over the radio live on the air. You can hear Z going, 'You fuckin' bastard!' in stereo. Gimpo, it seems, has won roughly three hundred quid – maybe not enough to retire on, but at least a sign. The rest of the game gets forgotten. Up till now we do not know what our new-found friends are called.

Introductions: the cheeky chappy is called Lars; the cuddly girl goes under the strange name of Tuna; as for the other lad, I forget. Lars takes charge; does a deal with Tuna. Gimpo gets his winnings out of the till and she will collect on his behalf. Tuna gets a round in on the house. I'm moved almost immediately to ask Lars what he does for a living – polite conversation or divine intervention?

'Ah, ha, ha!' he laughs. 'I'm a lighthouse keeper,' comes his reply.

'Where's your lighthouse?' asks Z.

'My lighthouse is on its rock!' laughs Lars.

'Give me your testament,' dread silence, 'and seek the Ocean of Wisdom!'

'Yeah, but where's that?' Z.

'It is the most northern lighthouse in the world.'

'You mean it's The Lighthouse at the Top of the World!' says Z. Z and I look at each other; we both instantaneously know. Distant stars align as interstellar ley lines quiver; St John the Divine gets the joke; Milton's eyesight is restored and Beethoven can hear the closing movement of his Ninth for the very first time.

I handed him the picture of Elvis and knew this was just the beginning. We had experienced hell and survived, laughing.

Divine Intervention Now. Fuck you, MTV. This is it: satori full on. We have arrived. We have found it. Or at least found our man, our keeper of Elvis. Gimpo is dispatched by Z back to the hostel to bring us our icon of the King. Meanwhile Z and I explode, our minds and voices cascading like fireworks over the White House lawns on the Fourth of July. This lighthouse at the top of the world is the most northerly pole in the world, is the North Pole we had longed for – true, true, true north. Standing there proud on its rock, phallic and strong, throwing out its beam of light into the night of darkness. Our ship may have its sails ripped and torn, all around us are heaving, storm-tossed, leviathan-infested seas, the charts lost; but that beam of light comes sweeping out of the infernal blackness, washing across our bows, bathing us in its strong, pure light, marking our point in an otherwise boundless ocean, illuminating hidden dangers, giving us hope but warning us not to come too near. Yes, I am now ready to confront Satan and tear down his majestic splendour. Z proclaims he knew his cards would come in handy.

I passed out.

I feel like becoming a Victorian hymn writer. Those thumping tunes well up in my breast:

> All people that on earth do dwell,
> Sing to the Lord with cheerful voice,
> Him serve with mirth, His praise forth tell,
> Come ye before Him and rejoice!

'Odin!' bellowed Ragnar, 'King of Hell, Lord of the Corporeal!' He cracked a massive, stinking, razzling fart and crashed like a felled oak to the puke-spattered floor.

CHAPTER ELEVEN

Ride the Moebius Rollercoaster and Twist Infinity
(Epiphany No. 2)

Gimpo arrives back. Z lovingly unwraps the Bon Scott T-shirt to reveal the truly magnificent visage of Elvis. Each plastic pearl on its encrusted frame shimmers with a thousand hues of pale pinks, blues and greens. Lars, we can see, is a moved man. He instructs Tuna to keep the King safely behind the bar until tomorrow, when the coastguard helicopter will pick him and Elvis up to take them to the lighthouse. Lars will give the King the place of honour above the galley dining table, where the Pirelli calendar is presently hanging.

My notebook is now open again, and between bouts of standing on the chair and singing favourite verses from *Hymns Ancient and Modern*, I pour out notes. Satan beware! Ready or not here we come, the Magi on a mission: our souls back or you die!

We get the latitude and longitude, the legends of these northern islands. Fruholmenfyr, 71°.06' north and 24°.00' east; 'the island of the mistress', Danish hussy, posh slag, banished to Fruholmenfyr to live out the rest of her life. I'm writing this down 'cause Lars is telling me it, but I don't know what it relates to. 'The sea took her,' he says. He then grabs my notebook, writes down his full name and address, gets Tuna and the other lad to do likewise. Tuna's name you can just about make out is spelt Tone, which is a bit of a disappointment. I will continue to spell it the more dolphin-friendly way. Z and I recognize through the haze of our unabandoned revelry that if it was not for Gimpo 'boldly going' this could not have happened. It was Gimpo who had recognized the importance, no, the absolute necessity, of us playing radio bingo.

Ride the Moebius Rollercoaster and Twist Infinity (Epiphany No. 2)

Phone calls are made. A taxi arrives. We bundle in, all six of us. We head into town. The taxi driver uses only the handbrake, letting the cab skim round the gentlest of curves. Gimpo, I'm afraid to report, is well impressed by this style of driving. No idea of where we're going or what we are doing. Feel I should describe the world outside – the houses, the streets, the weather, the view – but can't be arsed.

'The Corner Cafe' buzzes the neon light. We climb the stairs. Smoke-filled, jukebox rocking, Russian seamen ranting and drinking. We find a table full of Lars' best friends. There are now about a dozen of us, all blokes 'cept for Tuna who is there as the female mascot. She seems to be unattached and looks more and more attractive as the night wears on and the lager takes its toll. Gimpo seems intent on putting in some groundwork. Let him.

I go for a shit. In fact, I'm sitting here right now having my shit, jeans round my ankles, kilt on the floor, notebook on my naked knees. Two Russian seamen are having a piss. One starts banging on my door and shouting something. 'Can ya speak English?' I shout. 'Oh, English, ha, ha, ha. You English,' in heavy thick Russian accent. My shit smells bad.

Messerschmitts and Chinooks spun around the inside of my skull. The drummer from Megadeth was using my brain as a double bass pedal. Hangover. Antique electricity. 300-pound killer bees buzzing and jamming my synapses. I clenched my fists and screwed them into my frayed eyeballs, horror-movie moaning.

Through the fog I could make out weird Frankenstein machines: towering grey steel, crackling and spitting Van Der Graaf venom; glass orbs with ozone fire; black cables dangling from the high vaulted roof like ominous jungle vines. I half expected some Gothic electro-Tarzan to come spinning out of the strobe lights. Mad dials and switches danced and spun demented, epileptic circles. Cascades of sparks and red smoke illuminated the stone room.

Back in the bar and Lars is standing on the table, jar of lager in hand, conducting the community singing. I fuckin' hate lager, as I've most probably informed you on numerous previous occasions, but there is no stopping its flow. Tray after tray of brimming jars of the

145

stuff keep arriving at the table and I judge it would be well bad form to refuse the hospitality.

I was on a straw pallet surrounded by empty beer horns and vodka bottles. Over in the corner Bill and Gimpo were gibbering. Gimpo, yelling out catchwords from Northern bingo halls, appeared to have temporarily lost his mind. 'Two little ducks, ha ha. Kelly's eye. Legs eleven . . . ha ha! Blind forty!' I didn't take too much notice. Gimpo is a weird fucker under normal conditions, God know what tricks this Arctic weirdness was playing on our chum's hallucinogenic reality. I tipped the vodka bottles and beer horns to hopeful angles, looking for a little eye-opener. No luck.

'Skol!'
  'Skol!'
  'Skol!'
  The lad next to me (actually, he must be in his early forties so lad's the wrong description) wants to talk, ask questions; tells me of his trips to England, his love for Manchester United; how he came over for the FA Cup Final in 1977 when United beat Liverpool 2–1; how he fell in love with United after the Munich air disaster – Busby's Babes, Denis Law, Bobby Charlton, Nobby Stiles and of course, later on, George Best. Didn't ask him what he thought of Ryan Giggs, their new heart-throb star circa '92. We talk of distant wives and broken hearts and The Moody Blues, his all-time favourite band in the world. We talk of fishing and how, if I was to come back in the spring, he would take me fishing for trout in some of the hidden lakes. I learn his name's Olden and that Glasgow Rangers have just beaten Leeds United 2–0 in the second leg of the European Cup. Olden watched the game live on satellite. Olden is a chef at a small US air base over at Hammerfest on extended leave with a shoulder injury.

  The amount of meaningless information you can take in on nights like these! Z is somewhere down the other end of the table. At some point he gets the three of us together to put on a display of our Elvis to the Pole chant. The lager seems to have blurred the memory banks, so I'm unable to report if our hosts were impressed – I think there was a rousing cheer. The Zen sticks get passed around for inspection and I am aware that the intricate patterns on Z's are still making the most impression, and I am aware that this is still causing a very un-Zen like twinge of jealousy in me. Bastard.

Now, these blokes we are drinking with are all 'regular guys', buy their clothes from the local equivalent of Marks & Spencer's men's department. Some Russians join us. One can speak English. They are from Murmansk. Lars is back standing on the table again and has now broken into something that might be poetry. His voice rises to a roar, his palms gesticulating to great theatrical effect, guttural sounds cascading from his throat. The comrades are seemingly appreciative of these lines of Nordic rhyme. Mirth is stirred and Lars leaves gaps between his couplets for laughter and cheers. Olden has my ear and he is telling me that Lars spends many of his hours of lighthouse solitude dreaming up rhymes to embroider the events of their dull lives into epic sagas.

One of the Russian seamen is now up on his feet, banging his fist on the table, his sonorous voice booming over the jukebox, rhyming a rant of sprawling proportions. Those mountainous Arctic oceans must be home to some wild muse. He crashes back on to his seat; there is much banging of steins and 'Bravos! Bravos!'

Lars turns to me. 'Come on Bill, you must read us some of your poetry. Come up on to the table. We want true Scotsman poetry.' What the fuck should I do? None of the verse I've ever written, even if I could remember it, would stand up to this sort of public performance. 'Bill, you must tell us your poetry! It's your duty! We will be most upset if you don't! We are your hosts! You must obey!'

I catch Z's eye. He is grinning. His grin is saying 'Come on Bill, get up and give it loads!' I pull myself up to my full height and announce to the throng that I will recite not my own words but those of Robert Burns, words that they won't understand but which might be applicable on a night like this:

> When chapman billies leave the street,
> And drouthy neebors, neebors meet,
> As market-days are wearing late,
> An' folk begin to tak the gate;
> While we sit bousing at the nappy,

An' getting fou and unco happy,
We think na on the lang Lapp miles,
The mosses, waters, slaps, and styles,
That lie between us and our hame,
Whare sits our sulky sullen dame,
Gathering her brows like gathering storm,
Nursing her wrath to keep it warm.

That's all I can remember of 'Tam O'Shanter'. I once tried to learn the whole poem by heart to impress on nights like these. Of course, I accentuate the Scots. They love all that and there was much cheering; they aren't bothered with me giving a translation. I feel pretty pleased with myself as I sit back down.

It's Z's turn next. While he rises to his feet the jukebox plug is pulled and a hush falls on the bar. With no preamble Z intones in his droll Yorkshire accent, 'A cold coming we had of it,' etcetera. Well the first verse of it anyway.

Whether a word of what he says is understood by our comrades I doubt, but its manner of delivery certainly has an effect.

Jukebox plug rammed back in. Thin Lizzy's 'The Boys are Back in Town'. The lager flows; drunken banter bonds strangers and melts language barriers. A hand bell is rung and last orders are called. Lars protests, but even he can't hold the clock back; and when a landlord calls time and wants to get to bed, there is nothing to be done but to move on and find another place to continue the revelry.

The oak door creaked open. It was Ragnar. He looked magnificent: huge mirrored Viking helmet; massive reindeer-skin cloak and curly-toed, blue reindeer-suede boots. I noticed our Elvis portrait clutched under his tattooed arm. He was accompanied by two dwarves wearing gold lamé suits and plastic Elvis masks. 'Follow me!' Ragnar's black ocean voice boomed. The three of us rose to our shaky feet and followed the big man.

Z and I follow Olden out, up some back street and into the central square. On three sides of the square stand civic buildings of some sort; on the fourth is the waterfront, and there in the water, towering over us, is a Russian merchant ship. Every time I see a ship like this at close quarters I feel the urge to stow away. The urge is resisted. But a town square with a dirty great steamer towering over it is pretty impressive and, added to that on the impressive stakes, is the taxi cab that has just scud on to the square, spun round twice on its own axis and come neatly to a halt at our feet. It is only now that I notice we are standing at a taxi rank. This place must produce the world's best rally drivers. Where's Gimpo? Where's Lars? Where's the gang? Olden shoves us into the taxi and says it's all OK, everything's under control. We trust.

Off. Up through dark empty streets, mountains of snow-ploughed snow on either side, small houses huddling the frozen earth. Taxi driver performs feats of driving unknown in any other part of the world. Pull up outside non-descript house. 'Wait here. I will just be a few seconds,' Olden assures us in his confident English as he gets out of the taxi and disappears behind the house. Have I mentioned the temperature outside? Although there is little wind and no snow falling, it must be the coldest weather I have ever experienced. Z and I are silent knowing there's nothing to be said. The Wordsworth v. Blake case is temporarily closed.

We ascended a stone spiral staircase in hangover silence. It was freezing. My nicotine-racked lungs pushed curling vapour into the air where it seemed to freeze instantly. After 2,300 granite steps (I counted), we reached an oak door, where we rested an hour.

In about five minutes Olden returns. Back in the taxi, he pulls out from under his sports jacket (note: no quilted thermal Arctic coat) two large green plastic bottles of 7-Up. Why on earth all this mystery and time-wasting to pick up a couple of bottles of pop?

Ragnar passed around a foul alcoholic drink.

He offers me a swig. We are guests, I don't want to insult his hospitality. I take a swig. My tongue is on fire, my throat explodes and my guts erupt.

Bill threw up.   *

What the fuck have I just swallowed? It certainly wasn't any form of soft drink that I've ever experienced. Z has a swig. A broad grin breaks out across his face. The taxi moves off. Olden turns to us and laughs: 'Hooch!'

Our Viking pal wiped his beard with the back of his big fist. 'The machine,' he belched, 'it was made by the ancient ones.' His eyes were serious; he reminded me of Oliver Reed. 'It was written,' thick vowels, 'that you would come.' He pushed open the huge door.

Seems that Olden has just made a visit to the local dealer, The Man. Not quite Lexington 125, but then I'd go for the glamour of drinking hooch from a disposable 7-Up bottle in the Arctic with Lars and the lads any day rather than chopping out lines of coke back-stage in New York with Andy and The Velvet Underground circa '66. We're off. 'Cross town.

A wooden clapboard house. Over a snowdrift; up a flight of wooden steps. Front door open. The lads are all there, plus some of the Russian seamen. Hooch ceremoniously passed around. There seems to be all sorts of etiquette about how this is done. It's weird how any sort of illicit behaviour encourages etiquette, traditions and ceremony. Have you ever been round somebody's place when they're putting a bong together and all the rigmarole that goes with it? Do us a favour the next time you see somebody building an elaborate bong. Kick it over.

White light splintered into the dark corridor and speared my retina to the back of my skull. I screwed up my eyes and tried to peer into the brilliance through my fingers. I could hear a choir of angelic sopranos singing grandiose hymns in a far-away valley: Rhine maidens. A pulsating blue shape stood in the middle of the room. Ragnar handed us each a pair of Elvis-style aviator shades, the ones with the thick metal arms punctured with holes. My eyes adjusted quickly to the brightness.

In the middle of the circular room I made out some kind of solid plinth about eight feet long, four feet deep and four feet wide. It gave off a supernatural glow and a low hum. I realized that it was somehow connected to the weird occult machinery we had seen in the guts of the building. The gold Elvis dwarves started to dance excitedly around the plinth, cartwheeling and doing bizarre approximations of the King's dislocated, spaz-nigger jive. Ragnar was breathing heavily, his breath pluming into the cold air like ectoplasm. His eyes burned yellow. The angelic soprano choir was reaching its climax as Ragnar strode boldly towards the mysterious stone. Closing his eyes and curling his top lip, he purposefully placed the jewelled portrait of the King on the block.

And then it happened. Leviathan stirred in the Stygian depths of a black ocean; beachboy Apollo glided across the heavens on a gold surfboard drawn by swans; mountains imploded and stars fell from heaven. I left my body and circled the earth three times, faster than the speed of thought; snap, crackle, synapses popping like an electric toaster. Wagnerian Valkyries riding Harley Davidsons side-saddle sped across the Milky Way, lactating; the sun went nova; black lightning showered red sparks and set my hair on fire; the bible spontaneously combusted; a million angels sang hosannas to the sphinx. The past, the present, the future and something sideways spun backwards on a huge golden merry-go-round; the pantheon of every god and hero ever invented danced amongst the wooden horses. The pinball machine of creation banged out twelve million replays. I was speeding faster miles an hour on a moebius rollercoaster, twisting infinity. The music of the spheres had a Rock 'n' Roll beat. Teams of tag-wrestling Buddhist monks on flying carpets sent me reeling backwards with double cosmic clotheslines and I understood everything and nothing.

My entire nervous system unravelled like a wounded golfball and draped a dripping organic mesh around the perimeters of several alternative universes. I ejaculated a shower of twinkling platinum sperm and one hundred million tadpoles sang my favourite hymns in perfect harmony. I swam with dolphins for a billion years. Walt Whitman was orating the New York telephone directory with passion and conviction. He had stars in his beard. Spinning in the moebius rollercoaster, three monkeys hammered out the complete works of Marc Bolan on a Bontempi organ. My eyeballs swivelled in their sockets and I could see my brain. It looked like a video game about to explode.

One and a half nano-seconds later I was back in the strange white room. It was like hitting a brick wall. Stunned, I looked around. Bill, Gimpo, Ragnar and the dwarf Jordanaires stood there with big, cosmic, shit-eating grins. Gimpo farted.

The picture of Elvis shimmered gold. We were covered in fairy dust. A cold stain in my underwear told me I had come in my pants.

Whose house are we in? I ask nobody. An old man appears in dressing gown and pyjamas, slept-in hair and shouting. A young lad of about seventeen seems to be taking the brunt of the wrath. Must be his dad. Bad move on his part, bringing us all back here. Olden says back to his place. Off.

In silence we glided down the stone stairs, glowing inwardly with essential knowledge. We had experienced the ultimate epiphany, the Mike Tyson of religious experiences, 12,000 DMs in the eye. We were all communicating telepathically and clapping with one hand. I felt like the ocean.

Ragnar opened the door and we followed him into the pure snow.

Lars does a spectacular slide down the banisters of the wooden staircase, facing forward, legs wide apart and stretched out, arms spread-eagled. Have I mentioned his cowboy boots before? He wears the crappiest cowboy boots going. They match his lightweight slacks and all-round who-gives-a-fuck-about-the-weather-and-cosmopolitan-fashions attitude. His whole being screams: 'I'm Lars! I'm the Keeper of the Lighthouse at the Top of the World! I may be only five foot four inches tall, but I'm as cool as fuck. I've got four days' shore leave a month and everybody look at me!' He lands triumphantly on his feet.

I looked behind me at the building we had left, a huge white tower that disappeared into the sky. Obscured by clouds, a golden glow pulsated from the top of the huge ethereal construction with a deep God-bass rhythm. All around us was horizon. Three 5000cc snow-mobiles with extended front forks and apehanger handlebars sat purring in the snow. Black fumes fluttered out of the chrome exhaust pipes like exotic butterflies. The machines looked like fat steel insects. The rear tank tracks were black and covered in vicious iron studs. The bodywork was decorated with jewelled swastikas and magic symbols. They had double front headlights which supported a polar-bear skull between them. Eerie ice-hogs, a gift from the Sons of the Horned Ones. Ragnar laughed heartily and hugged each of us in turn.

We all cheer and clap. Then Z and I notice Gimpo. He's still up on the balcony and somehow Gimpo doesn't look too pleased with Lars' performance. Up he jumps on to the handrail, stands there fully erect, wobbles but keeps his balance, holding on to nothing but the way below zeros. He makes sure the whole gang are watching then swallow-dives, head first, as if from the top board of the civic swimming pool, fifteen foot up, down into the drift of snow below. We rush forward to make sure he is not dead. But he is up, laughing, knowing he outdid Lars and established his credentials in these northern parts as whatever it is that Gimpo feels it is important for him to be. Z and I feel proud of him. There was no knowing what life-taking lumps of rock and iron contraptions lay lurking in that snow drift that Gimpo landed in. Gimpo is heralded by all as the King of the One Louders.

We tramp up a hill. A gaggle of late-night revellers. Olden's place. A non-descript block of flats. The hooch is passed around. Some mix it with coke, others tomato juice. It obviously kills you. I drink strong black coffee (a rare thing for me) on the settee with Tuna on one side and Olden on the other, *Hooked on Classics* full volume on the stereo, Lars conducting.

Then it's The Moody Blues' 'In Search of the Lost Chord'. Z catches my eye. We know something is falling into place: that Chord has to be found and somehow this is all a clue. We've delivered Elvis to the Pole but now that Chord has to be found.

Gimpo is in the kitchen with Tuna, giggling. Lars confesses to being a Lapp himself; starts talking Lappish; threatens to cast shamanistic spells on the lot of us. Time to go.

*

He presented us with a final parting gift: three objects covered by reindeer hides. He pulled away the first skin. We all drew breath. The frost hurt my lungs. We were stunned. 'Bill, this is yours.' Ragnar made a grand gesture and pointed to the most beautiful thing I'd ever seen: a solid gold chainsaw. It was studded with diamonds and all manner of precious stones. Magical symbols and runes were intricately carved in the engine casing and the handles were covered with ermine. Inlaid with ivory along the blade of the saw, the word 'Lancelot' shimmered in an incredibly ornate Germanic typeface.

'Ragnar!' gasped Bill. 'What can I . . .'

'Say nothing, hero,' replied wise Ragnar, patting Bill on the back.

He removed the second hide. Jade, emeralds, gold and red enamel decorated Gimpo's saw. A huge gold pentangle was emblazoned across the engine casing, its name along the blade: The Gawainsaw. Gimpo picked up the Gawainsaw and stroked the teeth, cutting his finger on the razor-sharp blades. 'This is the saw that beheaded the Baptist,' said Ragnar, seriously.

I was almost pissing myself with anticipation. Ragnar ripped back the last hide. I almost fainted. The other saws were probably the most beautiful things I'd seen in my life, but this, this . . . this had not been made by humans. This was the work of the gods. Vulcan himself must have forged this blade, six feet from mink-covered handles to the tip of its adamantine blade. Platinum and rubies, ebony inlays, fantastic runes and strange magical symbols deliciously caressed the heavenly machine; adorning the casing, a huge black Hakenkreuz, the Nazi swastika. Its name, in a stern Germanic typeface: Parzival. The 'Z' was the largest letter.

My dick erected itself immediately. I was in love, in love with my chainsaw. Why, with this weapon I would be invincible! I turned to Ragnar, speechless.

'There are holsters on the ski-mobiles,' said Ragnar nonchalantly. 'You have your horses, the ski-bikes. These are your swords. You are warriors!'

We shuffled, a little embarrassed.

Ragnar spoke in a stage whisper: 'You are Dambusters, 666 Squadron, ja?'

'Huh?' said Bill.

'A little joke, my friends. Dambusters! Ha ha,' he laughed loudly, slapping me hard on the back.

Outside. Z, Gimpo and me: the Magi triumphant. We are high on a hill. Above, Orion straddles the sky and the friendly Big Dipper helps us find the Pole Star. Below lies the small town sleeping in its long Arctic night. The street lights still burn. Three ships in the harbour. Down there beyond the petrol station we can pick out Valanbo Overnatting. We do our Elvis to the Pole thing one last time before taking the direct route to Valanbo, tumbling down the steep rocky hillside, laughing and shouting. Gimpo has a throw-away camera from somewhere. He takes pictures as I crash down head over heels, kilt a-skirling.

Tears in his eyes, the man Ragnar smiled and pointed to the horizon. 'Follow any ley line,' he said. 'They all lead south.' He smiled cryptically and added, 'The world is safe. You will free the waters.' We mounted our iron steeds and set off home. I glanced over my shoulder. Ragnar, the dwarves and the tower had vanished. Obviously.

Lying in my bunk now. Can't sleep – coffee pumping around me like a dozen lines of speed. Gimpo is snoring and Z, dead (well, hopefully not). I catch up with these notes and wonder at the day's events. *In Search of the Lost Chord* – what a crap record. But somehow tonight it all seems so right. If we were armed with the Lost Chord, Satan wouldn't stand a chance! I had a mate at school called Stuart Hart. He had all the Moody Blues records. Wonder what he's up to now.

CHAPTER TWELVE

Bill the Ripper

Awake. Morning. No hangover. Room full of heat and farts. Off in search of a shower. Hammer banging nails into wood from some-where down below. Shower dries up whilst still covered in soap. 'What about the Baby Jesus?' The voice. Look, dear reader, get a bit more lateral. This journey ain't over yet. Me and my fellow Magi have just got past 'Go'.

Twenty minutes later, Gimpo gone. Me and Z all dressed up and out. Search for breakfast. Blue skies, glorious winter sun. Russian trawler leaves the harbour into the east. Water calm, molten with light. Hooded crow perched on telegraph pole. Three sparrows, feathers fluffed up. Clear, dry, still air. Sunlight on snow strains eyes. Children play. Rafts of eiders bob in the bay.

Gimpo turns up in the car. It seems we left it somewhere. Climb in. Gimpo in charge. Me at one with the world. Wordsworth is the best.

Small modernish hotel in centre of town for breakfast: fried eggs, tomatoes (what the fuck are the lettuce leaves for?), bacon, toast and tea. Gimpo tells us we had arranged with Lars and the lads to meet them here for breakfast; they meet here every morning. Their plan was to take us up on a trip to Nordkapp where we can view some magical islands full of Viking legend and lore.

Memories from last night soak through, bits of loose information. Each spring the Laplanders travel north with their reindeer and get them to swim across the narrow straits that separate Mageroya from the mainland, and for four months the island has a population of 6,000 reindeer. They get everywhere. The Lapps living in their wigwams, drinking themselves senseless whilst their reindeer wander into town, getting stuck in hotel lifts, falling out of second-floor windows, drifting into classrooms full of schoolchildren. Is this true? Don't fuckin' care, but got told it last night and am writing it down anyway.

World War II. The Germans evacuated the island; burned the whole place down 'cept for the church; put the population in a work camp somewhere in the south of Norway. After the war, the population returned to this bare rock of desolation and rebuilt it. Why come back when they didn't need to? There's nothing here. The human spirit. I'm awed. Memory of Olden telling me he was from the south but moved here because the people on Mageroya are the best people in the world. He's maybe right. Each summer the Germans return en masse as holidaymakers to visit Nordkapp, the top of Europe. A kinda John o' Groats vibe for them.

Ten to ten. Lars and the lads have not turned up. Z impatient that we should be heading off to get past the Road of Fear and Tunnel of Doom before darkness falls. Yeah, but I want to see this Viking legend place. We agree to hang on for Lars until 10.30, then if he's not here head up to the north of the island and get back in time for the 12.30 ferry to the mainland. Look about ground floor of hotel. On the walls, prints of Victorian etchings of life on the island, the natives all done up in Lapp clothes – huge fur-lined anoraks with fancy stitching – harpoons in hand, sledges, dogs, whale hunting, church, life. Wish I had some copies of these prints to show you. Pretty good.

Z and I strike up conversation about the relevance of the Lost Chord; reckon now that we have put world peace in motion by placing our portrait of Elvis at the North Pole, we should organize an expedition to find the Lost Chord. Conversation soon gets pretty strange. Maybe we have to find the three separate notes that make up the Lost Chord; to find each in the right order. The ends of the earth, all sorts of feats have to be accomplished – this could take years, a lifetime. Must be worth it.

We order more tea. I notice a stain on the front of my kilt. Scratch my head under my hat. Lars doesn't turn up. We are off.

Gimpo at the wheel and he is trying to drive the Escort like one of the local taxi drivers. Z and I attempt to insist he doesn't. Gimpo argues that it is the safest way to drive on these roads. He compromises. A bit.

We have a local map of the island from the hotel reception. Take the road out of town for Nordkapp. Sky still blue. Road along coast. Sea, a mysterious clear green. Small fish dart in their thousands as one – the Jacques Cousteau effect. Little wooden shacks hung with drying nets, harpoons and other ancient tackle. Landscape untampered by nothing. Snow, ice and black rock. Eiders make me laugh with their friendly sounds – what a lovely duck. Other strange northern birds tease me. I hope to see a seal's head bob up, or a school of whales breaking the brine. Small islands litter the horizon. Everything looks so gently serene. Transient or eternal? Who cares when we have now.

Our snow bikes carried us across the blinding white tundra. We kept close to the ley line, which glowed pale blue in the snow. I chugged steadily on a bottle of clear moonshine. The cold sun, a white disc in the frozen air, kept us company during the fourteen-hour journey.

We glide to a halt; get out of the car. Gimpo suggests a game to play: me and Z should crouch down at the back of the car, grip on to the bumper while he sees how fast he can drive it before we lose our hold. The trouble with Gimpo is that you have to go along with some of his suggestions, however death-defying or illogical, or your manhood is called into question. I mean, if we hadn't agreed with him about playing radio bingo, we would have never hit satori and saved the world. We have a go. It's fun. Yeah, we tumble off, bang our knees and bruise our thighs, but 'Are we not Men?' We have more goes, ice-covered road rushing under our feet, kilt trailing behind. Any loose lumps of rock or ice in our way could throw us off, loosen our grip. Acceleration; fear. He's not going to stop, must be doing about sixty mph. (Well, it feels like that.) We either let go now and survive with a few cracked ribs and a broken ankle, or we die. We let go at the same time; tumble head over heels, specs flying; come to a halt at a large rock at side of road, palm of hand ripped and bleeding, grit in cut. Z in similar state a few yards away. Gimpo reverses car back to us; out of the car and laughing at us. What do they do to squaddies to make them like this? And why the fuck do me and Z go along with it? I'm fuckin' thirty-nine years old for Christ's sake, a responsible grown man with a family. What kind of example am I?

Back in the car and heading to catch the 12.30 ferry. I pick grit from my cut, fret about the stains on my kilt and listen to stories about the Falklands War from Gimpo. He says this place looks like South Georgia. They had sailed there first in the *QE2* (being used as a troop carrier not a cruise liner) before heading over to Goose Green and all the Argie bashing. Did I tell you before that when they were heading down the Atlantic in the *QE2* they, the squaddies, had no idea what sort of place they were going to? South Georgia to Gimpo sounded like it might be near Georgia in the Southern States of America, all Southern belles and peanut plantations. Him and his mates would while away the hours reading Commando comics (kids' adventure combat comics set primarily in the Second World War, full of Tommies taking on the Bosch, Hun, Jerry, Japs and Nips single-handed and winning). Our boys, eh! And, of course, bashing the bishop.

There are a few other travellers on the ferry this time. The voyage is timetabled to take only fifty minutes. The sea is calm. We stand on deck, wave our farewells to the town of Honningsvag, the island of Mageroya and all our friends. We wave goodbye to Elvis Presley, the King of Rock 'n' Roll. We turn to face south, the future; our responsibilities concerning the Lost Chord, making it past the Tunnel of Doom and the Road of Fear before the Arctic night caves in and certain death takes us to her cold bosom.

Back on the mainland, we breeze south along the same road, but in a different lifetime from when we were headed in the opposite direction less than twenty-four hours ago. The southern sky is already turning pinks and golds, flurries of snow skim and tease the road in front of us, light shifts. We stop the car to watch the sun melt behind some far-off mountains.

This road in daylight has, in one sense, lost all of its life-threatening satanic forces in overload fuck-me-we're-about-to-die vibe. But a sort of contradiction to this is that now, in daylight, we can see that the road is in fact far more dangerous than we ever imagined:

two-hundred-yard sheer drops with no crash barriers are not a black, unfocused nightmare illusion; they are a reality. Even Gimpo takes this on board and drives with a lot more consideration for our lives and limbs than he did last night.

Worry that Tuna will forget. Her boss will turn up and dump Elvis in the bin along with what I didn't eat of last night's microwaved chicken.

Black wispy clouds. Distant islands float in Arctic mirages. A sea eagle soars. How the fuck do we finish this book? Z is writing. I wonder what he has got down. What visions are visiting him? I scribble more notes about the thousand shades of pinks, gentle oranges and soft turquoises in the snow, to be edited out later as I have done loads of the same before. I want to write something dramatic, earth-shaking; I want to reveal something that will change the course of history forever; and I just write down the shades of snow. I always want to skim the descriptive bits in books, just get on with the meat and plot. It might all make good writing, but who wants to read about the colour of snow? You want shagging and killing and taking loads of drugs.

> No drugs today.
> The dealer's gone away
> Stolen my dreams.

I sing to the tune of that song by Herman and his Hermits (average age seventeen years and nine months – a fact my sister told me). Start to read some of the notes I have made in previous twenty-four hours; notice a couple of lies. I never kicked over the chair or upturned the table. Must have been me trying to make my emotions seem more animated, make me look tougher and harder.

It's like all that over-emphasis on bad language and ungrammatical writing. At school I was always so bad at spelling, grammar, writing and stuff, and I was never allowed to forget it by my teacher or the other members of the class. When we did spelling or dictation the teacher took great delight in spelling out aloud my flawed attempts at the words in question, much to the hilarity of my comrades. So maybe now, all these years later, I am trying to get my own back. Now that I am in a position to be involved in writing a book, I'm going to write it in a way that I know those teachers would abhor. As much as I have always loved books and the use of strange and wonderful words – from Shakespeare, Milton, the Bible, through to Kerouac, Larkin and Burns – it was made very plain that it was not for me to attempt; and there was no way I was going to be seen attempting it and making an arsehole of myself and failing. So fuck the thesaurus, I'm going to stick to these oft-repeated simple words. To aspire to any more is to aspire to being like the teachers who taught me: bitter, twisted and misanthropic (a word that Z explained to me yesterday) – maybe. Or maybe I'm just trying to wring out your sympathy, win a few votes on the self-effacing ticket.

The Tunnel of Doom has passed by unnoticed.

2.17 p.m. Daylight drains from the sky. A small fishing boat chugs silently in the sea. A light on board illuminates a human soul out there earning a living. Stunted silver birches in a hollow, the first vegetation in what seems like months. A lone figure trudges along the roadside, clutching her shopping bag, momentarily caught in our headlights. Where has she come from? Where is she going? The moon makes its presence felt in the darkest part of the east.

'Oh, to be a classical composer, to capture all of this in a major work or at least a tone poem,' is a thought that drifts in and out before I can give it much thought.

Gimpo lets rip a corker. The radio is on. A Norwegian version of 'Ob la di, Ob la da'. I try to catch hold of the translation of the hook line, 'Life goes on, yeah', but cannot. Next, Michael Jackson singing 'Too Young to Love' – must be from his wilderness years, post-Jackson Five and pre-*Off the Wall*. Mind you, 'Got to Be There', 'Ben' and 'Ain't No Sunshine' were all from that period and they are maybe some of the greatest stuff he has ever done. The vocal performance on 'Ben' is breathtaking.

We stop for meatballs and potatoes in a huge empty hotel restaurant in Lakselv. We are served by a pair of sisters who snigger openly at our appearance. Can't even bring myself to write, 'They laughed at all the greats' with any conviction. Z and I enliven what has been a pretty dull afternoon with debate about Keith Richards' failure to find the Lost Chord; about the four million dollars cash he had offered the Lapp shaman only to be turned down, then on to Oscar Wilde and his mistaking Gimpo for Bosie.

Have I mentioned earlier how Z once had a cartoon published in the *Independent*? It was a drawing of Oscar on the phone. The caption read, 'Oh Bosie, it's me. I've been banged up for sodomy.' Why this should be funny I don't know, but at least once a fortnight while walking down some street I will hear Z's impersonation of Oscar going, 'Oh Bosie, it's me. I've been banged up for sodomy,' in my head, and I will laugh and laugh and laugh.

In the corner of this barren restaurant is a small stage. On the stage is a double bass drum kit, set up in all its pompous glory. On the front skins of the twin bass heads are written the words 'Molten Rock'. A couple of Marshall stacks stand idly by and effects racks await fiddling with. We can only guess at the sound that Molten Rock make. Do they write their own epic rock anthems about life in the Arctic wastes, tapping into their inherited myths and legends, or do they do cover versions of Led Zep's 'Immigrant Song'? Or does it get even sadder by exploring the ZZ Top and Van Halen catalogue for bar bands all around the world?

Z and I get to talking about the tragedy of Rock, and why the word 'sad' keeps taking centre stage. What does all this mean? Then Z wants to know who I think the world's greatest living poet is. He knows I think it's Ted Hughes, and I know he thinks it's William Burroughs, so all this predictably develops into another nature-boy versus the-road-to-excess-leads-to-the-palace-of-wisdom argument. But we find common ground and bond on the fact that both our favourite living poets found a certain weird arty-macho vibe out of the infamous and untimely death of their respective wives. Maybe dead wives are what we need if we are to take the poetry high road.

The conversation loses its focus and we all get lost looking for the bogs. Find them. Have a slash. Back out through an empty, cavernous reception: towering rubber plants, indescribable murals and huge plastic settees. Out through the smoked plate-glass doors. Why is this hotel here? Who stays in it? The questions fade. Gimpo runs back in to pay our bill. I can see the two sisters snigger one last time. The meatballs and mash were good.

Back in the Escort, heading south through the military zone. Darkness, silence. The radio crackles on. Z is in the front twiddling with the dial; must be trying to find the sorely missed Radio Mafion. Radio stations come and go.

The moon. The good moon rises, round and full, casting its silver magic, turning this landscape of certain death into a Disney winter wonderland. The much-mentioned pine trees, heavy with snow, frozen lakes and mountains, all bathed with this luminous lunar light.

Must have drifted into sleep and back. The lights of Karasjok up ahead. Remember me telling you on the way up that this was the capital of Lapland? It's only 5 p.m. but feels like it has already been dark for half the night. We drive around the empty streets looking for action. Most of the buildings are detached wooden houses, set back from the road in largish plots of land, and on each of these plots, amongst the pine trees, stands a wigwam. Each house has its corresponding wigwam. I know you're supposed to call them tepees, but wigwam is a much more beautiful word. No, not beautiful – more lost-continent-of-boyhood.

Now these wigwams, as already noted, are what the Lapps live in over the summer months while following their reindeer. But I do wonder, looking at the substantiality of these houses and the impressive Cherokee pick-up trucks parked up in the driveways, if these wigwams are just for show, just a symbol saying, 'Hey, I've not forgotten my roots' – like me with my kilt; or sticking a statue of Robert the Bruce in the front garden. Cultural solidarity and all that. Whatever the reasons, I like these wigwams there.

No action to be found. We're hoping to find somewhere to be staying for the night, like the cabin we had a couple of days ago. Everywhere seems to be closed down for the winter. We follow signs taking us on the west road out of town. The signs depict a little cabin and a tent. Hopeful. Follow signs off main road and down track. Cabins and campsite in darkness. We're getting desperate. We instinctively know there is no need to take the risks we took the night before: our mission has been accomplished. It would be foolish to let ourselves die of exposure out in the wilderness now.

We get out; check out the cabins. They are unlocked. Bunks but no bedding. This might be the best we can do. Find a fuse box, throw a switch, get the power on: lights, heating. But Gimpo isn't satisfied; he needs something more. He is off looking, searching, pushing at his hidden boundaries. I'm trying to get the cooker going. Z and I are making light of our miserable circumstances. Our Zen-stick Magi bravado is wearing thin.

Gimpo's back, grinning his grin. He claims to have found us our home for the night. We follow like followers do. At the edge of the forest, standing away from the cabins, Gimpo has found a wigwam.

It was twilight when we reached the tepee. It stood alone on the tundra, beside it a large supply of chopped firewood and a dead reindeer supper.

He lifts the flap and we climb inside. Z lights his lighter.

Inside the tepee a circle of stones acted as a rudimentary fireplace. There were plenty of reindeer skins to keep us warm.

It must be about ten foot in diameter at its base and about twelve foot high. In the centre is the remains of what was a large fire, circled with stones; the rest of the floor space is taken up with reindeer skins. Outside it is beginning to snow heavily again, the temperature is obviously plummeting, a wind is beginning to bite.

Z and I have said nothing. Gimpo is insistent that we stay here. I have a serious problem. I may as well be up front about it. I turn to Z: 'Zodiac, you must take responsibility for telling Gimpo we cannot stay in this wigwam for the night.'

'Why?'

'Because, Zodiac, Gimpo's your manager, brother-in-law and close friend.'

'So why does this mean you can't tell him?'

This is word-for-word. Gimpo in the meantime is chuckling at the both of us. Z has let the lighter go out so we are now in complete darkness.

'Look, Zodiac, I am unable to tell Gimpo we can't stay here because, if I do, Gimpo will have proved, unequivocally, that he is more of a man than me. So you have to tell him, thus letting me off my own skewer.'

Maybe the last line isn't word-for-word; maybe I beat about the bush more, but Z knows and fully understands my predicament and has that sort of evil mind which will make me pay for that small-minded, arrogant, twisted pride of mine. Z will turn the skewer all he can. Mind you, the last thing Z wants is for us to spend the night out here in this wigwam, but he so wants me to suffer as my Jack London/Up the Yukon/Call of the Wild type manliness is made to look hollow, fraudulent and soft.

Z doesn't have the same sort of problems about this stuff that I have. Z is more than ready to admit that he would desert from the front line and squeal at the first sight of the thumb screws; where I would have to be the first up and over the trench top when the officer had blown the whistle, the first to be shot down by the Hun's fire, just to make some sort of point.

We're both saved by Gimpo, who makes a convincing argument that we can build a large log fire, cook ourselves a splendid meal and keep the fire going all night long. We readily relent. Plans are hatched.

Into the Escort. Drive the three kilometres or so back to Karasjok. Find a small supermarket that is still open. Gimpo and I stack the basket with provisions for the night while Z studies the comparative proofs of the beers for sale. Turnip, potatoes, bread, a leg of frozen reindeer meat.

Back to wigwam, Gimpo in charge. I fall in behind him. Firewood first. Lucky for us, there's a great stack of logs piled up just outside the wigwam. I clear out the ashes from the previous fire, tear up our Arctic maps for fire lighter, snap kindling to manageable sizes and build the perfect campfire. We soon have an impressive blaze going. Get the logs on. Adrenalin pumps round our veins. We know this is the life. Z starts becoming animated as he is able to warm his hands and feet.

Gimpo soon had a homicidal fire going which threatened our eyeballs and scorched our livers. We hacked the reindeer into small pieces and placed the bloody meat on the fire. The heat was unbearable.

*

We soon learn that to stop the wigwam filling up with smoke and the fire dying down we have to keep the entrance flap open, thus feeding the fire with oxygen and creating an up-draught to take the smoke through the gap at the top. Our faces grin gold in the flickering light. We make up rules, like no boots on the reindeer skin and no pissing in the wigwam. The fire has a solid base of glowing logs. We snuggle in potatoes, onions and chunks of turnip (the big sort – what most people call swede), unwrap the frozen leg of reindeer and lay it across the top of the fire. When it comes to cooking, I like to be in charge.

Gimpo is off into the night. He returns a few minutes later. He's got three or four more reindeer skins. It seems he has found another wigwam that he is raiding. He makes a couple more journeys, returning with further skins. He then sets to organizing the interior design of our wigwam. All draughts, bar the entrance flap, are excluded. We now have enough skins to provide us with good all-round mattresses and blanketing.

We stripped to our by now quite filthy underwear. I passed the moonshine around. The heat and the hooch thawed us inside and out. The meat was soon cooked and we fell upon it like starving wolves, burning our fingers and lips in the process. The orange flames sent spooky shadows across our faces. Gimpo looked positively feral with grease and blood running down his unshaven face. Bill's hair was matted and had grown considerably. We resembled caveless cavemen.

The leg of reindeer sizzles and splutters. The essence of pine, burning reindeer fat and unwashed human bodies makes a heady mixture of aromas. I turn the leg; burn my left hand. Prod the flesh with my purple plastic-handled knife, brought over from my past life. Through the opening at the top, we watch embers rise and glow up into the night air and, way beyond them, we can gaze at the stars. Somewhere a dog is barking at the full moon. The cold seems far away.

We laugh, talk and lie. Gimpo tells tales of Goose Green, sleeping huddled and cold in a hole in the bog; of the one girl on the island who would let herself be shagged by the conquering squaddies; of an officer who . . . Z, of course, makes us laugh with his wise legends of debauchery and sadness. Topics sway and swirl. Poetry descends. We discuss the Lost Chord and the Lapp strip club that we were hoping to find – we'd had these fantasies about meeting up with these three Lapp babes all dressed up in their Lapp gear, out for a good time (of course, they would like nothing better than to come back to our wigwam and entertain us with their Lapp belly dancing and Dance of the Seven Blizzards before servicing our mannish needs); or the wise old Lapp shaman who'd enter our wigwam at the witching hour to tell us that we had been chosen, amongst all men alive, to be the recipients of the ancient secrets.

Out comes the last bottle of Blue Label and the bottle of red wine that Z and Gimpo had purchased as a gift for me somewhere in the dim and distant past. No cork screw. Gimpo is able to push the cork in with his little finger. The wine is the best I have ever tasted. We take turns in gnawing meat from the bone. Our faces drip with grease. No, that description of the meat is not right: on the surface it is burnt, then there is a thin layer of edible stuff, then underneath that it is still frozen solid.

Z recites a poem he has just written, dedicated to a life well spent. We retrieve burnt potatoes, cut them open and remove the delicate white flesh within, savouring each morsel as if it was the highest of delicacies and not a humble spud. I seem to be the only one willing to explore the delights of the turnip's sweet and succulent flesh.

Huddled around the blaze, chugging the moonshine and passing it around, the fiery liquid loosened our tongues and Bill's arse. He was rattling off a continuous rip-snort symphony of quacks, splats and long, slow, gaseous raspberries. Nobody commented; we were accustomed to the Scotsman's spectacular flatulence.

Swig the wine; pass the meat; stare into the flames and spin silently through space.

According to the original plan, The Book should finish when Lars takes the portrait of the King and with all that head-on satori bit. But here we are, and the adventure is unfurling more and more. We get introspective. Yes, Elvis is safely at the Pole and we have been freed to take the next step along the never-ending road to redemption. We talk of how much of the wonderfulness of life we have lost, get corny; how the further we get from the rawness of what we are feeling right now, the further we get from what man must have felt for millennia, stretching way back to the Garden, the tree and its apple. Z talks about life in India – his girlfriend is Indian and he spent last Christmas there visiting her extended family. He is convinced we should make up some reason why we should go on a pilgrimage to India, where life, he assures me, is still lived very much in the raw, and because of that it is far more vital, spiritual, real, vibrant and sexy. All sounds a bit hippyish to me – I hate all that Goa trip bit.

It was Gimpo who initiated the next slice of strangeness, one of his odd screwball sentences arising from nowhere and escalating into vast shibboleths of weirdness.

'What's the worst thing you've ever done?' he asked casually, passing Bill the moonshine. Bill was tight-lipped.

'I once killed a dog,' added the Gimp. Bill and myself gnawed and said nothing. Gimpo continued, 'I don't know why, I just did. I threw it over a waterfall. It drowned.' Why Gimpo felt the need, here at the top of the world, to unburden this ancient secret, I've no idea; but it opened a truly odd can of worms, that's for sure.

The fire roars.

A slow rumble from Bill's guts, followed by probably the foulest fart I've ever smelt in my life. It curled around the small tepee like some evil child-eating demon from the Old Testament. 'Hmmm.' It was Bill. He looked nervous, beads of sweat on his top lip. 'I, I, yes, it's all coming back to me now. 1888, the East End of London – Hawksmoor's Christchurch, Aldgate, Whitechapel. Yes, White-chapel, one of the most evil places in Victorian England. All those skulking denizens of that modern Gomorrah living under the shadow of fear, the fear of me, me and my pretty blades . . .'

Somehow we remember it's November the fifth, Guy Fawkes' night.

*

'Huh?' interjected the Gimp, confused by Bill's suddenly pompous tone.

'Aye, Gimpo. 1888, you heard me correctly, lad. It was 1888, November the fifth to be precise.' Bill noticed Gimpo's confused expression and clarified the nature of his soliloquy. 'Walt Whitman, you chump – leaves of grass, every atom of my body, that sort of thing, you know.'

This is the bonfire night I will remember above all others.

'Oh yeah, right,' answered Gimpo, somewhat condescendingly. Gimpo understood that the moonshine was weaving its dubious magic and had greased the Scotsman through the portals of his own unique temple of eldritch weirdness.

The fire danced and crackled, warming our bones. Stinker Drummond continued his tale. He raised his left cheek and forced an angry one. He was getting excited.

'So much blood, so much blood. Who would have thought the cunt would have had so much blood,' he misquoted Shakespeare and continued. '13, room 13, Miller's Court. A foul night in a foul city. Mary Jane Kelly, Scabby Mary as she was commonly known, had made a rendezvous for 2.30 a.m. at her squalid little flat. She wove through the labyrinth of malodorous back streets, avoiding the sprawled drunks and stepping over the piles of human ordure and vomit. She didn't usually work this late, but the tall Scottish gentleman had offered her a handsome sum for her services. Her five-year-old daughter needed new shoes and, after allowing for Mary's usual drink, there would be just enough left from her fee to buy little Jemima some pretty new boots. Mary sang to herself drunkenly as she entered the courtyard, "Only a Violet I Picked from my Mother's Grave", a popular song of the time.

'The whore didn't see me. I was standing in the shadows clutching my doctor's bag and wearing a top hat. I peered into my bag. The gaslight shone brightly on my fine collection of steel. I felt myself stiffen and followed her up some stairs. The bitch turned towards me. "Oh, there you are, sir. You startled me. Well, come on in. I hope you'll be comfortable."

'The room was disgusting – twelve feet square and it stank of sperm and onions, of rat shit and dirty linen. A single, soiled bed and bedside table, a small fireplace, a cheap print of *The Fisherman's Wife* hung above the bed. "Now, what was it you wanted sir? Bumhole through the knickers, wasn't it? Good grief sir, I larfed when I heard that one. No one's ever wanted to suck old Mary's bumhole through the knickers before. Most unusual, most unus . . ."

'The cunt didn't have time to finish. "Suck on this," I shouted. My blade arced through the twat-scented atmosphere of 13, Miller's Court, blue sparks of lustmort cracking from its razor edge. It sliced clean through her throat, the handle jarring my wrist as it scraped across the bones of her neck. A great spurt of black blood fountained across the room and splattered against the wall as she fell backwards on to the bed, legs akimbo, displaying her soiled underwear – she had shat herself. I thought of the horrible corpse-like drawings of whores by Egon Schiele – that's what she looked like, that's how I felt.

' "She is just a whore with a stinking womb and foul, milky, lactating dugs. Fucking whore slagbag vampire!" I shouted, stabbing my flensing knife into her left cheek.

'The blood made a crimson halo which spread around her head on the grey bed sheets. I looked into her dead eyes. By now covered in a light sweat, I noticed a chill coming through a broken window. The fire was getting low so I undressed the whore and burned her clothes to generate some heat. I removed the small frying pan from my leather doctor's bag and placed it by the fire.

'Yes, the eyes – why, only a minute ago they had reflected what I had come here looking for, what I sought in my incessant divine mission to rid the world of these creatures, these sucking vampires who drain the life from men, make us weak, mock us, shame us, spend our money, steal our sperm. Here, amongst the rat shit, dirty bed sheets, amongst the fart-dust and lust, amongst the beetles and venereal lice, I saw it in her cankerous eyes. Fear. Fear dancing amongst the reflected yellow flames of the fire. Just before the knife ended her suffering, when her slash of a mouth opened showing me the red of her insides, her fat wobbling tongue, the ribbed roof all wet and shiny, the caried teeth. "Oh my God!" she had gasped, "it's you, Bill the Ripper!"

'"Have a cigar," I laughed, just before the knife hit bone.

'I closed the curtain and knelt down by the side of the dripping bed. Tonight there was no need to rush – I had all the time in hell. I checked my pocket watch and lit a cigar.' Bill giggled and paused.

'Go on,' I said, fascinated by this grim secret history of my Scottish pal. Gimps farted excitedly and took a swig of the moonshine. I noticed he had tented his reindeer skin. Bill took the bottle from Gimpo, took a long chug and, wiping the excess from his chin with the back of his hand, continued. 'Yes – where was I?'

'You'd just hit bone,' said Gimpo, shuffling away beneath the flayed hide.

'Yes – and then I tidied up the room. I needed plenty of space for my work. I put a little firewood on to the fire, checked my watch again and then removed the skin from the whore's face. Two neat incisions under the eyes, sliced down beneath the chin and her flesh came off like a rubber mask. Her skull smiled at me – my pretty little friend had started to get the joke. I tossed the soggy mask on to the fire – no need to make any unnecessary mess; after all, someone at some time was going to have to clean this little lot up. I may be a homicidal maniac, but at least I'm a considerate homicidal maniac.

'Her eyes continued to look at me from the gristle and strings of the sockets. It disturbed me. I remembered when I was with the army in India. A wise thuggee told me that he always removed the eyes from his victims to blind their ghosts, thus preventing them from haunting their killer. Good thinking! I ruined both eyes with my knife and tossed the gristle in the fire.

'My attempts at keeping the place tidy were starting to become a little futile. The cunt's blood was all over the fucking place – a real mess.' Bill giggled and took a swig of the moonshine. 'A real fucking mess.

'I lopped off her fat tits. My ultra-sharp blade cut through the fat and milk ducts of the bitch's mammary glands as easily as if I were cutting through a hunk of warm butter. They felt soggy and jiggled in my hands. I licked one of the nipples. It tasted dusty and old, like sour milk and dirt. The bitch obviously hadn't bathed for months. I wrinkled my nose in disgust. I placed one – her left one, I think it was – beneath her head like a pillow; the other I placed on the table.

The reason I placed one of the breasts beneath her head is a Masonic secret and, I'm afraid, I can't reveal its significance.

'The two gaping wounds where her breasts had once been looked quite beautiful, like two terrible giant poppies. The fire was really blazing now. A red steam rose around the room like smoke. I was in hell. I was enjoying myself in the purifying flame.

'The smell, however, was not pleasant – blood and shit never are. I opened up her guts and held my nose. The overpowering smell of jellied eels, the whore's last meal, nearly knocked me out.' Bill shook his head at the memory and let fly a noisy rat from its drainpipe.

I grabbed the moonshine and took a deep draught. Bill's boy's own tale was starting to make me come over all funny. 'Carry on, Bill,' urged Gimpo. The familiar halo of blowflies had appeared around his head again and his expression was surfing feral dimensions.

'Yes, yes, all right. Well, when I had become accustomed to the awful fish odour, I got down to business: a large gash stretching from her ruined abdomen right up to between where her tits used to be. I opened her up like a book. Her ribs and innards shone in the firelight, steam rose from her guts.

'Well, to be honest, I lost it a bit here – indulged myself somewhat.' Bill tittered and continued. 'I removed my machete from the doctor's bag and hacked away at the ribcage, smashing through the bone and helping myself to a handful of guts, which I threw around the room. I draped all sixty feet of her intestines on the picture rail. It was nearly Christmas and I thought it added a nice festive touch, like paper chains. I placed the heart and the liver on the table in case I got peckish later – I could fry them in the pan.

'I was feeling a peculiar elation, and for some strange reason I proceeded to perform a little jig around the room. It occurred to me that my friend Mary might like to join me. I lifted her from the bed, held her messy body close to mine, and we danced a vigorous waltz. Such an intensity I had never – even during my previous murders – felt before. It was as if I had somehow purified this fallen creature, this woman of the night. I had returned her to the innocence she knew before birth. Innocence. Death. Innocence, birth, death . . . yes, that's it,' Bill meandered. He was rocking autistically.

Suddenly his mood switched and he angrily resumed his tale. 'I carved up her thighs like Parma ham and took the pieces back to my room. I like to eat the thigh meat with melon, raw, in the Italian manner! The place looked terrible, but at least there was one less female on the planet, one less whore in Emily Pankhurst's evil army!' Bill paused for breath and continued more calmly. 'I felt quite pleased with myself. My appetite seemed to have evaporated though, so I left the heart and liver on the table and, checking that I hadn't left anything, quickly departed.' He looked up and smiled, shrugged his shoulders. 'I'm a funny monkey, what can I say?'

Conversation becomes more sporadic.

I decided that the two dead newspaper delivery boys underneath the floorboards back home paled a bit compared to Bill's confession, so I decided to keep that little story for another day.

We bury ourselves deep beneath mounds of reindeer skins. The occasional log gets tossed on the fire landing with a thud and another shower of embers lifts up through the smoke-hole, glowing into the far-off yonder.

Gimpo gathered his skins about him and tried to sleep. I finished the moonshine and decided to do likewise.

Sleep welcomes me. Through the night I occasionally drift back into consciousness. It is at times like this that the waking hopes and fears mix freely with the dreams of sleep and the unconscious can exchange thoughts with the rational world.

I slept fitfully for a few hours. My dreams were of troubled hostile landscapes and strange creatures. A hideous woman with painted breasts and a bloody mouth dressed like a prostitute slunk across my dreamscape; severed heads dangled from her suspender belt and she was drunk on the blood of saints. Men called her Blasphemy. She danced lasciviously, laughed cruelly and faded to red.

*

Elvis keeps coming back. Something has changed; something has been locked away; something has been opened up: Elvis – past, present and future. I've held on to my innocent experience of Elvis throughout my cynical years, kept it untarnished by all the knowingness that has surrounded me and been part of me. Something has happened. In the handing over of our icon to Lars to hang in his Lighthouse at the Top of the World I was able to let something go; but in doing so I may have got a whole lot back.

There was a moment in my life which I alluded to earlier when I was going on about Elvis: at the age of seventeen, I was visited with the realization of what I wanted to be when I grew up. I was in this greasers' café in Cromer, on the Norfolk coast. I'd put two bob in the jukebox, enough for three selections. The first two were 'Green Manalishi' and 'Oh Well' (I was a big Peter Green fan). The third choice was a random one – I just pressed a couple of buttons to see which track came up. I watched the barrel of records crank round then shudder to a standstill. The arm lifted up to make its selection but, before it had pulled the disc out and flipped it on its side, I could feel, in the pit of my stomach, a brief epiphany coming on. The random seven-inch piece of plastic landed on the turntable. The needle found its groove. No intro. The voice came banging in, 'You ain't nothin' but a hound dog . . . And you ain't no friend of mine.'

The epiphany hit hard. It was a big one. There was nothing I wanted more out of life than to be the very essence of that record. It wasn't that I wanted to be Elvis or to be the writer of the song, or the guitarist on the session or the producer or the A&R man, or even Colonel Tom Parker himself. No, it was something beyond all of those things. Something right at the centre of the record's being is what I longed to become part of. At the time I thought it was maybe the black plastic that contained the true essence. I tried not to give this notion or desire too much thought – not the sort of thing you bring up with a career adviser.

But the notion didn't go away, and over the years I got closer and closer, bit by bit, to that thing that lay at the heart of that record. There was nothing I could do to stop myself. This may explain what seems a rather unfocused voyage through the world of Rock 'n' Roll.

No, I never wanted a career in a rock band, never wanted to strut my stuff, never wanted to be a manager, a singer, a producer, a publisher, a songwriter, an A&R man, a record mogul or even an outsider maverick. No, I was just trying to get to touch, to become at one with the pure essence that lay at the very heart of that record.

Working with Jimmy, I knew I was getting closer. We both shared a need not to fulfil any of the previously defined roles of what a person working in pop music should be; we shared an experience and understanding of a wide range of music; we had a knowing overview of the industry we were in; we were both old enough not to need peer-group pressure to keep us bound within any one confining genre of music; and both infantile and shallow enough to believe in and be swayed by whatever we heard on the radio or in a club that very day to dictate our direction. We were getting nearer and nearer all the time.

Then, at some point in 1991, we started working on our final record, 'America: What Time is Love?' A previous release, '3 a.m. Eternal', was riding high in the American Top Ten, we'd had No. Ones all around the world, our confidence was running over. We put everything we had into the making of 'America: What Time is Love?'; dug as deep as we could go, drew on every trick we knew, sampled the tunes that God whistled whilst creating new universes, used the toughest breakbeats Tony 'Moody Boy' Thorpe could deliver. Then, while we were nearing the end and Spike, the mix engineer, was fine-tuning the delays, it happened: we were there. It may have only lasted for ten minutes at the most, but for those ten minutes I was part of whatever it was that lay at the heart of 'Hound Dog' by Elvis Presley.

For twenty-one years I had been reaching for that thing, and that was it. And it was over. It slipped away. That didn't matter, these things are not supposed to last. The eternal found in the transient; the transient magnifying the eternal. But it takes some time to come to terms with what you may have gone through. Although you know it's over and it no longer matters, it doesn't all disappear in a puff of smoke. All those things that have built up around your core and define you to the world and to yourself are still there. You still carry on doing the things you have done.

Have I already mentioned about me wanting to chop off my hand live on stage and throw it into the massed ranks of the music business live on prime-time TV at the 1992 Brit Awards; about me ending up on top of the Pyramid of the Sun at Teotihuacan in Mexico, staring up at the New World, and the snake in the grass leaving my body after crossing the Rio Grande? But it was from that ten minutes at the end of me and Jimmy making 'America: What Time is Love?' that everything began to spiral out of control: the focus had gone; the end had been achieved. Jimmy and I had loads of other things we thought we wanted to do: massive world tour, multi-bulti-million selling follow-up to the *White Room* album, every track an international No. One and all that stuff.

Then after Jimmy and I had officially and rationally been able to bring it all to a close, delete our back catalogue and turn out the light, Z and I had started our correspondence. For a long time I had been fascinated by the idea of letters collected across the ages, countries and seas. It had an air of something ancient and honourable; also something out of control, where everything is up for grabs, everything at stake. Through these letters, Z and I tore each other apart and built each other up. They were written at a furious rate – as many as five or six a day would be sent; uncontrollable drunken rants, admissions of the most despicable deeds, egos out in the open pumping blood from their open wounds. And through these letters rose Elvis and this journey, neither of us defining what the journey was for or what either of us as individuals would get out of it.

If I've said any of this before I don't give a shit, 'cause that 'best red wine in the world' is still carousing round my veins. The firelight is bright enough for me to write and the other two are asleep and I feel the need to say it again. My thumb is aching from gripping my pencil too tightly. Of course we gave our reasons: saving the world, the Baby Jesus inside and any number of half a dozen half-baked ideas, all worth a journey to the furthest star in their own right. But has the real reason been for me to put to rest what the past twenty-one years have been about and get on with the remains of my life? Should The Book stop at the point that Lars took possession of the portrait of the King, heavy with all its loaded symbolism; or should it end now, as the embers glow, Gimpo snores, Z turns in his sleep and that far-away dog still barks at the moon? I put a couple more logs on the fire, prepare to bed down again amongst the reindeer skins and hope to get a couple more hours' sleep before dawn.

I woke at dawn, afraid. Bill, I was relieved to see, had packed away his grim memories and was boiling water in a tin pan on the fire. Gimpo was outside preparing more reindeer steaks.

We ate a substantial breakfast of burnt reindeer and washed it down with hot beer. We kick-started our bikes and pointed them towards the world.

Drummond's Log: Friday 6 November 1992

CHAPTER THIRTEEN

The Secret of the Lost Chord Revealed

Awake with the dawn and the cold and the sound of a car engine at close quarters. My bladder is bursting. The others are still asleep. Mild paranoia about car engine at close quarters.

Climb out from under the pile of reindeer skins and clamber through wigwam entrance. A middle-aged man is walking towards me. Behind him is a pick-up truck, its engine still running. I notice how beautiful the diesel exhaust fumes look rising through the clear, clean air. The man's face contains a smile – no obvious outward signs of malice towards me for trespassing on his property. He stretches out his arm. We shake hands. Without anything being said on my part, he speaks in a heavily accented English to ask if we are all right. He tells me we could have slept in one of the cabins – they leave them unlocked through the winter in case any travellers turn up needing a place to sleep for the night; his home is on the opposite side of the valley and his wife saw the slender plume of smoke rising from where they knew the tepee was and felt they should check to see if whoever it was was OK. We are. I try to offer to pay something but he is having none of it. I get the feeling he is rather impressed with our hardiness (or that's what I like to think). I wonder at the man's innate goodness, but acknowledge how all that would disappear if it was taken advantage of by packs of Brits abroad. He leaves.

Gimpo staggers out of the wigwam followed by Z. Nothing much is said and we are all looking pretty much the worse for wear. But we done it: we slept out in 19° below zero (a fact we learnt later). Now, that's pretty tough, that is something to tell the grandchildren.

Fuck the hit records, we slept out in a wigwam in the depths of the Arctic winter. Beat that, Martin Amis. We take it in turns to piss on the dying embers. The hisses and the steam billow up. We do our Boy Scout best to leave the place as we found it.

Back into Karasjok. No café open for breakfast. We stare through the plate-glass window of a closed-for-winter tourist centre. They are selling all the Lapp gear: funny four-pointed hats, embroidered fur boots with the toes curled up – all the stuff. I suppose the arsehole in me and Z wants to get the whole rig-out so we can dress up in it, pose and do a Literary Arseholes photo session.

Back in the Escort and heading south. We want to make Rovani-emi by nightfall so we can get the overnight train back down to Helsinki.

Our throbbing iron carried us through the white wasteland for three days and three nights with only the sun and stars for company. I had no alcohol, so I drifted back to some version of reality fairly quickly. The marshmallow snow became colder. I threw another reindeer skin across my shoulders and continued driving. For some strange reason I kept getting the feeling that there was a passenger riding pillion. My mind, although pretty much sober now, kept wandering. I would have conversations with a gentle voice that seemed to whisper behind my left ear. I would turn around, convinced there was someone there, but there would just be snow. There was something familiar about this phenomenon, but I couldn't quite place it. It reminded me of the world reflected in soap bubbles, of dreamfish swimming in an enchanted childhood pool.

As the powerful engine ploughed its way across the frozen tundra something warm flooded my consciousness, uninvited by maudlin shots of Pentangle vodka. That gentle voice. I remembered this voice. As a child I believed it was God. Here on the tundra, sober for the first time in over twenty years, I believed it was God once more. It was no big deal, I'd half expected the Holy spook to show up for some time. I gunned the accelerator and took the lead.

After a few hours God's gentle voice was really getting on my tits. I needed a drink – I figured that was the only way to get this sad bastard off of my fucking back. I don't know about higher powers and all that shit, but after four hours of the Holy creep's sanctimonious whingeing I needed to get in touch with my lower power, pronto.

Cross border into Finland at Karigasniemi.

Fortunately we'd arrived at a small Lapp town, a sort of crossroads with a few wooden cabins and a saloon on the corner.

We are drawn back to the café we had visited only two days previously, hoping to refuel our bodies before the long drive south.

I wandered into the saloon and ordered a bottle of cowboy whisky and three beers. I sank the beers and cracked open the whisky.

Nothing much had improved in what they had on offer. Don't their truck drivers expect better? Tepid tea and dried-out factory-produced pastries is yet again not what I need.

Half-way down the bottle God decided to take a hike and his bad pal Lucifer took up his regular position behind my right ear. 'Welcome back, cunt,' I slurred to myself. That old demon-fire warmed up my guts, and images of burning churches and raped nuns flickered across the screen of my inner cinema. I razzled off a real brimstoner, stinking the bar up real good.

Now the three of us are not on some spiritual downward spiral, but we all could do with a hot bath and a good square meal, and I now have to admit to another lie: the reindeer leg we had for our meal was, in fact, a leg of lamb, and we were unable to eat very much of it at all and the cooking of it was pretty much a failure. I suppose a leg of reindeer would be far too large to cook in the way I described, but it did sound so much more impressive.

Some locals chat. Laplanders, high cheek-boned, looking like they are each able to trace a straight ancestral line back to the Mongol hordes. Well, I suppose not, but they don't look like us or any other European.

*

Bill and Gimpo looked like zombies. We hadn't slept for three nights. Gimpo was asking the in-bred-looking barman if there were any rooms in town. No luck. 'Maybe the next town,' offered the weird-looking Lapp. We sat at a table next to a big log fire and worked on our alcohol. After a while I noticed a tall, skinny guy.

One of them is, strangely enough, tall and slim; early forties, short dark hair and a bit of a beat beard. He's got the intellectual Russian-dissident look. His hollow cheeks and gaunt frame give away the years he must have spent in the labour camps. His black eyes dart in a nervous way.

He was staring at the fire. The flames danced in his black eyes. He had a three-day beard and stank of blood. He said nothing. I noticed that he kept taking surreptitious looks at the three of us.

He keeps catching our gaze.

He was starting to make me feel uneasy. Bill and Gimpo must have felt the same way, because without saying a word, we all stood up and decided to leave. The spooky guy just carried on staring into the fire. Something about his eyes bothered me: they looked like they had seen too much. Just as we reached the saloon door a quiet voice like rats in a cellar skittered across the room.

'Excuse me.' I turned round.

'Hello, my name is Martti. Would you like to have a lift to Helsinki late tonight? I have a good Siberian car: a Lada.' Word-for-word, and it's all a bit much to take in at once. The Lada being described as a good Siberian car is the bit that strikes me most to begin with. For the past few years we have been so persuaded by whoever it is that makes these persuasions that the Lada is the ultimate joke car that for it to be pre-sented as anything but causes a certain amount of culture shock. None of us are able to answer him so he develops his theme. 'Yes, the Lada is built in Siberia to withstand Arctic conditions, that is why it is so good on the roads here. In fact, it is the best car for here.'

These stilted statements are still word-for-word. His English is confident, but I'm not too sure what Volvo would have to say about his judgement. Z and Gimpo seem to be still uncertain as to how we should react to our new-found acquaintance, so I explain we have our own hired Escort, but I thank him for his offer.

He beckoned us to his table and bought a round of drinks. 'I know of the Chord,' he said. A grand piano dropped from the sky and brained me.

'The Lost Chord?' spluttered Bill, choking on his beer. I had completely forgotten about this mystery. That terrible night at Oscar's bar, the mouldering Oscar, Keith Richards, the bad breath, the hideous evisceration Gimpo had performed on the supernatural remains of the legendary literary bumboy – it all came flooding back. Every atom of my body screamed at me to run, but Bill was having none of it. He gripped the thin man's arm, beseeching him to reveal what he knew.

'First,' announced our strange companion, 'we see where they catch the reindeer.'

'Do you want to see how they catch reindeer?' Another unexpected question.

It sounded like a riddle, some profound Arctic wisdom to be unravelled.

Z and Gimpo are looking negative. 'Who the fuck is this nutter?' might be the thought they share. Gimpo mutters something about the train we have to catch in Rovaniemi.

'It's only eight kilometres from here.'

'Come!' The thin man got to his feet. 'Follow me. It is not far.' We followed him outside. He saddled up his reindeer and set off into the forest at a steady trot.

Are we not Zen Masters? Is not this an unrefusable invitation to go boldly with the mystic flow? Martti carries on talking at us without expecting much back. It seems we have agreed to follow, to find out how they catch the reindeer, but first he must put up his poster in the shop across the street. Martti, as it turns out, is an intellectual; a Lapp native of these parts who headed south to Helsinki to follow his academic calling, but right now he is back home and tonight he is giving a classical guitar recital in the local church and, after that concert, he is driving the 837 kilometres back to the capital.

Z looks at me. 'He's a shaman. He knows the Lost Chord. We must get him to reveal it to us.' Now although Z and I both know that this is a joke, we also know that what Z is saying is the irrefutable truth. I don't think either of us believed that we would have the Lost Chord revealed to us so early in our search.

Martti returns from sticking up his posters for this evening's recital and beckons to us to follow his Lada the eight kilometres. We follow him like good Zen Masters do.

We kicked our bikes into second gear and followed slowly. The man left the main road and took us into a labyrinth of unmarked paths deep into the frosted pines. A light powder snow was falling, covering us in white dust.

The day is looking fine – high wispy clouds and low, low temperatures. Martti pulls up his Lada outside the white church I had passed comment on some time in the past to pin a poster on the notice board. He is leaving it a bit late to publicize his recital. Is there a big following in these Lapp parts for the languid Mediterranean works of classical guitar composers? We follow on, out of town, the road south. Conversation in the Escort turns from the Lost Chord to 'Are we being drawn into some horrendous plot involving bestial shamanistic black magic, culminating in our own ritualistic slaughter?' Ever seen *The Wicker Man*? Yeah? Well then, you'll get where our paranoia is coming from.

We drove steadily for hours. The orange sun hung low in the sky; the flickering borealis painted gentle swirls across the snow. I could hear the staccato shrieks of unidentifiable animals from deep inside the woods.

About four kilometres out of town and the Lada in front turns off down a track to the left. Follow on; bump and skid. The landscape is empty: large rounded hills blindingly white, a vivid blue sky reaching all the way over, no animal or vegetable life. The track twists and turns for three kilometres or so; up ahead it disappears around the shoulder of a hill. In the sky, circling above an unseen destination, are a number of large birds. Corny, but fact. Our almost forgotten Zen sticks are at the ready to ward off any evil. We round the hill.

At last we came to the far side of the pine forest.

A couple of hundred yards in front of us is our destination.

We drove on slowly, and eventually small figures appeared on the horizon. As we drew closer I saw they were deer, thousands of them. They seemed to be in some kind of pen, tended by small men dressed in yellow underpants and yellow wellington boots.

As we draw near we become fully aware of the horror of the open-air charnel house that we are about to enter. We pull up.

There is no way I have the narrative powers to describe the sights, sounds and smells that confront our senses. Best I just list them and let you slot your own adjectives in:

1. A lake of blood, thirty feet in diameter, dark crimson against the snow-white landscape.

A vast lake of blood. The deep crimson reflected the orange sunlight. It was strangely beautiful. The red blood on the pure white snow evoked all manner of religious imagery deep within me: holy wine and the communion wafer. The Saviour and his army of martyred saints sang amongst the symbolism. Tiny epiphanies started rolling down my genetic memory circuits bringing a religious tear to my cheek, where it froze.

2. A pile of severed reindeer heads, about ten feet high, eyes open, eyelashes that Bambi would kill for.

3. A stack of the lower half of the reindeer legs: the shin and the hoof. The stack is no higher than four feet.

4. A mound of intestines, offal and other assorted innards.

5. Three carcasses strung up from timber gallows, heads hung down, dripping blood from nostrils, antlers just touching the ground. Blood is trickling through the snow, these trickles banding together to form a rivulet leading to the afore-mentioned lake.

Around this lake of terrible beauty, crucified reindeer hung splayed on large Saint Andrew's crosses made from the local pine trees. Their bellies had been opened and the viscera tumbled gracefully to the pristine snow. The slaughtered animals resembled fantastic caskets of jewels: the liver and kidneys looked like large, wet rubies. Dancing stars of light glistened on purple intestines, all manner of bright colours flickered inside the splayed deer: sparkling yellows, sensual purples, crimson.

There was nothing sadistic in this slaughter. In fact, there was an intensely spiritual feeling to the whole scene, as if we were in a giant open-air cathedral. The steam rising from the blood and the animals' insides was reminiscent of incense in Catholic churches.

6. Rough-hewn wooden pens. The nearest to the gallows is about fifteen foot distance. It contains twenty-six live reindeer. They circle the inner circumference of the pen, single file, in an anti-clockwise direction. Fawns follow mothers. None make a sound. Round and round they go. A large male crowned with proud antlers attempts to keep order in his herd.

7. Three male Lapps all dressed head to foot in bright orange rubber aprons, waterproof overalls and waders. In their hands they clutch the tools of their trade. Their aprons are covered in blood. They grin at us as we approach.

The bearing of the small Lapp men dressed in yellow reminded me of holy men. They wore serene looks on their faces and recited some form of prayer before cleanly cutting the deer's throats. There was a tangible, tender bond between the men and the animals. The deer were very calm: no squeals or wide-eyed fear were evident here. They acquiesced willingly to the slaughter.

*

What does one say? What does one feel? Why on earth is God showing us this? Now I'm going to get confused here; or is it confusing?

Have you ever read *The Golden Bough* by Sir James Frazer? You can dip in anywhere and are likely to come out with a jewel of wisdom that reveals something about the condition of man, man trying to make sense of his place in creation and have some control over it. And why this book comes to mind as we Three Kings stand here staring across the lake of blood at the three Laplanders dripping death and the three empty gallows behind them is . . .

Well, maybe I have read about all of this somewhere in *The Golden Bough*. Or maybe, if I haven't, he should have written it. In one chapter, 'The Killing of the Divine King', he kicks into how past civilizations developed traditions, constitutions, religions in which kings served for a fixed term – as little as three years in one of the pre-Columbian Aztec-type Indian societies, where, some time around the age of puberty, a boy was chosen by the people and high priests. For a king to be truly a king, he must have divine right; without it, he is just another bloke, and that's no good 'cause blokes get things wrong.

The boy had to be beautiful in figure, fair of face, with a strong and healthy constitution. At the age of eighteen he became venerated as a living god-king and for the next three years toured the land being worshipped by all the people, whose prayers and thanksgiving were focused upon this young and beautiful man-child. In exchange, his every appetite was sated: young virgin brides-to-be were brought to him by their proud fathers so he could honour their virgin wombs with his deified seed before the girls entered matrimonial status with the local lads. He lived a life of splendour, opulence and indulgence. At the end of the three years, the high priests, with much pomp and circumstance, marched the lucky lad into a little house at the top of the pyramid and there chopped off his head with their ceremonial implements. They took his dismembered head out to display it to all the thousands of people who had gathered around the base of the pyramid for the show; then the priests proceeded to cut up the rest of his body into as many bits as they could and all the people got a morsel of flesh to savour. Next, the new young and beautiful eighteen-year-old lad was deified.

I can't recall all the facts, and the ones I have reported may not be totally correct, but I hope you get the picture. When I first read this passage, I was struck by its similarities with the pop-star system we have had for the past four decades, although the Incas had it all worked out in a far more refined way and enshrined it in holy law.

The thing they did best was the ceremonial execution. If only pop music could somehow clearly dispatch yesterday's pop stars so they wouldn't have to make their lives miserable by trying to kick-start their careers again, punishing themselves and those around them in the process. Imagine how amazing it would have been to have seen Jimi Hendrix or Jim Morrison at the height of their powers knowing that within a finite period, not more than three years thence, they would be dead. It would have bestowed on them, during their life-time, a double-top deity which, in fact, was granted only after their deaths.

The only thing that could have ever tempted me back into pop management would have been the reins on an indisputable talent who was willing to sacrifice himself live on stage at a given time within the not-too-distant future. At the final concert our indisputable talent would, before topping himself, introduce to the world his successor, who would have a three-year career before repeating the same ceremony. There would be world-wide pandemonium, hysteria like The Beatles never saw. Each and everything said by these young men during their short careers would be taken to be ultimate words of wisdom such as fall only from the lips of those that die young. And of course I, as the manager (read high priest in Incan times), would be able to exert considerable influence on the culture of the times.

'Basically, what's killing Rock 'n' Roll these days is there's not enough death any more,' a voice.

'Rock 'n' Roll deaths, how passé! Or are you being nostalgic for when Rock had some broader cultural importance?' another voice.

None of the above diversions alter the reality of the blood lake and waiting gallows before us. What I mean to say is, having delved into *The Golden Bough* over the years (and certain passages have haunted my dreams) we are now confronted with a situation that my fevered mind interprets thus: 'As the Magi of these latter days, we have fulfilled our function of laying to rest the primeval spirit of Rock 'n' Roll. We must now be ritually slaughtered so that our blood can feed the earth and the spirit can once again rise into a new shape, a new form, a new dimension.'

Well, that's what I thought. What in fact happens is that Martti steps forward from his Lada, shakes hands with the three working Lapps; some dialogue is exchanged. The men smile in our direction and proudly show us round their place of work.

As far as the eye could see, animal skins were spread over the ground and pinned to trees; small birds picked the flesh clean. Every part of the deer was used for something: the flesh for food, the horns and hooves for knife handles and buttons, the hide for clothing and footwear.

Our tall guide introduced us to one of the men. He grinned, rubbed the blood from his hand on to his yellow underpants and shook hands with each of us, welcoming us in his own language. A small boy of about ten years of age, also dressed in the yellow underpants and boots, ran up to us holding a tray with four cups of steaming broth. We accepted gratefully and sipped the hot blood soup.

What interpretation Z will put on all this I shudder to think.

I wandered around the lake for a while, muttering passages from the King James – Ecclesiastes, I think it was. I remembered that as a child I once found the body of a dead fox in a small copse near where I lived, and each day for that whole summer I would visit its decaying corpse, which vanished completely within six months. I loved the way it seemed to melt into the ground, the grass growing through its white ribcage, its skull sinking into the earth. It all seemed like magic. One day I saw a bird pick a worm from where the fox had melted and in my own ten-year-old way I understood the concept of reincarnation. Something of that ten-year-old's reverie came back to me as I stared at the lake of blood and the beautiful innards of the slaughtered deer.

I returned to the small shack at the centre of the camp. The men, about seven of them, were having their lunch of fried reindeer meat and blood soup.

One of the workers is a cousin of Martti's. It is explained to us that although the reindeer live completely undomesticated lives on land that is held in common by all the Lapp people, each animal carries the brand of its owner; once a year the herds are rounded up, the young kids are branded and a number of each herd are slaughtered; a Lapp's wealth is measured by the number of reindeer he owns. The part of us that cries at Bambi is happy to be told that the herd of twenty-six circling in the anti-clockwise death march is, in fact, not for the knife: they are only there so the kids can be branded.

Once over the initial shock and safe in the knowledge we are not to be made human sacrifices for the greater good of mankind, we kinda get to like the place. In fact, we love it. We learn that each and every part of the reindeer carcass is put to good use and that these people's lives revolve around the life of their reindeer. Z picks up one of the shin bones with hoof as a keepsake. I contemplate taking a head complete with antlers and dripping blood as a gift for Jimmy but think better of it.

We are soon frozen, and although Gimpo wants to stick around on the off-chance that he might get to kill one of these innocent beasts, we climb back in the car to try and find some warmth. We ask Martti about his music and, although we cannot stay for his recital this evening, we would love to hear him perform. His ego is adequately stroked and once again we fall in with his instructions. The Lost Chord must be revealed. Although Martti has not seen fit for us to be sacrificed, we are now convinced he is the shaman we had been expecting – all this intellectual classical-guitar-playing trip is just a convenient front he has to have so he can get on with the real tasks he has to perform for his people. Why else would he be allowed to roam freely around the country and escape the soul-grinding, back-breaking work that his spirit-fearing brother Lapps spend their lives doing?

*

The tall black-eyed man invited us to his brother's home. It was his brother, he informed us, who knew of the Chord. We finished our meal, thanked the reindeer men for their hospitality and set off to find out more of the legendary Chord. The boy gave Gimpo a lucky reindeer foot.

The Escort bumps and skids back down the track, leaving our three new friends to their work.

As we drove across the tundra our friend told us his name was Egil. His brother, the keeper of the Chord, was called Skalagroft and was the local shaman. Skalagroft was very wise and kept the tribe's magic safe. We drove for a further twenty or so kilometres and engaged in small-talk with our friend. He ceased to appear quite so strange. He told us he was saving his earnings from the reindeer harvest to buy a Harley Davidson to drive across the United States. He had relatives amongst the Pawnee Indians and wished to visit them. Lapps and North American Indians are closely related and share many cultural and religious beliefs.

Twenty minutes later we pull off the road again.

The light was fading as we reached his brother's home – a small log cabin in the middle of nowhere.

A short way up a track and we skid to a halt outside one of the sparsely scattered homesteads.

An oil lamp burning at one of the windows indicated that his brother and sister-in-law were home.

The cabin was surrounded by all manner of strange artefacts: flags, Arctic hieroglyphics, old drums and reindeer hides, rusty axes, saws, a huge pile of timber. The roof of the cabin was decorated with carved animal skulls and bone sculptures. Thick black smoke curled greasily from the iron chimney. The wind and snow had ceased completely, and when we cut the ice bikes' engines a supernatural silence descended. I looked at the night sky. I could hear the

North Star – it sounded like Chinese wind chimes. The aurora borealis threw gentle swathes of colour against the Prussian blue infinity. I thought I was in the most desolate and most beautiful place on earth. The air smelled thousands of years old. Peace and tranquillity. Egil's reindeer-skin boots squeaked in the tight snow as he walked to the cabin door. We followed him in to his brother's home.

We are greeted by barking dogs and what can only be described as a seriously inbred Lapp leprechaun.

The little smiling guy gave me a high five and asked me if I dug Metallica. I was dumbstruck.

He stands no more than five foot, could be of an age anywhere between thirty and sixty and has startling blue eyes that twinkle in his lined oriental face.

He welcomes us into his living room. The walls are painted a dirty sky blue, a log stove has its doors open revealing a warmth and welcome, the air is heavy with a high, sweet but savoury hum. A battered settee, a kitchen table covered with an oilskin cloth, a hand-tinted portrait of the Pope on one wall, the Virgin Mary on the other. Catholic enclave?

We had walked into an Arctic Graceland. The cabin's decor made Elvis's taste in interior design look sophisticated: velvet, nylon, plastic, leopard-skin settees, zebra-patterned wallpaper, huge round hi-fi speakers, massive TV built into the wall blaring out rock vids; cocktail bar, snooker table, tropical fish tank, red plastic light fittings, breakfast bar, fitted carpets that swirled around your ankles, and, reclining on a massive mink-draped waterbed, the shaman's babe, Claudia Schiffer with bigger tits and bigger hair. She giggled and waved her red fingernails. 'Hi!'

Gimpo was smiling at her reindeer-skin micro bikini, curly-toed thigh-high stiletto-heeled reindeer boots and see-through, black baby-doll nightie. The little shaman had bright green Elvis shades and a pony tail. He was wearing red leather trousers, cowboy boots and a

Nirvana T-shirt. He jabbed his TV remote and a video of Alice In Chains started blaring from the monstrous screen.

Cracked linoleum on the floor. Chairs are pulled up. Gimpo fetches a bottle of Blue Label from the Escort. The top is unscrewed.

'I love this band!' An American accent. 'You guys wanna drink? Jack Daniels? Jim Beam?' He turned to his Arctic bimbo. 'Honey, fix the guys a drink!' She teetered through some glass beads, wiggling her furry butt and giggling. I was still in shock. The hyperactive gnome ushered us on to his massive leopard-skin settee. I sat down and nearly disappeared into the upholstery. Bill was stuttering, trying to say something. Egil placed his hand on Bill's knee.

The Lapp leprechaun turns up the twinkle in his eyes.

'It was when Skalagroft got back from Vegas,' Egil said, as if this explained everything.

'Yeah, ha ha, Vegas!' butted in the dwarf. 'Kinda like a Rock 'n' Roll epiphany, if you get my drift.' The shaman had lost me. He was on a roll; there was no stopping him.

Good measures are poured into tumblers.

'All of the planet is connected to its heartbeat. Think about it. Om. What's that? It's the planet breathing, the lifeforce, Woodstock, African tribes, drums, that incessant rhythm, the blood flowing through your veins, pulsing in time with the primeval essence, the swamps, magic, ritual. It all means the same thing, banging those drums in the forest, dig?

'King Kong dug it – he is the rhythm, he is the great man. Iron John, fairytales, myth, the Fisher King, T. S. Eliot, Dante's *Inferno*, Milton's *Paradise Lost*, Walt Whitman, Walt Disney. Shit, man! The Devil as hero, Dionysus, Jim Morrison, Rock 'n' Roll, William Blake. If the doors of perception were truly cleansed then everything would be as it truly is – infinite, or something like that. Do you like AC/

DC? I love AC/DC, and of course, as you know, Elvis is Apollo, man.'

The hyperactive gnome drained his glass of Jack Daniels and continued. 'It all made sense – I won at blackjack, I won at the tables – I knew the force was with me; never again would I think that the shamanistic secrets passed down to me from generation after generation were the true designs of the great reindeer god. No, I knew all life was connected and that the great reindeer was indeed Kali, Buddha, Christ, Led Zeppelin and The Beatles. Do you know what I mean?'

The mystic dwarf pinned me to the settee with a bug-eyed stare. Hesitantly I stuttered, 'You mean, kind of, like that, erm, seemingly unrelated phenomena can become united into a spiritual whole by simply refusing to accept the constraints of language and linear conceptualization; and that by thinking symbolically and instinctively one can arrive at a spiritual non-system which decrees that all truths are, in fact, one truth, and that the details and dogma of any of these truths are wholly and totally irrelevant . . . sort of?'

'Yo, dude!' he exclaimed, slamming me a high five, 'I've been watching you cats on Channel Far Out, the extraterrestrial psychic channel. You can't get it on Sky, it's only accessible by magic. I videoed you!'

The dwarf punched in a series of commands on his remote. I noticed that instead of numbers on the buttons of his remote control he had painted runes and magic symbols. The TV set flashed a psychedelic swirl of day-glo static. 'There it is!' shouted our host. He was bouncing up and down on the settee. 'I love this magic eye stuff!' he laughed. 'Here, look!' he shouted. 'This bit in the tower, where you do the Elvis thing and get the rollercoaster zap . . . fucking brilliant!' He flipped the channel back to MTV. Metallica were singing a song about being scared of the dark. 'So!' shouted our fast-forward friend, 'how do you feel? Cosmic enlightenment, seeing everything in everything, Walt Whitman and shit – pretty groovy, huh? I remember when I was first tipped the wink, ha ha, scared me shitless . . .'

'It's all been a bit quick,' Bill sheepishly replied. 'We're kind of feeling our way . . . you know . . .'

'So you want the Chord?' The shaman was laughing and rummaging through a large box, throwing out tambourines and banjos and other small percussive instruments. 'In here somewhere!' he muttered. 'A-ha!'

We drink each other's health and Martti opens his guitar case.

He pulled out a battered Spanish guitar with four strings. 'That Keith Richards!' he laughed. 'What a jerk! He knew nothing of the secret art, ha ha. Trying to buy the Chord, what an asshole! Six million dollars! Heh-heh! He's lucky I didn't take all his money! Any dumb schmuck who reads comic books knows that secret knowledge can only be used for the good of mankind. It is a sin against God to use divine gifts for personal gain. Now, how does it go?'

The little guy was tuning the four strings to a tuning I'd never heard before. The top E was stretched almost to breaking point, the G and F were flopping all over the fretboard. The A string he snapped and threw behind him. He rummaged through his box again and pulled out an old calculator. He banged it on the table and made a few rapid calculations and fine adjustments to the strings of the guitar.

'Cindy!' he called over his shoulder. The ice babe teetered into the room.

'Yes, honey?' She pouted and started throwing game-show poses.

'Bring me my chainsaw! . . . The small one.'

Cindy brought in a dinky little chainsaw no bigger than an electric carving knife. The shaman placed his tongue in the side of his mouth and with great concentration carved the sound hole of the guitar into a rough approximation of a Star of Solomon. He tossed the chainsaw over his shoulder and, cocking his head at an angle, made some fine adjustments to the machine heads.

How important is the Lost Chord? How long has the myth of it existed? Is it the Holy Grail of music? Every musician knows it's a theoretical impossibility, but everybody that has ever sat down to write a song will know their fingers are constantly searching for that elusive Lost Chord, the chord that will turn a trite ditty into a work that contains the sacred mystery of creation. There have been times when musicians' minds have been momentarily distracted while their fingers have kept on playing. Fingers may then fleetingly stumble across the Chord but, by the time their mind is back on the case, there is no way of knowing where the fingers strayed. Some musicians are not bothered about tracking it down and are quite at ease with expressing all their wants, needs and passion in all the standard chords on offer; others, like Miles Davis, you feel have dedicated the whole of their life to its search.

'Trumpet players don't use chords.' The voice.

'Yeah, but what about the harmonics?'

None of this has any premeditated relevance to putting Elvis at the top of the world, but it somehow developed a parallel path of its own throughout our journey. And here we are in this run-down but friendly kitchen/living room probably about to have it revealed!

'There!' he said, 'the Lost Chord!' He strummed the guitar. It sounded like the opening chord to every great song that has ever been written, the opening note of every great symphony ever composed. The Walt Disney fairy dust was dripping off his hand and little Tinkerbells were flying from the fret board. I noticed that he had a halo floating above each of his fingers. 'There you have it. The Lost Chord, the secret of all music,' continued our magic sage. 'Music is the purest language. It is the true language, the language of the gods. It is also incredibly dangerous, just check out a Slayer gig if you don't believe me. Anyway, you have the Chord. Don't abuse it . . . Shit, man! Beavis and Butthead!'

Our friend flipped channels to his favourite cartoon. 'I love these guys!' The shaman started chuckling in a dumb Beavis and Butthead style and playing his guitar. He said 'cool' and 'this sucks' a lot. Bill gingerly picked up the battered Spanish guitar, examining it closely, fingering the sound hole and wiping the rusty strings.

Martti has a stack of dog-eared sheets of music, dense with black dots, staves and other coded lies. To our untutored eyes this is complete shite, and I remember how much I hate and resent classical music. This doesn't look too hopeful. He starts to play some unknown piece of turgidity as his eyes follow the dots. It finishes. He plays another; then another. We make the right noises of encouragement. Gimpo fills his glass. But we know this is not what we were hoping to hear. Z asks Martti if he writes any of his own music.

'Yes, I make songs, but they are Lapp songs.'

'Can we hear one?' mutters Z.

'Of course, I will sing you a song about the reindeer. It is about an old stag reindeer who has wandered the tundra preparing himself for death.'

Martti sings. The tune is very simple – no intricate guitar frills, just a stark, slow arpeggio accompaniment. It is a good and worthy song. We nod our approval. The Lapp leprechaun, whose name I can't even start to pronounce let alone write down, rises from his battered chair and, using sign language, offers to heat some scraps of meat that lie in a frying pan of congealed fat. Gimpo nods. He places the pan on the stove. The opaque fat melts, then splutters; a strong high odour is set free and finds its way to our nostrils. A greasy plate is taken from a bare shelf, the scraps of now hot meat are presented to us on the table. We eat with our fingers. Our palates are not used to such strong flavour – not even the gamiest of game matches this. I savour the taste and chew on the tough meat. My stomach will not be able to take too much of it. The vodka washes it down.

Z and Gimpo are also finding it difficult to indulge our Lapp friend's hospitality. I try not to stare at the Lapp leprechaun's boots, which are like a disfigurement that you try hard not to notice but your eyes keep straying back to. They are made, I presume, from reindeer skin, come half-way up his shins and have curled-up toes – very Disney. There is no fancy embroidery on them – just bog-standard pixie boots, but for real. I want to ask where he got them from but feel it would be like asking a hunchback where I can get a hunch just the same. So Gimpo asks him anyway. Martti translates and off he goblins through the door.

Some minutes later the door opens. In enters a female grand-mother hobgoblin, almost bent double with age, covered from head to foot in tattered and dirty Lapp gear, none of the brightly coloured clothes that we had seen pushing supermarket trolleys some time past: a national costume in the raw. Her eyes also do the twinkling through the dark lines of her aged face. She smiles and croaks a welcome to us all. Behind her she drags a large cardboard box. The box contains a huge loose bundle of these reindeer-skin boots. Martti translates and informs us this is his aged great aunt; she can only speak Lapp and all her life she has made reindeer boots; they are the best boots to wear in the snow; they must never be allowed to dry out; the skin has not been tanned; if you take them off you should leave them outside on your porch.

We start trying them on. The inside of them still has bits of flesh clinging to the suede. The great aunt then drags through another box. We find sizes to fit. The prices are reasonable. We purchase. Does this commerce sully the hospitality we have shown each other? I hope not. We comfort ourselves with the knowledge that Martti imparts: she makes these for the locals to wear; these are not the embroidered ones manufactured for the midnight-sun tourist trade.

Our host, the Lapp leprechaun, whispers something in her ear. She gives a coy giggle and pushes him away as if she was a teenage maiden and him a likely lad with a cocky wit, not his old mum. She looks up at us and a sound begins to rise from her throat, a sound that falls somewhere between the guttural soul-searching of the nightingale and the strained but moving intonations of Björk. An ancient melody slowly unwinds from her spirit, a lament so moving it would almost be worth having a massacre just to know that such beauty could be created. The bare unaccompanied melody is very simple, but each phrase is adorned with twists and curls that display a great technical talent along with a bottomless well of soul.

The Lost Chord. In all truly great music – music that has in some small but essential way changed the world, like the hypothetical butterfly's wing which started a tornado – the Chord has been in all those songs, usually accidentally, a strange discordant harmony from a rattling guitar string mixing with an out-of-tune piano or a rattle from a loose cymbal. This magic musical motif has the power to change people's lives, and in changing lives it in turn changes the world.

*

The song is short. Martti translates. It is about an ageing reindeer doe who was born many years past and now is ready to find a place to lay her weary body and die. We feel small. Martti explains in his rather formal English that his aged great aunt is the finest living female singer of traditional Lapp songs. We have no argument with this. He also tells us that her songs have been recorded for posterity as a record of a dying art by the Finnish government – her generation is the last that grew up in a Lapp culture unsullied by the modern world.

The Lost Chord cannot be used for evil. It features in many of The Beatles' best-loved songs. The Edge's strange guitar playing with his bizarre tuning and idiosyncratic playing style has ensured that the music of U2 has featured this divine musical feature in much of their work. Led Zeppelin, Prince and, surprisingly enough, AC/DC have also accidentally stumbled upon this secret combination of notes. Of course, Elvis had the Chord in every song he ever made, the reason being that his vocal pitch and vibrato almost always touched the three notes which make up the Chord. This is why he is known as the King.

It is no accident that in many Third World countries Elvis Presley is regarded as a saint. In the small, isolated villages of Northern Mexico special shrines are erected on lonely mountains to worship Santa Presley. Many peasants believe that St Elvis has the power to heal, and the blind in many villages wear the aviator shades beloved of their idol in the belief that it will restore their vision. Miraculously, this does appear to improve their sight by up to 20 per cent.

Bill gently strummed the battered guitar. Gimpo held his breath. The Chord hung in the air. It shimmered like ice and gold dust, the delicate intonation caressed me like warm hospital heroin and clean cotton bedsheets.

The credits rolled on the Beavis and Butthead cartoon and our wise shaman friend wiped tears of laughter from his eyes. He turned to us, chortling. 'Sorry, ha ha, I love that show! Anyway guys, tell me, what exactly do you plan to do with the Chord? That is if you don't mind me asking.'

Bill furrowed his brow. He always reminds me of Sherlock Holmes when he does this. He replaced the top of his gold Waterman fountain pen – he had been making notes on the exact tuning of the Lost Chord – and fixed our friend a serious look. 'We intend to destroy News International and all multinational conglomerates. Rupert Moloch, we believe, is Beelzebub himself. With the aid of this Chord we shall destroy Mammon and save the people of the Earth. But that is just the beginning. We intend to bring down Heaven. We will free the waters! We shall all of us return to the Garden! We shall not rest before global satori is achieved!'

Myself, Gimpo, Cindy and the shaman applauded Bill's statement and toasted the wise Scotsman with our whiskies. Bill nodded modestly and blushed. He fumbled with his leather doctor's bag and placed his pen and notepad inside it and pulled out the notes he had made about the Chord, a small jeweller's tool kit and a stylophone.

We spent the rest of the evening drinking and watching our host's extensive collection of psychotronic videos. He told us hilarious tales of failed pretenders who had tried to secure the Chord for their own selfish ends. Dick Scabbard, lead guitarist with Metal Submarine, spent years studying the magical theories of notorious necromancer Aleister Crowley. Dick conducted numerous ceremonies of homosexual magik in order to secure possession of the Chord. All he gained from his toil and tribulation were several years of psychotherapy and a severely battered ring-piece.

David Bowie also ventured into forbidden zones, utilizing a whole cornucopia of bisexual substances in his search for the musical grail. Mick Jagger? He was laughed off the astral plane. No, as I have said, the only musician who had ever known the secret of this eighth wonder of the world – before it was revealed to us – was the King, Elvis himself.

Skalagroft the shaman entertained us with many more tales of failed attempts at grasping the secret of this supernatural phenomenon. The whisky and beer flowed, our legs and minds became unstable.

Just before dawn an ice-cockerel crowed. The psychotronic film show had ended; Gimpo and Cindy had retired to the master bedroom (she and the shaman had an open marriage). A single candle dripped purple wax in the middle of a small round table. Skalagroft drew Bill and myself in close. He rubbed his grey beard and then, well in his cups, revealed another secret, a dark secret. 'My friends,' his Marlboro larynx creaked, 'before you leave there's one thing which I must warn you about.' An icy hand grabbed my testicles. Skalagroft continued in a whisper: 'The Anti-Chord, it . . .'

Something shrieked and whizzed around the room, interrupting the terrified shaman. The door crashed open, and with a yell the nether demon sped upwards into the aurora borealis. Skalagroft crossed himself, ran to the door and slammed it shut. The episode sealed his lips and he would speak no more of the dread phenomenon, the Anti-Chord, but left it hanging in our imagination to torment our dreams. Somehow I sensed that we had not heard the last of this mystery. I retired to my bed uneasy.

Bill studied his notes and tinkered with his stylophone. I could see him rewiring certain parts and switching various transistors. Gimpo worked on his Zen stick.

Bill produced a pack of tarot cards and was attaching them to the circuit board of the stylophone. I noticed he was using the darker elements of the major arcana. I got a little nervous when he attached the dread Ten of Swords to a makeshift aerial he had made from an old coathanger. He was stabbing at his runic calculator and muttering in Latin.

I sucked on the vodka; it made my stomach warm. Bill continued scratching and rewiring. I noticed he had broken into a sweat and there was something spooky about his expression. His matted hair was stuck to his forehead and his eyes looked wild; he was dribbling. I was becoming increasingly alarmed.

'Bill,' I said, 'what are you doing?'

He ignored me and carried on with his disturbing science.

'Bill!' I repeated. He looked up as if from a dream. I noticed his fingers were bleeding. He gathered his thoughts.

'I'm reversing the Chord. I think, I think I've done it,' he murmured. I knew what he was talking about but I dared not contemplate the implications – the bastard was searching for the Anti-Chord.

*

We say very little. We have to move on. We want to show our gratitude. We don't know how, and we don't really know what for. It feels as if we have been shown something that exists far beyond the boundaries of our own limitless ego-driven horizons. This aged great aunt, dressed in her ragged peasant dress, has spent a lifetime in this frozen wasteland rearing generations, making reindeer boots and singing songs that ache through the ages, heavy with Creation's secrets, while I can only patronize her by writing these lines and buying a pair of her boots.

We mumble our farewells. Martti writes down his Helsinki address and phone number in my notebook. We promise him we will return one spring to follow the reindeer north with him and his cousins. Martti spies Z's cards, which he has been aimlessly shuffling: 'You know, it is said that the tarot is the only book that the Magi took with them on their travels.'

Note: the only ever recorded example of the Anti-Chord appeared during the middle of the track 'Revolution No. 9' on The Beatles' White Album.

CHAPTER FOURTEEN

The Blaspheming Cunt of Sodom,
Plague Queen

Our friends prepared a fine breakfast: all the reindeer steaks we could eat, fried eggs and as much beer as we could drink. Between the three of us we polished off the best part of a whole reindeer. I drank a considerable amount of fine Lappish ale and had a good fug to insulate me against the harsh snows we were bound to encounter later that day. The shaman indicated a ley line that passed by his cabin. He told us to follow it for thirteen hundred miles, where we would reach the world. We embraced our friends and set off home. Skalagroft, Egil and Cindy waved till we were out of sight.

Back in the Escort, back on the road, me still in awed silence. Z turns to me and talks: 'Well, now we have heard one of the notes of the Lost Chord, there are only two more to go.' And yes, Z is correct: in the aged great aunt's lament lay one of the three notes of the Lost Chord. We have to hold that note in our hearts. It's a note that cannot even be remembered, but the note is now in there, embedded in our souls, resonating for as long as it takes to find the other two notes.

By my reckoning, each of these three notes must be symbolic of something. Must be birth, life and death. (This symbolism stuff is quite easy once you get the hang of it.) Now we have to find the note of birth and the note of life; and when all three notes resonate together in our soul, we shall experience the Lost Chord, the chord of resurrection. The only weird thing in all of this is, why was the Note of Death revealed to us first?

And yes, Martti was a shaman of the highest order, even if he played crap classical guitar: he showed us the way.

We pull up at the side of the road; all three of us puke up the putrid reindeer flesh we had been obliged to eat. No, fuck it! I've just realized that eating the stinking meat was not just them offering us some rustic hospitality – the reindeer meat must have contained all sorts of mystical trace elements, the gravy flavoured with rare tundra herbs; the Pixie boots we purchased and are now wearing like tourists' trinkets were magic garments; Martti's opening song about the dying reindeer was the subtle introduction to the final ceremony.

'Fuck me, Z! We've just gone through some weird initiation rite.'

'Bill, there is more to life than the ten o'clock news.' Z has a shit load of wisdom; and so has Gimpo.

'We have only five hours to make the overnight train to Helsinki from Rovaniemi,' imparts Gimpo. In fact, he didn't say that. He just put his foot hard down on the accelerator.

We drove for days, never straying from the blue hum of the ley line. I switched to auto-pilot several times. The computer locked on to the earth's magnetic field and cruised at a steady 30 mph. I tried to sleep in the saddle but it was impossible.

My dreams were skating nightmare: I was riding bareback on Fuseli's spectral horse and kept seeing the woman, the scarlet, bloody woman with the severed-head suspender belt. Her face constantly shifted shape; it moved like melting fat, blowing sickly black holes and popping viscous bubbles. She adopted the visage of pubescent beauty; it mutated into hag, dominatrix, Earth Mother. And always the snakes, purple and red, like shiny intestines. Music entered the swirling dreamscape – eastern, discordant, terrifying. The mystery woman started to dance. Her Gorgonic mane of severed penises writhed around her oiled hair, a Priapic Medusa jolting me into consciousness.

I was sweating and shaking; my heart pounded like death metal. The world was two days south. Bill and Gimp were also on auto-pilot, but judging from their seraphic expressions they were experiencing dreams less grim.

The pale disc of the sun was setting behind the swathes of snow. I noticed the snow's texture was changing; the dry powder of the more northerly climes was becoming wetter, our bikes cut deeper. Patches of grass were visible here and there. The odd bird sang amongst the pines.

We move south through the empty landscape, the sun heading west, shafting its rays to us through space and time in seconds flat. Einstein gets relative and time bends. Z in the front passenger seat fiddles with the radio dial, searching for Radio Mafia. He thinks he finds it. Friendly Finnish punk; but then bang into 'Ebeneezer Goode', the current chart-topper by the pop rave band The Shamen (their name is the ultimate misnomer).

Z is disappointed to find that Radio Mafia has begun to play dance music while we are on our voyage to the North. Now Z is pretty good at detecting the raw nerve in fellow travellers and knows that anybody who has ever been in a band hates any other band that threatens to move into its area. Both The Orb and The Shamen threatened Jimmy and myself in this way; and now that we were no longer putting out KLF records, they were instantly and successfully filling the gap we had left. Of course, I would like to think a Zen Master like myself should be able to rise above these smallnesses of the material world; and yes, I have to admit that 'Ebeneezer Goode' is a great dance/pop/rave record; but the terrible fact is that it has been at No. One for the past five weeks and we, The KLF, only ever managed a UK No. One for two consecutive weeks.

I don't know if Z knows all these details but he does hit the raw nerve. I try to dismiss his petty teasing as being infantile and way off mark. At last the record ends and we are released into 'Eight Miles High' by The Byrds.

Conversations drift: Tracey and her boyfriends. Tracey had been going out with this skinny American with a bad haircut who sang in an almost-made-it Irish band. It had been love and torment but he had left her for a maths teacher. She couldn't understand how he could be happy with a maths teacher. Now, I don't know this singer lad, but it seems I made some comment that he probably needed to go out with somebody normal; that mad people need to go out with normal people and normal people need to go out with mad people is the yin and yang of it. I'm not trying to get deep, but you know what I mean.

This conversation with Tracey has been lost in the dumping ground of my memory but Z feels the need to fight Tracey's corner. She is most upset that I think she is mad, and, 'Why can't she go out with crazy fucked up mad artist-types if she likes?' asks Z.

'Well, I haven't got a problem with that, but if she wants some equilibrium in her life why don't she go out with a regular geezer?' I can't believe I'm saying this. What do I know about relationships? Z's the only person I know that's fucked up more than me. Z reckons it's the other way round.

Enough, enough!

Gimpo was the first to spot him: a bronzed god of a man, an Arctic Adonis, a Nordic David, naked, arms folded, standing astride the ley line. He appeared to be carved from sandalwood. His waist-length hair hung in shining tresses upon a muscular torso; an iron jaw, eyes as piercing and blue as those of a desert nomad scouring pyramid horizons; massive knob.

We drifted the bikes to a slow halt to speak to this apparition from a bumboy's dream. The homo superior flashed a dazzling smile, his white teeth reflecting the light of a thousand suns. He extended a large bronzed hand. 'My name is Fabio.' A caramel baritone dripping quiet confidence. 'Forgive my attire, or . . .' he laughed, 'lack of it. I have been jogging. No one lives around here except my brothers and me, and,' he gestured nonchalantly, 'the polar bears don't seem to mind.'

I shook his hand. His shake was, as I had expected, firm but not aggressive. 'Come!' he continued in his seductive voice. 'You may dine with us – the monastery is not far.' Fabio broke into a steady jog, the shiny beads of a light sweat reflecting the orange sun as if they were a million amber diamonds. The dynamic force of nature trailed steam in his wake like the tail feathers of a phantasmagorical bird crossing the sky of an opium dream. We were still many hundreds of miles within the Arctic Circle, but this superman did not seem to notice the cold.

We kick-started the ski-bikes and glided parallel to our new friend. He radiated a beatific calm and did not seem the slightest bit homosexual.

We headed into the sun.

The day is dulling, the landscape losing its majesty. It is as if we are driving back from the match and, even though our team won, the post-match euphoria has dissipated and the dreariness of home life looms.

Fabio communicated by telepathy. He informed us that he was the spiritual leader of a group of warrior monks highly trained in esoteric and martial disciplines, sworn to celibacy and dedicated to saving the planet from an impending disaster predicted by the founder of their order.

When rave culture exploded out of the acid house clubs of 1988 and Jimmy and I were munching on our disco biscuits, Z stood firmly outside the whole dance-love-friendly-frenzy mess and sneered. 'I will commit suicide if metal bands start taking E, it would be the end of death metal. Love metal? Fuck that for an idea. Imagine Black Sabbath reforming then destroying their whole legend by recording rave-happy versions of their death-bell toll of a legacy!'

Darkness has fallen. Gimpo drives on in silence. My conversation with Z takes unmarked turns down Rock's more ragged roads: we relish each line from Sabbath's debut LP; we remember lost tracks by Budgie, the *Very 'Eavy, Very 'Umble* album by Uriah Heep; and had he ever heard of Stray? We must sound like a couple of old geezers discussing opening batsmen for lesser county cricket sides some time back before the war – long shadows, warm pints and all that. But that ain't going to stop us as we wallow in Rock's broken dreams, the call of Ozzy and the darkness that lurks inside. Yes, it's the greatcoated figure who is sentenced to shuffle aimlessly through eternity, his shoulders hunched, his long hair hanging lank hiding an adolescent countenance; and, under his arm, seven hard-fought-for albums by bands with names long forgotten.

Z asks about the *Black Room* album that me and Jimmy as The

Justified Ancients of Mu Mu started but were too afraid to complete. I tell him how, when I was standing in the twilight of the recording booth, the microphone in front of me, Jimmy's magnificent metal guitar riffs roaring in my headphones, a voice came out of me that I had never heard before, words flowed that I had never written and a precipice appeared before me. I crept forward and looked over the edge: the abyss. The Justified Ancients of Mu Mu's LP, *The Black Room*, was never finished.

But Z keeps talking and I'm warming to his persuasions. He feels that Jimmy and I are evading our responsibilities; we should return to our war horse and complete the task. And yes, right now I believe Z may be right. But maybe Jimmy and I should wait until we are both over fifty before we record the sound of us as battle-scarred veterans of a hundred mercenary campaigns, when the music would not be drawn from our fading libidos but from the horror of life spent confronting that abyss – kinda like Milton backed up by Megadeth.

It is feeling pretty snug in the Escort: fag packets, empty bottles, sweet wrappings high-tide the floor; the air is thick with farts and stale sweat.

'You know, Blake wasn't even one of the Romantics anyway. He was out there on his own,' Z.

'Yeah, but it was all at the same time he was reacting against the Age of Reason, like the others,' me.

'Well it's like trying to say The Stranglers were a punk band, when in fact they were just playing the same gigs,' Z.

'So where does that leave the argument?'

'Who cares?'

Gimpo is pulling into a service station. I intend to make a call to Ulla at Mega Records to tell her our mission has been completed and we are not dead. We also hope she will be the provider of entertainment for us. Inside the service station: lots of pink packaging and yellow things wrapped in cellophane, magazine racks and fridges full of soft drinks, a payphone by the check-out desk.

Ten minutes later, back in the Escort, my head is bursting. How to tell Gimpo and Z the news?

'Did you get through?' Z.

'Yeah,' me.

'So?' Gimpo.

'Well, she can't get together with us because she has got some other artists in town, who are doing interviews and TV appearances to promote a record they've got out and in the charts; and she doesn't think we would want to meet up with them. She's full of apologies and kinda embarrassed, even ashamed,' me.

'So, who are they?' Z.

'Guess!'

'Don't be a fuckin' Jessie. Just tell us,' Z.

'It's the most unlikely outfit in the world you can imagine us meeting after what we've been through.'

'U2?' Z.

'Even better,' me.

'Frank Sinatra?' Gimpo.

'No, no, better even than Frank.'

So before the stakes get too high I spill my news: 'The Chippendales – not all of them, just two – but Ulla says we can go to this party in the afternoon with Mulla and in the evening we can get together with her and the Chippendales, go to a night club, hang out.'

The order was known as the Rosicrucian Brotherhood of the Knights Chippendale or, more commonly, the Chippendales. Their spiritual headquarters, the Sugar Shack, was located in an austere temple here amongst the ice and snow, and it was at the Shack that the monks underwent their training for up to ten years, spending many hours performing prayers and meditation as well as following strict physical programmes, before they were allowed to preach their message in the south.

So maybe now I should try and define the place the Chippendales hold in our ever-shifting Western culture. By the time you read this, the Chippendales, if remembered at all, may be just a faded novelty item lost somewhere in the post-eighties fade-out years. But right now, for me, the Chippendales are more significant than The Beatles, more confrontational than The Sex Pistols and more alive than Elvis.

*

In their final year at the Shack, the monks learnt the specially coded magical dance routines. This powerful magic can only be performed before an audience of women, for the dances' purpose is to provoke hysteria. (Hysteria is the natural condition of woman and the mark of a man is how he deals with it.)

Yes, I know there have been male strippers providing the giggles at hen parties for years, but whoever lay behind the formation of the Chippendales knew what was out there, knew that the world was now ready for the Chippendales or, to be more precise, that half the population of the world was now ready for the Chippendales. The female half.

The Chippendales have not only learnt how to deal with the condition, but also how to harness it as a spiritual entity and channel it into a force for peace and understanding. In Chippendale churches the female congregation is rendered hysterical by the dervish-like dances of the men; their unconscious minds open like the rusty gates of Atlantis, and in this state they receive the divine preaching of the Brotherhood's current leader, the fourteenth reincarnation of the order's original founder, Fabio Bysalhaugo, whose name translates from the original Sanskrit to 'ocean of immaculate love'.

Never before in the entire history of mankind's existence on this planet has anything like the Chippendales been allowed to exist. Whenever the Chippendales hit town, paste up their posters and book themselves into the local theatre, coach loads of women travel hundreds of miles to witness their performances; and when I say women, I mean women of all ages – not just teenage screamers but grannies, even great grannies, down to girls not old enough to bleed. And there is nothing their menfolk can do about it. In the past, men would never have dared let the Chippendales exist. Now we don't dare to let them not exist.

The teachings of the original Dalai Chippendale, Fabio the First, instruct that only men are able to grasp the concept of divine love, and that to discover spiritual truth they must first declare their love for themselves and their fellow men (not as easy as it sounds – some novices take up to four years to discover this eternal axiom). To ensure that there are no distractions of the kind that polluted the philosophies of the early Greeks, the Chippendales must swear a vow of absolute celibacy, of total abstinence from all forms of profane earthly love. Any intimation of the Greek persuasion in the lads is punished by instant dismissal from the Brotherhood. The dreadful crime of sodomy is considered to be a mortal sin, homosexuality an irreversible cancer of the soul.

Fabio and the Chippendales believe that men should have sex for reproductive purposes only, to further the species towards the final meeting and reconciliation with the Holy Father, the ultimate Chippendale – God. This is why they have knackers the size of space hoppers. Women, although they are capable of the ultimate creative act – childbirth – cannot conceive of the concept of absolute truth. The Chippendales' ritualistic magical dancing enables women to grasp intuitively that Fabio, and therefore all men, are the incarnation of God, and that women should obey their man and treat him as their own personal deity – worship him, never criticize him, do the washing up, cook, clean, etc. – simple truths that many women in this pagan age of feminism seem to have forgotten.

This goes way beyond Clark Gable not wearing a vest in that film in the undermining of man's inherited self-confidence. Now I have no idea what goes on at these Chippendale performances, but they are able to provide something for our womenfolk that we are eternally unable to give. All I have learnt about them is from what I see on their posters stuck around our cities; and on these I see a collection of young men wearing nothing much more than dicky bows and winged collars, revealing well-oiled, smooth-skinned, muscular torsos. On some a gold mane flows and blue eyes pierce, lending credence to a Nordic bloodline; others have short, dark, well-groomed hair, a complexion more Latin than Lithuanian; and maybe sometimes a Negroid with a straight-from-the-plantation-and-into-the-boudoir vibe.

Are they providing some type of old-time religion revivalist meeting or is it a new-rule all-in wrestling? Maybe not. But whatever it is, us regular blokes know it is something we can never compete with.

We arrived at the Sugar Shack, a huge marble monastery, Grecian in style. Fabio informed us that the monastery was built in the twelfth century on the site of the original Sugar Shack, reputedly more than 5,000 years old. We were also told that the first Fabio, 'the ocean of immaculate love', was central to the spiritual tuition of both Jesus Christ and Gautama Buddha. 'Jesus a Chippendale?' exclaimed Gimpo. Fabio drew our attention to the Nazarene's superb physique. Bill and I nodded sagely. It all made sense.

We were greeted by two beautiful sylph-like lads of about twelve years of age dressed in cashmere jockstraps. They handed Fabio a silken jocker; Bill, Gimpo and I were handed plain cotton visitors' straps. We struggled into them uncomfortably, self-conscious of our un-Chippendale like physiques.

Fabio thanked the boys courteously and patted them on their bottoms. 'Run along, Joshua, Gabriel, and work on those pecs!' Fabio smiled affectionately. 'The future,' he added with a paternal smile. 'Come! The temple!'

Z's one-word answer contains all the justification that our insecurities need for defence: 'Jessies.' But Z doesn't stop there; he is off, and I will desperately try and keep log of what falls from his lips.

'Shirt-lifters of king-size proportions.' Z's Yorkshire-grit of a voice subsides into an affected West Coast, chocolate-rich seduction of a larynx: 'Hi, my name is Flare. Meet my friend Adonis. Great to meet you guys. Yeah, so you're staying in the same hotel as us – fabulous! Have you been down to the gym? Adonis and I were down earlier working on our pecs. Look, have a feel. What do you think? A bit more work and I should be back up to what I was like last summer.'

All memories of Rock's great tragedy and who was and who was not a Romantic have been left behind. There is no way I can keep these notes up as Z entertains us with Flare and Adonis (1990s West Coast Julian and Sandy) memoirs of life as serious artists in the modern entertainment industry. Z, providing all the voices, is on a roll with this stuff. Should I apologize to whatever gay friends we may have left for all the homophobic fun we are having? No point. It's us that are the sad fuckers.

Our cultured host gave us a guided tour through his temple of masculinity, where young athletes trained and sweated in this incredible gymnasium of the soul and body, each one striving for physical and spiritual perfection.

First we saw the solemn dining room – a long hall with an oak table where a vegetarian meal was served once a day on silver plates, the monastery's only concession to luxury, as silver does not contaminate their extremely healthy food. Every novice Chippendale is required to know the exact calorific intake required to build stunning muscles and must be able to calculate the exact number of calories in any piece of fruit or vegetable by sight alone. Chippendales only ever drink Perrier water.

We then arrived at the velvet-covered doors of the inner sanctum, through which only the highest adepts of the order may pass to meditate upon the Himalayan virtues contained within the catechism of the Chipps. Fabio informed us that inside the sanctum sanctorum (which we were not allowed to enter) lay the original weights used by the 'ocean of immaculate love' 5,000 years ago. Legend has it that the original Dalai Chippendale continuously pumped iron for months at a time beneath the sacred Bong tree to develop his superb physique.

We moved on to the Chapel of Saints, where there were small shrines decked with flowers. The drifting intoxicating aroma of incense licked its way around the revered images of legendary Chippendales who achieved sainthood within the order. I noticed a small picture of the American muscle band, The Red Hot Chilli Peppers. Fabio explained that some graduate Master Chippendales preferred to perform their missionary work in a clandestine fashion, and that provided they could prove their intentions to the Council of Elder Chippendales, were then allowed to do so. 'The Pepps', as they were affectionately referred to amongst the novices, had chosen this path.

Amazingly I spotted a painting of that gnarled old slash-and-burn pyro-rocker Iggy Pop. 'Yes, Iggy too!' added Fabio, a moist tear dampening his chiselled features. 'Iggy, Ocean bless him, was late to the cause. He had terrible problems with those dread demons, drugs and alcohol. But one day, like a flash of sunlight on a bottle of baby oil, the calling reached him and he knew he had to follow the light. He graduated in just under three years, a truly remarkable man, one of the most brilliant novices I have ever trained.'

Sylvester Stallone in his silken novice jockstrap smiled youthfully from a student group shot. I noticed a remarkably under-developed Arnold Schwarzenegger standing nervously behind Sly. 'Arnie and Sly, excellent Chipps!' Fabio informed me. 'Wonderful dancers! So graceful.'

We left the Chapel of Saints to visit the prayer and fitness rooms. The sweet smell of baby oil, testosterone and sweaty butt clefts was overpowering. Huge, naked men and slighter boys heaved with arse-clenched determination at colossal weights and clanging slabs of iron attached to pulleys. An older Chippendale with a white beard who wore the red leather jockstrap of a Master Chipp inspected the novices' straining flesh. He applied baby oil to the younger boys, shining up their pectoral muscles, and instructed them on the importance and intricacies of pectoral and abdominal shine.

The car speeds on through the premature night. I fail to notice traffic signs or moonlit landscapes. Just the radio playing some forgotten melody and the tales of Flare and Adonis reaching further heights of unreality.

Fabio invited us to dine in his private meditation suite. It was elegant yet austere, manly and calm: leather and tubular steel, Bauhaus furniture; the walls were hung with framed Athena prints of leaping dolphins and sparkling oceans; the only frivolous items were a couple of cuddly Garfield cats on Fabio's monastic waterbed. A matt black hi-fi pushed low-volume Simply Red tunes. Fabio draped a silk kimono across his perfect body and sat cross-legged at a low Japanese table. A young novice brought in four small bowls of rice and a tray of sushi. We drank modestly of the mulled sake and ate the delicious fish.

Fabio related the tale of the famous Japanese samurai Chippendale intellectual, Yukio Mishima, who was revered amongst the Brotherhood for the stylish way in which he had eradicated the shame of his sad infatuation with the Greek persuasion – he had chosen *seppuku* as punishment for his sodomistic pursuits.

I was enjoying the delicate texture of the sushi when the genial tone of the conversation switched moods. A dark orchestral malevolence like the wings of a giant bat pulled the room into shadow. Fabio's black irises surrounded by their pale blue whites fixed me with a serious stare. My heart stopped beating for five seconds. Valkyries trilled in the background; white curtains fluttered in a haunted house; Van Gogh's *Starry Night* hovered madly on the Prussian blue sky; dusty silence. Spiders' feet negotiated the hairs on my arms. A wet fart of fear dribbled from my butt.

Reality. We pull into the snow-bound station, dump the car, drag ourselves aboard the night train for Helsinki, dump our bags in the reserved cabin and retire to the buffet, where I am now catching up on these notes. Déjà vu?

One last point to make about the Chipps before we face them in person tomorrow evening: the Chippendales have saved us regular blokes from feeling bad about our bodies because we make the obvious assumption that all Chipps are homosexual. Thus, any geezer with a good body must be a homosexual as well, thus not a real man like me and all my mates; and what women really want is a real man and not some vain poof who spends too long down the gym. So if you've got a beer gut, wear it with pride. Something like that anyway.

Boredom. Our conversation spirals downwards. Pale insipid-looking beer flows.

Fellow passengers? Not much to report: a haggle of neat soldier boys, a pair of teenage spunkers who seem to hold Gimpo's attention. He regales us with some squaddie story of his days in Port Stanley after the Argies had flung in the towel: there was this girl in town, she worked in the fish 'n' chip shop; fat, face like the back of a bog, but she was obliging. According to Gimpo she obliged all of our squalid conquering regiments of squaddies. Gimpo knows a spunker when he sees one. Gimpo also comes up with a worthwhile theory. It goes something like this: 'Girls like you to have a bit of a gut 'cause it makes them feel OK about their cellulite.'

And so to bed. In our bunks we sing Johnny Cash songs and Z tells us the edited highlights from the life story of the Love Reaction's faithful roadie.

'You know of the whore?' said Fabio in a hushed and reverent whisper.

Now Johnny is six foot four and built like a granite wall and he's a half caste. His father went AWOL, his mother couldn't cope, so Doctor Barnardo's took care of Johnny. Like all kids he watched kids' TV, he watched *Blue Peter*.

'The whore?' questioned Bill. A piece of wet mackerel flobbing on the end of his chopstick paused between bowl and mouth.

And Johnny got angry.

Fabio shook his head resignedly; a slight tremble rippled his muscles.
'The Plague Queen? The Purple Whore drunk on the blood of saints? You know nothing?'

If you are a British reader, you will know what *Blue Peter* is; if not, all you need to know is that it represents all the values that our Royal Family once personified: God, country, service, citizenship, thriftiness and the centrality of the family. In those days *Blue Peter* had a regular gardening slot. The Blue Peter garden was in the back lot of BBC TV Centre. Young folk in our green and pleasant land were encouraged to give their dads a hand in their gardens at home. But Johnny didn't have a dad and Johnny didn't have a garden. And Johnny got angrier.

One night Johnny broke into the grounds of BBC TV Centre down at Shepherds Bush; he found the Blue Peter garden and trashed it: he ripped up all the flowers and shrubs; he smashed the greenhouse; he burnt down the shed. The tabloids made it front-page news. The next edition of *Blue Peter* was a black day, almost as bad as the day Shep died (Shep was the show's pet dog).

I don't know if Johnny was caught and brought to justice, but his actions were a pivotal point in the history of children's television in this country: from that time on, in came the mixed-race and minority representative presenters, accents from far-flung outposts of our land who instructed us on what could be made from discarded washing up liquid bottles and sticky-backed plastic; and the Royal Family lost it.

But Johnny's influence on the cultural life of our country was not over.

Fabio's voice had the distinct quaver of approaching fear.

Bill stood to his full seven foot height, adopted his familiar noble pose, wiped a large glob of horseradish sauce from his mouth on to the back of his sleeve. 'Reveal this knowledge, friend! We are ignorant of this person.'

Anger kept growing, and once he had attained his full height and had fists as big as market-stall cauliflowers he made his move: he joined the National Front. Now, you may remember he was of mixed blood: his hair was in tight black curls and his countenance as dark as a light-skinned kaffir. According to Z, this was no ironic statement on Johnny's part: he joined the National Front as the toughest skin-head in White City – any fellow member who challenged his birth-right to join would have met those above-described fists at close quarters. But the majority of his fellow Fronters were able to empath-ize with Johnny's situation: his pure-bred English rose of a mother had been violated by the seed of a black man. Who, if not a mother's son, can seek justice through revenge for their mother's lost purity? If Johnny was not to know who or where his father was, what better way of channelling this revenge than taking up the cross of St George, wrapping himself in the Union Jack, reading *Mein Kampf* and joining the National Front in an attempt to rid this sceptred isle of its impurities?

'The Great Purple Whore of Babylon, the Plague Queen, destroyer of worlds, goddamit! I'm talking about the Evil Blaspheming Cunt of Sodom! It is in your King James Bible, no?'

Bill placed his chin between thumb and forefinger. 'The Bible is full of evil women, Fabio. In fact some people – my friends and I included – believe that all women are evil and that a septic line runs directly from Eve and her befriending of the Evil One through Salome, Delilah and Emily Pankhurst right up to our modern plague of harpies, the feminists, fucking bunch of lesbians! . . . Bitch! Slag!' yelled Bill, shaking his head and regaining his composure. 'I digress. Exactly what or who are you talking about, Fabio?'

Fabio stood. He was scared. His fear manifested itself as a green nimbus of steam around his manly frame. It was contagious. Gimpo skittered a fearful fart. 'The Cunt of Sodom! The Baphomet of Mendes! El Diablos! The Princess of Darkness! Keeper of the Anti-Chord! Dammit, you fools, I'm talking about Satan herself! The Vision told us you would help us!' Fabio slumped to the ground, head in hands. A blue spark popped.

Bill rummaged through his battered leather doctor's bag and pulled out the weird stylophone and several ancient books bound in human skin. I noticed the titles: *Malleus Maleficarum*, the dread *Hex Hammer, Hammer of the Witches, De Occulta Philosophia* by that terrible practitioner of the black arts Cornelius Agrippa, *Theisoid Aichidoxis Magica*, a first edition, printed in Basel, Germany, in 1590. Bill scrabbled through the pages making furious notes. He jabbed at his runic calculator, eyes bulging, forehead vein pounding. 'God in heaven!' he ejaculated, 'The Sabbat!'

Fabio leapt to his feet, tears welling in his eyes. He embraced Bill. 'Then you are the ones! The Sons of Presley!' Fabio fell to his knees, crying. Bill quickly returned to his grimoires, flicking madly through the pages. He stopped halfway through a copy of Collin de Plancy's *Dictionnaire Infernal* (1863) and spread the leaves flat with the palms of his hands. My heart stopped beating when I saw the terrible engraving. Icy needles of sweat pushed their way through my skin, the room spun: it was the woman in the dream, the Plague Queen, the Blaspheming Cunt of Sodom! Intense eastern music skirled from the ether. Fabio fled from the room and returned with a CD sleeve. He jabbed at the sleeve; he was salivating. His usually seraphic composure had shattered and he was a twitching wreck. 'Shape-shifter!' his cracked voice spluttered. 'Her, her earthly . . . earthly guise!' I looked at the sleeve. It was *Erotica* by Madonna. Madonna was the Devil herself?

I had always suspected as much – those pointy iron tits, those weird demonic dancers – it all made sense. Bill had produced several star charts, compasses, dividers and a Bunsen burner on which he was scorching ancient parchments. He made notes and started digging at his runic calculator with complete, almost manic concentration. Finally he looked up: 'Tomorrow!' he exclaimed, his hair stuck to his forehead. 'The Sabbat!'

Dust motes floated in the still air; a fly prowled across my cheek, the tension tangible. Bill continued: 'The Sabbat begins at midnight. It is to be conducted under the guise of an MTV party. We have eighteen hours to reach Helsinki.' He clicked shut his leather doctor's bag and headed purposefully to the oak door. We followed.

Outside, thunder cracked and lightning strobed. The elements configured foreboding; the wind threw millions of needle-sized icicles into our eyes. Dawn was struggling through the tempest, the sun a dull ball of ice sporadically visible through the black clouds.

Anyway, Johnny's tale doesn't end there. By the time I met him, he was of a quiet and gentle disposition, nurturing a keen interest in collecting small firearms and seemingly at one with the world. His taste in music varies from a love of Johnny Cash, through to the white-hot metal of the more extreme Aryan Rock bands. In his wayward honour, we have just sung the Johnny Cash classic 'Understand Your Man'.

We have now fallen into silence. Gimpo's gentle snores rise to harmonize with the trundle of the tracks. I turn to switch off my lamp and think about the great meeting with the Chipps that awaits us in the morning.

Two hundred robust Chippendales lined up in strict formation, barely perceptible in the violent morning twilight. They were dressed in traditional battle gear: naked except for a small black tie, shirt collar and cuffs, black war-trunks and Chelsea boots. Fabio, composure regained, inspected his brave troops.

'Present arms!' The men held out their chainsaws for inspection. Fabio presented a warrior-like silhouette against the sunrise. 'Saddle up men, it is time for war! Death to the Blaspheming Cunt of Sodom!' The men returned the call as one in a fearsome battle cry: 'Death to the Blaspheming Cunt of Sodom!' They raced to the stables. Bill, Gimpo, Fabio and myself strolled behind them admiring their youthful vigour.

When we arrived at the stables all two hundred lads were sat astride fantastic white horses whose hot breath pushed psychedelic swirls on to the mythic landscape. They stamped the ground, throwing up clumps of hard earth and snow, straining at the bit; their eyes burned like destiny. The scene reminded me of Géricault – those visionary steeds suspended in the primeval moment when lightning rips the sky and that finite crack between the real and the unreal becomes tangible, terrifying and exhilarating.

A non-homosexual tumescence disturbed my underwear. It was the electric connection between myself, the elements and destiny. I noticed Bill adjust his sporran; he too was inspired. We mounted our china white horses and, following the blue throb of the ley line, headed into the dawn, the sound of 200 white horses, holy thunder. In Valhalla, fallen warriors toasted us and bid us victory; Odin sipped from his horn and Loki danced like a madman; Thor cast his hammer and the thunder heralded our departure from the Sugar Shack. Lightning shot across the sky like serotonin through a madman's brain; the aurora borealis screwed nova. Victory would be ours; victory or death. No quarter would be given, none received. We were warriors; we knew the rules. Beowulf laughed in a parallel universe.

Even though there's all the Lost-Chord-strumming dragon-slaying stuff to be done, we have returned to being just the regular bunch of misogynistic homophobic bigots that we are. The higher-plane stuff seems to have taken to the sky and I contemplate whether I should have a wank or not. Sleep overtakes me before my guilty hand makes me cum.

*

'Lancelot!' screamed Bill. His gold chainsaw drew down a bolt of lightning on to its sparking blade.

'Gawainsaw!' There was another flash of lightning as Gimpo crashed the blade of his saw against Bill's.

'Parzifal!' I yelled and added my blade to the avenging trio of flashing fire.

'Death!' roared two hundred Chippendales.

We joined the chant: 'Death to the Blaspheming Cunt of Sodom! Death! Death! Death!' And we fucking meant it.

Over and out.

CHAPTER FIFTEEN

Homogeddon

Daybreak.

Helsinki.

Helsinki Central. The night has rumbled by. Woke once at some forgotten station. We are the last off the train, harried by the guard. The air is almost sultry (above zero). Bulging and gaping bags on the platform around our feet. I'm still half-dressed and Z is in a concerned state searching for his lost Zen stick. Gimpo is unfolding a street map of Helsinki. I make these notes. Z finds his Zen stick and we stoiter down the station platform, dragging our luggage behind us; start a conversation about taking post-modernism to the bushmen of the Kalahari. Gimpo hails a taxi.

    We had decided to award ourselves a night in this hotel for having survived the months of our Polar exploration. It's the major Rock 'n' Roll hotel in Helsinki, it's where all the visiting stars stay. It's modern and huge. It commands a view across Helsinki's Amsterdam-like inner-city waterways; colossal ugly bronze statues grace its forecourt. Open-plan reception area and restaurant: exotic vegetation grows to jungle proportions, monolithic shards of glass hang from the lofty ceiling, attempting to define the future of chandelierdom. A back-lit waterfall and accompanying interior design divide this massive lobby.

A hotel.

*

Z's flies are undone. My kilt is ragged and stained. We approach the check-in desk. On the whole I find the classic Nordic ideal of womanhood very unappealing, all that Swedish blonde bit very unstiffening – give me a dark-haired, dark-eyed, rounded real woman any lifetime. And yet, and yet . . . Behind the check-in desk is a vision of Nordic beauty with a painted smile reaching half way across the lobby to welcome the guests, her natural blonde hair piled high, gleaming teeth, sparkling blue eyes, cheeks radiant and . . .

Madonna, pop idol and Satan herself, sniffs the air. Her flared nostrils pick up something, an aroma from an astral plane. She is perturbed; something is not as it should be. She sips a chilled glass of human blood and prepares a bath of warm goat's sperm. The Plague Queen was in her earthly guise, holding an informal meeting with the Oberführer of her dread Homoschutzstaffel, Queeny Felcher, leader of the foul SS army of gay black dancers, all expert warriors trained to black-belt standard in the deadly martial art of vogueing.

'Meine Führess, something is wrong?' asked Queeny.

'Fuck it, Queeny!' She drained the blood from the champagne flute and tossed it at him. It missed and smashed against the wall. 'Yes, something *is* wrong, you black cocksucker!' The Blaspheming Cunt of Sodom kneed the ubiquitous nigger in his black nuts. He crumpled in a heap at her feet. She placed her mouth two inches from his ear. 'But I don't know what, and I don't like it! Get up, you black bastard! You disgust me!'

Queeny was au fait with his mistress's notorious temper, so he was neither surprised nor offended. Besides, the bitch paid well. The poof shuffled to his feet. He was in full Homoschutzstaffel uniform: thigh-high patent-leather stilettoed boots, black rubber jockstrap, SS officer's black cap, Nazi armband, black leather belt and shoulder strap. 'Would Madam like me to suck her bumhole through her knickers? That usually calms you down, darling,' offered Queeny who, despite his homosexuality, regularly had to perform perverse sexual favours for his evil mistress.

I hate it when a woman can have that effect on me before she has even opened her mouth. I put mere physical charms pretty low on my list of what makes a woman desirable – I usually go for attitude. But for the moment I can't deny I am bewitched.

'Good morning, gentlemen. Can I help you?'

'Yes, we have a reservation. Three rooms, under the names Goodrick, Manning and Drummond.'

Queeny obediently proceeded to stick his expert tongue up the Devil's arse.

The Queen of Hell writhed in appreciation as Queeny's snake-like tongue probed the inner recesses of her satanic shitlocker. She reached over to the bedside table and grabbed a twenty-two-inch black dildo and stuck it into her evil hell-cunt. She shuddered to orgasm and shat into Queeny's mouth. The Blaspheming Cunt of Sodom then wiped her arse on the silken bed sheets, got to her feet and strolled to the window. She was on the twenty-third floor.

Outside, a gaggle of young Finnish kids had gathered in the snow, eager for a glimpse of their pop idol. Madonna looked down at their innocent, excited faces, waved and smiled. Under her breath she murmured her true feelings: 'Pathetic scum! A plague on all your houses!'

Queeny lounged on the huge bed. The twenty-two-inch dildo was rammed to the hilt in his distended bumhole, humming merrily away. His right hand casually twanged away on his ugly cock. He spurted lazily on to the back of his hand and offered it to his mistress. She refused, so Queeny ate his own spunky oyster. The Plague Queen was obviously deeply perturbed. Ordinarily she was a vigorous sperm-eater, able to identify with stunning accuracy the sperm donor's exact diet during the previous twenty-four hours. Yes, Queeny could sense there was something troubling his diabolical mistress.

She presses a few buttons on her computer keyboard. I watch the light from her computer screen dance in her china-blue eyes.

She pulled back a greasy bang from her wrinkled brow and slammed a scarlet-taloned fist on to the glass dining table. The glass splintered.

She cursed and licked the green blood leaking from a nick on the side of her hand. 'Damn! Fuck! Anal cunt! Bollocks!' she cursed.

'I'm sorry, sir, there doesn't seem to be any reservation made under those names.'

'There's something very wrong, Felch. My demonic supernatural antennae are picking up bum vibes. Something out there is planning to harm me. Something powerful, powerful enough to erect a substantial psychic wall around its intentions and its location.' The Plague Queen shook her head and snapped out of her perturbation. 'Fuck it! Is Ernie coming to the Sabbat?'

'Yes, madam,' answered Queeny, relieved. 'He will be here. He's got a new boyfriend, fourteen years old . . .' Queeny squealed with perverse delight, slapping his limp-wristed hands together and batting his heavily made-up eyes, 'with tattoos!'

'Good, good. I was thinking of promoting him. Rupert is very pleased with his contribution to the destruction of the moral values on which Western civilization has been built. Maybe I'll give him another castle or something . . . hmmm.' She changed her train of thought. 'Have the necessary preparations been made?'

'Yes, madam. The men and Mr Moloch are working on them in the basement right now.'

'Excellent. Nothing must go wrong. This is to be a very special meeting.'

'Aren't all Sabbats special, mistress?'

'Yes of course, of course. But tonight I plan to wipe out a significant percentage of humanity. I have a craving for new souls . . . I am preparing to use the Anti-Chord!' Madonna, the Blaspheming Cunt of Sodom, threw back her head and let out a spine-ripping devil laugh.

She is still smiling her lovely warm welcoming smile as she delivers the above line, but my paranoia detects some other thought patterns filling her unconscious mind, and they go something like this: 'How the fuck can I get these three urine-stinking, bad-breath-stenching, grime-encrusted bums out of the lobby of this internationally regarded, pristine-presented cosmopolitan hotel lobby for which I am currently responsible?'

Queeny fell to his knees. His mascara had run and he appeared to be crying black blood.

Now, we had been planning on paying with the cash float that Gimpo is carrying, but in case of an emergency like this I have in my sporran the KLF Communications' platinum American Express card. I pull it out and lay it on the counter.

'Oh madam, madam. The Anti-Chord! How wonderful! What will it be? A natural disaster? An earthquake? Famine? Pestilence? How about a nuclear holocaust? You have been promising that one for years!'

Her eyes spy its colour, her fingers tap a few more digits on her keyboard, her face beams and her lips move.

'Exactly, Queeny! The Anti-Chord is tuned to spontaneously trigger the nuclear arsenals which my evil generals have hidden all over the planet in a chain reaction that may just bring Leo Silek's terrible vision on the stairs of the British Museum into three-dimensional reality, ha ha har! With a little diabolical luck, I may succeed in destroying the entire world!'

'Ah yes, sir. Here we are. I seem to have made a mistake. Goodrick, Manning and Drummond, you said. Smoking or non-smoking rooms, sir? Just fill out your details on these forms. Do you need any help with your bags? I hope you enjoy your stay.'

'Oh, mistress, I am so happy! Please, please, your arse, I need to eat your shit!' Madonna pulled apart her cheeks and Queeny fell upon her bumhole like a hungry seagull.

You get the picture.

*

Bad Wisdom

Two hundred miles north, Bill, Gimpo, the Chipps and myself thundered across the tundra with the wind and snow whipping our slit-eyed faces.

I am now in my private suite on the seventh floor. The bath is filling to overflow.

Our steeds raged; we were the holy defenders of the faith; we were armed to the teeth: we had chainsaws, we wore battle trunks, we had the Lost Chord. God was on our side.

A basket of fruit, a bowl of fresh-cut flowers, a king-size bed bigger than most bedrooms, a brace of armchairs, a glass-top table with an array of international magazines and *What's On in Helsinki* tourist guides.
    I'm sure the allure and loneliness of the modern international hotel has been well documented before by the likes of the Gavin Youngs and Eric Newbys but . . .

The fucking bitch didn't stand a chance.

Back in a second.

The staccato chatter of Madonna's stilettos clattered along the marble floor, echoing off the cold walls as she made her way to the subterranean gymnasium she had commandeered to prepare her diabolical magic. Low green sparks flew from her high heels; her teeth looked sharp. She needed more power. If her regular intake of human plasma was not replenished hourly, the magic which afforded her a human appearance would fade and she would revert to her hellish splendour, her Priapic hairstyle writhing like bad acid. She ran a finger over her demonic canine teeth, cursed and kicked open the door of the gymnasium.

Just gone into the steam-filled bathroom to switch off the taps. The room is laden with the ubiquitous body gels, bubble baths, shampoos, conditioners, bath caps, luxuriant white towels, bath robes.

*

Hell was here. The tortured wails in the gymnasium swirled like a tiny Auschwitz. The Plague Queen smiled, slammed shut the door and stepped into the red mist. Truly the Nazis would have been proud of this playground in hell. The beaming Madonna's spirits lifted as she wandered through the labyrinth of inventive tortures. She was always amazed by the ingenuity her beloved Homoschutzstaffel showed in harnessing the pure power that innocent souls provide.

'Ha ha!' she giggled, closing her eyes and savouring the tortured chorus. 'Is Rupert here?'

All over the world there are these hotels competing with each other to fill their rooms with more and more complimentary luxuries. But none are able to achieve what I assume are their aims: to make you feel welcome and fill that lonely hole. Yes, maybe these hotels are too easy a target for those that have spent any time in them but, if you have, you know how lonely they are, with their windows that don't open and their adult movie channel.

Rupert Moloch, Head of Propaganda in Madonna's diabolical army – the satellite Goebbels, the Mephistophelean multi-media techno-baron who preaches envy, lust and greed to the four corners of the world. 'Mistress,' purred the cigar-chewing mogul, 'everything is prepared. The studios are ready, the Sabbat proceeds at midnight.'

'Excellent!' said the Blaspheming Cunt of Sodom as she menstru-ated heavily on to the wooden floor.

I unstrap my kilt, leave my soiled clothes where they fall and lower myself into the depth of the bath. I wallow and watch my ageing flesh lose the tautness of youth. My belly spreads and bollocks shrivel, a small navy blue ball of fluff rises from my belly button to float, a dark grime lurks between my toes.

A hidden speaker pumps out the blare of the twenty-four-hour-a-day, three-hundred-and-sixty-five-day-a-year MTV soundtrack from the television that I have left on in the bedroom.

On the blasted, barren tundra one hundred miles away, the Three Wise Men, Fabio and two hundred semi-naked Chippendales charged on thundering hooves towards their confrontation with destiny: death or glory; freedom or slavery.

My diatribe against MTV three days ago may have seemed unfocused, the rage of a sad man; but now I ruminate in the womb-warmth of these deep waters. MTV:

Madonna and Moloch, the Queen and King of Sodom and their manifesto of useless aspirations and avaricious materialism; a diabolical duo dedicated to razing the world down to their level.

America's last stand and maybe its winning hand. It may not work against the Japanese, who at some point in the next thirty years will doubtless buy it out, but the Communist block has already fallen to the blue jeans, Big Mac, Coca-Cola and Marlboro man. The spreading empire of Muhammad and his fundamentalist prophets – from Bangladesh in the East to Marrakech in the West – leading the old Third World's retreat into pre-modern Muslim certainties, is in full sway. When those lands realized they were not invited to join us at the top table of the Western-liberal/free-market/protectionist/democratic/republican gravy train, they found comfort and strength in the words of the Koran, the harsh Holy Laws, hands chopped off for criminal crimes of theft, women sentenced to life in purdah and all that stuff. It can frighten the shit out of us in the West: with Allah on their side, how can we stop these infidel nations holding the world to ransom with their oil-rich lands and atomic-bomb-proliferating practices? But whatever laws a fundamentalist state passes to prevent the import of corrupt Western ways, they can't stop the satellite spinning overhead in space from beaming down its missionary zeal.

MTV: Missionary TeleVision, the main weapon of their evil campaign, pushing superficial fast-edit messages of global peace and racial harmony whilst carrying a slime-covered subtext of rampant materialism and loose morality, of impotent rebelliousness, of selfish individualism, a debauched sucker fish swimming beneath innocent teenage minds, preaching sex, misery and guns as fashion accessories.

*

Across the Muslim world, makeshift dishes made from dustbin lids gaze to the heavens, picking up Madonna, Prince, Niggers With Attitude, Guns 'N' Roses, Bon Jovi, Pearl Jam and the latest from Boyz II Men. And the seeds are sown, the damage done: young folk with the Koran in one hand, Kalashnikov in the other, eyes transfixed on the cathode ray of Madonna singing 'Like a virgin, touched for the very first time' as her right hand performs a self-inflicted fake orgasm while her body writhes in simulated ecstasy on a bed placed centre stage of a huge arena in front of 50,000 willing voyeurs.

The unholy trinity: Madonna, Moloch and MTV.

Then, in between the video clips brimming with every post-modern irony and teenage temptation, is all that one-world, green-conscious, peace-now bonhomie schlock and the 'You too can be like us and join the United Colours of MTV' of it all. South-east Asia, the sub-continent, Africa, South America stand in line and pray for deliverance from the one great god in the sky. 'A satellite of love,' as somebody once said.

Tonight at midnight, the witching hour, the fate of mankind would teeter on an unstable fulcrum. We would be there.

Look, my body is getting shrivelled and the bath water going cold, my log book damp as these notes are scribbled in this bath. My belly is sending messages to my brain: 'Fuck the MTV tirade and get downstairs for a full-on breakfast!'

We pulled into a roadside café to discuss battle plans. An old Lapp woman, detecting our noble auras and psychic power, smiled.

Downstairs in the split-level restaurant, I choose from the display of pan-European serve-yourself cold breakfast delights: freshly squeezed orange juice, a bowl overflowing with stewed apricots, unsweetened muesli, natural yoghurt with a dusting of wheat germ. I feel like being healthy. The table set for four, heavy with pastel linen, welcomes, and so does the waiter: 'Tea or coffee, sir?'

'Tea.' I weaken to the way he just assumes that the only truly international language is English.

She brought us a rich broth of reindeer flesh and offered us her teenage daughter. We gratefully accepted the broth and declined a go on the girl.

But should I feel guilty, make an apology? To be honest, I have just stuck that guilt bit in as I make these notes while the waiter is off getting my pot of tea. At the moment of him asking me if I wanted tea or coffee, it never crossed my mind that he would ask me in any language but English. Same goes for that now-forgotten girl at reception.

There is a white grand piano on an elevated podium. It's 8.20 a.m. An evening-suited piano player plays 'As Time Goes By', and I'm not making this up. Through the wall of smoked glass I can see a world of people going about their business. Wind and rain, umbrellas and overcoats.

I look up. Gimpo is crossing the room to join me. 'Way up, Bill. Do they do cooked breakfasts and do you know which room Z is in?' We order up cooked breakfast: it's American-style bacon fried to a cinder, pancakes, eggs over easy. Gimpo and I settle into a rambling conversation. He plans to spend the day sorting out his receipts, putting together the accounts for our trip. It's good to have Gimpo putting our journey of world-saving enlightenment into the practical terms of a short Rock tour. He has a rubber-banded wad of receipts, each one numbered and ticked off in readiness for the future inspection of one of Her Majesty's Customs and Excise men. Is enlightenment VAT-exempt or not? Does the Baby Jesus carry Excise Duty? Into which earnings-related tax band does world peace fall?

Gimpo's father has recently died, leaving Gimpo and his numerous half and full siblings with a whole stack of affairs to sort out. It seems his father owned numerous properties in Victorian Manchester, had interests in a number of questionable businesses. His father had lived life as a maverick, had many hidden dealings that are only now coming to light; he had also been a Tory councillor. The idea of

Gimpo's dad being a Tory councillor at first seems so unlikely but, within moments of Gimpo telling me, it seems strangely apt that Gimpo is the product of such a Dickensian-sounding scoundrel's loins.

Gimpo is talking to me. I'm trying to make sense of it. Stuff to do with his position as manager of Zodiac Mindwarp and the Love Reaction; about the eager young rock-chick who had elected herself to the position of his assistant; about how she had just turned up from somewhere in the East Midlands with her cute little arse and 'Can I suck your dick' smile and was willing to do anything. The band all loved her, A&R men loved her, metal-rock journalists loved her. But Gimpo could sense something being undermined, something sliding away.

Shit. I don't want to write this stuff about this girl. It's unfair on her, the band and Gimpo. It's just that Gimpo has things on his mind. We are nearing the end of our journey and he must be contemplating the return to the on-going wrangling about his father's estate and the nightmare of managing the Love Reaction. Gimpo is now sitting in silence, staring out through the smoked glass at the miserable wet day outside. I am trying to keep these notes in order. I'm losing patience with them. My hand has cramp from holding the pencil for so long.

Gimpo turns. There is no Gimpo grin filling his face; his blue eyes do not sparkle. He is talking about me and Z and Z's girlfriend who shares an office with him. He is telling me, in a way that assumes I already know, that she distrusts me, suspects my motives. It seems she read some of the correspondence between Z and myself and could not comprehend our relationship; was worried that we are both, at some very deep level, homosexual; that we fear this reality so much that we bury ourselves deeper and deeper into our macho male fantasy and the only way we can deal with it is through these male-bonding misogynistic adventures we make of our lives. This is not the case, but it does bring up the problem of women and what to do with them.

Bill clicked open the doctor's bag and produced a blueprint of the Helsinki MTV studios. There were only three entrances, each of them heavily guarded by Madonna's Homoschutzstaffel. Bill took a pen from his sporran and clicked out a small aerial. He talked into the pen in an obscure Russian dialect. The pen crackled static and a tinny voice fizzed in response. Bill pushed the small aerial back into the pen and informed us that we were outnumbered by at least four Homoschutzstaffel to one Chippendale. This, according to Fabio, was equal odds. I was not so sure, although the Chippendales were probably the fittest, both mentally and physically, army on earth. The HSS was not a corporeal enemy. Madonna was a god, and the Homoschutzstaffel demons. Even Bill was not entirely sure what powers this infernal force of nature possessed.

The plan was simple and Bill had several pounds of semtex. As there was no possible way we could storm any of the three entrances, Bill, myself and Gimpo would blag our way into the studios using our pop-star costumes – Bill in his orange monk's robe with the big horn on his forehead, me in leather trousers and sunglasses and Gimpo in a T-shirt that said 'Crew Filth' on the front. Once we had gained access, we would take out the west wall with the semtex; Fabio and the Chipps would then storm the breech and, God be with us, we would exterminate the entire termite's nest. Fabio had ordered his lads that no quarter was to be given; all must die by the saw, absolutely no mercy whatsoever was to be shown. It was a hall of devils; our chainsaws were instruments of God. We would send them all back to hell and, if needs be, follow them there and finish the job.

Yeah, I've been pretty flippant with my use of the word 'misogynist' in these notes. Women enjoy using it as one of their armoury of barbed words to throw back at men. For me, misogyny is as natural as having a wank: something I recognize, tolerate and attempt to keep under control. To try and deny it doesn't get rid of it.

Bill made a few minor adjustments to his stylophone, rearranging the tarot cards and sellotaping various magical parchments and trinkets to the frail-looking plastic casing. We had decided to use the Anti-Anti-Chord. If Madonna used the Anti-Chord, the Lost Chord would simply negate the Anti-Chord and, in theory, the Anti-Anti-

Chord would eliminate the arch fiend and all her stinking breed. But this was just a theory. The supernatural powers of the Homoschutzstaffel might tip the balance in their favour, and we could not risk this. We were operating in the realm of gods, where nothing is real or unreal, true or false. Indeed, there was always the chance that the Anti-Chord and the Anti-Anti-Chord would feed off of each other and destroy the entire universe. It was a chance we had to take.

Bill crossed himself and placed the fragile, somewhat pathetic-looking stylophone reverently in his doctor's bag. Who would ever have thought that the fate of the world, if not the entire universe, would depend on a small musical toy beloved of that strange Australian, Rolf Harris. We left the roadside café, bidding our charming host a grim farewell. She wiped a tear from her craggy face. She knew we were men of destiny on a serious mission.

All men are born of women: that's where it starts to go wrong. For the first few years of life we are totally dependent on them for our survival: that's as nature ordained; it's the same for all mammals. I'm told that in primitive societies, when lads hit puberty they are forced to go 'walkabout' or are thrown into the jungle or some other barbaric method is used of making them get out there and survive away from their protective mothers. This, I suppose, helps break the mother–son bonds and turn them into self-sufficient men.

But we live in a society where males are encouraged never to break those bonds with the female. While the humiliating neediness we have for our mothers is still in place during adolescence we are entranced and lured into this other thing, this sex thing. And once this has got us, we let the female entrap us in all sorts of other ways: as homemakers, bed-warmers, sympathy-givers, clothes-menders, bill-payers, better halves. And to make sure they keep us there, we let them undermine us, make us feel inadequate, clumsy and juvenile, the implication being that we could never survive without them. They say they want a strong man and then do everything possible to chop him down. So of course I have these urges to get my revenge on women. Most of the time it's under control. I can usually deal with it by suppressing my sexuality, putting my balls in the freezer. But fuck knows what side effects that has.

Most women think men just want to get inside their knickers. Well, bitch, you got it wrong. I would never give you the satisfaction of thinking that you got something I need that bad. You either beg for it, or I cut you up. Well no, hopefully not that extreme; more, you want it or I ignore you. For me the idea of chasing after women is humiliating. Yeah, I know I've done it, but it's humiliating. I hate myself for it. So for the past few months I've been trying to carve out an existence where I'm not dependent on women in any sense – no, not just in a cook-for-myself, mend-my-own-clothes, come-and-go-as-I-please and wank-without-guilt way, but something far deeper than that. Is that what this journey is about? Not some spiritual odyssey at all, more an aborted attempt at my walkabout that I should have been forced to do at thirteen.

Maybe some men in our society find a way out of this messy dilemma through homosexuality. Lucky them. For me, my hormones ain't lined up that way. If I open the freezer door I can hear them scream for more of what's in the honey pot.

Lately I've been able to dump most of the guilt that has clung to these conflicting urges, but back in the winter of '78, when I was twenty-four and living in Liverpool and they hadn't yet caught the Yorkshire Ripper, I began to wonder, was it me they were searching for on *News at Ten*? Was I their man?

It was 20.00 hours when we struck camp five miles outside Helsinki. Here, we would make final battle arrangements and drink soma, a powerful magic potion made from the mushroom amanita muscaria. The shamen of the Lapp people believe that, when imbibed together with certain secret roots and plants, it enables the eye of a truly pure soul to perceive absolute objective reality; no magic, not even the foul web of Maya, that infernal spider of illusion spun by the Dark One herself, could blind the eye of a pure soul drunk on soma.

Fabio prepared a small fire and placed a cauldron over it. In this he placed snow, the mushroom and some strange-smelling herbs. Bill, Gimpo and I then joined him in making a small incision in our wrists with a curved knife; we dripped our blood into the brew. The whole ritual was very matter-of-fact, almost like making a cup of tea. Fabio explained that the purpose of the incantations and esoteric ephemera of much magic was to baffle children and confuse the ignorant; for a real magician, magic is matter-of-fact and, funnily enough, very much like making tea.

Twenty minutes later the soma was ready. Fabio's nonchalance did not prepare us for the spectacular effects the soma produced on our perception of reality. No more than twenty seconds after tasting the sweet, coppery brew, I noticed a distinct shifting of my senses. We were all communicating telepathically. Until I had tasted soma I could only receive messages; now I found myself able to send them as well. 'Good,' communicated Fabio. 'I, of course, had no doubt that you were all pure of soul, but one can never be too sure. Drinking soma has terrible consequences on anyone whose soul is less than 100 per cent pure. It can cause hellish visions, rampant fear, crippling paranoia and ultimately an irreversible condition of total insanity.'

Was I the Ripper? Maybe, somehow, after my wife and I had fallen asleep, I would awake and taking just my coat and whatever tools were needed, would cross over the Pennines, down into those Yorkshire towns, do my deeds and be back in bed asleep beside my wife before dawn thawed the frost from the cracked window pane. There was no logic to these feelings – it would have been impossible for me to get over the Pennines – we didn't have a car – but the fear and the guilt were real. There was a song that I wrote entitled 'Shallow Grave', but the band I was in at the time refused to perform it.

On the *Today* programme on Radio 4 one morning back then, Brian Redhead interviewed a police psychologist about the Yorkshire Ripper whose concern seemed to be that their man's hormones might settle down before they could catch him; meaning, once the hormones had settled he would lose the urge/need to kill 'those' women.

'And at what age might you expect a man's hormones to settle?' asked Brian.

'Forty,' answered the police psychologist.

Forty! The number ricocheted around my skull. I've sixteen fucking years to go before I'm free, out of the woods, clear of these terrible hormones and those women that need killing and God telling me it must be done. (The God bit is supposed to be ironic.)

As you know, Peter Sutcliffe stood trial and was found guilty for being the Yorkshire Ripper. I was mightily relieved: it seemed it wasn't me. But as for the next sixteen years, I could only take things one day at a time. Since then, the age of forty has meant freedom; the time in between, my sentence. I am now thirty-nine; there are five months to go before my fortieth birthday. As you may remember, I bought that plastic-handled knife a few days ago; I stroked the blade and felt my cock harden. What was that about?

The thing is, I have never indulged in any sado-masochistic fantasies, or even ever wanted to smash anybody's face in. The trouble with me is that I find it impossible to have fantasies: if I wanted to hit somebody I would go and do it; if I wanted to rape a girl, I would go and do it. Nothing in my head gets shoved away as a mere fantasy. Once any thought, wish or desire surfaces to the conscious part of the brain, I have to go and at least attempt to fulfil it. That's what has caused many of the problems in my life. So what if those Ripper-like thoughts and desires started popping up, what then? I haven't got the wherewithal just to push them away as far-out fantasies; a little voice inside me would be going, 'OK, if that's what you want, Drummond, go and do it! Come on, are you man enough or are you just a weak peely wally shilpit slaister of a man?'

Five months to go: can I make it? Am I able to keep whatever dark demons that are down there from surfacing into this side of the conscious world? But what strange creature lurks below that now familiar scrap heap? None of which helps with the problem: What to do with women?

'Is he being knowingly provocative here?' a voice.

No, that's just the way it came out, but now I have written it I have to deal with it: none of that glib can't-live-with-them, can't-shoot-them stuff is going to help here.

Women have got it easy, even if they don't like it or want to admit to it. They have been given a clear-cut purpose, they know why they are here: they have to breed, to create. After life itself, God's greatest act of creation was to make it possible for us to re-create ourselves. But other than the spunking up bit, men's whole role in the affair is pretty non-specific, or even irrelevant. All the creating bit is done by the woman. That's where all the magic goes on. Yeah, yeah, I can hear all those cries of derision thrown at my shallow over-simplification of the whole male–female messy business, but stay with me . . .

Us men, we don't know why we are here; we have been given no clear-cut purpose. So we attempt to discover meaning, devise laws, invent gods; we dream up ideals and carve out countries that we have to go to war to defend; we form football leagues we have to win. And because we cannot give birth, yes, create in the truest sense of the word, we go out endlessly and pathetically writing our Fifth Symphonies, painting our Sistine Chapels, writing our Rise and Falls, tending our lawns to be the most perfect in all England. But in the end they are like so many dry wanks. There is not one artistic achievement by any man that has ever walked this earth which can compete with what nearly every woman can do. We keep trying and we applaud those that have tried harder than us; we bestow upon them fame and fortune and maybe a place in history, to be remembered for all time. The time and effort we pour into all this, and yet we never have been and never will be capable of true creation.

All of the arguments about why the great works of art and other historic achievements were produced by men are redundant. No, it's not because man kept woman down, banished her from the battle-field, the studio, the court, the coal mine or wherever else greatness was being created; but because she wasn't arsed, she knew it was pointless when she could create the greatest of creations right there in her belly. Yeah, I know there have been genius women writers, artists and composers, but all of them produced their finest work while neither bearing nor rearing children. I would go further than that and say, show me a female writer, artist or composer and I will show you a barren belly, a lesbian or a sad, fucked-up wallflower. And yes, the world would be a far drearier place if it were not for those great women. We need the woman's angle on things, but, on the whole, they don't need all this shit.

'Patronizing bastard or what!' a voice.

Of course, from time to time our culture makes demands on women to get ahead in a man's world, to smash the chains that bind them to the kitchen sink; which is, of course, only right, because who wants boring women who only want to talk about babies and how Johnny's doing at school and other such topics?

But let me turn the spotlight on us poor, pathetic men, waving our dicks, spouting our half-baked wisdom/lies, competing with each other to get in the Great Bores of Today column of *Private Eye*. Ever since the sixth day when God uttered those terrible lines, 'Let the earth bring forth living creatures . . .', and it did, women have known what to do: have babies; and men have had no idea what they should be doing. Yeah, we keep pretending, coming up with cultures that demand to be fulfilled; but we insist on changing the rules; we keep losing the plot, not knowing what our continuously evolving societies will demand of us next.

I look longingly back over history to times of apparent certainties. In my grandfather's generation it was simple: men went across the sea and gave their life on a foreign field for God, King and Country. But the war was won or lost, so what next; where then? When Neil Armstrong took those first steps on the moon, he should have said, 'One small step for man, one giant dry wank for mankind.'

In front of my cottage are two fields. In one of the fields there are forty-four ewes and seventy-two lambs. Each ewe has given birth to at least one lamb this year. Through the daylight hours the lambs drink goodness and life from the ewe's udders, and through the night the ewe keeps her lambs warm. In the next field are seven rams. For eleven months of the year these seven rams do nothing but challenge each other to head-butting contests. The winners move up the strictly kept league table and the losers drop down. During those eleven months each of those rams knows exactly where it stands in that league of seven. For the twelfth month of the year the farmer opens the gate that divides those two fields and those seven rams go shag crazy with those forty-four ewes. After the month is up, they go back to their mindless existence of head-butting. I exaggerate: for most of that eleven months they are not head-butting; they get on with each other fine and dandy, probably discuss the meaning of life, the role of God, the politics of the farmer, EC subsidies, the mutton mountain and who's got the biggest balls.

From my smoking pencil, I look up. A lift door opens; out steps Z. He looks around, sees Gimpo and myself, weaves his way through the emptying breakfast tables. 'Do you fancy going to look for some porn shops?' Gimpo makes his excuses. He plans to spend the morning getting some kip.

Z and I leave the hotel in search of hard-core European porn. Z is my leader. Eject ourselves through the revolving doors. The day hits us hard. My knees shiver as I realize I have dispensed with my undergarments of long-johns and Levi's and am now wearing my kilt in the more traditional fashion. My overcoat has been left on the floor of my hotel suite for the maids to hang in the wardrobe. Z leads the way up through some unlikely streets, me shivering, clutching my notebook and pencil.

Nervous intrepidation: there are no neon lights, no visible signs of back-street sleaze. But Z is not concerned: he has a nose for these things; something about enlightened states not needing to hide their porn away in small, guilt-ridden neon-lit quarters of their cities.

Fabio warned us that when we entered the studio in Helsinki, the horrors we would encounter might prove too great for us to withstand in our present enlightened condition, despite our fearless courage. Although Madonna's magic would give an illusory vision of a splendid MTV party to the rest of the world, with our soma intelligence blazing on full power we would perceive its true depravity. He gave us each a pair of absolute-reality deflector shades; these looked like ordinary Rayban Wayfarers, but in fact they acted like a kind of dimmer switch; instead of seeing absolute reality we would see the illusion, the web of Maya, Madonna's magic. Fabio advised us to put them on before we entered the hall of Sabbat so that the shock of the very physical presence of evil would not affect our composure and give us away to the ultra-perceptive eyes of the Homoschutzstaffel.

The Chippendale army pulsated light; a visionary battalion swathed in gold, they mounted their white charges and rode on to Helsinki, trailing stars and dripping heroic music. In heaven, God commissioned Gustav Klimt to be our war artist.

23.50 hours. Helsinki. With our forged invites we entered the TV studios in our pop-star disguises. We had taken Fabio's advice and were wearing the ARD shades, so everything looked normal:

rubber-necking air-kissers chattering and looking over each other's shoulders to check if there is anyone more glamorous around; people drinking free beer and watching the hunted make a dash for the VIP lounge. Our expertly forged invites granted us access to this hallowed area, but before we scuttled into the celebrity ghetto I couldn't resist a peek at the ordinary punters over the top of the ARD shades. They were all beautiful, about fourteen years old and looked like black and white footage of Beatles fans. I was confused. Fabio had warned us of horror, but these people were gorgeous; they radiated a child-like innocence and a purity of soul that almost brought a tear to my eye. Could it be that the Master Chippendale had been mistaken? Maybe we were the fucked up ones. Maybe Madonna wasn't the Devil. Was all this some kind of collective hallucination? My mind reeled.

It seems a futile cause. Each corner we turn reveals just another respectable street of grocers, banks, newsagents and scrubbed-clean stone apartment blocks. I'm kinda hoping we don't find one. I'm all for just hanging out in a café watching the Helsinki world drift by and pondering on the lost role of man in God's creation and how crap post-mo . . . We turn another corner. Nothing. But before it has time to shrink back into the respectability of another row of worthy shops, Z spies our prey: FUCK NOW proclaims the neon. Z turns to me. With a serious resonance in his voice he offers a bit of manly advice before entering this portal to an unknown world. He tells me of a strict code of conduct – this is a very serious affair: there must be no talking loudly, no running about and, above all, no laughing; all business is carried out in the hushed tones of a gentlemen's club; other patrons' choice of literature must never be peeked at or commented upon; and lastly, ultimate decorum and respectability must be observed at all times.

Z pushes open the glass door and we step inside.

I put the shades back on and walked through the green velvet curtains into the ultra-exclusive VIP lounge. Everything seemed normal: glamorous celebrities in expensive clothes with expensive women drinking expensive champagne; elderly record-company executives wearing too much gold and too much cologne; waitresses wearing humiliating costumes being jostled by slightly inebriated younger record-company executives; the latest pop stars with that far-away look in their eyes, still unable to take in quite what has happened to them. I was worried. This was not what I had expected – Fabio had told us of evil beyond all comprehension.

From floor to ceiling the walls are racked out with video cassettes and printed publications.

And then it clicked: I was still wearing my absolute-reality deflector shades. I took them off.

Z purposefully moves to his desired section and begins to browse studiously through the literature on display. I quietly step to an unoccupied section and self-consciously begin to follow suit. Although I am still clutching my notebook and pencil, I feel I must refrain from making notes while here; my mind tries to hold these observations in place to be put down on paper at a later stage. I pick up a publication racked up in front of me. Each is sealed in a clear polythene envelope.

I wished that I hadn't. One minute I was looking at a waif-like Sinead O'Connor, thinking that she was pretty fine looking for a bald chick. There she was smiling shyly, drinking champagne with her record-company people, the silver ice-bucket twinkling under the candelabra; then the next second I went straight to hell. Sinead was strapped to an iron chair, naked, covered in horrible purple bruises, red welts and open sores. Pipes attached by huge steel needles trailed from every major artery; the needles drew the poor drugged girl's blood into a rusty bucket from which the naked record-company executives filled dirty wine glasses and then drank. She appeared to be about seven months pregnant, though it was hard to tell because of her emaciated state.

We can only judge the contents by the title and the cover shot. Am I shocked by what I hold in my hands? Well, I suppose I am.

*

It was truly horrible, like something from the diseased imagination of the medieval church. Sinead was slipping in and out of consciousness. One of the men kept injecting heroin into her glazed eyeball. The other middle-aged men, their putrescent bodies like fleshy bags of congealed blood, sucked on her breasts and defecated gold coins. One ugly bastard was inserting a bloody crucifix into the Irish Catholic's ripped vagina; he forced it in up to the crosspiece, jogging her into painful consciousness. She let out a piercing Edvard Munch scream. At this howl of agony one of the vile bastards shot steaming globs of grey sperm over her bruised face. It hit the skin and started burning the flesh like hydrochloric acid. Thin grey smoke and bubbling fat sizzled from the wounds and dribbled on to her ruined breasts. A fat, long-haired guy with soiled buttocks, naked apart from a grubby silver tour jacket, was kicking her in the stomach. He looked like a tour manager.

At the next table Sting was tied to an artificial tree; he too was emaciated and covered in sores. He was punctured by small arrows. Sat a few feet away, the naked, ugly record-company men were decorated with what appeared to be Amazonian tribal paintings daubed on to their fat pale flesh. Instead of the bright colours of the Indians, however, these designs were made from human faeces. The vile shit-men had blow pipes and were firing evil little darts at the green singer. The blood from the arrows ran down his once-athletic frame and gathered in pools at his feet. Two gnomes dressed in dirty McDonald's overalls were fishing gold coins out of the pools and placing them in hessian sacks. I instinctively surmised that this money was going to be used to produce arms to sell to Third World dictators. Bob Geldof looked on enviously at his martyred chum, a bag of unsold records under his arm and a fallen halo around his scrawny neck.

We all know this stuff exists, but being able to walk down an otherwise respectable street and walk into a shop called FUCK NOW, pick up a copy of *Sadistic Rape* and purchase it as if it were a magazine on classic motorcycles of the fifties before returning home to your family for some relaxing reading throws up some disturbing contradictions. When Mrs Gilchrist taught us the letters of the alphabet in primary 1 back in 1958, did she imagine that her young pupils would put her imparted knowledge to such uses?

Other titles catch my attention: *New Cunts, Big Mamma, Anal for Beginners*. I notice that Z is at the counter with half a dozen or so periodicals which he is purchasing. I pick up these other titles, studying the information in the international language of the pornographer, English. I return to *Sadistic Rape*, looking for tell-tale signs of irony. You might be thinking, 'What's the big deal? Hasn't he ever been in a porn shop before?' Look, I'm a Presbyterian; we try to ignore the existence of sex. (I'm afraid I've allowed some overstated irony to creep into the last sentence.) What I have in my hands are the facts: no excuses, no cover up, no beating about the bush – the title tells us all clearly and unequivocally what this publication is for.

The photograph on the cover is of a young woman who has been bound and gagged; she is front-side down on a table, naked apart from her bonds and a tightly bound, partly revealing face mask. A naked overweight male is standing between her legs. In one of his hands is a hank of her hair; using this he has yanked her head back. We are led to believe he is taking her from behind. Whether this is up her arse or her cunt is unclear – the pain that can be detected on the visible part of the woman's face leads one to think it's the former. Standing by the table is another male watching and holding a stick. I now notice that her back is badly bruised and partly lacerated, but it is the agony on her face that holds my attention and, as I make these notes some hours later, is still there in every last detail.

If men were able to give birth, would they ever want to treat a fellow human being like this? Is this, too, born of the search for fulfilment, meaning and true creativity that is to be eternally denied to myself and my brothers? So I try to convince myself how wonderful it is to have this little enclave of paganism, where we men can come and worship at the altar of some primeval female goddess. It doesn't wash.

In a dark corner, Michael Jackson. A paper-thin mask covered the fragile bones of his skull. I could see the red and white blood corpuscles pumping through transparent veins. His eyes reflected the road of a man travelling the labyrinth of a personal dream. Michael is a man who has reinvented the world within the cryogenic emotional landscape of his own aspic; he is stranded in pre-pubescence. His libido, however, has led him into the real world. Personal planets are ill-equipped for the armed forces of reality. He sat alone, shunned by the cash vampires who feared that his Midas touch had been reversed and that everything the golden boy now touched would turn to shit.

I joined him at his lonely table, unplugged his drip feed and offered him a cigarette and a swig on my bourbon. He looked startled and then started to cry. I put my arm around his fragile shoulders and looked him straight in his bewildered eyes.

'Michael,' I said quietly, 'you have been fucked. You see those fat naked men with the gin blossom on their faces, the ones with the shrivelled genitals, the ones with the gold coins leaking from their irrigated colons? They are your enemy, Michael. They did this to you.

'When you were a small boy they banished you to a cockroach-infested dungeon and told you it was a palace. They stole your soul and moulded it into a commodity. They stole that child within you, Michael. They tied it to a tree and then fucked it until it was dead. They are evil, Michael. They are the servants of the Devil. And do you know something else, son? They are still fucking that dead child's mouldering corpse.

'Do something! Join us. Destroy them. Do it for your love of God, your love of Walt Disney. Do it for love, for truth and the un-American way, for the world, for me; but most of all, Michael, do it for yourself!'

Reality beckons. I can feel that something has stirred in my loins and is pushing itself upwards. Luckily my sporran is in place, and with a little pressure from my left hand I hold it down. I return *Sadistic Rape* to the racks, move slowly across the shop to the door. The chill of the outside air freeflows through the pleats of my kilt, subduing my readiness, and I wonder at the fate of man, the Zen Masters, the Three Kings, the Baby Jesus inside. And what if that Scots woman who had been on the bus from the airport had just

seen me leave this FUCK NOW shop? Would I be banished forever
from God's own country?

Z appears, brown paper parcel in hand.

Swirling hero music bellowed out of the ether. I recognized the score
as it swelled to its grand climax and the vertigo violins and clashing
cymbals almost deafened me – Mussorgsky's *Night on the Bare Mountain*.
Michael began to cry, great geysers of tears jetting from his eyes. I
handed him an honorary Chippendale jockstrap. A smile cracked
his tissue-paper skin.

'It is you, isn't it?' asked Michael.

I didn't understand the question.

'You are, aren't you?' For some reason his question frightened me.

'Who do you think I am, Michael?'

He smiled a spooky skeleton grin, bent his knee and took hold of
both my hands. 'You are . . .' he hesitated, 'the Nazarene!'

Gimpo fell to his knees. 'Master!' he ejaculated, bowing his head,
'I always knew!' Bill looked envious and fiddled with the semtex,
cursing under his breath.

We discuss visiting art galleries, museums, cathedrals; but I'm frozen
and ashamed. I want to return to the warmth, comfort and safety
of our hotel.

Back in my hotel room MTV is still on. 'Smells Like Teen Spirit'
by Nirvana.

Back-stage in the main hall, the Homoschutzstaffel are flapping like
schoolgirl turkeys. The twenty-four members of Madonna's ultra-elite
bodyguard dance squad prepare for the big performance of the
evening: a lavish, Egyptian-inspired interpretation of the title track
of the Plague Queen's new album, *Fist Fucking the Stupid Thwarted
Womb*. This, of course, is the ultimate-reality version of the album
title; the mass hypnotism, cosmodemonic black magic weaved by the
unholy trinity of Moloch, Madonna and MTV has given it the
innocuous title of *Bedtime Stories*.

Prolapse Pete, the prima donna of this debauched dance troupe,
is beside himself with excitement. Dressed in a tutu tailored from

the flayed hide of a dead leper, he is hopping from foot to foot, stroking his tumescent crotch.

'Oh, Felchy! Queeny daaahling.' He stretches the last word, camping up the vowels. 'Is it true? Is it, Queeny? Is Madam planning to use the chord? The divine Anti-Chord?' The overexcited nigger pansies gather around Queeny excitedly, dancing and feeling each other's arses.

'Queeny! Queeny! Queeny!' squeals Fellatio Joe. 'Do tell! Do tell! Is she? Is she?' The whole bunch of sodomistic ballerinas – Rectum Steve, Cocky Paulo, Shitstabber Jacky, Bummer Nige and the rest – are beside themselves. They break out in a little nursery rhyme sing-song:

> She's going to use the Chord,
> She's going to use the Chord,
> Destroy the whole world,
> Destroy the whole world,
> Armageddon!
> Armageddon!
> We all fall down.

They perform a little balletic jig and burst into a fit of girlish giggles.

'Well, ladies,' says Queeny checking his eyeshadow in a small compact mirror and snapping it shut with a dramatic flourish, 'between you and me' – the Anal Ballet giggle conspiratorially – 'I think it's going to be the Big One. I saw her programming her keyboard this morning and girls, believe me, the amount of infant plasma Madam has been consuming recently . . . well, put it this way, I would be very surprised indeed if we don't see a little occult nuclear action. Poof! There goes the sub-continent!' The Queens are now bordering on hysterical.

'Tell me,' interrupts Bummer Nige, 'will this be global or local?'

'Hard to tell,' answers Queeny, 'but who cares, petal? Several thousand or several million – innocent death is innocent death. I know I'll be masturbating furiously over this incident.' Queeny mocks a quick one off the wrist. The dancers squeal delightedly and practise their lascivious dance routines, thrusting, fisting, fellating.

*

My soiled clothes have been hung in the wardrobe and the cover of the bed has been turned. Fully kilted, I tumble in and fall into the deep sleep of the innocent.

The phone rings. It's Mulla. Are we going to the party? He gives me the address. I make some brief notes about the morning's exploits, to be sketched in later; phone Gimpo. He wants to get his accounts done. Phone Z. He is up for the party. Rearrange my kilt, cock my hat at a jaunty angle.

Z and I in the back of a cab heading across town to an unknown party full of unknown people.

Front of house trembles with anticipation. MTV cameras are primed for the event of the decade. Bill, Gimpo and myself mingle with the predominantly teenage audience. Bill flashes me a secret hand-signal indicating that the semtex is in place. I notice that he is sweating and clutching his bag nervously. Gimps is ogling the secondary sexual features of the flowering teenage girls in the audience. On stage, in the blackness, Madonna's sinister keyboard glows blood red. My palms are wet and my mouth tastes of tin and LSD.

Back-stage, the evil one primes her dancers and menstruates heavily. She is in her earthly guise, sipping from a pint of human blood. She radiates satanic confidence. Green steam hovers in her wake; a faint smell of brimstone stings the eyes. *Night on the Bare Mountain* thunders from the Empire State PA.

Z, it seems, has started the introduction to his half of the book. Should I wait until he has finished his tale of mystery, debauchery and imagination, so I can read his stuff before I attempt to turn these notes into a work of crude literature? He reads me what he has written.

The huge velvet curtains part. The stage billows smoke; red lasers call down hell. The black fag dancers vogue their way on to the stage. It is saturnalian. They mince all kinds of perverted gay sex shit in time to the deafening classical score. My sphincter clenches angrily. Queeny's face glows yellow in the Stygian darkness. He grins; his teeth are pointed. Queeny is being serviced by Fellatio Joe, who has somehow managed to insert his entire head up his perverted Überführer's butthole. Mincing Mary is stuffing live pitbull terriers up Fellatio's arse in some horrible serial sodomy dance. Those poor animals. I feel physically sick.

Suddenly, babies start dropping from the ceiling. They are still alive, on fire and screaming in agony. Everything smells of fire and shit. Classical music builds to its deafening climax. Twenty-four Homoschutzstaffel dancers writhe in a vile sodomistic orgy, stuffing animals up one another's arses in time to the demonic rhythms. Strobes, dry ice and laser beams conjure up flashing images of a homosexual Auschwitz Disneyland.

The music stops dead. A single bass drum pounding slowly like the sound of a sodomite's nuts slapping into a dead arse creeps out of the madness. The Plague Queen herself – iron tits, penis snake hair writhing – undulates out of the smoke like some vile eel swimming through a lake of Swarfega and excrement. She is surrounded by blowflies and blue fire, blood drips from her mouth. Black gas and words escape: she is singing the title track from her *Thwarted Womb* album.

'I am death,' she hisses.

Blue paste dribbles down her chin. The audience is mesmerized. Multiple black epiphany.

'The stinking foul womb of all perverted desires.'

The place stinks of unwashed cunt.

'You will believe in me.'

Like Grace Jones, only more evil.

'All my debased misery I share with you. Don't be satisfied with what you have!'

She takes a huge brass crucifix and rams it in her flapping cunt and starts to masturbate in time with the music. Blood hits the stage. Screaming, the dancers skitter round her licking it up. 'Why be satisfied with what you have?' she choruses, flicking into a horrible dislocated dance routine, her arms and legs at weird Egyptian right angles. She whips off her steel bra and starts squeezing her poisonous dugs. Green acid lactates at high velocity across the stage and hits one of the dancers in the eyes. He starts screaming and falls to the ground twitching. One of his comrades leaps upon him and stuffs a skinned emu up his behind to revive him. Madonna turns her back to the audience, bends over and farts purple ectoplasm at them.

Screaming babies are still dropping from the ceiling like hellish cherry blossom. A huge wall of fire burns in the background. The audience, completely under the brainwash spell of Rupert Moloch and his cronies are, of course, seeing something entirely different; Bill and I are able to witness this ultimate reality only because of our special vision, gift of the sacred Lapp mushrooms. The Plague Bitch moves towards her sinister engine: the synthesizer. Bill twitches. His face is sweating; his Andy Warhol-style glasses keep sliding to the end of his nose. I place a calming hand on his shoulder and tell him to move towards the PA stack.

The music ends abruptly and the stage blacks out. The Bitch announces her next song: 'I'd Rather Have an Abortion in Hell than be a Mother in Heaven'. The music crashes in, stinking up the hall. The Bitch's head starts spinning 360-degree circles, the Gorgonic penis mane spurting fountains of poisonous black semen. She resumes the dislocated Egyptian spaz dance. The dancers bugger each other with wild abandon. A rocket of vomit scrapes up my throat. 'Girls, do ya wanna have fun?' Her Minnie Mouse voice echoes around the black hall. 'Flush your foetus down the toilet, ha, ha. Are you in control of your body? Do you want to have eternal sex, spinning on the infernal storms with Francesca da Rimini? You do? Yeah! Well . . . Murder your baby! Ha, ha! We can dance . . .'

I vomit down the back of a teenage girl dancing in front of me. The whore cartwheels across the stage to her synthesizer and raises her arm to strike the dread Anti-Chord. I scream across the room to Bill: 'Now!'

He depresses the plunger. The wall explodes. A concrete cacophony of light, dust, noise; a seraphic mushroom cloud. The teenage audience flees screaming, leaving the battlefield clear. Madonna brings down the hammer: the Anti-Chord. India and half of Africa explode into oblivion; the dancers simultaneously orgasm; fountains of brown sperm rain on the fleeing teenagers.

Three single notes hum across hell on earth. The low frequency: a tectonic grumble, deep beneath active volcanoes, grinding and shifting. One million sperm whales evacuate their bowels. The noxious, greasy bubbles of trapped fart-dust and whale shit slither from the bottom of black oceans and explode to the surface, stinking of rank plankton.

The high frequency: a billion castrated pigs career out of control in a million farmyards, screeching as their ragged scrotums flap beneath red curly tails. Plagues of locusts with rasping teeth grind out babies' eyeballs. Ten billion butterflies on fire scream in paradise.

The mid frequency stenches up the astral plane: human offal discarded on a hot summer's day; Dennis Nilsen's loft insulation; Idi Amin's cannibal farts.

How could I compete with such polished prose embroidered by adjectives unknown, spinning tales of heightened unrealities?

My mind reels.

We pay the cab driver and climb the stone stairs.

The air is sucked from my lungs.

The apartment door is open. Hip, early nineties acid jazz music flows out. A spacious but crowded high-concept flat. We follow the music into a throng of the highly fashionable people of Helsinki.

My spinning eyeballs, like the silver orbs dancing around on a multi-ball fever-pitch quick orgasm, lock on to the epicentre of this calamity: a jagged hole in the wall. Mounted Lone Ranger, Trigger Roy Roger horses rampant on hind legs, the Chippendales, Fabio at their head. Kinetic Spielberg strobe lights silhouette the heroes; soaring Dambuster music.

The in-crowd is made up of types you would have imagined soirée-ing at a mid-eighties *Face* party. This description is pretty two-dimensional and ultimately unfair on the people.

We feel aloof: we have taken Elvis to the Pole, we have saved the world. But Z and I feel like the outsiders, so we believe we have every right to criticize this crowd of friendly individuals in this clichéd way.

'I hate parties.'

The dynamic troops gallop through the breech, chainsaws held aloft, sparking like thunderbolts from God. Fabio, hooves thundering, leans from his magnificent white horse, slicing off black bumboy heads: Death, the gardener, cutting back black pansies. Slow-motion Jackson Pollock arcs of blood paint Auschwitz expressionism. George Grosz, naked, armed with a knife, slices in a mad frenzy, his street-pizza corpse dragged lynch-mob-style through the bad paranoia landscape.

That's me repeating to myself my battle cry of the dour self. I hate all that 'Fight for your Right to Party' and 'Freedom to Party' Criminal Justice Bill stuff. What the fuck are parties for?

I smash a queer's head into the floor. Flecks of blood and bone cling to his Maori demon face. I laugh insanely as his skull comes apart in my hands. I slice and dice, ripping off penises and stuffing them down their owners' queer throats. I feel like Lawrence of Arabia. The eroticism of battle! My pants bulge with Spartan lust. This is the life! Death, death, death! In the name of God, kill a queer for Christ! Annihilate anyone who disagrees! Rip their nuts off; slice their eyes out; trample on their kid's pet hamster! Are we having fun yet!

You just meet people you haven't met since the last party you went to, talk a load of rubbish, try to impress people, go home miserable and wonder why you are such a social failure.

On and on it goes . . . chainsaws spurt fire; erotic pyrotechnics call down hell; blood flashes wet and shining; tattered tissue slithers across fetid panoramas of feral realities. Gimpo fans scat fountains across the uncensored cinemascope of the Marquis de Sade's bad dreams.

Who the fuck wants to be a social success anyway?

*

I am knee-deep in gore; and slightly bored. I reach for Bill's leather doctor's bag and pull out a frying pan and a half pound of lard. I catch a passing kidney flung from the battle and fry it on a small fire made from slippery bones and pubic hair. It smells like delicately cured bacon. I reach again into Bill's leather doctor's bag and find some HP sauce. It compliments the human offal rather well.

Objective reality, that dangerous spiritual goal of the East, can only ever be like this: laughing with Friedrich Nietzsche, talking to horses, as mad as war.

Here, within the insane decor of Jumping Jack Flash's infernal restaurant, there is human flesh for breakfast. Eyeballs? Now that, my friend, is indeed a delicacy. Fried eyeballs in vinegar, lice and child rape sauce? A favourite of Queen Victoria's, so it's said. Boiled nipples with bumholes à la grecque? Slit gizzards with piss, sperm, faeces and homosexual onions? – Boy George's favourite. How about arse-cream mayonnaise poured across fried Italian scrotums and leper scabs? Jellied tampons? Carcass vagina stew – a peasant favourite from Eastern Europe? No? Then perhaps Japanese schoolgirl's sphincter with teriyaki sauce served with spider's legs and woodlice syrup? Faeces-encrusted anal hair lightly fried with ginger? – a little like fried seaweed, so I'm told.

Z and I are nibbling from plates of quiche, chicken legs and salad dips. A young lady hands us glasses of wine. Mulla joins us with a warm welcome, asks how we got on, if the Pole found us, introduces various party goers to Z and myself. Some of them attempt to engage us in conversation. I think they vaguely know who we are. Some bloke with a baseball cap on is trying to talk to me as I make these notes in a corner of the kitchen, talking about techno music, about how he is a DJ and has a sampler and is hoping to make a twelve-inch and maybe I would like to hear his cassette – he has one right here. Should I tell him I fuckin' hate all forms of dance music or just techno in particular?

The battle rages on, a maelstrom of severed limbs and crashing steel. The Homoschutzstaffel, each armed with two katanas – the long curved swords used by Japanese samurai – fight viciously. Their martial vogueing, combined with the swords, proves particularly deadly. Queeny, I notice, is particularly effective at this ancient homosexual martial art. He spins like a miniature tornado, bringing down several of the Chippendale horses in one sweep. Dreadful hand-to-hand combat: chainsaws versus katanas. One of the fag S S slashes Gimpo across the face. So incensed is my friend that he disembowels his assailant with his bare teeth. He tosses me the queer's appendix. I lob it into the frying pan, where it pops and spurts greasily in the hot fat.

Two more glasses of red wine are thrown down my throat. Z is likewise engaged in conversation with some bloke with the currently fashionable version of flares on. It is too easy to slag these people off, but what do you expect from us? Only moments ago, it seems, we were receiving shamanistic rites in the warm welcome of a Laplander's home, eating their reindeer, drinking their health and listening to their songs; here we are now, stuck with this bunch of would-be *i-D* readers who must long for the day the *Face* or any of those lost magazines from the previous decade does their 'Visiting Clubs Around European Capitals' piece, so they can all get in the picture. The note of death is still ringing in my ear, the eternal quest calling.

Out of habit, Z and I hang on, as if something is going to happen, as if the ceiling is going to roll back and the archangel Gabriel is going to lead us all in some celestial community singsong, or the floor will open up and Dante take us on a trip round his Inferno. But no, it's just another fuckin' party.

'Yeah, but what about the girls?' A voice.

Last thing I need to be doing right now is getting the hots for some foreign bint. It would just make me feel like a lumbering lump of sexless shit. And what do you want me to do with her anyway?

The Plague Queen continues to perform her vile songs. She is wailing a mantra-like chant to the accompaniment of the single, droning Anti-Chord. 'Rivers of blood from my stinking cunt shall baptize you at the Sabbat at the end of time,' moans the hell bitch.

Cut out her insides with my virgin purple plastic-handled knife?

*

Outside the battle arena the world is slowly burning.

Yeah, and of course they all want to know about the kilt. And yeah, my ego does get stroked by somebody telling me how great the KLF records were.

Z wants to split. So do I. We split.

The thing is, as Z and I make our way down the stairs, I realize that we must have appeared as two rather dull blokes with not much to say for ourselves. I hate meeting people who already have some preconception of who I am – I feel they are going to expect me to be witty, interesting, radical or at least weird – and all they get is this vaguely amiable, inarticulate bloke. Fuck all this egocentric 'me, me, me' shite! Z and I, with the help of a tourist map of the city, make our way back to the hotel through failing light and sporadic rain.

Back in the hotel suite MTV is still on: Simply Red. Mick Hucknall is for real. You might think his music is bland, but Mick means it. I vaguely knew him years ago when he was the singer with the Frantic Elevators. They used to do this cover of The Beatles' 'Don't Let Me Down' – it was heart-stopping stuff. He was just this fat, scruffy, carrot-top teenage urchin, but when he hit that song all the pain of the rejected child came out. But the warm feelings don't last long. MTV refuses to be switched off like the serpent in the tree; it will not take no for an answer.

What about Kate and James at home? I haven't written them any postcards, bought them any presents, and anyway what could I write to them on a postcard that would be honest and that they could understand? What the fuck will they make of all this when they read it one day?

Catch up on these notes. Time drifts by, boredom shimmies about. MTV drawing me in then letting me go. Then Gimpo phones. It's Chippendale time! It seems that Ulla has called and we have to meet up with her and the Chipps at some restaurant and then we are going on to a club. Forget what I wrote above, I'm up for a night out! Who needs that line of coke when the adrenalin starts coursing through the veins?

Ring Z's room. His receiver is picked up and before he has time to say anything, I can hear 'Highway to Hell' by AC/DC coming through on the ear-piece. It's *Head-Bangers' Ball* on MTV, and they're playing some all-time metal classics. Z's droll Yorkshire drone cuts through on top. 'Hallo?'

'You comin' to meet the Chipps?'

'Nah, I think I'll stay in. I've got started on the writing, it's going good. Do you want to hear some?'

He reads. It sounds brilliant, all about the Lapp Pygmy Chainsaw Fishermen or something, and he's got this idea about these Viking Bikers and this Nazi Sex Bitch from Hell. Did all this stuff really happen? Must have.

Basement of pizza parlour: me and Gimpo, loads of the groovy people from the party this afternoon. Somebody's birthday. No Chippendales, no Ulla, but everybody is really friendly. They all seem to know about our successful mission and already they say the world is feeling a safer place to live in: the Middle East should be sorting it out soon, Northern Ireland getting it together, Bosnia might take a little longer, Africa could do with serious Elvis vibes. Yeah, flippant stuff, but you wait and see. If I stop clapping, Tinkerbell dies. So baby, right now, I'm clapping. (Reality check: using words like 'baby' in this prose might give you the wrong idea of what type of bloke I am.) There are these good-looking women that have just walked in and joined our table and I'm in a good mood. Time moves on and it's time to move on to the club.

Through the wet cobbled streets. We arrive, welcomed in by this spectacular-looking queen of a doorman. It's all very neo-New Romantic, with a genuine weird outer edge of Europe vibe – what you imagine a decadent party in a 1990s Moscow to be like, if the 1917 Revolution had never happened. I mean, that looks like Crown Prince Alexandre over there, and isn't that the Countess of Push-kinskiye? Techno music is pumping at a massive volume but never feels threatening; marble staircases sweep us to higher levels; court jesters giggle; B Boys bounce around; what appears to be a swarm of supermodels breezes by. Gimpo is off to look for Ulla. A huge cascade of fresh flowers headies the air. A Leigh Bowery-type charac-ter with a light bulb on his head and an ermine robe queens by. I move from room to room, now making these notes from a small corner of the bar as I wait to be served. Maybe I should be hating all of this. Surely this club should be depicted as Sodom and Gomorrah in full swing. I mean, isn't that a golden calf over there?

Inside, the hero Fabio, leader of the Chippendales, God's third in command, slices his way through the tempest of destruction. He is dressed in blood and honour. He holds his chainsaw aloft in his left hand and points at the Hell Queen. 'Blaspheming Cunt of Sodom!' he bawls, his manly voice stilling the swirl of battle. Madonna turns towards him, a supercilious grin curled across her inhuman visage.

'Oh, hi Bill! Here, meet Vince and Larry. They're big fans of The KLF. I've told them all about your trip to the North Pole with Elvis – they loved it!' It's Ulla looking radiant and gorgeous and this must be the two Chippendales. Ulla is getting the drinks; Vince, Larry and myself fall into conversation.

'Hey, Bill, I just love that "Last Train to Trancentral" track. We flew out from the West Coast yesterday. We heard it in the car on the way to the airport.' I kinda nod and smile and wonder if I've heard their record. I'm vaguely aware that Pete Waterman has made some high-energy track with them that's sort of made the charts in Britain.

'You look nothing like what I expected somebody in KLF to look like.'

The hero continues. His manly baritone silences the carnage. All ears heed the battle speech, chainsaws stop sparking, queers stop vogueing.

> 'Author of Evil unknown till thy revolt
> Unnamed in heaven, now plenteous, as thou seest
> These acts of hateful strife, hateful to all
> Thou heavest, by just measure, on thyself
> And thy adherents; how hast thou disturbed
> Heaven's blessed peace, and into nature brought
> Misery, uncreated till the crime
> Of thy rebellion? How hast thou instilled
> Thy malice into thousands, once upright

And faithful, now proven false? But think not here
To trouble Holy rest. Heaven cast thee out
From all her confines. Heaven, the seat of bliss,
Brooks not the words of violence and war.
Hence, then, and evil go with thee along
Thy offspring, to the place of evil, Hell,
Thou and thy wicked crew – there mingle broils
Ere this avenging chainsaw begin thy doom,
Or some more sudden vengeance, winged from God,
Precipitate thee with augmented pain.'

Gimpo scratched his head and farted. I, too, was clueless as to what the fuck our seraphic hero was talking about, but something about him reminded me of the archangel Gabriel. Madonna strolled to the front of her blood-spattered gore platform. The room hung silent. Her black eyes focused on Fabio and she spake thus:

'Nor think thou with wind
Of airy threats to awe whom yet with deeds
Thou canst not. Hast thou turned the least of these
To flight, or if to fall, but that they rise
Unvanquished, easier to conquer me,
That thou should hope, imperious, and with threats
To chase me hence? Think not that so shall end
The strife which thou call'st evil, but we style
The strife of glory; which we mean to win,
Or turn this Heaven into the Hell
Thou fablest: here, however, to dwell free,
If not to reign. Meanwhile thy utmost force
And join him named Almighty to thy aid
I fly not, but have sought thee far and nigh.'

I still had no idea what these fuckers were talking about, but Madonna's poetry had certainly pissed Fabio off big time.

'You mean I look older?'

The heterosexual warrior leapt to the stage and sliced off both her tits with his chainsaw.

*

257

'Well, no, not exactly, but . . . ah . . . kinda.'

The Homoschutzstaffel were on him instantly. Before the Chipps could reach their leader, one of the evil arse-bandits had Fabio's battle trunks down and was slipping him the salami – the ultimate insult for a Chippendale.

'Yeah, I know what you mean.'
    But, dear reader, I must interject some opinions into this night-club conversation: Vince and Larry don't look that much like what you'd expect Chippendales to look or even sound like. Vince is only about five feet sevenish, has short wavy hair and round wire-rimmed spectacles; he is wearing a modest T-shirt and regular slacks. Larry looks more the part: he is taller, has a mane of dyed black hair, a fake sun-tan and shirt buttons open to reveal a well-groomed chest. But neither are 'drop dead gorgeous'. I think that's the circa '92 phrase that women use.

I had had enough. I entered the faecal mêlée, ripping and gouging with my chainsaw, Parzival. I felled twelve or so homos, straddled the corpses and pointed at the hell bitch. 'Back thee! To chains of darkness and the undying worm!' I don't know where the words came from, but the bitch looked scared.
    'My God!' she stuttered, 'the Nazarene!'
    I leapt on the cunt without saying a word. I grabbed a handful of the penis snakes writhing on her head and slammed her face hard into the floor. It split like a melon. I worked on her eyes with my knife, raped her in every orifice including the ruined eye sockets, and pulverized her into hamburger.

'So, Bill, at your gigs you must be pulling in about 10,000 punters a show. We can get in about 800 to 1,000, but it's growing gig by gig.' This is Larry talking. And I'm thinking, 'He's talking as if we were both in Rock bands, climbing the ladder to stadium success. No mention is made of what constitutes a Chippendales gig. For all I know, they may in fact actually be a would-be stadium Rock band and are going through a misunderstood period as exotic male dancers. Or is it a post-modern comment of theirs on the state of popular entertainment and mankind's place in it. Are they outdoing Jeff Koons at his own game?'

A heavenly music arose from nowhere: Bill had plugged the magical stylophone into the PA. Madonna's synthesizer exploded, her Anti-Chord silenced. The Lost Chord swirled in the ether, the sound of angels and singing whales, dolphins and sunlight, The Beatles, U2, AC/DC, Led Zep and Elvis, all rolled into one; blue oceans, children singing love, peace and hosannas to the Lord. By some divine accident Bill had used the Lost Chord instead of the Anti-Anti-Chord; and it had worked.

Larry's head is turning. He is surveying the scene.

The hamburger bitch was gurgling; the arse-bandit army were terrified. Green fire, thunderbolts, laser beams and smoke sliced out from behind the Empire State PA.

'There are some real Shetland ponies here. I wouldn't mind getting me some. Have you seen that little miss lady over there? I bet she gives good.' Well, that's one comforting illusion of mine shattered: the Chippendales are not gay. Larry takes a wander, looking out for the 'real Shetland ponies'. It's funny how, as soon as three or more blokes get together for any length of time, they will invent a term of derogation/endearment for the female sex. But how come 'a real Shetland pony'? I mean, what's all that about? Vince and I try to find common ground, try to bond in that strange way that one always feels is necessary. But me and one of the Chippendales? What on earth could we bond about? What common ground could exist?

'Larry is full of shit. He's just a Chippendale. I'm an actor. Yeah, I was in the Chippendales, but the whole thing sucks. I only came out on the promo trips 'cause they paid me 5,000 bucks. I've had it with them telling me to get down to the gym and work on my physique. I mean, I like to work out, keep my body in shape, who doesn't? But hey, they tell us they have done this survey to find out what women really want in a guy's body and have done this photo-fit picture of what this perfect physique is supposed to look like, and that's what we're to aim for. I ain't taking it any more. Once we're back from this trip I'm through with the Chippendales. I'm an actor. I got a career. I got self-respect. They can go fuck themselves!'

Who's this anonymous 'they'? I have no idea. Maybe it's Jeff Koons and La Cicciolina? Maybe they manage them? But Vince doesn't seem too happy about the 'they'. I just nod, take a sip from my glass and say something like, 'Yeah, sounds pretty bad, acting seems to be the right thing for you to be doing.' Vince really wants to be friendly. Ulla arrives back. Other people drift in and out of our conversation. The music pounds, time drifts.

A huge rip in space opens behind the stage. It is full of stars.

And our precious icon of Elvis has been lifted through the dark sky. Hopefully it is now hanging on a bare wall in an unlit galley, its secret power rising up the tower to be cast out with the searching beam from the top of the world, across the heaving sea, bathing the storm-tossed whalers, the Russian merchants, the Nordic lands, onwards, outwards and downwards. But the epic visions flicker and fade. Larry is back; Vince is off. Ulla is talking to one of her many socialites. I see Gimpo's Cheshire-cat grin hover above the crowd.

Outside in the world, joy riders spontaneously combust; sodomite vicars are ripped apart by the resurrected victims of paedophile rings: Myra Hindley, Ian Brady and all the other dark apostles of the Plague Queen choke on their own black blood; politicians of every creed die agonizing deaths and all their sins of greed and self-interest manifest themselves as voracious insects gnawing and chewing away at their rancid genitals with pincer teeth; and all their children die with them. All just, all correct! The waters are set free, the wasteland drinks!

Larry talks: 'You after any pony, Bill? Man, that guy Vince, he's a bore. He don't know a good thing. The Chippendales is one hell of a thing to be part of – we get good money, travel the world and all the tail we can take. Man, he just ain't good enough. That's his problem.'

And I think, that's as maybe, but I want more than this mindless chitchat on a Helsinki night. This meeting the Chipps should be the catalyst for some great truths to rain down; or at least I should be using this here and now as a backdrop for some unlocked wisdoms spilling forth. But I'm tired and lonely and want to go home. Gimpo wants to stay. I shake Larry's hand and give Ulla a hug, promise to send her a copy of the book when it's finished. Leave.

From out of the black hole charge purple flaming skeletons riding black horses with bat wings, clutching huge, bloody lances. A massive, rushing vacuum pulls the screaming Queens into the maelstrom. Madonna, terrified, is dragged screaming and flailing into the black hole. The hole rips shut with a white crack: Hell reclaims the bitch.

The night is raw.

We stand still amongst the silent spooky carnage. Gimpo is slightly wounded; Bill, myself, Fabio and most of the Chipps seem to be OK. All trace of the Plague Queen and her Homoschutzstaffel has vanished.

My knees rattle.

The Chipps are not fond of long good-byes and offer manly handshakes and phone numbers. 'If you ever need us . . .' says Fabio in his deep voice. 'Silver, away!'

Street lights dance on the wet cobbles. Late-night revellers make me feel conspicuous in my proud plaid. A huge billboard poster: a now familiar character grins down at me with his sly, knowing face; he wags his finger as if to say . . .

'Adios, amigos, adios!'

*

Well, fuck knows what he is trying to tell me, but he is trying to tell me something.

The Chipps wave and gallop into the sun.

I pass on by, but that sly grin and wagging finger stay with me.

I turn to Bill, serious. 'We did it, Bill!' Bill punches the air and freeze-frames.

The hotel room. MTV beams out its secret and evil messages. I watch to see what the next video clip is. The kilt falls to the floor. 'If I Could Turn Back Time' entertains me in the dark. I hit the off button and sleep drags me under.

The credits roll.

CHAPTER SIXTEEN

Back to Kansas

The telephone rings in my dreams. Cher refuses to answer it. I stretch out my arm, knock the handset from its cradle.

'Good day, sir. This is your morning call. The time now is 6.25 a.m. The airport bus will be leaving in thirty-five min . . .' Cher seems to have left. Fuck that. I'm making this Cher bit up. I never had a dream about her – I never have sex dreams at all – but I do love Cher and love that video with the battleship for 'If I Could Turn Back Time': she is so much bigger than all the ludicrously tacky costumes. She's a great actress, gives everything to even the most unglamorous of parts which somehow, set against the Vegas qualities of other areas of her career, makes her even more of a star. Compared to Madonna she . . . What the fuck does any of this matter? I'm supposed to be getting dressed. Stuff my bags and down to reception, trying not to justify why I think Cher is great.

'I thought he said he didn't have any fantasies?' A voice.

The lift door opens. Gimpo grins. He's already settled up. It was Gimpo that put the wake-up calls in for us. He is now going back up to bang on Z's door. It seems Z's left his phone off the hook. I wait in a heap in reception. Gimpo and Z arrive. A fierce wind and pelting rain hit as we take the three small steps for mankind from the hotel foyer to the airport-bound courtesy mini-bus, dark blue with the name of the hotel in gold down its side.

Z mumbles. It seems he has not slept at all. Harnessing the powers of the complete contents of the last bottle of Blue Label vodka, his newly purchased hard-core porn and the twenty-three satellite channels available, Z had not only been able to uncover the plot by the pop-singer Madonna acting in cahoots with the world's leading media mogul to bring about Armageddon, but with the use of his pen had foiled all their attempts at this apocalyptic meltdown. There is no trace of irony in Z's voice, his faith in the power of his pen is total. He reads me something about a blaspheming cunt of Sodom and her vogueing Homoschutzstaffel. I try to tell him about Vince and Larry. He grunts something about how I've got it wrong – he was called Fabio. A waking Helsinki sweeps by beyond the tinted windows.

The airport. I make a call using all the Finnish change I have left to Jet Taxis in Aylesbury, England; negotiate a price (twenty quid) then book a cab to be at Heathrow when we arrive back. Baggage; embarkation; the plane. I have an aisle seat. I'm shagged out. The plane taxis, the cabin crew does its display, seat belts are checked. Acceleration. Take off. Steep incline. Tiredness. Far-away thoughts.

The hum of the aircraft is comforting. We are going home, back to families and loved ones. It had been a strange trip. The air hostesses glide up and down the aisles. I can hear static electricity as their nylon hosiery rubs together beneath the tight blue skirts. They bring me dozens of bottles of miniature Pentangle vodka; they're cute, friendly little fellows, warming the belly and cheering the soul.

I am admiring the gentle sway of one particular hostess's shapely arse when Bill starts pontificating.

'Madonna, the Plague Queen, the Blaspheming Cunt of Sodom: how many of us can say that the bitch is not in some way a part of our nature, if not in fact a large part of our true selves?'

Gimpo joins the symposium: 'Yes, Bill. As you know, I have often thought that religion, or more specifically the moral and ethical restraint inherent in religious practice, somehow, how can I put it, limits one's experience of true existence and that if . . .'

Bill interrupts: 'Yes, Gimp, I see what you're driving at: that if we did not have these moral and ethical certainties, these policemen of the soul, then man could be truly free to his essential nature.'

Gimpo: 'Which is, unfortunately, somewhat bestial, animalistic – evil, in fact?'

Bill: 'Not quite, old chum. Animals are not evil; evil is a human concept. The serpent, the apple, the knowledge of good and evil, the fall – human concepts, dear boy. And of course, the case of our friend Madonna proves beyond doubt that if man is permitted to indulge, indeed to revel in his most basic desires without restraint, the restraint inherent in spiritual principles, that . . .'

Gimp: 'You mean like buggering dead babies and shitting on supermodels' faces?'

Bill: 'Exactly, young fellow. Such things lurk within us all, and it is only the teachings of our spiritual leaders which prevent normal people like you or me or our chum Z from indulging quite freely in these normal human activities.'

I butt in here: 'Buggering dead babies and shitting on supermodels' faces?'

Bill: 'Yes. Rape, torture, murder, birds' nesting and camping . . . Perfectly healthy, youthful activities.'

This sage dialogue goes on and on. Only when Bill starts expounding some bizarre theory about Sonic the Hedgehog being God do I drift off into my own reveries.

I've just woken. Z's sleeping.

The twenty-third miniature Pentangle hits the spot. I dream of the Baby Satan inside us all, an innocent little fellow, a Blakean chum, the Byronic and Miltonesque hero, the rebel with a cause lighting fires just to admire the wonderful colours; starting wars for fun, dipping pigtails in inkwells, watching *Beavis and Butthead*, inventing slavery and shitting in little Beckie's mouth.

Gimpo is staring out of the window, looks like he's deep in thought. I need a shit.

I'm sitting on the bog again, notebook, as you'd expect, on knees, pen in hand. Aeroplane toilets are always a problem: those collapsing doors, the cramped space and hidden flush handle, the fact that there is a queue and the next in will know it's my stench.

I slam the big-arsed air hostess with the mostest into the small lavatory and kiss her hard on the mouth. She melts like warm butter. I tear open her thin cotton shirt and bite hard on her left tit. She moans. I can smell female rising from the intricate incarceration of cotton and nylon. I drop to my knees, mad with lust, and rip down her skirt and pants. Her pubic hair smells of soap and desire. I ram my face into her cunt and my mouth sucks hard on her plump twat. I stick my tongue hard into the sopping hole. She squirms and moans. My hands maul her breasts.

On the radio last week there was an interview with the actor Simon Callow who was writing a biography of Orson Welles. They were talking about how Welles had been such a mythologizer of his own life that the lies he told of his exploits contradicted each other on a daily basis. The interviewer thought this must make Welles's auto-biography a worthless source of reference. 'On the contrary,' argued Callow. 'You can learn as much about a man from the lies he tells about himself as from the objective realities of his day-to-day life' (not verbatim). I've tried to keep the lies to a minimum in these notes, but sometimes I just can't help myself.

I am losing control.

I just hope that when you detect a lie it won't undermine the spectacu-lar truths. OK, my knob wasn't hanging out in Oscar's restaurant when my kilt fell to the floor, and there wasn't a Leigh Bowery look-alike with a light bulb on his head, and all those 23s were just shoved in for the junior members of the Numerology Club. What you've got to watch out for though is all this self-effacing honesty stuff. Anyone who writes about themselves is obviously trying to get you, the reader, to like, admire, be amused by, even love them; and because we all know we are fundamentally not very likeable people, we try to pull the self-effacing honesty trick.

I leap to my feet and slap her hard on the mouth, drawing blood. My own mouth falls on her bloody lips. I can taste salt and primeval forests. I grab a handful of her hair and ram her head down on to my dick. She takes it down the throat to the nuts. I manhandle her roughly and grab her once more by her hair, pulling her foolish head up close to mine. I kiss her deeply; my thrusting tongue tastes my own semen, it sears the back of my throat and tastes like grapefruit juice and piss-flavoured vodka. I kick into psycho gear and bite off one of her nipples. I spit it in her face. The fucking whore loves it. She writhes in atavistic ecstasy, a rippling tiger bitch on meltdown heat. I smash her hard in the face and push her dumb head down the khazi.

'Well, at least he's being honest with us.'

I am basalt hard. The evil porno Medusa has scoped my monkey spanner. I smash it into her virgin butthole and bugger her in a mad pneumatic frenzy. The slag panics and lets loose a sloppy barrage of black diarrhoeic shite which covers my stomach.

In fact, I'm not sitting in an airplane bog, thirty-odd thousand feet above the North Sea on 7 November 1992: I'm sitting in a café in Aylesbury and it's 1996 and I'm editing these notes before publication, and I've just decided to put this honesty bit in.

I pull out my Spam javelin and wipe the faecal matter on the cunt's hair. She looks at me with melting submissive admiration. 'OK, bitch,' I remember thinking, and ram my iron-bar cockhammer hard into her sliding snatch.

'Do you believe him?'

Jungle heat rises; macaws and chimpanzees scream in the primal forest. Somewhere in Africa a volcano explodes; tectonic plates grate beneath boiling oceans. The evil serpent bangs up into her ovaries and lets fly a barrage of cosmic tadpoles; they fly to the waiting egg and the Darwinian spunk-gizzard breaches the membrane.
    The cunt is pregnant and she knows it.

All that nose-picking and farting stuff peppered throughout was stuck in as just a bit of a debunking trick.

*

Like my friend Bill, I am super fertile. (In my brief rock-star career, I have fathered over two thousand illegitimate sprogs.) Her eyes swim in their sockets. Flushed, her blonde hair sticking to her perspiring forehead, she dabs her wounded breast with cotton-wool. I am breathing heavily; sweat clings to my large black crucifix chest tattoo. She licks the sweat from my bare chest. 'My hero!' she purrs.

Not only have I read the Bible from 'In the beginning . . .' straight through to 'May the grace of the Lord Jesus be with you. Amen', and found not one recorded snot-picking; but also Bret Easton Ellis documents every conceivable form of misogynistic sadism possible in *American Psycho* as an allegory of the state of his nation and not once does he record that his nose needed picking or the satisfaction to be gained from such a small pleasure. All that coming clean about sordid secret sexual fantasies is old hat. But what I want to know is, is nose-picking and the eating of snot one self-effacing honesty step too far?

'The child, what shall I name the child?' she adds, instinctively knowing she will never see me again but knowing she is indeed privileged to have been impregnated by one as noble as myself.

Where are the boundaries set?

I smile and tease her. 'Honey, name the kid after me.'
  'But hero,' she replies, 'what is your name?'
  I snort a derisive chuckle and casually toss her an obscure epigram: 'Babe, I am all things to all men. I am legion.'

On re-reading these notes two and a half years after they were first jotted down, there is lots that has dated, doesn't stand up now, looks naïve. But if I were to tamper with it any more than the odd nose-pick or post-modern visit to the bog, the whole thing would start coming apart at the seams. In that Rock 'n' Roll death bit, I would like to have predicted its revival, naming the bloke from Nirvana, the guitarist in The Manic Street Preachers. Have I broken the spell?

*

'He is legion,' sighs the fucked air hostess.

'Yes,' I thought. 'Yes, I fucking am.'

Back in the bog, my ablutions complete. I find the handle, work out the mechanics of the inward-folding door; return to seat.

I walked back to my seat. Bill was asleep, one hand down the front of his kilt, the other lazily hanging by one finger from his left nostril. Gimpo was concentrating hard, dripping into the techno universe of his Gameboy. Planet Earth was safe. As long as great men like myself and my comrades walked this hallowed earth, mankind had nothing to fear. I nudged Bill in the ribs to wake him from his slumber.

Fasten safety belts. Descent. Disembark.

It is time for farewells. We shake each other's hands, feel a bit embarrassed. Z and Gimpo are to get the Underground back into London. What should we say to each other? 'See you soon,' seems to do.

'Fly the black flag, lads,' I said, symbolically. 'There's a swallow nesting on my roof.'

Bill laughed and answered, 'I see an elephant with its trunk held aloft and Madame Sosostris deals me the temperance card.'

Gimpo looks up from his Gameboy. 'I am,' he says, fist held aloft, 'Donkey Kong!'

I can already see the friendly and familiar face of Faizal approaching me through the throng.

In the passenger seat of Faizal's minicab. We exchange pleasantries. He asks me how my business trip went, I ask after his family. I'm now tending to these notes. We past under the M4 and up towards a still-raining Uxbridge.

On the seat beside me is yesterday's copy of the *Daily Jang* – it's an English/Urdu paper for the thinking Pakistani abroad. I pick it up, flick through its pages, glance at the headlines: 'Benazir Bhutto plans to meet Bill Clinton'. My eyes wander to a column on the opposite page: 'Egyptian Couple Jailed for Public Circumcision'. I read the article. I'm shaken and shocked like any good Western liberal. I ask Faizal if I can keep his paper as I want to rip this column out and stick it in with these notes.

This is what I read:

CAIRO: A Cairo court has sentenced a barber and his wife to two years' hard labour for circumcising a girl in public during a religious festival . . . The court said the couple had violated the fourteen-year-old girl's humanity and insulted her pride by performing the procedure in front of passers-by and had endangered her life by using unsterilized instruments . . . The couple had circumcised the girl late last year in a small tent set up during the festival to celebrate the birthday of Sayyeda Zeinab, the granddaughter of the Holy Prophet (peace be upon him). Many traditional barbers in Egypt double as amateur surgeons, performing male and female circumcisions.

A film showing the circumcision of a ten-year-old Egyptian girl broadcast by the US Cable News Network during a UN population conference in September embarrassed the Egyptian government . . . Female circumcision is a traditional ritual signifying a rite of passage into womanhood and is considered highly desirable.

It almost makes me want to throw away my purple plastic-handled knife. I don't.

My mind drifts back to the last few days. What now of the Magi returned, we Three Kings, the Baby Jesus inside, Elvis to the Pole and his magic rays that were going to leak peace down through the longitudes? Did all that just serve as an excuse for a lads' night out? Or will this journey of ours be seen in the future as the moment in history when post-modernism was symbolically cast aside as an empty and useless thing; when the humour of the knowing reference and sly nod were seen as a dead, dated, pathetic cul-de-sac? Do we need another reminder that the past glories of modernism were just monuments to man's vanities, and the pre-modern world where all was safe in the cruel, strong, loving hands of God, Allah, the Chief, Mother Earth, YHWH or a million other spirits, hobgoblins and water sprites, is just a distant memory?

And do I have to answer to my female friends who say it is their right to explore and exploit their bodies in whatever way they want. They don't need a repressed, moralizing hypocrite telling them how they should be having sex. If they want to be buggered by a fat man whilst being battered black and blue, it's none of my business. It's between them and Nancy Friday. And yes, of course I've knowingly over-used the words 'post' and 'modern' in these notes. What do you expect? Why bite the hand that has fed you when you can rip it right off and throw it to the dogs? But what next? The time must have come to turn the page of history. The next chapter in man's eternal search for meaning beckons. This one is boring.

Or was our journey a farewell to those gods of our century that have done their time, served their master well and held us, their worshippers, enthralled? So it's bye-bye Mickey Mouse, Charlie Chaplin, John Wayne, JFK, Malcolm X, Miss Monroe, Courtney Love, Louis Armstrong, Doctor Spock, Doctor Leary, Captain Kirk, General Ike, Superman, Spiderman, Batman, Marlboro Man, Cassius Clay, Fritz the Cat, Iron Mike, Ronald Reagan, Coca-Cola, Henry Ford, Big Mac, Bob Dylan, Jimi Hendrix, James Brown, Spike Lee, GI Joe, Charlie Manson, Bette Davis, Hank Williams, Ice T, the Man on the Moon; but most of all, it's goodbye Elvis. Or is it just me wanting to lay to rest my youth and young-man days before I face the responsibilities and adventures of the middle years? A mid-life rite of passage 'thang'?

Well, we got Elvis to the Pole, even if we didn't get there ourselves. The Baby Jesus inside? Yes, I think we found him. If I listen hard enough I can just about hear 'that still, small voice'. No, not the voice I've used as a corny device throughout these notes, something far smaller.

But like Z said, it's the deal we struck with the Devil. We've got to go and find him and sort it out. As for women, it's going to take more than my purple plastic-handled knife to even the score there.

Faizal is not looking. I try once again to pick the encrusted bogey in my left nostril. It's not there; gone; made off. To a better place?

The taxi pulls up outside my cottage, the twenty quid fare is paid. I cross the country road to see where I cut down the small tree earlier in the week, half hoping to see that it has shot forth fresh shoots and its leaves are unfolding their pale green newness to brighten this dull, dark winter's day; but, no. In the field, the rams earn their keep and the ewes give chase. I'm tempted to document some gauche remark like, 'The dance of life goes on, what other meaning do we need?', but that would just be a lie.

I turn, cross the road, push open the door of my cottage. On the mat lies a picture postcard, a midnight sun, postmarked 'Honningsvag', dated Thursday the fifth. In Z's distinctive hand, the following words of the magus: 'We returned to our palaces, these Kingdoms,/ But no longer at ease here, in the old dispensation.'

Shantih, Shantih, Shantih.

I dump my haversack and shuffle through to the kitchen with one thought in mind: to fill the kettle and make a pot of tea that will last a lifetime. Yep, the journey has just begun to trick the Devil and get our souls back.

It is raining.

Thanks for the postcard, Z.

Bill's Leather Doctor's Bag
Its mysterious origins and secret history

When James Brown, soul singer and secret occult scientist, sang the line 'Papa's got a brand new bag', he wasn't singing about a Tesco's carrier bag and he wasn't singing about his father either. No, the wise black seer was speaking hermetically, revealing in a coded fashion his knowledge of the existence of a very strange and mysterious object – an object of reverence and awe whose existence has stretched down the aeons from times before the birth of our Lord. Some say the object is even older, dating from beyond the Dark Ages to the days of the Druids and Stonehenge; but my research has shown that the earliest reliable records go back to the Old Testament, and specifically to the times of the law-giver himself, the man Moses.

I will show that Bill's leather doctor's bag is, in fact, the Bag of the Covenant and that the mystical object was the original sanctum sanctorum, the Holy of Holies, which contained the tablets of the law brought down by Moses from Mount Sinai. Through careful study of records kept by an ancient order of Jewish magicians, whose name I am sworn on penalty of terrible death to keep completely secret, I was able to establish that when the Bible was being translated from Ancient Hebrew into Greek, the words 'bag' and 'ark', both having three letters, somehow became confused. But more of this later.

The question most pertinent to this journal is how did my friend, the wise Drummond, and his clan come to possess this powerful object, this Bag of the Covenant? The story begins in Africa – Ethiopia, to be precise – and Bill's great-great-grandfather, Mungo McDrummond of the pygmies. Mungo was a famous Scottish African explorer, ivory hunter and slave trader. He made his fortune after draining nearly half of Central Africa of natives by sending them to work on the sodomy ranches of the southern states of America.

These poor unfortunate young blacks were sold as eighteenth-century rent boys to rich cotton barons who would pleasure themselves for a few weeks with their young buck, kill the poor unfortunate and then order up more of the delicious black meat. Mungo was more than happy to provide the morsels these depraved displaced Europeans required. It was also rumoured – but never proved, I hasten to add – that Mungo himself was of this anal persuasion.

But back to the Bag of the Covenant. Apparently, Mungo was given the Bag in return for sparing a young black from becoming an arse-slave in America. The boy's father, the local witch doctor, revealed to Mungo the history of the Bag: how, after Nebuchadnez-zar's destruction of Jerusalem, the lost tribe of Rastafari had brought the Bag to Ethiopia, where it had been guarded over the centuries by one priest after another, until it had eventually come to him. At some point during this time the Christian faith deteriorated back to its pagan, idolatrous roots, and the Bag, because of its obvious power, became a fetish for the tribe which had been entrusted with its welfare all those years ago.

Mungo inspected the frayed and maltreated object. There was, he felt, something to the man's story. So, true to form, Mungo welched on the deal, killed the witch doctor and his son, stole the very Bag of the Covenant, the Holiest of Holies. What's more, to compound the blasphemy, Mungo had the witch doctor flayed and used the poor man's hide to re-cover this, the most holy relic of all time.

Thereafter, the Bag took on a darker aspect; its pure and holy power was infused with the knowledge of more sinister divinities. Mungo returned to his native Scotland two years later, where he began to drink heavily. He was often to be seen burning small bundles of pound notes in the street and mumbling curses under his breath about the Dark Ones. He became obsessed with the Cthulu Mythos and went insane and finally shot himself in 1784.

Little is known of the Bag until it resurfaced over a hundred years later in the possession of the self-proclaimed Ipsissimus magician, the great beast 666 himself – Aleister Crowley, notorious practitioner of evil arse-bandit magik. Crowley found the Bag in the attic of his Loch Ness mansion, Boleskine, and instinctively and immediately recognized the sinister powers of this dread object. By now it was becoming clear that the Bag of the Covenant possessed some form of a curse. Crowley, in his *Book of Lies*, describes how his downfall into penury and heroin addiction can be blamed entirely on 'that damned Bag'.

It is also known that Oscar Wilde once had possession of this ancient artefact. After Oscar's reported death, Lord Alfred Douglas, or Bosie as he is more commonly known, told a terrifying story of how one evening after, as he puts it, 'one or seven bottles too many of champagne', a terrible incident took place involving the Bag. Douglas continues: 'I staggered, somewhat the worse for the Bollinger, into Oscar's boudoir for a little goodnight kiss. We had stopped indulging in our Greek pastimes by this time as Oscar had become singularly unattractive, ever since, now I think of it, he recovered the Bag from the bald fellow with the bulging eyes. What's his name? Crowley or something, I believe. I pushed open the door and, well, gosh, I nearly fainted. I knew Oscar had been dabbling with hobbies more esoteric than mere pederasty, but I didn't know it had reached this stage. He was standing in the middle of a huge pentagram drawn with what I suspected to be the South American stuff. What's it called? Ah yes, cocaine.

'He was completely naked, candles flickering in the green light, and, horror of horrors, he was up to the nuts in a floating disembodied black arse. I noticed he was bleeding from both nostrils.

' "Bosie!" he screamed. "Leave me alone! It's dangerous! Don't enter the circle!" Well, he needn't have bothered warning me. That mumbo jumbo stuff puts the willies right up me, and I was off down the stairs and into my hansom cab as fast as blazes, I'll tell you!'

This account of Oscar's terrible decline into drug abuse and sodomistic sorcery came immediately before his incarceration in Reading gaol.

Again, mysteriously, all records of the Bag disappear until 1933, when the mysterious object turns up in the hands of a famous collector of religious artefacts. The German collector was none other than

Adolf Hitler, future chancellor of Germany and instigator of the Third Reich. Mr Hitler had for a long time been interested in the magical powers inherent in religious items; it was rumoured that he had in his possession the 'Spear of Destiny', the original spear used by the Roman soldier Longinus to pierce Christ's side. Hitler had this weapon of infamy, symbol of the crucifixion, under safe lock and key in his Bavarian mountain hideaway known as the Wolf's Lair, along with Christ's foreskin. The combined magical power of these holy items together with the Bag of the Covenant nearly destroyed the world. After the suicide of the Führer, itself echoing the dark end of Mungo McDrummond fuelled by madness and failure – much like Crowley and Wilde – the mysterious Bag disappears once more.

Rumours in London literary circles suggested that the next possessor of this dread magical curse was the Welsh poet, Dylan Thomas. After a heavy drinking session one Friday evening in London's Fitzrovia the genius, well in his cups, let rip a large Guinness fart and followed through, black diarrhoeic shite trickling down the back of his legs. The intellectual giant was heard to moan despairingly, 'It's the damn bag, the damn Bag of the Covenant. I'm ruined. I can't control the power – it's too great!' Mysteriously, four weeks later Thomas was found dead in New York. Yet again, following the enigmatic pattern, the Bag disappeared.

In 1969 W. E. Drummond was visiting America, researching female writers for his burgeoning interest in the newly emergent feminist movement. Bill was eighteen years old; he had little money. His father afforded him a small allowance but not nearly enough for his sea passage to America. Like his hero Jack Kerouac, the young Bill had worked his way across the Atlantic on a small steamboat as cabin boy.

In Los Angeles he met occult film-maker and expert on Aleister Crowley, Kenneth Anger. Anger presented Bill with the Bag of the Covenant and informed him that his recent astrological calculations indicated that he, and only he, was the true owner of the magical Bag. For Bill this was a revelation. He had read family histories and had always felt an affinity for his long-dead great-great-grandfather, Mungo McDrummond of the pygmies. As a boy he had dreamed of finding this lost family treasure, and here in LA the bummer cinematographer, who was also to die in suspicious circumstances, presented the object to him with a stern warning of the negative powers attached to the relic.

Bill was unconcerned. He knew the reason it had had such a devastating effect on the previous owners was entirely down to the fact that they had no right to its power. He and he alone, the last living male heir of the great Mungo McDrummond, was entitled to the Bag. He took the precious object back to his motel room, placed it on the bed and fondled the soft, strange black leather. It appeared to have small scars worked into the surface.

Bill gingerly closed the cheap plywood motel door. Anxious William sat on the bed full of trepidation and no uncertain amount of fear. He unclipped the solid brass clasp, and the black leather doctor's bag, the Bag of the Covenant, Holiest of Holies, slowly yawned open. Bill cautiously peered inside. He could see stars, spiral galaxies. It was a hole in space! Bill's bag was full of the universe. It smelt of jasmine and apples; it smelt of summer and warm sunlight. Bill instinctively knew he would never have to worry about money as long as he lived. He placed his hand inside the Bag. He could feel a strange, electric vibration. It was the earth's magnetic field, this he knew. The Bag spoke in a gentle voice like a Mediterranean wind over a field of poppies, only not words, more like feelings.

Bill knew what he had to do. He unfastened his battered old typewriter and placed in it a sheet of clean paper, smoothing it down roughly. He placed the black leather doctor's Bag of the Covenant on his head like a hat. Knowledge and erudition flowed into him.

Four days later Bill had written the book that was to establish his literary reputation around the world. That book was called *Born a Cunt*, a stunningly perceptive history of the plight of women in the Western world. Bill was heralded a genius, and by the age of twenty-two had created and defined the women's movement. His follow-up books went straight to the top of the best-sellers list in over 260 countries around the world. His master trilogy dealing with the subject of women and creativity, *Triumph of the Womb*, *Bun in the Oven* and *Up the Spout*, won him a Nobel prize for literature. His populist feminist self-help books, *Women Who Create Too Much*, *Fear of Farting*,

The Female Bumhole and *The Ugly Myth*, won him a dedicated following of intelligent young women eager to sit at his feet to learn from the master.

But Bill tired of feminism; went on to even more complex and deeper theories, his quest for erudition and learning aided by the magical properties of his new-found friend, Bag. Bill's later books, *Bog Off: How I Invented the Liverpool Punk Scene in 1981* and *On One: How I Invented the Rave Scene in 1987*, further widened his fan base. Although the Bag granted him wisdom, it seemed to have a perverse sense of humour, and not all its gifts were benign. Some say it was hubris; others that the Bag started to play practical jokes, but his most recent work, a 25,000 page autobiography, *I, Bastard*, was a publishing disaster.

The book (which, incidentally, I consider to be a masterpiece) contained all of the genius of Bill's brilliant theories – including his correction of Einstein's Blunder of Relativity – and apparently was so advanced in its thinking that it simply left the majority of its readers flabbergasted. Indeed, some critics said it made Stephen Hawkings's book on the theory of everything seem like a light-hearted holiday romp.

Bill took the news stoically, however, and decided that, like most geniuses, he was ahead of his time. He comforted himself with the thought that mankind would obviously not be ready for an intellect of his stature for at least another century.

He threw himself into his next work, *Why I Am So Clever*, but unfortunately this *oeuvre* has been interrupted by the pressing urgency of the tome you now hold in your hands.

All of the master's writing can be found in the Drummond wing of the British Library.